\7~\4

# PRAISE FOR JEREMY BURNS'S PREVIOUS WORK:

"With *From the Ashes*, Jeremy Burns establishes himself among the best authors of taut, historical thrillers. In this gripping debut, Burns lays bare a fascinating conspiracy of deceit, full of action and twists. You'll find yourself rooting for his heroes, repulsed by his villains, and rethinking what you think you know about one of history's darkest times. Truly, a must-read for fans of suspense, action, and history."
– Robert Liparulo, bestselling author of *The 13th Tribe, Comes a Horseman*, and *The Dreamhouse Kings*

"*From the Ashes* is a thrilling race against time to expose a diabolical conspiracy that would shatter everything we think we know about the 20th century. With clever puzzles, enigmatic clues, and hidden secrets, Jeremy Burns re-imagines New York's landmarks so vividly that you will want to explore them all over again."
– Boyd Morrison, #1 *New York Times* bestselling author of *The Ark* and *The Vault*

"A book for fans of Steve Berry and Raymond Khoury, *From the Ashes* is well-written and impeccably researched with great characters and a conspiracy that is frightening in both its implications and plausibility. Jeremy Burns is an author to watch."
– Ethan Cross, international bestselling author of *The Shepherd*

"*National Treasure* meets *The Bourne Identity* in this riveting debut. Blending history, suspense, and adventure, Burns takes readers on a nonstop thrill ride through some of the country's most famous sites – and infamous periods of history – ensuring that you'll never look at New York City, the 1930s, or the name 'Rockefeller' the same again. Not to miss!"
– Jeremy Robinson, bestselling author of *Threshold* and *Secondworld* on *From the Ashes*

"Amazing historical research, very frightening agent-types and some people just trying to do the right thing and led into it quite nice by author Burns. Even if you don't believe in secrets, this is a story of the first-order and if you like mysteries pick it up. You won't be sorry."
– Cheryl's Book Nook on *From the Ashes*

"Start early as this is definitely an intriguing story that will have you muttering 'oh, no' as you are reading as fast as you can to get to the next page. For interesting plot and edge-of-your-seat, nail-biting suspense, *The Dubai Betrayal* is definitely the book for you."
– Vic's Media Room

"Will leave fans of Daniel Silva and Brad Thor breathless for more."
– Mark Greaney, #1 *New York Times* bestselling author of *Back Blast* on *The Dubai Betrayal*

"Combines history, secrets, and conspiracies in an entertaining and intriguing tale."
– Steve Berry, *New York Times* bestselling author on *The Flagler Hunt*

"A treasure-hunter's dream read."
– Carter Wilson, USA Today bestselling author of *The Dead Girl in 2A* on *The Flagler Hunt*

# THE FOUNDING TREASON

# THE FOUNDING TREASON

A Jonathan Rickner Thriller by

## JEREMY BURNS

THE
ST RY
PLANT

The Story Plant
Studio Digital CT, LLC
P.O. Box 4331
Stamford, CT 06907

Story Plant hardcover ISBN-13: 978-1-61188-263-6
Fiction Studio Books E-book ISBN: 978-1-945839-26-9

Visit our website at www.TheStoryPlant.com

First Story Plant Printing: June 2019

Printed in the United States of America

0 9 8 7 6 5 4 3 2 1

To Meredith
For all the adventures we've shared
and all our adventures yet to come

# PROLOGUE
## *December 1799*
## *Château de la Grange-Bléneau, France*

Gilbert du Motier, the Marquis de Lafayette, realized something was wrong before he even saw the courier. The messenger, about five years the marquis's junior, had a distinctive cadence to his step, one Lafayette's trained ear had learned to recognize in bloody revolutions across two continents over the past fifteen years. Now, on the cusp of a new century, new conflicts had replaced old ones, with an uneasy peace having settled over Lafayette's native homeland with Napoleon Bonaparte's seizure of power in the guillotine's wake. But the streets of Paris still stank of noble blood, and the marquis, deprived of his civil rights and citizenship though allowed to remain in France for the time being, prayed for the dawn of the nineteenth century to be free from the horrors of bloodshed he had witnessed. So much sacrificed in the name of peace. So many slaughtered on the altar of freedom. May the year 1800 mark a new era, full of the life, liberty, and pursuit of happiness he and his friends had fought for so dearly.

As Eduarde approached, clear hesitance in his footfalls, Lafayette knew it was not to be.

"Marquis," Eduarde said, bowing his head reverentially to his employer.

"What news, Eduarde?"

"Sad tidings, I'm afraid. General Washington has died."

The gardens blurred as Lafayette reeled at the news. His old friend and commander George, dead? Washington may have been in his sixty-eighth year, but he was the pinnacle of health, always active on his plantation in Virginia, horseback riding daily, enjoying his well-deserved retirement.

"How?" Lafayette asked as he regained his composure.

"Reportedly, he caught fever while riding through a storm. A few days thereafter, he passed on."

He couldn't believe it. Washington had been one of his closest friends. They had fought as brothers, saw their men die together, raised up an army and a nation. And unwittingly set in motion events that could lead to that very nation's downfall. Without Washington, anything was possible.

The marquis thought back to their last conversation, walking through the orchard at Mount Vernon, discussing Washington's fears for the secret legacy he would leave behind. Lafayette tried to assure him that his concerns were unfounded, but to little avail. Then, just a few months ago, a sheaf of parchments had been delivered to the marquis's estate, accompanied by a letter and a key. The letter, penned and signed by Washington, contained instructions, a last request from his old friend and brother-in-arms. Upon reading through the accompanying papers, Lafayette realized there might be more to Washington's fears than he had given him credit for.

And now he was dead.

"What of Bonaparte?" Lafayette asked. "Will he give me leave to pay my respects in Virginia?"

Eduarde looked sullen as he shook his head, ashamed to have to compound his employer's sorrow with further ill tidings. "With the naval war still raging between us and the Americans, I fear he will not." He swallowed at a lump in his throat, but said nothing else.

"There's more, is there not?" Lafayette asked.

Eduarde nodded. "Perceptive as always, my lord. Yes, there is one more thing. Bonaparte is holding a ceremony in Paris to honor Washington. You are officially not invited."

Lafayette expected Bonaparte's snub, but it still hurt like a gut punch. Washington meant more to the marquis, and vice versa, than to anyone else in Paris—certainly more than to Napoleon Bonaparte or any of his allies. To be shunned like this was pouring salt on the wound.

But there was more to do than just sulk over Bonaparte's underhanded slap in the face. Washington's papers, letter, and key were locked in a chest in the chateau, but soon the war with America would be over. The two nations were sparring over whether or not America's debt to France had been canceled by the success of the French Revolution. President John Adams argued that the debt had been owed to the previous regime, an entity that Robespierre, Bonaparte, and the rest had erased from the earth. Paris had emphatically disagreed.

Still, the war wouldn't go on forever. There was too much at stake—particularly with Bonaparte's desire to expand the new French empire across Europe—for France to be distracted with a petty war over a decades-old debt. Napoleon would turn his sights elsewhere, and Lafayette would be able to fulfill his friend's final wishes.

And he knew just the man to help him finish the job.

≈ ≈ ≈ ≈ ≈

## February 1865
## Philadelphia, Pennsylvania

Nicholas Longworth Anderson held tight to the reins, praying his hired horse wouldn't be spooked by the latest flash of lightning. The horse raced on, tensing at every boom of thunder, beating through the empty streets and splashing puddles in all directions as its master urged him onward. Why this meeting couldn't wait until more favorable weather was beyond Anderson's understanding. But Powell had been adamant. The future of the Union was at stake. So he raced on.

Minutes later, the home of Hiram Powell materialized through the haze of rain-soaked night. The three-story mansion was dark save for a light that burned in a second-story window. Powell's den. Anderson handed the reins of his horse to the stable boy, then rushed to the door. He used the knocker to rap the agreed-upon pattern, then checked his pocket watch. Ten minutes late. Considering the weather and how far he had come, surely the others would understand.

A Negro servant answered the door and took Anderson's coat and hat. Anderson knew the way to the den. He also knew that whatever was going on in there was for members' ears only. Powell wouldn't trust anyone outside the circle—not even his own wife—with their secret business. So Anderson saw himself up.

Arriving at the entrance to the den, he paused. He could hear indistinct voices through the heavy oaken door. A heated argument. Something big was indeed going down. He brushed in vain at the water soaking his trousers and shirt, then rapped the secret tattoo upon the wood. The voices stopped immediately. Moments later, the door creaked open and the broad face of his friend Jeremiah Burkett greeted him.

"Come in, Nicholas, quickly."

Immediately, Anderson knew something was amiss. There were far more brothers here than he had expected, including a number he had never seen before. They must have come from another chapter of the society, which made the urgent business Powell had called the meeting for all the more mysterious. The room was charged with a curious energy, not unlike the air shortly before a storm struck. Burkett's normally jovial face was pinched with worry. Anderson surveyed the expressions of his fellow brothers as he took his seat. An array of emotions bedecked their countenances. None were pleasant. Anger, frustration, and disbelief made multiple appearances. But most prominent of all, an underlying emotion seemingly present on most of the faces here, was a fatalistic resignation.

"Nicholas, so nice of you to join us," Powell said. Anderson was about to reply with an excuse about the weather, but Powell didn't give him the chance.

"Gentlemen, the path forward is clear. The only question is, do we have the courage to take it?"

"What you're proposing is treason!" countered a thin man with a New England accent.

"We were born in treason," Powell countered. "We had to defend against allegations of further treason throughout our early years. And yet, we remained stalwart. Our forefathers made the difficult decisions necessary to defend our nation. Shall we cast off their sacrifice and disgrace their legacy, in this, our nation's hour of need?"

Most of the room shouted "no!" But a few dissenters remained. Anderson, for his part, remained silent, unsure what Powell was proposing.

"How do we know this won't make things worse?" asked a white-haired man with a bushy mustache and an aristocratic South Carolina accent. Anderson blinked in confusion. A Confederate brother? Had Powell actually managed to get brothers from Confederate-held chapters to attend his secret meeting? How big was this plan of his?

"The war is drawing to a close, but there are those who remain dedicated to rebellion at all costs. When the time comes, my plan will be the only thing that can prevent the Union from dissolving again. The successor has his issues, but he is from Tennessee and will be much more palatable to those who would tear us apart again. And need I remind you that the election four years ago was what spurred your great state to turn its back on our nation in secession?"

The man from South Carolina assented under his breath. In a group whose founding had been built upon a series of treasonous acts, the reminder of a more recent treason against everything their forefathers had built was more than enough to silence him.

"You know Hamilton Fish won't stand for this," argued a brother from Maryland.

"He doesn't have to. Gentlemen, I called each of you for a reason. All of you are powerful men of finance and influence, chosen from each of our thirteen chapters. If it comes to it, those of us in this room—and our sons in the years to come—can stand alone. Our forefathers fought valiantly to create our nation. Now we must become the vanguard to defend it from the enemies lurking within our very borders."

A murmur grew among the members as they debated Powell's points. In the lamplight, their faces appeared curiously contorted, deepened shadows flickering until obliterated by the occasional blaze of lightning from the windows. Anderson took the opportunity to whisper to his friend.

"Jeremiah, what is Powell talking about?" Burkett leaned toward him and opened his mouth to speak, but Powell's booming voice cut through the discussion before he could answer.

"I propose we put it to a vote," Powell said, raising his hand. "All in favor of proceeding with my plan to defend our nation and the legacy of our forefathers, raise your right hand."

One by one, hands went up across the room. Anderson, still ignorant of the plan Powell was proposing, saw Burkett's hand raised and realized that only one hand was not raised. Slowly, Anderson lifted his hand, trusting that a unanimous vote in spite of the contentious discussion had to signify the plan was the right decision.

Powell looked from brother to brother, letting the gravity of their decision sink in. Moments later, he finally spoke.

"Then it's decided, my brothers. History shall never know of our actions, but our nation will survive because of your boldness. May it ever be so. In order for the United States to survive, President Lincoln must die."

≈≈≈≈≈

## November 22, 1963
## Dallas, Texas

Lee Harvey Oswald climbed the last few steps and pushed through the door into the cavernous expanse of the sixth floor of the Texas School Book Depository. His Carcano M91/38 bolt action rifle was in hand, and his mind kept going over the details of his mission. It was a brilliant plot, and he was determined to see it through. The risk was astronomical, but then, so was the payoff. And they wouldn't have given him the job if they weren't confident in his ability to succeed.

Oswald had already staked out the sixth floor and prepared his sniper hide, hidden behind a pallet of books. With the incoming dignitaries on the street outside and the day shift's lunch break coming up, he would have the entire floor to himself. He went to the far wall, cracked open a window, and began setting up his weapon—assembling the rifle, affixing the telescopic sight. He drew a test bead on one civilian standing along the parade route, then another, whispering "bang" as he envisioned his target's head exploding in a crimson blossom of bone and brain. He checked his watch. The motorcade was nowhere in sight. He loaded the rifle, chambered the first round, and gazed east down Houston Street where the cars would soon appear. With everything ready except his nerves, all he could do now was wait.

The past few years had been preparing him for this moment. From his career as a Marine sniper to his covert work with the CIA to his time in the Soviet Union, all coalescing into this one point in time. A chance to finally break free of the past and move into a glorious future, both for himself and for the nation. They had made him great promises, and all he had to do was shoot one man. The politician was as mortal as any other, and though he was a public figure, they had promised to protect Oswald from any fallout that might stem from the man's assassination. He had a million questions, but there was so much that went on behind the scenes, so many pieces to the geopolitical puzzle, that very few knew the fullness of its master design. After today, Oswald would be one of those few, and he would see how the killing of this one man fit into their plans.

The exuberant thrill of cheers echoed from down Houston Street, followed by the distant rumble of motors, each growing louder by the second. Dozens of men, women and children lined the streets outside, jockeying for position to get a good view of the presidential motorcade when it came into view.

The car came into sight, and he saw his target, smiling and waving to the gathered crowd. It was a brilliant plan, really. The ultimate obfuscation. He moved his finger from the trigger guard to the trigger itself, then back again. They were coming up too fast. The drop angle was changing every second, and he needed to make his first shot count. Once gunfire was heard in the plaza, the chaos that ensued might preclude the chance for a second shot.

He waited until the car slowed at the corner below the book depository, keeping his sights on the man's head all the while. The car turned the corner, and he wrapped his finger around the trigger. Moment of truth.

He had the sight lined up on his target, but the car was now moving away from his position. Oswald didn't know why they wanted Texas Governor John Connolly dead, but it was his ticket to the big time. One shot, and his world would be changed forever. And killing him when the president sat just feet away was even more brilliant. Who would suspect that Connolly's murder wasn't just an attempted presidential assassination gone wrong? Kennedy's presence provided the perfect smokescreen.

He tightened his finger around the trigger, the pressure just shy of firing. The car was moving too quickly. It was now or never. He took a deep breath, held it, and, doing a quick calculation for the motion of the car and the angle of the shot, he squeezed the trigger.

*Bang!*

Connolly jerked, but then, so did everyone else in the plaza. *Gunfire?* they must have been thinking. *Or a car backfiring?* Oswald checked his target through the scope. Had he killed Connolly, or was another shot required?

*Bang!*

Another shot, but Oswald hadn't pulled the trigger. This one from somewhere closer to the car itself.

*Bang! Bang!*

Two more in quick succession, the reports echoing off the buildings of the plaza, making it impossible to get a read on where they were coming from. Cops? Secret Service? What was going on? He had to finish his mission and get out of here.

The motorcade accelerated, racing out of the plaza. Oswald sighted his target again, but instead of focusing on Connolly he saw someone else entirely. He had hit Connolly, but the other shots had hit a different target.

President John F. Kennedy.

The leader of the free world was slumped over in his seat, part of his skull blown off, Jackie scrambling toward the back of the vehicle.

The president of the United States was dead.

Oswald felt his face grow hot, ice dripping into his fingers. His legs and spine were tingling with overactive nerves as the fullness of what had just transpired sank into place. There was no time for clean-up, no time for careful exfiltration. He could no longer count on his contacts to protect him. In fact, the very people he had been counting on to get him out of here, the ones who had set him up with this mission in the first place, were the last people he could depend on right now.

Oswald had been horribly betrayed. The president of the United States was dead. The crime would be pinned on him. And *they* would make sure he wasn't long in following Kennedy to the grave.

## PART ONE
### *KENNEDY*

"I thought they'd get one of us, but Jack, after all he's been through, never worried about it. I thought it would be me."
– Robert F. Kennedy

"Things do not happen. Things are made to happen."
– John F. Kennedy

# CHAPTER 1
## Present Day
## Washington, DC

Making history could ruin your life, even if you stayed in the shadows. Jon Rickner knew this all too well. His current circumstances could certainly be worse, but he couldn't help reflecting on what could have been. What *should* have been.

"You planning on getting any work done today?"

Jon turned from his task to see the corpulent brown face of his supervisor, Loretha Hayes. Earlier in his short employment here at the National Archives, Jon had made the mistake of replying about how very busy he had, in fact, been. The torrent of verbal abuse that followed, coupled with the admonitions from his coworkers not to argue with Mrs. Hayes, had taught him very quickly to shut up when she decided today was your day. It was Jon's day more often than not.

A thousand snarky remarks came to mind, brilliantly sardonic retorts that would make his coworkers bowl over with laughter and finally wipe that smug look off Hayes's face. But he needed this job. The past few months had taught him just how bad.

"Yes, ma'am," he said, pretending to redouble his efforts as he sifted through a file cabinet. "I'll work faster."

"That would be lovely, Mr. Rickner. You may be here against my wishes, but this is not a charity case. Bear that in mind if you value your future here."

Jon watched as she shuffled off down the stacks to micromanage some other fully capable underling. Her calling him *Mr.* Rickner niggled at him, as she knew it would. He had worked hard for his doctorate in history, graduating first in his class from Oxford following a Summa Cum Laude undergrad degree from Harvard. But instead of top-tier universities throwing tenure-track positions at him in an academic bidding war, as might have happened with a similarly credentialed candidate, he found himself universally rejected out of hand.

He should have been on the other side of the counter, out front like the professor he was retrieving materials for, requesting documents to further his own research. Instead, he was relegated to a relatively menial role, finding, retrieving, and archiving historical documents for his true peers. Technically, he wasn't even all that qualified for this position. Most of his coworkers had graduate degrees in library sciences. The historians employed by the National Archives were the resident researchers, digging through the stacks in search of new insights, forgotten documents, puzzle pieces thought lost to time that would further the understanding of America's past. That was the job he was qualified for, perhaps more than any candidate they had considered in years. But his unique credentials were also what had blackballed him from the career he so desired.

Two years ago, he had been involved with the takedown of an elite government killing squad, one tasked with keeping hidden a secret dating from the Great Depression. When Jon had uncovered the proof of the organization's existence and revealed the decades-old secret to the world, much of the country revered him as a hero.

Others called him traitor.

The federal government largely fell in the latter category. Certainly they disagreed with the way the so-called Division had been killing its own citizens to protect a long-forgotten secret, but his public airing of their dirty laundry hadn't gone over well, even if they had already killed his brother and were about to kill him. The powers-that-be had let it be known—through unofficial channels, of course—that Jon Rickner was a pariah, and any institution that hired him might find themselves under closer scrutiny from all manner of federal inspectors. Before Jon had even finished his doctorate, he was unemployable.

But just as he was about to give up stateside and see if he could land a teaching job at a university overseas, the National Archives called. Supposedly, someone in the administration had decided to throw Jon a bone and pulled some strings to get him a position with the National Archives. According to the call, he was going to be a researcher, helping to flesh out the historical record in more universally beneficial ways. Though it wasn't exactly what he was looking for, Jon jumped at the idea. Not only could the job itself be tremendously edifying for his insatiably curious brain, but it could also be a launching pad to an actual teaching position once the furor over his role in exposing the Division gave way to some newer contributions to the historical record.

When he arrived for his first day of work, he was notified that his job would actually be as a retrieval archivist. A glorified librarian assistant. The one or two publications that were still following his tragic fall from accidental stardom found the twist humorous. Jon disagreed. He still hadn't found out exactly who had leaked the news to the press, but he had a pretty good idea.

Loretha Hayes had taken a particular dislike to him. She was certainly efficient at maintaining the stacks and the researcher service desks up front, but her people skills left something to be desired. A careerist with two master's degrees and no political savvy, she had been in her current supervisory role for twenty years. Her refusal to play the great butt-kissing game so prevalent in DC had stalled her career. Instead, she made the most of her little corner of the Archives, putting her own indelible mark on it. And, by most accounts, she wasn't even that bad a manager. She just really hated that the very bureaucracy she had refused to kowtow to at the expense of her own career had foisted an inexperienced and underqualified new employee upon her. Jon's hiring was a constant reminder that her professional domain was not hers after all. And she hated him for it.

In the two weeks he had been here, Jon had become convinced that his demotion from the promised researcher job had been no accident. Perhaps whoever had pulled the strings originally had been overridden, only able to offer this position as a consolation prize. Perhaps it was another mean-spirited joke by the bigwigs on Capitol Hill or in the current administration, suckering him in before pulling the rug out from under him yet again. Either of those might be true, but, more likely than not, the powers-that-be just wanted to keep an eye on him. He had already proven dangerous to the status quo as a twenty-four-year-old grad student. Running free with a newly minted doctorate and a grudge to bear against the government that had blackballed him, Jon Rickner could be a dangerous character indeed.

Or so Jon liked to think.

He finally found the document he was looking for. A 1779 letter written by Benedict Arnold to Major John André, one of the first known communiqués between the infamous traitor and his British handler. As with most of Arnold's letters—and indeed with many important messages sent by leaders on both sides during the American Revolution—the missive was written in code.

Jon missed that world. He and his brother had grown up adventuring around the world with their archeologist parents and continuing into adulthood, but that all changed two years ago when Michael had been murdered. Since finally bringing his brother's killers to justice by exposing the Division, Jon had retreated into his studies, focusing on finishing his doctorate and eschewing most social and recreational activities. There hadn't been time for exploring exotic locations or diving into the harrowing world of historical secrets and hidden codes. Or perhaps he had simply chosen not to make time for it.

Tomorrow. He would finish out his shift today, and tomorrow morning he would place some calls to universities and institutions overseas. Even America's closest allies wouldn't stand by their defense of the Division and the horrible deception it had been formed to protect. He would be able to find the career he was looking for elsewhere. He just wished it could have been in the country he called home.

Fresh with renewed hope for the life that should have been, Jon carried the Arnold letter to the clean room where researchers were required to study the most valuable and fragile documents. An original letter penned by the most infamous traitor in the nation's history before the country even existed certainly qualified on both counts. The researcher, a thin, bespectacled professor with short hair graying at the temples and a goatee, was already waiting inside. He offered Jon a curt thanks before turning to the document.

Jon gave a wry grin to no one in particular. So close. So far away.

Leaving the professor to study in private, Jon eased the door shut and headed back up front. His colleagues, Angela and Jessica, were helping other researchers. The lobby was otherwise empty, save for a young woman dressed in what Jon had come to call "research casual." Stylish but comfortable black flats, yellow button-up blouse, black slacks. More attractive than many of the researchers that came in here as well, but then, most of them were significantly older than his twenty-six years. Male, too.

She was biting a nail, staring at the floor as she subtly swayed to an unheard beat. He hoped she wasn't a crazy person. Most people who got this far had to display some sort of credentials, if not an outright appointment. Still, it wasn't as though the university system didn't have its share of oddball faculty members and graduate students.

"Can I help you?" Jon asked from his side of the desk.

The young woman looked up. Her eyes flashed with recognition as her mouth abandoned its fingernail chewing and grew into a smile. She approached the desk.

"Dr. Jonathan Rickner?" she asked, though her expression said she already knew the answer.

Jon tried not to grin at being called by his title. No one around here did. Following the boss lady's example, he supposed. Still, his name badge just said "Jon R." She knew him. But did he know her? He tried to place her face, but couldn't. She looked far too young to be a university dean, but maybe she was some sort of recruiter. Hope springs eternal. Maybe he wouldn't have to go overseas to get back in his element after all.

"That's me," Jon said with a friendly smile he hoped wasn't too effusive. "How can I help you today?"

She slipped a piece of paper across the desk.

"I really need to take a look at these particular items."

Jon flipped over the paper and read the few words she had written. Not quite what he had expected.

"Can I see your university or institution ID?" he asked.

She pulled a card out of her clutch and handed it to him. University of Iowa. Chloe Harper. Student. So much for her being a recruiter to help change his stars. She was probably just another fan who had followed his exploits from two years ago and hadn't realized that he just wasn't that interesting anymore. Back to Plan A for tomorrow morning's job search then. Jon typed the info into his computer and returned the card.

"I'll be right back, Ms. Harper."

# CHAPTER 2
## *Hyattsville, Maryland*

Anthony Kellerman answered his phone on the first ring, activating his Bluetooth earpiece so he could continue chopping vegetables. The caller ID was blocked, but only a few people had this number. All of them had caller ID blocked.

"You'll never guess who's in town." Kellerman immediately recognized the voice. Stanton Gaines.

"Bugs Bunny," Kellerman replied.

"Don't be stupid."

"Don't waste my time with guessing games. I'm busy."

"You're about to get busier. It's Chloe Harper."

"And that name should mean something to me?"

"Jack Harper's kid."

Kellerman cursed. *That* name *did* mean something to him.

"What's she doing? Sightseeing or shopping, I hope."

"Would I be calling you if she were? No, the daughter of our dearly departed Jack just showed up at the National Archives."

Kellerman fought the urge to curse again. Once was enough in a single phone call, particularly with his girlfriend's kids in the other room, but the longer this conversation went on, the more virulent the strain of expletives he wanted to let loose grew.

"There's more," Gaines said. "She's apparently got a co-conspirator now. Jonathan Rickner."

"From the Rockefeller thing a few years back?"

"The same. Apparently he got a job at the Archives recently."

"A perfect cover."

"That's what we were thinking."

"Is there anything for them to find there?"

"That's the million-dollar question. We had thought everything was purged before Jack got his hands on what he did."

"So there might still be a thread out there."

"No one's found one yet."

"That could be because no one has looked in the right place yet."

"Exactly."

"And you think these two might be onto something?"

"I doubt she's there playing tourist."

Kellerman lowered his voice as he heard his girlfriend's key in the door. "Extreme prejudice?"

"Whatever it takes. Just end this."

He flipped the knife in the air and stabbed it into the scarred cutting board with a flourish. "That's what I do."

# CHAPTER 3
## *Washington, DC*

The public face of the National Archives was one of pristine displays artfully showcasing the nation's most famous documents. The rotunda, made cinematically famous in the blockbuster film *National Treasure*, showcased the US Constitution, the Declaration of Independence, and a handful of other key documents in the framing and development of the fledgling nation, all wrapped in a dramatic presentation of awe, respect, and importance befitting such historic artifacts. But down here in the stacks, Jon had quickly learned not only how incredibly vast the Archives' collection was, but also how disorganized the repository had become.

Millions of documents, letters, executive orders, newspaper articles, photographs, audio recordings, newsreels, and myriad other types of media were held by the National Archives Administration, and, with countless more being added each day, it was impossible to keep up. With many of the less obviously important artifacts, the best the archivists could do for the time being was categorize them into boxes and shelve them for the mythical someday when they'd finally have time to fully catalog and organize the massive backlog.

Jon's first fifteen minutes of searching told him that Ms. Harper's request was not among those properly cataloged. That figured. More digging. And yet, it was in these moments, tedious though they could be, that Jon found himself distracted by the hope that in this labyrinth of poorly cataloged artifacts could be something incredible, a long-forgotten document of true historic impact. Something that could redeem him in the eyes of the academic community. A golden ticket out of his professional purgatory.

Thus far, the most impressive document he had stumbled across was an official menu for Thanksgiving dinner at the White House in 1897. Apparently Mrs. McKinley was a big fan of minced lamb and pumpkin pie. Even so, he held out hope. He had managed to get into plenty of trouble discovering lost or forgotten things with his brother, but the spark had been gone since solving Michael's murder. Maybe it truly had died with him.

In the distance, Jon heard Loretha Hayes berating one of his colleagues. At least he wasn't the only one receiving her ire. Misery loving company and all that. Still, he had been gone for a while now, and if he didn't find what Ms. Harper was looking for soon, Mrs. Hayes would be tearing him a new one for wasting taxpayer money and her man-hours.

The request was interesting, if unusual. A slim, pocket-sized volume of John Buchan's *The Thirty-Nine Steps* and a silver Kodak film canister with a regal-looking coat of arms engraved in the screw-top lid. Both of the items had apparently been donated by the estate of the late Senator Ted Kennedy several years earlier, though Jon could find no mention of the donation. Either it didn't exist, or the Archives' infamous backlog was rearing its head once again.

Either way, Jon would give himself a few more minutes, then head back up front. He had been on thin ice with Mrs. Hayes since the moment he got hired. He couldn't afford to be wasting hours on a wild-goose chase.

He had been digging through boxes marked "Sen. Edward 'Ted' Kennedy" to no avail. There were eleven boxes in total, shelved in two tall stacks in between stacks marked with his brothers' names. Despite his importance in the national memory, John F. Kennedy only had two boxes with his name on them. Presidents, particularly ones whose life—and death—cast as large a shadow as JFK's had, typically got moved to the top of the cataloging pile. Without doubt, the pair of boxes had also been sifted through thoroughly, resulting in nothing of particular historic import. But, with all the controversy surrounding the president's life and death, the Archives had been reluctant to get rid of anything related to the man. God forbid the conspiracy nuts get wind that the federal government destroyed documents related to the JFK assassination. Of course, as Jon had found, the Archives rarely got rid of anything that might be historically important to someone, somehow, at some time in the future. Hence, the millions upon millions of documents in its collection that was making Jon's newfound career an exemplar in wasting time.

Eight boxes in now, Jon had stacked the no-gos in the aisle in order to reach those on the bottom of the shelf. Mrs. Hayes would probably classify it as a fire hazard, blocking access to emergency egress points, but there really wasn't a better option. Besides, in a few minutes he'd have everything stacked back again, with no one the wiser.

As he opened the second-to-last box, he grinned. There, half covered by a manila folder full of newspaper clippings with Ted Kennedy's opinions scrawled in the margins, were the sought-after items. Jon retrieved them from the box with care. The film canister felt weighty, made of actual metal, unlike the modern plastic versions popularized in the '80s. The screw top had a coat of arms custom engraved, as Ms. Harper had said, while the side of the canister sported the embossed letters "KODAK." Jon's best guess was that it dated from sometime in the 1960s. The book, meanwhile, looked even older. Curious, he flipped it open. According to the copyright page, the volume was printed in 1924.

Ted Kennedy's commentaries. A film canister from the 1960s. And an adventure novel dating to the Kennedy brothers' childhood. What on earth was Ms. Harper researching?

He heard footsteps approaching. His instinct told him that, crazy or not, whatever theory tied these items together could be dangerous. Against protocol, he pocketed the film canister and the book, then put the lid back on the box and braced himself as the footsteps rounded the corner behind him, heading straight for him.

# CHAPTER 4
## *Washington, DC*

A nthony Kellerman climbed the stone steps at a side entrance to the National Archives. This entrance was a more sedate affair, its presence only denoted by the sign hanging overhead, directing tourists and others without official research business to the larger main entrance on Constitution Avenue. His business was research of a sort. And though he didn't have a university research pass or a proper appointment, far more depended on his success here than a doctoral dissertation or another white paper to be published, filed away, and forgotten.

National security, for example. Something Kellerman knew all about.

He had served in the Marines for six years, achieving the rank of captain before he led his company into a Taliban ambush outside of Kandahar. Eleven Marines were killed in the bloodbath, with another eighteen seriously injured. Though one of his men had read the intel wrong, Kellerman took responsibility for the attack, blaming himself for not double-checking the intel himself.

Despite his bravery in saving four of his men at great personal risk, he received a court martial instead of a medal. At minimum, he was facing a dishonorable discharge. At maximum, twenty years in Leavenworth Military Prison.

His father, a retired two-star general, called in a favor to chief of the Marine Corps, who once had been a young cadet under then-Major Theodore H. Kellerman. Charges were dropped on the condition that Anthony Kellerman retire from the service immediately. A lifetime in military prison had just turned into an honorable discharge. But a promising career had also gone up in smoke. A civilian for the first time in his adult life, Kellerman needed a new calling to replace the one that had slipped away.

And he found it.

Kellerman flashed his ID at the security guard just inside. Secret Service, it said. Had his picture and everything. The ID was real enough, but Kellerman didn't work for the Secret Service. Just another perk of the job.

"National security," Kellerman said. "Don't let anyone in or out of this door until you hear from me. Do you understand?"

"I'm going to have to clear that with my super," the guard stammered.

"Do that." Kellerman walked around the metal detector and past the checkpoint, giving his pace and posture just the right amount of professional urgency.

When he reached the lobby of the research center, he scanned the faces of everyone on either side of the counter, comparing them to the photos of Jon Rickner and Chloe Harper that Gaines had sent to his phone. They weren't here.

Three possible options.

One, Gaines had been mistaken. Kellerman dismissed that possibility immediately. Gaines didn't make mistakes. Certainly not ones that threatened to expose his agents.

Two, Kellerman was too late. He didn't even want to think about the ramifications if Harper and Rickner had already found what they were looking for and were now in the wild. He tried to reassure himself that if Gaines had intelligence sources to confirm when Chloe Harper arrived at the Archives, those same sources could have alerted him when she had departed. He decided to table that option until proven otherwise.

Which left option three. Rickner and Harper were somewhere in the stacks, looking for any last remnant of the thread that Jack Harper wouldn't stop pulling.

Kellerman gave the lobby one last sweep to make sure he hadn't missed them on his first pass. He hadn't. Option three it was.

He walked to the edge of the counter, reached over the railing, and opened the waist-high door preventing access to the other side.

"Excuse me, sir," a bespectacled middle-aged archivist began, turning from the patron she was helping.

Kellerman flashed his badge toward her, not stopping to make eye contact. "National security, ma'am." He continued on his way, not giving the archivist the opportunity to press him further. One of his regular tactics, demonstrating the grave importance of his work by not being able to stop to further explain what he was doing here. But depending on what Jack Harper's daughter had managed to piece together, they may well have a national security crisis on their hands.

He entered the stacks, looking around to orient himself. He knew the subject of Jack Harper's obsession. Kellerman just didn't know how far down the rabbit hole the man had dug before his death. Or how much his daughter had discovered since. Kellerman decided to start with what he knew that Jack Harper was digging into. The public records request Chloe had made through her friend—*did she really think that would fool them?*—also lined up with that. He started moving again.

He was unfamiliar with the filing system used by the National Archives. Some sort of Dewey Decimal hybrid as far as he could tell. But it couldn't be that hard to figure out by context. The problem was the size of the collection, one that spanned a dozen sites across the nation. But the most important were kept here. And though no one here had realized the true importance of what Chloe was after, it was likely piggy-backing on something that people did believe was valuable. Something tied to an event, project, or person of national historic significance. And, judging by that fatal public records request Chloe had farmed out to her now-dead friend, that person was likely Senator Ted Kennedy.

Someone with whom Kellerman and his colleagues were quite familiar.

Kellerman passed boxes and files dating from the Great Depression and on into World War II. This wing, at least, seemed to be chronologically dated. He was getting closer.

His row dead-ended at a long rack of shelves that stretched twenty feet in either direction. He looked both ways, scanning the labels and deliberating which way to go. Then he heard it. Voices coming from the other side of the shelf. Arguing.

Kellerman leaned over and peered through a gap between two boxes, only to find his view blocked by boxes on the opposite side. He removed a box from his side, taking care to place it on the floor as silently as possible. Through the gap on the other side, halfway down the next row of shelves, he could see a short black woman in a gray pantsuit taking someone to task. Possibly some sort of manager or director for the unit. She seemed like the sort of person who wouldn't be bowled over by his badge or urgent pleas of national security. She would demand proof, and he had neither the time nor the desire to appease someone like that.

He would have to avoid her while he tracked down Jon Rickner and whatever he was retrieving for Chloe. Hopefully this argument would engage her for a while. It didn't look as though she planned on letting up anytime soon.

And then the recipient of her ire moved into view. Standing there, with a longsuffering expression barely masking the contempt he clearly held for the woman before him, was Jon Rickner.

Kellerman had found his target. But the woman's presence created a significant complication. Fortunately, significant complications were the reason Kellerman had a job.

He studied their positions once more, replaced the box he had removed, and began to move.

# CHAPTER 5
## *Washington, DC*

Chloe stared at herself in the restroom mirror, letting the water flow over her hands. She splashed some on her face, hoping the cool liquid would help her focus. But there was so much going on. So much at stake. Far more, she was sure, than even she realized.

Her father had believed this quest was important. Important enough to ostracize his wife to the point of an uncontested divorce, to get fired from his job, to eventually lose his life over. He had even lost his daughter until Chloe finally realized that he wasn't crazy. But by then it was too late. He was dead. And the answers he sought remained hidden.

But maybe not for long.

She dried her hands and dabbed at her face with a paper towel. Hopefully Jon would have returned with the items she'd requested by now. He was taking longer than she had expected. But then, if the items had previously been identified as part of the standard cataloging, they would have been destroyed almost immediately. The Archives' decades-long backlog could be the only thing keeping this faint thread of truth from disappearing forever.

She stepped out of the restroom and froze. A man in a government-issue suit was surveying the counter. Looking for someone.

A stab of recognition jolted her as she caught a solid profile view of his face. She backed into the cover of the restroom, closing the door to a crack. She would never forget the face of the man who interrogated her after her father's death. Asking all the wrong kinds of questions about a purported suicide. She had known he was something other than what he presented himself as then. And his presence here confirmed that he was, in fact, an enemy to her cause.

The man flashed a badge at someone beyond the counter and walked authoritatively toward the stacks.

Toward where she had sent Jon.

She waited a beat before emerging from the restroom. Walking across the lobby, she glanced up at the surveillance cameras ringing the room. Perhaps that was how they knew she was here. Big Brother was watching. Always.

Next to one of the corridors leading out of the lobby, she found what she was looking for. A gray plastic placard, required by the fire marshal of all public buildings. A fire escape route diagram. She studied the map, considered what she knew of the Archives' layout, and decided on a plan.

It was a long shot, but it was all she had.

# CHAPTER 6
## *Washington, DC*

Jon was struggling not to roll his eyes and walk away from Mrs. Hayes's unrelenting tirade. He didn't deserve her berating. It wasn't right that he had been blackballed from the academic community, and it wasn't right that he had to suffer the scorn of a little tyrant supervisor who decided that his presence there was anathema to everything she stood for. A stint teaching at an overseas university was looking more appealing by the minute.

But the mystery of whatever tied together the film canister and the book secreted in his pocket buzzed in his mind, giving pause to his plans of fleeing his archivist job in hopes of once again discovering something incredible hidden within its collections. So long as Mrs. Hayes didn't fire him first.

"I don't know how long you expect me to put up with this, Mr. High-and-Mighty, but just because some politician thinks he can dump you in my lap doesn't mean you deserve to be here," she chastised him. This deep in the archives, none of the researchers or other members of the public could hear her tirade, so she was making no effort to limit her volume.

Jon swallowed his retort that his doctoral degree, recent or not, put his educational qualifications above several of his colleagues, as well as Mrs. Hayes herself. He wasn't quite ready to tell her where to stick this job, though she was pushing him closer by the moment.

"I was just finishing up here, Mrs. Hayes," he said, adopting the most conciliatory tone he could without drenching his words in sarcasm. "I'll be back up front as soon as I can."

"A lot of good it'll do you. Your patron already gave up and left. Looks like you're too slow for everybody these days."

That gave Jon pause. Why would Ms. Harper leave so quickly? Jon checked his watch. Just over half an hour had passed since he had left her. Longer than he'd anticipated. Clearly, digging through boxes upon boxes of Ted Kennedy's effects had set his mind awash with possibilities as he tried in vain to connect the dots behind her request, and he had lost track of the time. Even so, he had never had a patron leave mid-stream. If a researcher came to the Archives, they were there for a good reason. Something integral to their research could only be found in the Archives' collections, and they were willing to dedicate the time necessary to find and retrieve the item from the vast repositories. Most researchers made appointments ahead of time to allow archivists to prepare the request beforehand, reducing the time spent waiting on the items. Walk-ins like Ms. Harper happened, certainly, but it was understood that retrieval time would be increased.

Yet, according to Mrs. Hayes, Chloe Harper had already left the lobby. Was that it, then? His interest in the seemingly disparate items piqued by a practical joke? A waste of time rather than a mystery to be uncovered? Perhaps a lifetime traveling to archeological hotspots with his parents and digging up historical mysteries with his late brother had poisoned his mind to see adventures where there were none. After all, Chloe had come specifically to him. The man who had unmasked a deadly government conspiracy just a few years before. A prime target for practical jokesters preying on his passions.

And he had fallen for it.

Suddenly, Jon's pocket felt very heavy. The purloined book and film canister may not have held any history-changing secrets, but they certainly held sufficient cause for Mrs. Hayes to fire him on the spot.

A man Jon had never seen before turned into their aisle. He was about Jon's height, 6' 2", with a muscular build, no facial hair, and a serious demeanor. The freshly pressed suit completed the image. Mrs. Hayes had already called in security. How had she known about the items? He hadn't heard her mention them, but he had largely zoned out from her screed ever since she mentioned Ms. Harper leaving prematurely. Perhaps she was building her diatribe up to knowledge of the theft, wanting to spring it on Jon as a final gotcha before ordering him dragged ignominiously from the building.

That impression didn't last long.

"Jonathan Rickner?" the man asked as though he knew the answer.

Mrs. Hayes whirled around, ready to accost the newcomer for invading her space. "What are you doing back here?"

The man flashed a badge. Secret Service? What did they want with him?

"National security, ma'am. It's urgent, though."

She chortled, half-turning back to Jon. "I knew you were no good." Then she faced the agent again. "I'm afraid you'll have to wait. I'm dealing with my employee right now. When I'm done, he's all yours."

"Ma'am, this can't wait. I'm sorry, but national security supersedes your employee dispute. I need to speak with Dr. Rickner. Now."

Now facing Jon, she rolled her eyes. "When. I'm. Finished."

Behind her, the agent pulled a gun and aimed it at Loretha Hayes. "That's now."

But instead of giving her a chance to comply with the newly enforced demand, the agent fired. With an accusing glare at Jon for whatever he must have done to lead to this turn of events, Loretha Hayes fell dead at Jon's feet.

"Finally," the agent said, his gun now aimed at Jon. "Now we can talk."

# CHAPTER 7
## *Washington, DC*

Kellerman watched as Jon recoiled from the sight of his freshly murdered boss. Death had a way of emphasizing the urgency of Kellerman's position. And the lengths he was willing to go to get what he wanted.

"Who are you?" Jon asked.

"Secret Service."

"Secret Service agents don't shoot career service government employees in the back."

Kellerman gave him a simpering grin. "She was interfering with a federal investigation. Though that story might change if you don't cooperate."

"Change?"

"It didn't sound like she was a big fan of yours. Workplace violence is on the rise. Such a shame. But considering your controversial past, not completely surprising."

Jon's face flushed with impotent anger. Kellerman had him right where he wanted. But he had to hurry. His suppressed gunshot may have sounded like a heavy box hitting the floor—not an uncommon occurrence in the stacks—but someone would likely stumble across them before long, especially considering their supervisor was now missing.

"The important question now is what you found in that box."

"Which one?" Jon asked. "If you hadn't noticed, there's quite a few."

The agent glanced behind Jon, confirming the archivist's point. "Cute. I don't have time for cute, though. The woman who made this request of you is not who she presented herself to be. She is a federal fugitive, considered to be a threat to national security."

"There was a time when some would have said the same of me," Jon retorted, unmoved.

"It may be again very soon if you don't help me out."

Kellerman noticed that Jon was looking him in the eyes rather than at the gun. He had encountered that sort of defiance before, but not often. So if fear wasn't an effective motivator, perhaps another tack would get him results.

"Look," he said, lowering the gun slightly to get Jon to subconsciously lower his guard somewhat. "I know you've been dealt a bad hand since your encounter with the Division and that Rockefeller thing. You just got your doctorate, one of the most highly qualified new candidates in academia, only to find doors closed in your face at every university in the country. After the incredible impact your father has made at Cambridge, it's only natural you should be upset at being denied what you've worked so hard for. I know you see Uncle Sam as the enemy here, but we can help pry those university doors open for you. All we ask is a little assistance in return."

Jon looked thoughtful. "You can get me back into academia? A teaching position at a real university?"

"Not me, per se, but my boss has the ear of the president. Universities are fearful of government reprisals considering your activities in New York two years ago. A green light from the president would dispel all of that. The world would be your oyster. As it should be."

Jon appeared to be wrestling with Kellerman's promises. Clearly, the agent had tapped the right nerve. This was the delicate moment. Because if he had to kill Jon right here to dig through the boxes himself, pinning Loretha Hayes's murder on the young archivist would become more difficult. And without Jon's help, Kellerman would have no idea where to start with the boxes. Something important was in there, but it wasn't obvious enough for Kellerman's colleagues to have found it on their initial pass. Which meant Kellerman, in a public building next to two dead bodies, would be even less likely to identify it. If it came to that, more serious measures would have to be taken. His goal now was to ensure that it didn't.

"What did she do?" Jon finally asked.

"Who?"

"Ms. Harper."

"She's responsible for the deaths of three people that we know of. The details are classified."

Jon's brow furrowed, wrestling with this new information. Time to seal the deal.

"You're not the first she's duped, Dr. Rickner," Kellerman said. Ever so subtly, he emphasized Jon's title, reminding him what was to be gained by cooperation. "But she is planning something big, something sure to add to her body count. We need your help."

A breakthrough. Jon nodded, slowly, but with growing conviction. "All right. I'll help you."

# CHAPTER 8
## *Washington, DC*

Jon turned his back to the agent and began to rummage around in one of the boxes. He didn't for a moment believe that the man was there on national security business. And he had no illusions that the agent would allow him to walk out of there alive. Jon was already having flashbacks of his encounters with the Division two years earlier. But something about this guy felt even more dangerous. He had murdered a career federal employee in a government building in the middle of the day. That took balls. Or desperation. Or both.

"What did you find, Dr. Rickner?" the agent pressed again.

"I haven't found it yet. My boss"—Jon swallowed—"interrupted me in the middle of my search."

"What did Ms. Harper ask you to find?"

"A couple of newspaper articles," Jon lied.

There were plenty of newspaper articles in the box he was digging through. There was also the flask and the old lighter. Jon sloshed the flask from side to side. Not much inside, but perhaps it was enough. The lighter also seemed to have a modicum of fluid within it. But could he really destroy these historical documents? His whole academic career had been devoted to the preservation and advancement of historical knowledge. For his audition piece to get back into the university circuit, could he really turn his back on all of that?

He steeled himself. No, this was different. This man's desperation testified that the items Chloe Harper wanted were of importance somehow. And if Jon didn't do what was necessary to protect them from the so-called agent, they would be lost forever. Plus, Jon really didn't want to die. He had to believe that if the man didn't need the information that he had, Jon would already be dead.

Jon took a fistful of decades-old newspapers, annotated in the margins by Ted Kennedy's own hand, and twisted them into a makeshift wick. He needed some sort of distraction. If the agent thought that his intel was about to be destroyed, he would lower his defenses enough for Jon to make his escape.

Or so he hoped.

He unscrewed the flask, wincing at a squeak that to Jon's ears sounded like nails on a chalkboard. He prayed that the agent hadn't heard it and doused the newspaper bundle with whiskey.

Then he froze as a gun barrel, still warm from its last firing, poked the back of his neck.

"Wrong move," the agent said.

Jon flicked the flask skyward as a distraction and grabbed the lighter, flicking it once, twice, three times. Nothing. Not even a spark.

The agent kicked Jon to the ground. Jon spun around, staring down the barrel of the gun. "Last chance, Dr. Rickner. Your life for what you found."

He was trapped. The agent stood just far enough away that Jon couldn't kick him or the gun. And his last means of diversion had sputtered out, spilled from the toppled box that had fallen with him.

A deafening siren began to blare throughout the building. The fire alarm. Not his doing, but he'd take it.

The agent looked up at the flashing emergency lights overhead. It was all the distraction Jon needed.

Jon scrambled forward and swept the legs from beneath the agent, being sure to connect with the gun as the other man fell. The weapon tumbled from the man's hands and fell behind him, out of both men's reach. But the agent wasn't on the ground long. In less than a second, he had recovered from the surprise attack and was climbing back to his feet.

Fleeing was the obvious choice. So Jon did the opposite.

Jon lowered his shoulder and charged into the agent's midsection. The agent looked like the sort of guy who could take a gut punch if he saw it coming. He didn't see Jon coming.

The agent let out an *oomph* as he toppled to the floor. Jon landed on top of him. His advantage wouldn't last long, so he had to seize the moment. He had no idea where the gun had fallen, but the agent had other tools and weapons on his utility belt. He grabbed the first item he could get his hands on, a mace-sized cylinder, and snatched it free. The device wasn't like any pepper spray dispenser he had seen before, but all he really needed to do was figure out which end to point toward the other guy's face. He squeezed the trigger.

Nothing sprayed out the other end. He checked it for some sort of safety device. The agent was wrenching his arms free, recovering from the impact to his solar plexus. Jon couldn't see a safety switch or button. But he did see a small silver pin slip out and fall to the floor.

It wasn't mace after all.

It was a grenade.

The agent just missed Jon's chin with his first punch, but connected with his side on the second. Jon dropped the grenade.

Jon scrambled up, his shoe kicking the grenade and sending it skittering across the floor. He had to get out of here. Everyone did.

He ran down the aisle and made the first turn he could. A second later, another bullet report rang out as the agent's shot just missed him.

A second after that, all hell broke loose.

The grenade, instead of exploding with the percussive burst of a flashbang or a frag, detonated with a terrifying whoosh. Almost immediately, Jon felt the heat from the blast, and flames began to devour boxes of centuries-old papers and effects.

What was a federal agent doing with an incendiary grenade in the middle of Washington?

The answer, unbidden, came as quickly as it was foreboding. It was for covering up the evidence of his crimes. The body of Loretha Hayes. Of Jon Rickner. And anything he didn't need from those Kennedy boxes so no one could tell what he had stolen.

Only Jon had screwed those plans up. And now the entire section—thousands upon thousands of historical documents and artifacts—was about to go up in flames. All because of him.

An emergency exit beacon on the ceiling ahead beckoned him to the left. He darted down that aisle, then ran full bore into the emergency exit. Another alarm began ringing from the crash bar he pushed through to open the door, but it was dwarfed by the building's alarm and the growing roar of the flames behind him. Apparently the fire suppression system was poorly equipped to deal with whatever accelerant had been used in the grenade. Jon wished he could turn back the clock and redo that whole encounter, but it was too late now. The die was cast. And he was on the run.

He ran down a short flight of stairs to the sidewalk, drawing stares from pedestrians not used to such a ruckus coming from the normally staid National Archives. Now where? With the fire alarm blaring, HR would want to ensure that all employees were successfully evacuated and accounted for. But with his pockets still full of the items stolen from Ted Kennedy's effects, the agent on his tail, and the terrible fire that he had played a role in starting, it seemed clear that such a course of action would quickly land him in handcuffs.

Or worse.

He had to go to ground. But where? He hadn't planned for these sorts of contingencies. He didn't know that he needed to. But he couldn't stand out here on the street all day.

A decade-old Honda Accord screeched to a halt at the curb. Jon instinctively jumped back, then saw the face staring at him from the open car window.

"Get in!" Chloe Harper shouted.

Grateful and confused all at once, Jon did exactly that.

# CHAPTER 9
## Washington, DC

Kellerman staggered through the smoke, popping off a couple more shots before hearing the emergency exit door open. He ran to the door just in time to see a white sedan screech down the street and turn the corner. Too far away to get a read on the license plate, but he could definitely see the silhouettes of two occupants in the car. There was no doubt in his mind who they were.

How had it all gone so wrong? Now that Jon and Chloe were in the wind, his first thought was to try to save whatever he could of the documents his grenade had set ablaze. But no, his mission remained in force. Gaines would never forgive him for destroying so many of the nation's historical records, but preserving the integrity of their overarching mission was paramount.

As it had been since the beginning.

Either the documents Chloe had been seeking were being devoured by the fire, or Jon had taken them during his escape. Or they never existed at all. Option one and three contained the threat. But if Jon had just delivered them to Chloe, everything they had worked for could unravel in a hurry. It all depended on what they had found. And how quick they were to decipher its meaning. His colleagues would surely have swept through the Archives' collection of Ted Kennedy's effects before now. The Kennedys had caused plenty of trouble for the Society through the years. So whatever was there—if anything—wasn't immediately clear as a threat to the Society. But if Chloe Harper was after it, and if she had specifically targeted Jon Rickner as an ally to her cause, there was *something* there. The Society had gained a lot of powerful enemies over the centuries. A necessary consequence of their mission, regrettably. But they had fended off efforts to derail the Society's plans every time.

Or had they? Had one of their enemies in years past planted a time bomb that could destroy everything they had built? Had one of the Kennedys? The Society couldn't afford a breach. Not now, when they were this close to their biggest operation in more than half a century. If Jack Harper had proven anything, it was that he could be clever and resourceful. Not resourceful enough to save his life, but then, few were when faced with men of Kellerman's caliber. Yet both Harper's kid and the infamous Jon Rickner had managed to escape his grasp, possibly in possession of something that could complicate matters for the Society's upcoming operation.

He was going to have to rectify that.

But first, he had to clean up this mess.

Crouched to avoid the smoke and carbon monoxide gathering overhead, Kellerman made his way back through the building. He ignored the distant screams and groans echoing from the epicenter of the fire and the area beyond. Unfortunate casualties. They were an ever-present fact of war. And make no mistake, this was a war.

A guard was just exiting the Archives' security office as Kellerman arrived. Upon seeing that this was far from a drill, he panicked, forgetting to ensure the auto-locking door was shut before running for the exit.

Kellerman snagged the door handle just before it closed. He slid inside and was happy to see that it was empty. A bank of monitors filled the wall, with a number of computer towers and keyboards dotting the desk in front. He slipped a miniature flash drive from his pocket and inserted it into one of the computer towers.

According to the man who had given it to him, the virus should only take about ten seconds to upload. It was disguised as a common script automatically run by the operating system whenever a user logged in. As soon as the next guard logged into the system, either here or remotely, the virus would wipe all of the surveillance footage for the past week.

It would look like a glitch, a user error, or a consequence of the fire, but the length of the deletion would seem less like a targeted attack by the perpetrator of today's disaster. Or, if they did suspect a purposeful erasure, they would suspect someone who had made a previous appearance at the Archives' surveillance footage earlier in that longer window. Not someone like Kellerman, who hadn't been here in years before today.

Enough time had lapsed. He unplugged the drive and pocketed it. Sucking a deep breath of less-tainted air, he opened the door with his jacket sleeve and eased back into the smoke-filled hallway. He was careful to wipe his fingerprints from the outside handle of the security room door where he had grabbed it earlier.

No trace. He was never here.

The way it had to be.

Firemen in full tactical gear ran past him as he hustled down the hall and out of the building. Joining the mélange of terrified researchers, archivists, and tourists in the evacuation, he kept a handkerchief pressed over his nose and mouth. It didn't help filter his breathing much as far as he could tell, but it certainly provided a plausible excuse to hide his face from anyone who might remember it. He had tried to make as brief an impression as possible on the way into the building. A repeat appearance might help to solidify his features for the staff, who would inevitably be questioned in the coming hours and days.

All except for one.

Jon Rickner was on the run. And it was now Kellerman's job to find him, Chloe, and whatever it was they had found before it was too late.

# CHAPTER 10
*Prince George County, Maryland*

For the past twenty-five minutes, Chloe had remained silent, speaking only to rebuff Jon's demands for answers to what was going on. She was focused on getting out of town, navigating packed streets filled with lost tourists and frustrated commuters. She tensed up at every siren, clenched her jaw at every set of flashing lights. And they never seemed to stop. Whatever had happened in there, it was bad, and she didn't want any part of it.

"Did you get them?" Chloe asked once they were out of the city limits and in Maryland.

"Hey, look!" Jon said. "She speaks!"

Chloe ignored his sarcasm. "Did you get it or not?"

"I got something. You want to tell me what's going on?"

"What happened inside there? Why all the police?"

"Did you pull the fire alarm?"

"I saw . . . a man. Someone I've seen before. He had no business there unless he meant trouble for me. And, by association, for you. So I tried to get you out of there."

The day she last saw that man was the day after her father died. Gunshot wound to the temple in his study. So stereotypical of suicides it was almost a cliché. Chloe had her doubts even then. Those doubts had ballooned seriously once she realized her father's fanatical obsessions were not as crazy as everyone had said. And seeing the man in the Archives today all but confirmed her suspicions. Her father had not killed himself. He had been murdered.

"Yeah, we've met," Jon said, rubbing his side.

"Did he start the fire?"

"He had a little help, but yeah. He had an incendiary grenade on his utility belt. It exploded and . . . well, with all the paper in there, the stacks are a tinderbox."

A grenade. That explained the cops.

"He's serious trouble. I overheard him talking to someone on the phone the first time I saw him. He answered the phone with 'This is Kellerman.' Don't know if it's an alias or what, but death seems to follow him."

"I know the type," Jon said wearily. "Listen, Kellerman or whatever said some pretty serious stuff about you. He may be a bad guy, but I'm crossing state lines while fleeing a crime scene with you, and I don't know anything about you except that you're a Hawkeye."

Chloe frowned. "Actually, that was a fake ID. I'm not a student at the University of Iowa."

Jon threw up his hands. "So the single thing I thought I knew about you is a lie. Is your name even Chloe Harper?"

"Yes, it is," Chloe said, kicking herself that things had turned out this way. "Look, I didn't mean to involve you in this."

"Sure you did. You walked right up to my counter and asked for my help."

"But not like this. I thought you could locate those items in the Archives that everyone else had overlooked."

"What everyone else?"

"The people who don't want us to know. People like Kellerman."

Jon rolled his eyes. "And down the rabbit hole we go."

Chloe felt a lump in her throat. Had this all been a big mistake? "I would have thought you'd be open to the possibility of government conspiracies."

"Sure, they happen. But there's an entire cottage industry of two-bit hacks who believes wholeheartedly that they have the answer to the all-powerful Masonic order that rules the world, or the secret alien technology hidden at Area 51, or who really killed JFK. Not everything is a big government conspiracy. Sometimes, things just happen."

"And a purported government agent setting off an incendiary grenade in the National Archives, the same man who probably killed a retired FBI agent last year, that's not proof that something strange is going on?"

Jon shrugged. "Something's definitely going on. But your trustworthiness as a source is really suffering right now. Come on, tell me something true about yourself."

Chloe paused. "I've lived in nine different states, but I've never been to Iowa."

"Kellerman said you were responsible for three deaths thus far."

"That dirty, lying son of a . . ." Chloe took a breath and thought. "In a way, I did get my friend Riley killed. She submitted a Freedom of Information Act request for me. Because my name would send off warning lights to Kellerman's people. And just after she received the info, they killed her."

"Kellerman shot my boss when she wouldn't let me talk to him. That's two. Maybe I was to be the third."

Chloe shook her head. She hadn't killed anyone, but, in a way, Kellerman was right. He may have pulled the trigger, but she had put them in the line of fire.

"I'm sorry, Jon. I never should have involved you. I never should have involved anyone. Whatever this is, I should have just let it die with my father."

Jon turned his body toward her. She felt his eyes studying her, scrutinizing her for deceit. After what had happened over the past hour, she couldn't blame him.

"Well, I'm involved now," he said. "Kellerman, assuming he survived the fire, is not going to just let you and I ride off into the sunset. And I don't particularly feel like undergoing police interrogation without knowing who he is and why he attacked me. My claim of a secret government agent bringing the grenade into the Archives will probably get me a lot of eye rolls and a long prison sentence without proof. For better or worse, I've been associated with a lot of government conspiracy crazies ever since New York two years ago."

"Present company excluded on the crazies bit, I hope."

"Jury's still out. But I did get your goods from the Archives. I'll even show them to you if you can tell me what this is all about."

Chloe grimaced. *Here goes nothing.*

"Do you want to know who really killed JFK?"

# CHAPTER 11
## Pittsburgh, Pennsylvania

Stanton Gaines hated bad news. Worse yet was poorly timed bad news. Anthony Kellerman was delivering a hefty dose of the latter.

"You do realize what's at stake here, don't you?" Gaines asked, the cell phone pressed tight to his ear.

"Of course," Kellerman said from DC. "The importance has not escaped me."

Gaines stood up from his desk and paced the length of his oak-paneled office. He had taken off his shoes earlier, and gripped the centuries-old Persian rug with his toes as he walked. The desk and office had been created by the same artisan, a one-of-a-kind set specifically created for Gaines's great-grandfather. They were both hand-crafted affairs, inlaid with gold filigree and replete with a level of ornate detail rarely seen in modern furnishings.

Though the Gaines dynasty had been one of Pittsburgh's first families since the end of the eighteenth century, this house only dated to 1874. The three-story Victorian mansion was built for F. Byron Gaines as he finally capitalized on the success of his factories and erected a palatial home to match his kingly standing. An industrial titan dwarfed only by the likes of Carnegie and Rockefeller, F. Byron Gaines left quite the legacy to his great-grandson. And though Stanton Gaines, one of dozens of great-grandchildren sired by F. Byron, didn't own quite the commercial empire that his great-grandfather once presided over, the Gilded Age magnate had left him a legacy far greater than mere money.

"So were they working together before this?"

"Doubtful. There was no reason for Harper to show up at the Archives and expose herself if she had already given Rickner instructions for whatever she was looking for. But they're certainly together now."

Kellerman had already told him about the sedan that had sped away from the Archives' emergency exit. Gaines was having traffic cams scrutinized for the car, but without a license plate, he had little hope of finding them before they were out of the city. White sedans were a dime a dozen. Chloe Harper had chosen her getaway vehicle well.

"What were they after?" Gaines asked.

"Something to do with Ted Kennedy."

"*Ted* Kennedy?"

"Yes, sir."

"Not the brother I would have expected."

"Maybe that's why we missed it the first time."

In the digital age, everyone constantly demanded access to everything all the time. The very existence of the Freedom of Information Act made Americans think they were entitled to any information they wanted, whenever they wanted it.

That wasn't how classified information worked. But it didn't stop the clamoring from growing.

Thankfully, the information Gaines held wasn't sitting on some NSA server for the next Edward Snowden to come along and share with the world. It was far too dangerous for that. And far too important for the future of the country.

Unfortunately, thousands of recently declassified documents had just become available for public disclosure. Though he and his allies had fought against it at the time and ever since, there was no publicly acceptable reason why the documents should remain classified after so much time had passed. So, in 1992, Congress had passed the President John F. Kennedy Assassination Records Collections Act of 1992, which didn't officially go into effect until 2017. There was nothing particularly damaging in the files, of course. The truly damning ones had been scrubbed decades before, while dozens more had been flagged with national security concerns and were slated to remain classified until at least 2021. But with such a massive number of documents, even the most minor reference within them could open doors that would set off the conspiracy nuts.

Or someone like Chloe Harper, whose access to her father's research might provide insight into the documents that even Gaines didn't have.

He walked back to his desk and flipped through the files he had pulled on Jack Harper, Chloe Harper, and now Jon Rickner.

He didn't know what they had found or even how it pertained to the documents Chloe had acquired through an FOIA request last month, but he knew it spelled trouble.

"Is there any indication they know about our plans?" Gaines asked.

"None. She seems to be fixated on the Kennedy assassination. Just like her old man."

"Still, we don't need any unwanted attention. Especially not now."

"Understood. I'm already working to find them and put a stop to this."

Gaines told him he'd be in touch and hung up. His analysts would coordinate tracking with Kellerman. The agent had all the resources he needed to find and capture Chloe and Jon.

But there was another problem, one that niggled at him day and night. In declassifying the JFK assassination files, something had gotten out. Somewhere in that trove of reports, memos, and archival evidence, there was a hidden weakness that someone might know how to exploit. Gaines didn't know where that weakness would hurt them or even if it could, but he had to find out soon. Too much was riding on the next few days. Chloe and Jon were one problem, but another, more tangential problem existed that could cause irreparable harm, undoing nearly two and a half centuries of sacrifice. The weakness had to be discovered, analyzed, and destroyed.

Gaines began to search for a number in his cell phone. It was time to mix things up.

# CHAPTER 12
## *Baltimore, Maryland*

Jon rolled his eyes.

"Ha ha. Let me guess, you also know where the moon landings were faked and where the Founding Fathers held their secret cache of Templar gold."

Chloe didn't say anything for a minute. Jon turned and saw that her expression was anything but amused.

"Wait, you're serious aren't you? All that back there, all that was for some JFK assassination theory?"

"It's not a theory. At least three people have gotten killed over this in the past year alone."

"Just because you've got a psychopathic killer on your tail doesn't mean you've solved the JFK assassination. Lots of people over the past sixty-five years have thought that. And they've all been wrong."

Chloe clucked her tongue. "I figured you of all people would be open to a new theory. Especially after all the proof we've seen."

"Kellerman means something's going on. It doesn't mean he's defending the JFK killers. I mean, come on, everyone who could possibly have been on the grassy knoll or wherever is either dead or in a nursing home by now. There's a reason why they just declassified all the files on the assassination. Because there's no one to protect anymore."

"A, they didn't declassify everything; B, documents from that mass declassification are how I ended up at the Archives in the first place; and C, there's always someone to protect."

"Who?" Jon felt heat rising in his face. This was exactly the kind of nutjob conspiracy theorist he had tried to avoid since becoming the face of the Division's downfall two years ago. "JFK assassination theories have become an industry all to itself. Everyone has the answer, and the proof to back it up. Only none of those stories agree. First it was the Russians, then Castro, then the Mafia, then the CIA. The narratives always shifted to blame whoever the boogeyman *du jour* was. The only thing they can agree on is that there *was* a conspiracy, because otherwise they'd be out of a job."

Chloe choked up a bit, though her voice took on a more defiant tone. "I've gained nothing from this quest and lost everything. My father. My best friend. And, after that snafu back there, I'd imagine my freedom is on the chopping block next. Unless Kellerman decides to snuff me out entirely before that."

"Look, I'm sorry about your dad and your friend. I know all too well about loss." Jon's older brother, Michael, had been murdered at the hands of the Division, which, ironically, had been the catalyst that put Jon on their trail in the first place and ultimately led to their downfall. A decade before that, his mother had been killed in the Yucatan on an archeological expedition. In a way, Jon had lost his father that day as well, as Dr. William Rickner had never really come back from that failed excursion into the jungle to find his wife. Her shredded and bloodied backpack, along with the lack of a body, had not only seeded William's darkest fears, but had also prevented closure. William had retreated more and more into his work, leaving his sons to rely on each other.

Tears brimmed in Chloe's eyes. Jon felt awful.

"Hey, look, I'm sorry," Jon said. "All right, tell me your theory. I've heard plenty over the years, but I'm betting yours has a unique spin I've never heard before."

Chloe sniffed. "That's the thing. I don't have a theory. Neither did my dad. He was investigating. That's what he did. He was a special agent with the FBI. Twenty-eight years with the Bureau. And then they fired him because he wouldn't stop digging into the JFK assassination."

"Seriously? Was he doing it on his own time?"

"Yeah, mostly. But he was using classified FBI records to supplement his research. And that didn't go over well with the higher-ups."

"So what did he find?"

"It's more a question of what he didn't find. A lot of this is public record by now, but his initial investigation followed what the House found in '78."

"The House Select Committee on Assassinations," Jon said.

The committee, convened in 1978 with the intention of finally putting to rest the public's conspiracy-laden fears in the throes of the Cold War, capping a ten-year span that had seen America's out-and-out military defeat—and an ugly, televised one at that—alongside the assassinations of presidential candidates and civil rights leaders, actual government conspiracies like MKUltra, the ignominious resignation of a president, revolutions and growing unrest in Latin America and OPEC nations, and a growing counterculture that sought the downfall of the traditional order. But instead of dispelling the notion that there was a conspiracy behind JFK's assassination, the committee had only added fuel to the fire. Their official findings that Kennedy's assassination was likely the result of a conspiracy only served to validate the fears of millions of Americans. But the committee was unable to answer the biggest question of all.

Who was behind the conspiracy?

Even more problematic was that the committee's findings said that virtually all of the usual suspects were not likely to be the culprits. The FBI, the CIA, the Secret Service, the Soviet Union, Cuba, anti-Castro forces, and organized crime were all vindicated by the report.

So who did that leave?

Chloe nodded. "My father found a copy of a letter from J. Edgar Hoover telling Robert F. Kennedy to lay off investigating his brother's assassination. Dated 1964, just a few weeks after the Warren Commission presented their conclusion that Oswald was a lone gunman."

"Wait. RFK was the attorney general. He would have been Hoover's boss. How could the director of the FBI give orders to the attorney general?"

"It wasn't exactly orders. It read more like a thinly veiled threat."

Jon was well aware of J. Edgar Hoover's legacy. He had served for over a decade in the twenties and thirties as the last director of the Bureau of Investigation. For the next forty-seven years, he forged the newly christened Federal Bureau of Investigation into his own personal kingdom. By abusing the power of his position, he had built files full of compromising information on congressmen, senators, cabinet secretaries, titans of industry, and presidents. Wielding his extensive collection of blackmail material, Hoover was considered untouchable, bending men who were technically far more powerful to his will on a regular basis. His career helming the top law enforcement agency in the nation spanned more than half a century, serving every president from Coolidge to Nixon. Only death could wrench him from his throne, and it finally did in May of 1972, just weeks before the Watergate break-in sent a series of Hoover's less-formidable successors on a collision course with the White House.

"J. Edgar was blackmailing Bobby Kennedy?" Jon asked.

"Maybe. It was essentially a 'drop it or else' demand. The 'or else' could have been blackmail. Or it could have been something else."

Jon swallowed. The thought that the FBI could have been behind the death of not just John F. Kennedy in 1963 but also of his brother five years later was unthinkable. Bobby Kennedy, then a US Senator and a front-runner for the Democratic Party nomination in the 1968 presidential election, was gunned down by Sirhan Sirhan, a Palestinian who purportedly confessed to killing the senator because of his support for Israel. The assassination, occurring on the one-year anniversary of the Six-Day War that ended with Israel regaining its ancestral lands in Gaza and the West Bank at the expense of Palestine, changed the face of the 1968 election, eventually resulting in a fractured party base that helped Nixon defeat Hubert Humphrey in November.

"Sirhan Sirhan said he didn't have any memory of killing Bobby," Jon said. "Conspiracists have pointed to MKUltra, which was still an active project at the time, as being potential evidence of a government operation behind the assassination."

MKUltra was a top-secret CIA project that used a combination of psychotropic drugs, controversial technology, and pseudoscience to experiment with mind control. Founded in 1953, the project was one of the most controversial projects of the Cold War, with American and Canadian citizens duped into participation on false pretenses. With forced drug abuse, psychological torture, and deceptive practices all orchestrated by the US Government against its own citizens, the program was proof positive to countless conspiracy theorists that Washington was perpetually up to no good. The project's results were mixed, but by the time it was finally exposed by the Church Committee in 1975, MKUltra's greatest impact was shining a spotlight on the terrible lengths to which those in power would go to secure victory in the Cold War.

However, Sirhan's claims of having no memory of the attack, as well as a quickly given and just as quickly retracted confession of the crime, echoed the brainwashed assassin at the heart of Richard Conlon's recent bestselling novel and subsequent film adaptations, *The Manchurian Candidate*. Years later, once the horrors and goals of MKUltra were finally revealed to the world, Sirhan's claims started sounding less like fiction and more like a plausible government conspiracy.

Jon knew that one infamous instance of J. Edgar Hoover abusing his power with blackmail to coerce high-level figures transpired just a matter of weeks before he would have sent the letter to Bobby Kennedy. Hoover also took a short-term, limited surveillance warrant for Martin Luther King, Jr.—one approved by RFK in his role as attorney general—and illegally expanded it to track every aspect of his life indefinitely. In the wake of MLK's assassination, just a couple of months before Bobby Kennedy was himself gunned down, King's widow received a mysterious blackmail package with a threatening typewritten note and a tape recording of one of her husband's sexual affairs. Coretta Scott King immediately suspected the FBI was behind the threat and the blackmail material—which was acquired via J. Edgar's illegally expanded wiretap—and, a decade later, several years after death had wrenched the reins of power from Hoover's iron grip, a copy of the letter would be discovered in the files of Deputy Director William C. Sullivan. In the 1960s, Sullivan served as Hoover's director of domestic intelligence, a relationship that extended back to World War II.

All the more reason for the House of Representatives to convene their Select Committee on Assassinations in 1978. And all the more reason that effort backfired.

"So the FBI, or J. Edgar Hoover specifically, could have been behind the three biggest assassinations that defined the 1960s?" Jon asked.

"The Kennedy brothers and Dr. King? It certainly seems so."

"Okay, but how would you prove that?"

Chloe smiled. "My dad found a memo written by Robert F. Kennedy in 1968, just weeks before his assassination. It referenced an important package he was going to send to his brother and fellow senator, Edward Kennedy. Ted. He didn't write down what the package actually contained in the note, but he mentioned it as items 231 and 497 in a personal effects inventory done in the wake of Jack Kennedy's assassination."

The pieces started to click together. "The FOIA request you did?" Jon asked. "Was that for the inventory?"

"Sure was."

"And let me guess. Items 231 and 497 were a century-old pocket edition of John Buchan's *The Thirty-Nine Steps* and a 1960s-era Kodak film canister."

Chloe grinned. "You're even better than advertised."

Jon pulled the book and film canister from his pocket. "And the next piece of the puzzle is revealed."

Chloe took her eyes off the road to finally see the items she'd been seeking. She let out a little squeal of delight.

"Don't you want to see what's here?" Jon asked as Chloe passed by yet another exit off I-95.

"Were you able to figure anything out yet?"

"I just got a moment to look at it before my boss came up. And then Kellerman. And then the fire. I've been a little busy. But based on the inscription and the publication date, I'd say the book fits with your theory of it belonging to the Kennedy brothers."

"Any notes or anything inside? Photos or pieces of paper slipped between the pages."

Jon spread the cover spine up and shook the book. "Nope."

"What about the film canister?"

"I'm kind of afraid to open it without a darkroom setup. There's definitely something inside, but if the film hasn't been developed, whatever's on there will be ruined if I open it now."

"Good point."

"So where are we going?" Jon finally asked. "We're well out of DC Metro Police's jurisdiction. Heck, we're almost out of Maryland too."

"We're going to Delaware."

"Delaware? What the heck's in Delaware?"

Chloe smiled enigmatically. "Our escape route."

# CHAPTER 13
## *Marseilles, France*

P atrick Molyneux stared at the phone in his hand. Though the call was now disconnected, his mind replayed its message incessantly. He certainly knew the name Stanton Gaines, but he didn't realize that a man of his stature would be the one to invite him into the fullness of the Molyneux family legacy.

Molyneux dodged a bicyclist racing along the coastal boardwalk. The pristine waters of the Mediterranean crashed against the wooden supports below his feet. Fitting that the call had come while he was visiting here.

He came back to Marseilles every year. The same hotel. The same café. The same boardwalk pier. What had begun as a family vacation twenty years ago was now a solo ritual. Although this year, perhaps things had come full circle. He was the only family he had left.

Patrick Molyneux was born in New Orleans, but his father had ensured the entire family made regular pilgrimages to their ancestral homeland. A lifelong military man from a long line of military men, Colonel Cyrus Molyneux dragged Patrick, his mother, and his older brother Kyle across the globe from one US Air Force post to the next. By the time he graduated high school, Patrick had attended eleven different schools in nine different countries. He had rarely lived in any one place longer than a year, and never more than two years.

With so much constantly changing in his life, it was only natural that Patrick would latch on to the one geographic place of constancy throughout his childhood. Marseilles had been his mother's favorite place in the world. She had grown up in the nearby village of Saint-Savournin, and had frequented the city throughout her youth before immigrating to the United States to attend Louisiana State University, where she met her future husband. As such, Cyrus made it a point to bring the family to the seaside resort city every year, no matter where in the world they currently called "home."

For twelve years they came to Marseilles, stayed at L'Hotel Ciel D'Azur, ate breakfast at Charisse's, and walked this very stretch of beach. And then, just weeks before Patrick graduated from high school, Heloise Molyneux died of a heart attack at the age of forty-six.

Cyrus never again visited Marseilles. A hard man at the best of times, his wife's unexpected death dried up the last shred of emotion he shared. Kyle, a first lieutenant in the Air Force, was already deep into making his own military mark on the world, the next in a line of distinguished military officers stretching back to the Revolutionary War.

So Patrick was left alone. And without the influence of his father or his brother, he did the unthinkable for a Molyneux.

He pursued a career in academia.

Neither Cyrus nor Kyle could be bothered to make an appearance when he earned his bachelor's in political science from Stanford in three years. Nor did they show up when he earned his doctorate in American history from the University of Chicago at the age of twenty-five. Summa Cum Laude, graduate with honors, and the youngest in his class. But because he wasn't on the battlefield commanding troops in defense of Uncle Sam and Lady Liberty, he wasn't a real Molyneux man.

So it was these trips to Marseilles that kept him connected to his family. Back when that word actually meant something. Before his mother died, and his father and brother abandoned him. All through undergrad, all through his doctoral program, Patrick made his annual pilgrimage to his last tangible vestige of grounded happy times.

Then fate decided to throw him a curve ball.

A year ago almost to the day, Major Kyle Molyneux was killed by a sniper's bullet outside of Kabul. As the firstborn, the Molyneux birthright should have been Kyle's. He was actively pursuing the legacy left by his forefathers, with a promising military career and the blessing of the family patriarch. But a Taliban sharpshooter changed all that. Now Patrick, the civilian academician who had never known battle or basic training, would be the one to inherit his father's place in the courts of history.

A month after he buried his son, then-retired Colonel Cyrus Molyneux died of a heart attack himself. A lifetime of stress and bitterness had taken its toll, and the knowledge that his family legacy would be left to his *other* son was simply too much to bear.

But Patrick had never heard anything about that birthright. He thought that his father might have cut the lineage, forgoing the Molyneux seat at the controls of history so that his traitorous son would not ruin the legacy his family had built. Though the thought of being written off so blithely had angered him, Patrick never looked into the status of his membership. In fact, he preferred not to think of it at all. Did he desire that membership? Of course. Having learned so much about history in his studies, the opportunity to be a part of it as something far greater was incredible. But he was sure that if he sought out the truth, all he would find would be disappointment. His suspicions that his father had closed that door to him were painful enough. But despite his estrangement from his father and brother over the past decade and change, the pain of their deaths was still fresh. A confirmation that his father had thought so little of him as to destroy his most prized possession rather than bequeath it to Patrick would just be too much.

Only his fears were completely unfounded. This call from Stanton Gaines changed everything.

Patrick left the boardwalk and headed back to the hotel. He had a plane to catch. His destiny as a Molyneux awaited.

He would make his father proud.

# CHAPTER 14

## *Wilmington, Delaware*

Chloe pulled into the parking lot of a busy strip mall and instructed Jon to get out with her.

"We going shopping?" Jon quipped.

"Already went," Chloe said, popping the trunk. She lifted the lid and retrieved two suitcases, handing one to Jon.

"You were planning on this all along. On me coming on the run with you."

"No," she said. "I was hoping you would want to help me, but everything that happened with Kellerman and your boss was entirely unplanned."

She had already seen enough to know that preparing a contingency plan like this was necessary when playing with whatever political plutonium her father had unearthed, but she thought it best not to voice that right now. Jon was already suspicious of everything that was going on. Given his history, he had reason to be. But then, that was what made him such a valuable ally right now.

Kindred spirits trapped in a nightmare world of conspiracies and deception.

She pulled a screwdriver and Pennsylvania license plate from the trunk and swapped out her car's Virginia plate. The Pennsylvania plate had expired last year, so no one would be looking for it, but she had applied a new date sticker to prevent suspicion by a passing cop. A trick she learned from her dad, not just swapping the plates with another nearby car. Most people didn't look at their own plates often, but some did. And if they noticed that their plates were missing or had been swapped, the first number they called would be the police. She thanked her lucky stars once again that she'd had the foresight to plan ahead. She only hoped it would be enough.

"So do you have another car waiting here or something?" Jon asked.

"Not quite." Chloe tossed the Virginia plate and screwdriver into the trunk and shut the lid. Rolling her suitcase behind her, she stepped to the curb and hailed a passing taxi.

Once their luggage was secure in the trunk and she and Jon were seated in the back, Chloe gave the driver their destination.

"The airport?" Jon asked. "You don't think they'll be looking for our IDs?"

Chloe glared at him and motioned toward the driver. Jon seemed to get the message. He shut up and looked out the window for the duration of the drive.

Twenty minutes later, they exited the cab at New Castle-Wilmington Airport.

"Let me guess, you've already booked our flight, too?" Jon asked once the taxi driver had left.

Chloe smiled. "We're not flying out of here. They haven't had any commercial passenger flights at this airport since 2015. In fact, Delaware's now the only state in the country that doesn't host any commercial passenger flights."

"Seriously? So why the heck did you bring us to the airport?"

"Because that's not the only way to get out of here." She pointed to a sign and headed toward the building.

Trains.

Because of the unique situation Delaware's airports found themselves in, and because of the abundance of passenger trains in this part of the Atlantic seaboard, many Amtrak routes were considered "connecting flights," given official flight numbers by United and other airline carriers as part of a larger travel route. Thus, the first leg of their journey would be via rail.

"Your new ID is in the small zip compartment on your suitcase," she said, withdrawing her own from the bag.

"You've got one too?" he asked. "Why didn't you use that at the Archives instead of using your real name? If Kellerman was looking for you, if your name was the red flag that brought him down on us, all of this could have been avoided if you'd just used your alias there. Couldn't it?"

She frowned. "I had to know."

Jon froze. "You had to know whether they were looking for you?"

"Yeah."

"Well, clearly they are. And now my boss is dead, half of the stacks is a charred husk, and . . . Oh no."

Chloe looked to see what had caught Jon's attention. A television, mounted on a post for passengers waiting for their train. The TV was muted, but the screen's news ticker and images spoke plenty.

At Least Twenty-Five Dead in National Archives Inferno

Oh no, indeed.

Jon dropped his suitcase and stared at the screen slack-jawed. At first, she wanted to warn him not to give himself away by his reaction. Then she realized that his reaction was not the betraying factor she feared. This was news of a major national tragedy in the heart of the country's capital. There weren't many people in the terminal, but most of those who were also seemed aghast at the news. Jon's reaction, Chloe realized, went far deeper, though. He felt guilty. He felt the weight of those dozens of deaths on his conscience.

Chloe, however, knew better.

"Come on, Jon," she whispered close to his ear. "We have to go if Kellerman and the others responsible for all this are going to be stopped."

Hearing her voice the possibility that someone other than him might be responsible for the disaster seemed to snap Jon out of his horrified daze.

"At least twenty-five dead," he said distantly.

"Far more than that are dead because of whoever Kellerman works for. But we have the tools to stop them now."

Of course, it went without saying that their bed was now officially made. They couldn't go to the police about what had really gone down. They would assuredly end up in a jail cell awaiting charges of arson, murder, terrorism, and a host of other federal crimes. Depending on how ambitious the prosecutor might be feeling, perhaps even some crimes against the state, like good old treason. Not that they would ever have their day in court. Lee Harvey Oswald hadn't. And with Kellerman's penchant for gaining access to secure government facilities, she had no doubt that the agent would see that neither she nor Jon ever saw the inside of a courtroom—or anywhere else for that matter—again.

Like the trooper she expected he would be, Jon picked up his suitcase and gave her a nod. She walked to the board and checked the departure times. The next train to Philadelphia was on time and arriving for boarding in less than ten minutes.

"Erik Weisz?" Jon said, reading his new driver's license once they'd reached the platform. "Seriously?"

"Who better for achieving the impossible?" she said.

"I just hope there aren't too many Houdini buffs on staff here." Harry Houdini had been born in Hungary as Erik Weisz before immigrating to the United States and legally adopting his alliterative stage name.

She smiled and showed him her new ID.

"Pauline Schmidt?" he asked.

"One of the first female professional magicians. Made a name for herself in the late nineteenth century performing across Scandinavia. Back then, of course, professional magic wasn't exactly considered a noble endeavor, especially for women, so she dealt with that stigma both during and after her career."

"Is that you?" he asked, his voice thoughtful. "Ahead of your time, looked down upon by society for your ambitions, to be proven a true pioneer once history has run its course?"

She bit her lip. Apparently she had chosen her new moniker well.

"Something like that," she said.

The intercom announced the impending arrival of their train. Seconds later, the gleaming Amtrak liner blew into the station and screeched to a halt. Tickets in hand and luggage in tow, Chloe and Jon boarded the train.

Two hours later, they were in Philadelphia, transferring to another train.

"Newark?" Jon asked.

"Not our final destination."

"Where is?"

She glanced around the compartment, careful of any prying ears. "Dallas," she said.

"Because that's where it happened? JFK's assassination?"

"Not exactly."

Jon didn't look satisfied with her answer.

"Yes, that's where it happened," she said. "But we're going to meet with one of the foremost experts on JFK conspiracy theories."

"Oh really? And what makes him so much more of an expert than the thousands of other tinfoil nuts?"

She gave him a grin. "Because he was there back in '63. He saw Kennedy die. And he saw who really killed the president."

# CHAPTER 15
## *Washington, DC*

A bathroom stall in the Archives Metro station had been his workshop. Anthony Kellerman emerged with a new face, and a new ID to match. Now it was time to return to the scene of the crime.

Emergency vehicles surrounded the National Archives, with police roadblocks securing a two-block radius around the building. Fire engines had their hoses tapped into nearby hydrants, though the lack of visible smoke seemed to indicate the fires had finally been extinguished. Ambulances clotted around every exit, half of them screaming off to the nearest hospital to save their injured occupants, the other half remaining to treat the less severely wounded.

And clustered across Constitution Avenue on the grounds of the National Gallery of Art was the huddled mass of evacuated Archives employees and patrons. Kellerman headed their way.

It was a sorry sight. Virtually everyone he saw fell into one of three camps. Those who mourned their dead coworkers—unless they were so dedicated to their job that the objects of their mourning were the historical documents and artifacts lost to the flames. Those who were visibly in shock, shaking their heads back and forth at the ground, muttering to themselves, or lost in a thousand-yard stare. And those who were frustrated at being detained while the investigators tried to get some idea of how this tragedy had happened.

All of them were useless to Kellerman. But there was at least one exception to the rule.

Kellerman recognized Phoebe Iacocca from a biopic the *New Yorker* had published a few years back. Rather than falling into one of the three camps that represented the bulk of her employees' reactions, the deputy chief for Cold War studies looked in control of her faculties. She walked from person to person, offering whatever consolation she could, all while fielding questions from Metro police officers, the fire marshal, and her own supervisors via her cell phone.

Kellerman waited until the coast was clear of other authorities and approached Iacocca.

"Ms. Iacocca, my name is Scott Hall," he said, presenting his fake National Archives ID. His new name and face were designed to be inoffensive, generic, and utterly unmemorable. "I'm from the Archival Recovery Team, and I'm investigating the potential loss of some documents."

"Now?" she asked, her eyes blearier than her take-charge demeanor suggested. Between the fire, the deaths of her colleagues, the cops' questions, and the burden of being in charge during a disaster, she looked as though she needed a three-week nap. Which was exactly what Kellerman had been counting on.

"Time is of the essence, I'm afraid. The fire has shorted out College Park's connection with your local servers, so I need your access to understand what might have happened." College Park, Maryland, was the site of the official headquarters of National Archives, though its original home, as well as a significant chunk of its more famous holdings, remained here in the heart of the nation's capital.

"Fine," she said, pulling her secure tablet computer from her bag. "Can I ask what we're looking for?"

Kellerman gave her a sympathetic smile, with just the right smidge of condescension. *This is a need-to-know investigation. And right now, you and your people are potential suspects. So, no, you can't ask.*

"Ah," she said, comprehending his expression and too drained to fight him for more information. She logged into her account and handed over the tablet.

Kellerman keyed in what little he knew of Chloe's exploits and the boxes Jon had been rifling through before their confrontation literally exploded. All permutations combining the JFK assassination with Senator Edward Kennedy turned up a handful of Senate reports and memos, a pair of letters between Ted and JFK's widow Jackie, and a few newspaper reports. All of it fully digitized and in the public record. None of it was even remotely useful for conspiracists or dangerous for the Society.

He tried a few different combinations of Bobby Kennedy with his older brother's assassination and his younger brother's senatorial career. Nothing particularly useful there either. Then he tried a different tack.

He knew which boxes Jon was looking through. So whatever he had found would have been in there. He recalled the catalog number on the end of the box Jon had tried to use as his distraction. Kellerman had always prided himself on a near-photographic memory, and it was once again proving helpful.

The contents of the box appeared on screen. Theoretically, it could have been any of the eleven boxes that came in this posthumous set of Ted Kennedy's effects, as Jon had set a number of other boxes aside as he looked for whatever Chloe had sent him to find. But here was as good a starting place as any.

Kellerman resisted the urge to scratch his face. Sweat was starting to trickle down the bridge of his nose beneath the false one he had affixed as part of his disguise. Iacocca may have been beleaguered, but if her interrogator's disguise fell off in front of her, Kellerman had no doubt she would be very quick to call upon the swarm of cops still lingering nearby. He had successfully undergone far worse physical ordeals on a regular basis for most of his life, so he could ignore the itch long enough to complete his search. But if his sweat began to degrade the adhesive holding his disguise in place, his own willpower would be of no help in maintaining the ruse.

He had to hurry, or all would be lost.

He scrolled through the inventory of the box. Nothing looked particularly noteworthy, no secret manifesto or coded message that might explain Chloe Harper's interest. He was about to navigate to the contents of one of the other boxes from the set when something caught his attention.

He had gotten a fairly good look inside the box when Jon had tried to use the old whiskey bottle and a bunched-up newspaper to start a fire as a distraction. The newspapers were completely unrelated to anything having to do with JFK's assassination—or with even Kellerman's colleagues' earlier efforts to silence President Kennedy's brothers. Kellerman had thus already written off Jon's choosing them for the burning material as nothing more than a target of opportunity.

He had also gotten a decent, if brief, look at the items that had spilled from the box during their scuffle.

Two items from the inventory listing were conspicuously missing from his memory of the box's contents. And they could both be easily concealed within a pocket.

Bingo.

He read through the catalog entry for each item. Neither was particularly detailed, nor did either offer any immediate insight into what made those items—a 1960s-era film canister, contents unrecorded, and a century-old novel—of pertinence to the JFK assassination. Did the film canister contain previously undiscovered images from Dealey Plaza that day? The FBI had been thorough in locating and seizing any and all cameras immediately after the assassination, only releasing those images that didn't contradict the official story. Had one slipped through somehow? If Ted Kennedy possessed the smoking gun that could bring down the whole house of cards, why had he remained silent, cowed into compliance by the power wielded by men like Stanton Gaines? Perhaps even he realized the importance of their mission. Or perhaps he just remembered the corpses of his two older brothers and decided it wasn't a battle worth losing his life over.

Kellerman's phone rang. He copied the listings to a single-use digital dropbox site which routed the info across eight servers across the country before finally depositing it on another secure site where he and Stanton Gaines could access it at their leisure. Then he closed the search window on the tablet to not immediately betray what he had been looking at. He thanked Iacocca, handed back her tablet, and walked toward the National Gallery of Art, putting some distance between himself and the chaos of the National Archives. When he was a safe distance away, he finally answered the phone.

"Took you long enough," Gaines said.

"I was working. I may have found what Rickner took. A book and a film canister. I've sent the Archives' listings on the items to the online dropbox."

"Any idea why Harper was interested in them?"

"Not yet. But I've got some theories."

Gaines grunted. "You'll have a chance to test them out soon enough."

"You found them?"

"Facial recognition picked them up at Newark International."

That was one of the things Kellerman loved about his job. Access to near-infinite resources made tracking his quarry so much smoother.

"Destination?"

"Dallas. Get over to Reagan National ASAP. Your flight leaves in an hour."

# CHAPTER 16
## Dallas, Texas

Jon didn't know exactly what he expected Vance Nicholson to look like, but the man standing before him wasn't it. Tall and lean, clean shaven and well dressed, with a full head of gray hair and alert hazel eyes that seemed to size up Jon in an instant. He was far and away from the stereotypical conspiracy theorist, living out of a trailer, off the grid, with an unkempt beard and crazed eyes. Instead of a trailer, Nicholson's home was a modest-sized mansion in one of Dallas's oldest gated communities. For Jon, Nicholson's seeming respectability almost immediately gave Chloe's theories a little more credibility.

But just a little.

"Chloe, welcome," Vance said, embracing his traveling companion. "I must say, I was surprised to hear from you."

"I figured, who better than the man who aided my father on his own descent down the rabbit hole."

"I still grieve for what happened to your father. First losing his job at the Bureau, then his death . . . I tried to warn him about being too brazen in his quest. But Jack wasn't the type for subtlety."

Jon tried not to smirk. *Seems to run in the family.*

"He didn't kill himself either, Vance. They killed him."

Vance's expression grew even more somber. "I've suspected as much."

"Who?" Jon finally asked.

"Ah, and you must be the famous—or infamous, depending on who's asking—Jonathan Rickner. *Dr.* Jonathan Rickner now, if I'm not mistaken."

Jon accepted Vance's proffered hand and shook it. "Call me Jon." The title that niggled at him just hours earlier no longer seemed nearly as important. Being attacked by government assassins and accidentally killing dozens of your coworkers in the process had a funny way of putting things in perspective.

"Very well, Jon. I hear you're helping Chloe here." Vance leaned in close. "Be careful with this one," he said in a stage whisper. "She's a heartbreaker." He winked at Chloe as she gave him a faux scowl.

"As for your question," he continued, straightening up, "'who?' is, of course, the quandary of the ages. Who had motive to kill a president? Plenty, unfortunately. The sixties were a turbulent time, and virtually everyone who had motive then has a counterpart today who would want to ensure it remains covered up. The Soviets have a newly ascendant Russia, Fidel Castro remains a god to Cuba's elite, and, of course, the various governmental suspects—the CIA, the FBI, the military, and so forth—have only grown in power in the decades since."

"We may finally have a clue to answering that question," Chloe said. "But we'll need your darkroom."

"Film?" Vance asked. "A new Zapruder, perhaps?"

"We can only hope," Chloe said. She held up the film canister that Jon had relinquished after landing at Dallas-Fort Worth. "Recently acquired from the estate of Senator Ted Kennedy, care of the National Archives."

Vance's face fell. "Please tell me that's not related to the tragedy this morning."

"A man claiming to be an Secret Service agent attacked me in the stacks after murdering my boss," Jon said. "He had an incendiary grenade. His cover-up techniques seemed to lean toward the scorched-earth variety."

"He was there, Vance," Chloe said. "Just before my dad died. And then he questioned me afterward, saying he worked for the Bureau. I know he was involved somehow."

Vance shook his head at the ground, the slow, resigned motion of a man who had seen too much tragedy and knew better than to expect the fount of sorrow to run dry anytime soon. "Come on," he said. "Let's check out your film."

He led the way through the house. Other than the den, with its wall-to-wall built-ins crammed with hardbacks on history, politics, and a smattering of technothrillers, the house felt soulless and empty. The dining room held a long table with eight seats. All but one chair, sitting alone at the end, was draped with a white cloth. Another drop cloth covered a sideboard. The outlines of a pair of picture frames could be seen beneath the cloth, whatever memories contained within hidden from view.

The sense of loss was permeable. It didn't seem recent. But it didn't have to be to feel permanently fresh to the bereaved.

Jon could testify to that himself. As could his father.

"Watch your head," Vance said as he opened a door and led the way into a darkened room. He flipped a switch and red light illuminated the room. Counters that lined two walls were largely empty, save for a few shallow tubs used for chemical baths in processing pictures. A lightboard not unlike those used for displaying x-ray results in a radiologist's office was installed on one wall. Clotheslines crisscrossed the room just above eye level. Most of them were devoid of anything save a string of empty clothespins, but one at the far end of the room displayed a trio of recently developed prints, now finished drying on the line.

"Anything interesting?" Jon asked, motioning to the hanging prints.

Vance glanced across the room as though he didn't realize what Jon was talking about. "Oh, those? No, I'm afraid not. Just some blurry pictures sent in by a fan of my radio show, purporting to show the real shooters behind JFK's assassination."

Jon did a double take. "And that's not interesting to you? Chloe here led me to believe that was your bread and butter."

Slipping on a pair of sterile gloves, Vance gave him a sympathetic smile that only served to confuse Jon further. "Let's see what you've got there."

"Moment of truth," Chloe said as she unscrewed the end of the film canister. Inside, Jon saw from over her shoulder, was a vintage roll of film. She tilted the canister and dumped the contents into Vance's gloved hands. As Vance began to unspool the first few inches of film, the room went quiet as everyone collectively held their breath.

"It's already developed," Vance said.

"What?" Chloe asked. "You're sure?"

Vance stretched out the film, perhaps a yard in total.

"Absolutely. Get the light there for me, would you, Jon?"

Jon flipped another light switch next to the first one, bathing the room in a pinkish hue before he flicked off the red light. Vance was already clipping the film to the lightboard. He turned the backlight on, retrieved a magnifying glass from a drawer, and squinted at the film.

"It's the Kennedy brothers," he said almost immediately. "Jack, Bobby, and Ted. Family portraits. The three of them playing football on the lawn at Hyannis Port. Swimming in the surf at Palm Beach. Sailing in the Charles River. Posing in front of a Christmas tree. Celebrating Jack's election to the Senate. Everything looks like it's from after World War II, when Joe Jr. died, and before Jack even launched his presidential campaign in 1960. But they're all out of order chronologically. Images from across fourteen, fifteen years. Across the country. All innocuous family life stuff. Nothing related to the assassination."

"What do you know about *The Thirty-Nine Steps*?" Jon asked.

"Is that a new self-help plan?" Vance asked. "Just kidding," he said before Jon could respond. "You'll forgive an old man his sense of humor. Can I assume you're asking in the context of JFK?"

"You can."

"Well, then, that's easy. John Buchan's prototypical thriller novel was a favorite of the Kennedy boys, as it was of many in those days. But with their political upbringing, global travels, and far-reaching aspirations, the international thriller spoke to them in a special way. And, considering how the book's driving force is a lethal case of mistaken identity, some conspiracy buffs—myself included—have found an ironic parallel in Oswald's own claim of being mistakenly identified as JFK's assassin."

"So you genuinely don't think Oswald killed JFK?" Jon asked.

"No, I don't."

"Why not?"

Vance looked at Chloe. "You haven't told him?"

Chloe shrugged. "I tried."

"Told me what?" Jon asked.

"Why I do what I do. All this crazy conspiracy stuff. It's the same reason why I know the blurry pictures I've got hanging up over there don't reveal the true assassins of JFK."

Vance leaned in. "Because a lifetime ago, little eleven-year-old Vance Nicholson was standing in Dealey Plaza, waving at the presidential motorcade. Because I'll never forget the confusion and horror I felt at seeing the president's head pop like an overripe tomato. And because seared into my mind forever are the faces of the men who really murdered the president."

# CHAPTER 17
## *Dulles, Virginia*

Patrick Molyneux already missed Marseilles. A summer heat wave was already topping out thermometers in the upper nineties, and while southern France could certainly get hot, the Mediterranean breeze mitigated the heat in a way that the Chesapeake never could. Plus, it was a beach resort. People came there to enjoy the warmth and sunshine.

Washington, replete with some of the world's finest museums, home to all three branches of the world's most powerful government, headquarters to the world's most dominant—and expensive—military, and capital of the free world, had no business being as hot and muggy as it was today.

Washington was an indoor city. Unfortunately, Molyneux was stuck outside, waiting for his private chauffeur while the taxi stand beckoned just yards away.

His flight from Marseilles by way of a layover in Paris was uneventful, leaving him to his ruminations about this recent turn of events. His career in academia had been brief and unexceptional. Bachelor's at twenty-one, doctorate at twenty-five, then taking a string of one-year visiting professor positions at mid-tier universities across the country. He was smarter than his professional track record implied, but he had been in the grip of ennui long before he ever defended his dissertation. He felt lost, adrift. Ever since his family had shuffled off this mortal coil and left him alone, their disappointed ghosts echoing eternally in his skull. But perhaps he hadn't been a complete disappointment to his father. After all, of all the academic fields Molyneux could have chosen, American history was the one closest to his father's heart. Perhaps the old man hadn't lost hope for his second born after all.

And now, Molyneux was getting the chance to marry his love of history with his father's lifelong passion. He was finally in the family line of work. Though why Stanton Gaines had contacted him of all people remained a mystery.

But not for much longer.

As the Airbus 380 had made its final approach, Molyneux had gazed out the window at Washington's skyline. It was unlike any other in the world. While most of the world's capitals featured dozens of skyscrapers jostling for prominence, many of DC's most prominent buildings dated to nearly a century before late-Gilded Age building booms in Chicago and New York introduced the world to the term. And while many of the world's capital cities also doubled as one of, if not the, biggest cities in the country, Washington was content to leave massive tracts of land undeveloped, preserving the original design of the city from more than two centuries earlier. Neoclassical temples for each of the three branches of government, as well as for national heroes like Jefferson and Lincoln, made this a city where, unlike most metropolitan areas in the world today, history remained king.

Of course, most Americans remained oblivious to the true history behind their country's inner workings. His father had trusted him enough to share that much about his family legacy. That most of his countrymen would be shocked and appalled to learn the horrible, necessary truth.

Molyneux had packed light, so once the plane landed, he bypassed baggage claim, wheeling his carry-on to the pickup area. After an interminable wait in the unseasonable heat, he was pleased when a short man with a walrus mustache and a pale green polo called to him before shuffling in his direction.

"Blaine Curtfeld," the mustachioed man said by way of introduction before handing over a black duffel bag. "I was told to give you this."

"What's in it?" Molyneux asked, starting to open the bag.

"Not here." Curtfeld reached his hand to stop Molyneux. "When you get to your room."

"And then what? I thought I was meeting with . . ." He trailed off, wary of the countless ears that could overhear in a place like this. He was also cognizant of his mildly French accent, a remnant of his Francophone mother's influence on his speech from a young age. He didn't want to screw this up before he had even started by drawing undue attention to himself.

"You are. But he's not in town yet. For now, everything you need is in there. Intel on your targets, briefing on your mission, new credentials, a burner cell phone . . ."

"Wait, what now?" Molyneux asked, confused. "'Targets'? 'Mission'? What exactly was I brought here to do?"

Curtfeld smiled. "The same thing we've always done, Dr. Molyneux. Save the free world."

Forty minutes of DC traffic later, Molyneux was ensconced in his room in downtown Washington. He was so close to it all, surrounded by centuries of history. His history. His and his forefathers. But sightseeing would have to come later.

He finished emptying his carry-on, storing his clothes in the heavy oaken armoire by the window. There was no more delaying. The moment of truth had arrived.

The black duffel Curtfeld had given him sat patiently beside the bed. Hidden from view, just in case the authorities should burst into his room, guns drawn. But that was ludicrous. No one suspected a thing. Not yet anyway.

En route from the airport, he had poked through the bag in the backseat of Curtfeld's car. The windows were heavily tinted, so there was no real danger of anyone seeing inside, but he was hesitant nonetheless. He still wondered just how deep his father's rabbit hole went.

Molyneux got his answer when the first things he saw in the bag were a brick of hundred-dollar bills and a black handgun. With quivering hands, he zipped the bag shut and placed it on the next seat, as far from him as possible.

Now the time had come to see just what Curtfeld and Gaines had in store for him.

Glancing at the door to ensure it was securely locked, he unzipped the bag and set it on the bed. Then, one by one, he withdrew the contents and placed them on the bed as well, dropping the bag on the floor once it was empty.

Other than the gun, the items were fairly innocuous on the surface. But, as a whole, knowing what little Molyneux did, it looked like Jason Bourne's go-bag. Two passports, one American, one French, both in fake names. Two driver's licenses in the fake American name, one from Maryland, one from Colorado. Three bricks of cash, totaling $30,000 according to the paper tape that wrapped each bundle. Press credentials from the *Washington Post* and the *Denver Gazette*. And official-looking IDs for the FBI, the CIA, the Secret Service, Homeland Security, and the US Marshals. All bearing his image.

What in the world had he gotten himself into?

The last three items were the gun, which he had set farthest away from him, the cell phone that Gaines would be calling him on, and a sealed manila envelope.

The promised intel on his mission. And his targets.

He grabbed the envelope and sat down in a newly reupholstered wingback chair. A luxury from a century before. Just like the rest of his accommodations. An antique letter opener lay on the adjacent table. He picked it up and flipped over the envelope. Sealed not just with adhesive, but with the seal of the Society.

Molyneux smiled, despite his reservations about everything spread out on his bed right now. He was part of something bigger now. Bigger than himself. Bigger than today. He was dipping his toes into the pool of history itself.

He broke the seal, feeling a little rush as he opened the envelope designated for his eyes only. He may not have shared his father's or brother's affinity for combat or weapons, but he understood the value of secrets. And being entrusted with one that was surely significant to the nation's future made him at once exhilarated and nauseated.

Inside were three dossiers. The first was for a Jonathan Rickner. Molyneux recognized the name, and once he began reading the file, he realized why. Rickner had been behind the big exposé of a secret government assassination squad operating out of the CIA a year or two back. That case had involved a historical cover up as well, so it was clear why Rickner was on the Society's radar. The file ended with his current employment at the National Archives. The televisions in the Paris airport had been playing footage from a fire at the Archives this morning. Molyneux wondered if they were related.

The second dossier was on a Chloe Harper. Her file was smaller, but appended to it was a brief on her father, former FBI Special Agent Jack Harper. Dead by suicide last year, though the more Molyneux read, the more he doubted that was the case. Apparently he had taken an unhealthy interest in JFK assassination conspiracies that had led to his ouster from the Bureau. The official police report concluded that the shame of his firing likely provided the catalyst for his suicide. Molyneux's reading between the lines made him think it might have been the man's obsession with forbidden knowledge that had proven fatal for him.

The third file was significantly shorter. Really more of a fact sheet than a full dossier. A known associate of Jack Harper, someone Chloe might turn to in her investigation of her late father's theories. Even with the short length of the file, however, several sections were redacted. He was a conspiracy buff, apparently, so perhaps some of his theories had come too close to the truth for committing to paper here. The preservation of its history was one of the Society's goals. But the dissemination of that history was another matter altogether.

Still, Molyneux stared at those blacked-out portions of the third dossier and wondered what this Vance Nicholson had discovered.

# CHAPTER 18
*Dallas, Texas*

Chloe felt a growing something in the pit of her stomach as she walked toward the plaza. Not fear or dread exactly. Somewhere in that ballpark though. Not that danger awaited them now. But, rather, that she was approaching the place that had stolen a president's life. And, half a century later, had also stolen her father's.

It was bright and sunny today in Dealey Plaza, just as it had been that fateful November morning in 1963. And though some of the geography had changed in the decades since the twentieth century's most infamous assassination, the plaza looked largely like it would have when Kennedy's motorcade rolled through. The events of that day had frozen the site in time, a secular shrine preserved in memoriam of a youthful president murdered at the height of his power.

"I was right over there," Vance said, pointing to the sidewalk near where Kennedy's driver had begun accelerating toward the hospital. "With my mom, my dad, and my little sister. Millie."

Vance was getting misty-eyed as he seemed to travel back in time. She knew from her father's notes that Vance's parents were long dead, while Millie, knocking on the door of sixty, was serving thirty years for a murder charge in California. The recent loss of his wife likely increased his sense of being alone. Something that no one wants to experience, much less someone of Vance's relatively advanced age.

She felt sorry for the man. But she was also glad she had come to him. Not only did he seem enlivened by their company, but the opportunity to talk about one of the foundational moments of his life seemed to give him new purpose.

Jon was wide eyed at being here, tagging along with the wonder of a tourist seeing the Taj Mahal or the Eiffel Tower in person for the first time. He wore the unmistakable expression of someone trying to take in the reality of being somewhere he had seen on film or in photographs many times before. That feeling was undoubtedly exacerbated by recent events upending his perception of what had really happened at this site half a century ago.

Chloe knew that feeling well. She had experienced it here just a few months before her father got fired from the Bureau. She had come, trying to make some sense of her father's claims of a conspiracy. Or maybe to confirm that there wasn't a nefarious man behind the curtain, that sometimes truly awful things just happen. Regardless of her intentions, she left here a year ago convinced that her father was throwing his career and his life away. Chasing at ghosts and invisible fiends that had eluded truth seekers for half a century for one very good reason: they didn't exist.

Now, she wasn't so sure.

All signs pointed to Kellerman being one of the very fiends she had so long denied. But he was far too young to have pulled the trigger on JFK. Or on Bobby. Was he working for the FBI? Or was someone else carrying on J. Edgar Hoover's lethal legacy?

"So this is it," Jon said, his voice tinged with awe as his eyes swept the plaza. Vance had led them to a spot perhaps a hundred yards down the motorcade route from the infamous curve that fronted the Texas Book Depository. The Warren Commission had determined that all three shots had come from a sixth-floor window, from a Carcano rifle fired by former Marine sniper and communist sympathizer Lee Harvey Oswald.

The Commission's report, like many such cover-ups, was a pile of bull, shaped into something that could pass for the truth if left unscrutinized, and signed-off on by a slew of purportedly respectable leaders.

Created by one of President Lyndon B. Johnson's first executive orders just days after his predecessor's assassination, the President's Commission on the Assassination of President Kennedy became more commonly known by the name of its leader, Supreme Court Chief Justice Earl Warren. The other six members gave every semblance of a professional, unbiased tribunal: a bipartisan delegation of two senators and two representatives, including future president Gerald Ford, plus Allen Dulles—the CIA director who had overseen the failed Bay of Pigs invasion of Castro's Cuba that JFK had hamstrung at the last minute—and Council on Foreign Relations chair John J. McCloy.

The last two members were particularly interesting additions. Though Dulles would have had ample resources to dig into Oswald's purported Soviet connections, he also possessed a motive for revenge against JFK for the president's constant conflicts with the agency.

Meanwhile, McCloy's leadership of the Council on Foreign Relations and previous tenure as president of the World Bank, both mainstays in global conspiracy lore, was suspect, as was his proximity to a string of presidents over two decades. He served as an advisor to JFK, then to Johnson, to Nixon, and, once the vice president ascended to the presidency upon the ashes of Nixon's ignominious resignation, to fellow Commission member Gerald Ford. And just a week after the Commission was established, President Johnson bestowed upon McCloy the Presidential Medal of Freedom with Distinction, the highest civilian honor in the country.

A bribe? Or something else?

"This is the place," Vance said. "I can still remember the moment I heard him coming. The cheers swelled as the rumble of the motorcade's engines drew nearer."

Chloe tried to imagine the scene. The only film that existed of the assassination was a home movie made by Abraham Zapruder, a Dallas dressmaker who was a staunch admirer of the president. Standing just across the road and halfway up the infamous grassy knoll, Zapruder had been the only one to record the audacious murder that shook the world. The Zapruder film had no sound and was only 26.6 seconds long, with a few crucial frames missing, but its imagery had become an integral part of the American zeitgeist and a lynchpin for all sorts of conspiracy lore.

Being here alongside an eyewitness seemed to open the scene before her. She imagined the families and workers, clad in their best early-1960s apparel, smiling and waving to the First Family as they passed through the plaza. Televisions still were not in every living room, and color televisions were a rarity, as were color broadcasts. For most, this would be the first time they got to see a president moving and reacting in living color. And to see him actually waving at them was an unheard-of honor. The Kennedys were the youngest and most popular first family ever to grace the White House, owing in part to their youth, photogenic nature, and frequent use of the magazines and television programs that adored them. From Jackie's tour of her hand-picked White House furnishings and dress collection to demonstrations of Jack's virility and charisma, the Kennedys were perhaps the closest the presidency had ever experienced to the fawning adoration lavished upon Prince William and Princess Kate's growing family. Chloe could only imagine the excitement these people must have felt to be just yards from American royalty.

A few bullets later, that dream had twisted into a nightmare. The unthinkable had happened, and they were witnesses. A president, *their* president, murdered in broad daylight, right before their eyes.

But who? And why?

In front of them rose the grassy knoll, topped by a fence behind which—according to conspiracy lore—two mysterious men shot the president. The fence had become a pilgrimage of sorts, both for the vantage it afforded the historic plaza and for the wonder held by the purported gunmen.

"It had been raining that morning, and the air was cool and pleasant," Vance said, transporting Chloe and Jon back half a century. "Of course, that was why Zapruder almost didn't come out with his expensive new camera. But once the sky cleared, everyone showed up."

Ironic, Chloe mused, that had the weather remained unpleasant, the top on the president's car would have been up, protecting Kennedy from an assassin's bullet. That beautiful weather had changed history forever.

"Then, finally, there it was. Unlike these days, the president's car was the lead automobile, boldly helming the motorcade. Tiny American flags flew on either side of the car's hood, waving in the breeze as they heralded the arrival of the leader of the free world. My dad boosted me up on his shoulders so I could see. In those days, every little boy wanted to be president, especially after the charisma exuded by JFK's ascension to the office. I could see him, smiling and waving. Jackie, too, of course. I turned toward my mom and sister, making sure they could see him, that they weren't missing it.

"And then, as I turned back toward the president, I saw them. Three men, just beyond the fence that topped the grassy knoll. Wearing suits, looking official. I didn't think too much of it at the time. Similar men in similar suits ran alongside the motorcade. Just more security for the visiting president."

Vance bit his lip as he recalled the next part. "But then I saw the rifle. I didn't comprehend it until the explosion. I stared in disbelief for a moment before I realized that there were more explosions, coming from everywhere it seemed like. Then JFK's car went flying by, newly decorated with chunks of the president's brain strewn across the trunk."

"You actually saw the grassy knoll shooter?" Jon asked, incredulous. "Why didn't you tell someone?"

"I did. Of course I did. But they found Oswald so fast, so the official version was written long before I could tell anyone of significance. My parents listened to me, and actually believed me long enough to issue a statement to the FBI when they came asking for witnesses and film from the assassination. Of course, I was an overly imaginative little boy, while they had a Soviet sympathizer in a jail cell and a discarded rifle with his prints on it. Then Ruby shot Oswald and tied up that loose end, sealing the narrative.

"My parents persisted on my behalf until the Warren Commission report was complete and its conclusion made public. Then it became un-American to question the martyrdom of President Kennedy, as though questioning the official story was tantamount to supporting the traitor who murdered our nation's leader. They really picked a winner with Oswald. A communist traitor, who defected to the Soviet Union right after leaving the Marine Corps, assassinates our photogenic president in broad daylight at the height of the Cold War. McCarthyism may have been dead and buried, but the Soviets had a foothold in the Caribbean and we were on the cusp of war in Vietnam. In many ways, Kennedy's murder brought us closer together as a nation and focused us on our external enemies. The CIA gets their revenge for JFK hamstringing the Bay of Pigs invasion and nixing Operation Northwoods, defense contractors get fat off the growing war in Vietnam, and a million young men are sacrificed upon the altar of greed in a festering jungle halfway across the world."

Jon thought about this. He had heard most of these arguments before, but never from a purported eyewitness. Apart from his role as attorney general, Bobby Kennedy had been one of his brother's closest advisors and had played a role in virtually every controversial decision to come out of JFK's administration. Perhaps whoever had killed JFK had wanted to ensure his similarly aligned brother didn't get into the White House to push similar policies.

But that was just crazy. Wasn't it?

Could the US Government really be responsible for the murder of its own president? And the subsequent cover-up?

"Isn't it possible," Jon said, playing devil's advocate so he could stay on the sane side of the rabbit hole as long as possible, "that the men you saw on the grassy knoll really were there for protection. That they left so quickly because they were trying to set up a perimeter to find the real shooter or something?"

"I saw their guns fire, Jon. Right before the president's head exploded. So no."

"If it was really a conspiracy, why hasn't the truth come out after all this time. Surely someone would come forward after all this time."

"People have come forward. And they were immediately discredited, just like always. Others have been bought off to change or retract their stories. Others still have met sudden and mysterious deaths. Then you've got the entire cottage industry of JFK conspiracists blaming aliens and lizardmen and the British Royal Family and the Knights Templar for the assassination, branding anyone with legitimate theories a kook in equal measure."

Vance gestured to the scattered groups of tourists exploring the plaza, cameras and guidebooks in hand. "Most of the people around us believe JFK's assassination involved a conspiracy. In polls taken over the past two decades, more than two-thirds of Americans believe he was killed as part of a conspiracy. Even the House Select Committee found this probable. But believing isn't proving. And whoever killed the president, be it J. Edgar Hoover, the CIA, the Mob, the military-industrial complex, or mole people, they were darn effective at covering their tracks. I mean, after all this time—"

Vance's tirade was cut off mid-sentence as he collapsed to the ground. Chloe dropped to the ground to check on him, and Jon did the same. Heart attack, he suspected. And then he saw the blood on the old conspiracist's neck.

Someone had shot Vance.

Jon looked across the street. Atop the grassy knoll, a figure was partially concealed behind the fence.

Kellerman.

And he was adjusting his aim.

# CHAPTER 19
## Pittsburgh, Pennsylvania

S tanton Gaines had less than an hour before his plane left. His limousine was parked outside the terminal, engine and air conditioning still running. His driver and security detail, however, he had asked to leave the vehicle before making a few calls. They understood the sensitive nature of his work, and though they had taken their own oaths of silence after passing stringent background checks, there were certain things he didn't trust even them to overhear.

His conversation with Anthony Kellerman just moments before was one of those things. Kellerman had tracked down Jon Rickner and Chloe Harper in Dealey Plaza of all places. If that was where they thought the clues ultimately led, they were no different than thousands of lost truth-seekers, chasing shadows in the dark. Kellerman had a clear view of Jon and Chloe, along with Vance Nicholson, a local conspiracist who had been acquainted with Chloe's father and had been on the Society's radar since childhood.

Suffused with a sense of historic purpose, much like the rest of his brethren, Kellerman had taken up a position atop the grassy knoll, just like his rifleman counterparts more than half a century before. Then he called Gaines for authorization to shoot, a big ask for a public plaza in the middle of the day, especially one with such close ties to another famous shooting under similar circumstances. Gaines trusted Kellerman's judgment. If that was how the apprehension of these fugitives needed to go down, Gaines gave his consent. Kellerman would ensure that his role remained unknown. Nothing would be traceable back to Gaines or the Society.

Just as it had always been.

But it wasn't that simple, Gaines realized. While he had no doubt that Kellerman would pull off his part of the mission without a hitch, that wasn't necessarily the end of the story. The mass declassification of JFK assassination documents in 2017 had been a weak point from the beginning. And while his associates had worked hard to ensure that nothing could even remotely connect the Society to the assassination or its aftermath, clearly something had gotten through. It wasn't obvious enough for his team to find it in the National Archives before or after declassification, but it was there. And if Chloe Harper was smart enough to find it, she could be dangerous enough to do some serious damage if she figured out what it meant. Especially with Jon Rickner at her side.

And with the operation set to move forward in a matter of days, now was not the time to play fast and loose with national security.

Another approach was needed.

Gaines dialed another number and waited until the French-tinged voice answered in English.

"Dr. Molyneux, I believe you know who this is."

"I do."

"There is a very specific reason I summoned you stateside on such short notice. I presume you've received and read your mission briefing?"

"I have, sir," the historian said. "Although the briefing certainly lives up to the brevity implied in the name."

*A punster*, Gaines thought. *Wonderful.*

"Certain details, as I'm sure you can appreciate, are too sensitive to commit to paper. Especially outside of controlled environments. I'm heading into Washington this evening and will personally brief you on the rest of the details at my office."

"Your official office, sir?" Molyneux asked.

"Why not? What we will be discussing directly impacts national security, so I see no problem with the location."

"Nor do I, sir."

Again with the *sir*. He had chosen Molyneux because of his reputation as a forward thinker. And because of his heritage, of course. But the man on the phone sounded like a sycophant. And a nervous one at that.

"Good," Gaines said. "Be ready for my call in a few hours. I look forward to meeting you."

"As do I, sir."

He *would* manage to sneak one last "sir" in there before hanging up. Gaines decided to chalk it up to nerves. He knew Molyneux's history with his father, how he thought his family legacy would be given to his brother, then lost entirely. Gaines's call had given him new hope, and Molyneux didn't want to screw that up. His cloying obeisance was annoying, but Gaines couldn't write him off based on that alone.

Truth be told, he needed Molyneux and Kellerman to be at the top of their respective games. Because now was the absolute worst time for someone like Chloe Harper or Jon Rickner to have uncovered a weak spot.

The Kennedy assassinations were ancient history, with most of the conspirators in the grave or long out of power. But in the next few days, the fate of the free world would hang in the balance once again. And no one could be allowed to stop what Gaines had planned.

# CHAPTER 20
*Dallas, Texas*

"Come on!" Jon shouted, tugging Chloe from the fallen body of Vance Nicholson. Finally she relented, following as Jon ducked behind a confused group of high schoolers on a field trip.

"It was Kellerman," Jon said in a stage whisper.

"Here?"

Jon nodded. "Up behind the grassy knoll fence. We need to get out of the plaza. Fast."

Chloe dared a look toward the fence. "I don't see him."

Jon frowned. "Neither did Vance."

"We can't stay behind these kids all day. We're just going to put them in danger. Besides, I don't think we can pass for high school students anymore."

As though to emphasize her point, a chaperone started heading their way from one end of the group, a stern look on her face.

Jon looked around the plaza. They were maybe eighty yards from the overpass. Kellerman wouldn't have a shot once they were past there. The problem was, they'd be sitting ducks for each of those eighty yards. Unless he had completely abandoned his post already, Kellerman would have plenty of time to pick them off. And the high school group they were using as cover was moving away from the overpass, making the impossible eighty-yard dash even more lethal.

Then he saw his opportunity.

"How's your cardio?" he asked Chloe.

"My cardio?"

"Just follow my lead and keep up."

Jon peered through the throng of students who were increasingly eyeing him with suspicion, then darted around them toward a bus. A chorus of screams echoed behind them as Kellerman's next shot just missed his ear and found a high school girl, sending her crashing to the ground. Jon hated that he had put any of them in danger. But he stopped that guilt train before it could leave the station. After all, he wasn't the one pulling the trigger.

In this day of lone-wolf terrorists and random crazies, there was no way the bus driver would stop to let them board in the middle of the road. But the vehicle was tall enough and long enough to grant them cover from Kellerman's aim. If they could manage to run alongside until it reached the overpass, they would be safe.

No problem. If you were Usain Bolt. Or a cheetah.

"Stay beside the bus!" Jon yelled between breaths.

"Got it!" Chloe yelled back.

Behind them, cars began to honk at the crazy tourists trying to catch a bus while it cruised down the road at thirty miles per hour. Jon didn't care. He had bigger things to worry about right now. They were still forty yards from the overpass. Besides, maybe the honking would get the bus driver's attention, cause him to slow down.

It had the opposite effect. Jon locked eyes with the bus driver via the side-view mirror. The driver's eyes widened in surprise. Then the bus's engine began to roar more loudly as he stepped on the gas.

Their cover was accelerating away from them. Still thirty yards to go for the overpass. And in seconds, Kellerman would have a clean shot at them. A shot he had just proven he was ready and willing to take.

"Book it!" Jon yelled. His legs and chest burned as he sprinted as hard as he could. They were almost there. But the bus was almost past them. The people in the second-to-last seats stared down at them. *Crazy people*, they were surely thinking.

If they only knew.

The shadow of the overpass crossing the road beckoned to Jon like a finish line.

So close now. Just a few more yards.

Jon and Chloe were in line with the engine compartment now. Another few seconds and their cover would be completely gone.

A wave of cool hit Jon as they entered the shade beneath the overpass. The bus roared past as Jon slowed to a jog then darted across traffic to safety.

Kellerman would not give up so easily, though. And without Vance, they didn't have a next move.

# CHAPTER 21
## *Dallas, Texas*

After escaping from Dealey Plaza, Jon and Chloe agreed that they had to find somewhere safe and figure out what to do next. They had settled on a Chipotle on the other side of town. The route they took to get there, however, was anything but direct. They had hopped in the first available cab, taken it to the closest bus station, and taken a bus to an outdoor shopping mall across town. The restaurant had three exit doors, and the open-plan environment and noisy kitchen area met the needs of their conversation, crazy-sounding though it surely would have been for potential eavesdroppers.

"I can't believe he's dead," Chloe said, staring at her food.

Jon decided against saying he was sorry for her loss again. It wouldn't make her feel any better than it had the first eight times. As he had discovered years before, occupying yourself with an intellectually taxing project could be a great tool for deferring mourning. And when that project is designed to exact retribution upon those who caused that mourning, it became all the more effective.

"His death won't be in vain, Chloe. We'll figure this out. We know what's on the film and what's in the book. We just have to figure out how it all fits together."

"Yeah," she said without conviction.

Jon pulled out the book and the film canister and set them on the table.

"Look, the film is already developed and safe to open. Which means we can now figure out why Bobby Kennedy told his brother these items were so important."

"But the images don't mean anything," Chloe said, grasping at the film canister and screwing it open. She unspooled the film and stabbed a desperate finger at one image after the next. "It's just family portraits. No secret 'here's who killed my brother' message, just a bunch of pictures that are probably in dozens of books on the Kennedys."

Jon looked at the film. He had missed it in Vance's dark room, but in the well-lit restaurant, he identified the tiny breaks in the film where the frames had been expertly spliced together. That was why everything was so out of order. But why had someone Frankensteined all these seemingly innocuous images into a single roll of film?

"Nothing obvious in the pictures themselves," he muttered to himself. He studied each frame, but just like back at Vance's house, he found nothing out of the ordinary.

Then he saw it. The haphazard order of the pictures spanning more than a decade finally made sense. But it couldn't make sense on its own.

He thumbed through the old copy of *The Thirty-Nine Steps*, scanning each line until he found what he was looking for.

"L," he said, proudly pointing to an underlined letter on the page.

Chloe wrinkled her nose. "What?"

"Look," he said, "we have to assume that Bobby didn't specify these two objects for his brother to look at without reason. These pictures are all out of order because someone put them that way."

"But the pictures don't mean anything. They're just everyday, publicly available pictures."

Jon smiled. "You're right. The pictures don't mean anything. But the numbers do."

"The numbers?"

"Look right here." Jon pointed along the top edge of the film. "These numbers normally correspond to the frame number. But there's too many of them, with most frames having an extra number or two hand-written above. And, just like the images, they're all out of order."

"And you think . . ."

Jon pointed to the numeral "1" above the sixth frame, a picture of a shirtless JFK sailing off Cape Cod. "The first letter underlined in the book. An L."

Chloe leapt out of her seat and grabbed a fistful of napkins from a dispenser. She returned to the table with a pen she borrowed from an employee behind the counter.

"All right, let's puzzle this out." She spread the napkins before her. "I'll start writing the numbers out, you find the letters."

Buoyed by her newfound enthusiasm, Jon resumed scanning the book. He had read the story years before, and tried not to be sucked in by the narrative again. They may have hit a breakthrough, but time was short. Kellerman was still in town, after all.

"E," he said once he reached the second underlined letter. Chloe wrote it under the "2" on her makeshift worksheet, which corresponded with a handwritten "2" above the thirteenth frame, a candid shot of JFK and Jackie in Newport on their wedding day.

It was a variation on a book cipher, one of the most secure encoding methods of the pre-digital age. Benedict Arnold had used them to secretly communicate with his British contacts during the Revolutionary War, while the second of the mysterious Beale Ciphers had been encoded with the Declaration of Independence as its key text.

Usually, the code denoted the position of certain words within a readily available text, such as a book of the Bible, the dictionary, the works of Shakespeare, or other standard volumes that both sender and recipient would be able to access. Chapter, verse, and word position for Bible users, sonnet number, line, and word in Shakespeare, or, if it was an agreed-upon common edition of the same book, page, line, and word.

The trick was picking the right text. Too obvious, and the code could be intercepted and cracked. Too obscure, and the recipient might not be able to decode the message.

But there was another issue to take into consideration when choosing a text. Not every text contained all the words that the sender would want to include in the message. Which meant the sender either had to get creative in how to write their message with the words available, or they could get even further down in the weeds and spell out the message letter by letter. This, it seemed, was what Bobby Kennedy had done. But his choice of text was almost perfect. By underlining individual letters, it meant that only the specific copy of *The Thirty-Nine Steps* that he had left for his brother would translate the encoded message.

Which meant it was either incredibly personal, or incredibly dangerous.

Or both.

Jon continued feeding Chloe letters as he found them. As she slotted them into place, a cryptic message began to appear.

"That's it," Chloe said as she put an "R" under the number seventy-five. Jon closed the book and looked at the decoded message.

wherehiswordsliveonhechangedtheworldinsideiswhat-
countscarefultheyrewatching

"I'm guessing this still needs a little work," Chloe said.
"Spaces and punctuation at least."
Jon took the pen and a fresh napkin to tweak the message.

Where his words live on, he changed the world.
Inside is what counts.
Careful, they're watching.

"How's that?" he asked.
"Still cryptic, but more legible at least."
"The last part seems straightforward enough. Bobby is warning Ted that whoever killed their brother is still out there and has their eye on them."
"Which makes sense why Bobby was being all secret squirrel with his coded messaging and all."
"Clearly, they're not done watching yet," Jon said, thinking about Kellerman's relentless pursuit.
"'Inside is what counts' sounds like some sort of feel-good encouragement, which seems out of place here."
"It does. Hardly the kind of message worth going to all this trouble. So perhaps it means something hidden inside of something."
"Useful," Chloe said, shooting him a teasing glance.
"But 'where his words live on'? There's got to be dozens of monuments and memorials to JFK. Heck, I just about tripped over one back at Dealey Plaza when we were hiding behind those kids."
A spark of recognition illuminated Chloe's face. "The Oral History Program."
"The what now?"
"Bobby Kennedy's pet project to honor his murdered brother. It's a collection of hundreds of interviews conducted and recorded before and after JFK's death about him and his life. It was his ultimate memorial."
"Words live on," Jon said, stroking his chin. "The miracle of voice recording. That's genius, Chloe. But where is it?"
Chloe smiled. "You're lucky I got us those fake IDs, Mr. Weisz. Next stop, Boston."

# CHAPTER 22
## *Zrenjanin, Serbia*

W ayne Wilkins wiped the carving knife clean of prints and blood before hiding it under the bed. The freshly dead corpse of Ljubomir Prajlak stared at the ceiling of the apartment in which the young Serbian terrorist had been building a dirty bomb. Wayne had crossed Prajlak's hands across his chest in a sign of respect. Not that Wayne had any for the man. But it was just the cultural touch needed to deflect any suspicion that a CIA agent had been responsible for the kill.

Prajlak's target would have been Pristina, the capital of neighboring Kosovo, the breakaway state that Serbia claimed as their own. But the United States and her allies didn't need more instability in Eastern Europe, a region that was still struggling to pull itself out of the quagmire of Soviet oppression. Serbia may have been willing to turn a blind eye to Prajlak's actions against their erstwhile countrymen, but President of the United States James Talquin was not.

The knife also was intended to mislead. Not only was it locally sourced from Prajlak's own kitchen, but its haphazard hiding place showed panic at what the killer had done, not the cool-headed focus of a trained assassin. A crime of passion or opportunity by a fellow Serbian, not one planned an ocean away in a Langley briefing room a week earlier.

The Geiger counter in Wayne's pocket remained blissfully quiet. Only the occasional short crackle from where some second-hand radiation had once come into contact with the bomb components. Nothing major, though. Wayne felt fairly confident that he wouldn't be developing stage-four cancer in the coming days as a result of this visit.

He switched off the Geiger counter as he exited the apartment, keeping his head low as he descended the stairs to the street. He avoided eye contact once on the street, though that was common enough with the locals. His Serbian was at least proficient enough for brief bouts of everyday conversation, though there were only so many practical uses for "Where is the toilet?" and "What time does the train leave?" Black-haired, with ice-blue eyes, he could pass for a local if he avoided closer scrutiny.

His phone buzzed in his pocket. He ignored it. Whoever wanted to talk to him surely wanted to do so in English. And that might invite the sort of attention he sought to avoid.

Four blocks from Prajlak's apartment, Wayne climbed in the back of a waiting sedan. A local CIA asset named Filip drove off as soon as Wayne had closed the door.

"Did you have a good meeting?" Filip asked.

"As good as could be expected."

Wayne trusted Filip to drive him, not to share operational details with. Langley had listed Filip as one of its most longstanding and trustworthy assets in Serbia outside the capital of Belgrade. But Wayne knew the dangers of trusting blindly. Even those you thought were on your side could be there just to stab you in the back.

His phone rang again. Wayne pulled it from his pocket.

"Stop the car."

Filip pulled to the side of the road. "Everything okay?"

"Fine. Please exit the car and wait over there until I signal for you. I need to take this call in private."

Looking confused, Filip nonetheless complied with Wayne's order.

The caller was one person Wayne did not have trust issues with.

"Jon?"

"Wayne, it's good to hear your voice. Where are you?"

"Better you don't know," Wayne said.

Two years ago, Wayne had plied his assassination skills for a government agency known as the Division. It had been a low point in Wayne's life, lower even than when he had joined the military out of anger after both his parents had died in the 9/11 attacks. In returning to New York City as an agent with the Division, Wayne had hoped to find some sort of redemption from the desert warzones he had lived in for the previous decade. He found it, but not through the secret government killing squad. He found it in Jon Rickner. He had saved Jon's life, but, in many ways, Jon had saved him as well. In helping Jon bring down the Division from within, Wayne had been set free from a decade of festering anger and consuming hatred at those who had stolen his family from him.

But it had been Jon that had helped open the door to healing from the wounds of the past, Jon that had inadvertently shown him the greatness in humanity that years spent dwelling in killing fields had a way of masking. And that was a debt Wayne could never repay.

"Is there anything you need?" Wayne asked. Though he had given Jon his contact info after the dust settled from the Division's dirty laundry being aired on the nighttime news, they hadn't spoken in over a year. Wayne didn't think anything of the silence. Just the two of them getting busy with their respective lives, though it was an unspoken assumption that Wayne would be there if Jon needed his skillset or connections in the future.

Which was what Wayne feared this call might herald.

"I'm in a bit of trouble," Jon said. "Did you see the news this morning? In DC?"

"Afraid not." Wayne immediately wished he had access to a reliable LTE network so he could see what Jon was referring to. "I'm overseas at the moment."

"Some federal agent-looking guy killed my boss and attacked me at the National Archives. Things got out of hand in a hurry, and, long-story short, an incendiary grenade he was carrying killed dozens of my coworkers and burned down half the stacks."

Wayne was momentarily speechless. Not at all what he was expecting.

"Are you in custody?" Wayne asked, imagining that he was his one phone call.

"No. This is bigger than the Archives. The agent guy, Kellerman or something, he followed us to Dallas and just shot a friend of ours from the grassy knoll."

Deeper and deeper. "Whoa, hold on a second. The grassy knoll, like in the Kennedy assassination? And who's 'we'?"

"At Dealey Plaza, yeah. Her name's Chloe. Her dad was an FBI agent. Jack Harper. Fired from the Bureau early last year, dead a month later. Coroner ruled it suicide, but . . ."

"Yeah," Wayne said. Jon's own brother, Michael, had been ruled a suicide after he had started digging into the Division's secrets two years ago. But it wasn't a suicide. In fact, the man who put a bullet in Michael's head had been a fellow Division agent.

"So how would you like me to help?" After most missions like the one he had just completed, his bosses gave him a week off to regroup and get his head together. Filip was taking him to exfil from the country now, to debrief at Langley before giving him his much-needed respite. Though it sounded like that break would be less relaxing than he'd hoped.

"For starters, can you look into Jack Harper's termination from the Bureau? He was researching the Kennedy assassination, apparently convinced there was a conspiracy to kill JFK, and, later, Bobby."

Wayne grimaced. "Okay, I'll bite. Did he have a theory as to who was behind the curtain?"

Jon hesitated. It sounded like Wayne wasn't the only one skeptical about all of this. "J. Edgar Hoover."

"The head of the FBI."

"Which would, theoretically, give the FBI incentive to keep that covered up. And Jack Harper threw a monkey wrench into all of that."

Deeper and deeper down the rabbit hole. Though this wouldn't be the first time Jon had managed to discover the impossible.

"Who exerted pressure on whom to get him kicked out?" Jon continued. "It sounds like there was a concerted effort to blacklist him and destroy his credibility, which made it easier for people to swallow the suicide theory."

"Do you think this Kellerman guy is a fed as well?"

"Worth looking into, but I've got a bad feeling he may be off the books."

Wayne knew the type. He *was* the type.

"All right. I'll be coming back stateside soon, but I may be unreachable while in transit. I'll do some digging and get back to you as soon as I can."

"Thanks a million, Wayne. I owe you."

"You don't owe me a thing. If this is what you say it is, then someone in the FBI poses a threat to American lives and to the rule of law. Stopping people like that is my job description."

A pause on the other end of the line. Then Jon said, "I don't need to tell you to be careful. You'll be probing the very institution that may have killed a president and a presidential candidate, and has gotten away with it for more than fifty years."

"And I don't need to tell you to be careful, with this Kellerman on your tails."

Another pause. "Be careful, Wayne."

Wayne smiled grimly to himself. "You too."

# CHAPTER 23
*Dallas, Texas*

Anthony Kellerman jumped back as Vance Nicholson's arm flew defensively into the air.

"Easy there, sir," Kellerman said. He had quick-changed into a paramedic's uniform, acting and looking as though he belonged. An authority figure, above question. A professional performing his duty, not worth remembering beyond the role he played. "Let's get you someplace safe."

Vance wiped at the smear of blood the miniature tranquilizer dart had left on his neck. "What's going on?"

"Just a minor injury from your fall I imagine, sir. You really should be more careful out in this heat. Here, let me help you up. I've got a ride ready to take you to the hospital if you'd like."

"Sure, sure," Vance said, absentmindedly.

The student who had been shot by the second dart had swatted it away as soon as it struck her, limiting the amount of sedative delivered and accelerating her recovery. Kellerman had plucked the fallen darts from the grass nearby without anyone noticing. Then, he offered to help, claiming to be a nurse, much to the relieved surprise of the gathering crowd. The girl recovered more quickly than Vance, suffering only a mild headache, a scuffed knee, and what was sure to be a hefty dose of schoolyard teasing in the days to come. He had used a penlight to check the student for a concussion before suggesting she get some rest and stay hydrated.

As the school group moved on, he had turned his attention to Vance. Confident that the fallen man was in good hands, or at least confident enough that they weren't going to spend any more of their time worrying about a stranger, the small crowd that had been watching dispersed. Kellerman led Vance to the conspiracist's own car, parked nearby.

"I think I'll be driving," Kellerman said. Vance nodded his assent and handed over his keys.

Once they were safely inside, Vance glared openly at Kellerman.

"You were supposed to shoot *them*," he said, bile dripping from his words.

"You weren't supposed to move in the way at the last minute," Kellerman returned as he pulled into traffic. "I appreciate your activating your tracker once you had them with you, but why did you have to go all zealot in the middle of the operation? Still trying to win more converts?"

"Old habits die hard, I suppose."

If all had gone according to plan, Jon and Chloe would be unconscious in the back seat right now, on their way to a safe house to interrogate and eventually dispose of them. Instead, Kellerman was chauffeuring Vance while his targets were in the wind. But Kellerman already saw a way to turn this mistake to his advantage.

Kellerman looked sidelong at him. "Is it hard? Professing to know the revolutionary truth, but having to leave out the end of the story?"

"What, that I really know who shot JFK? Or that I've turned informant for them?"

"Both, I suppose. It's just funny to me. You develop a reputation as someone who has secret knowledge and you proselytize anyone who will listen, but you keep the most shocking secrets to yourself."

Vance gritted his teeth. "I do what I must to survive. You know that better than anyone."

"So, what did they learn?"

"Beyond what I've told them? Not much. They had an old book with them and a spool of developed film full of Kennedy family portraits."

Kellerman turned and stared at Vance for a moment too long. He slammed on the brakes as the truck in front of him stopped without warning, prompting an angry symphony of horns from behind.

"So that was what they were after at the Archives. And these items, you examined them?"

"Of course. But there was nothing much to see. The pictures were just regular family photos, most of which I've seen in magazines and books over the years. And the book was just an old novel. Nothing written in the margins or hidden in a carved-out compartment inside that I could see."

"Something had to be there. They risked life and limb to steal those items and bring them here to you. They wouldn't have done that if there was nothing conspiracy-related in there."

"They would have if they didn't know there was nothing."

Kellerman had to concede that point. Still, Gaines's concerns wouldn't be put to rest by the threadbare assurances of a begrudging informant. As long as Jon and Chloe were at large, they remained a threat to the Society's mission.

"You need to ingratiate yourself back into their quest," Kellerman said. "Tell them you survived and are recuperating in the hospital, but that your mind can still be an asset to them. If they find out something, you need to be the first person they call."

"And you need to be the first person I call after that," Vance said in a listless tone.

"See? You might prove your worth to me after all. Just remember, I'm the only one that stands between you and a bullet to the brain. If I decide you're just not worth keeping alive anymore."

"I understand, I understand," Vance countered, suddenly more enthusiastic.

"Good." Kellerman turned into Vance's driveway. "Now go make that call."

# CHAPTER 24
## *Washington, DC*

Stanton Gaines beamed a politician's smile as he shook hands with his visitor and invited him into his office.

"Please, sit down," Gaines said, closing the door behind Patrick Molyneux.

Molyneux gingerly sat down in an antique wingback chair, as though he was afraid to damage the furniture.

Gaines crossed to the sideboard. "Anything to drink? Water, tonic, something stronger?"

"I'll just have what you're having," Molyneux said.

*Of course you will*, Gaines thought dryly. *Again with the nerves. Again with the deference. At least he's dropped the arbitrary* sir *now.*

Gaines poured them two fingers each of scotch in etched-glass tumblers. Perhaps that would help calm the historian's nerves.

"So," he said, lowering himself into his overstuffed office chair. "Welcome to Washington."

"Thank you, sir."

Gaines grimaced. "A toast," he said, raising his glass. "To your entry into our storied ranks."

"Cheers." Molyneux leaned forward to clink glasses across the desk before leaning back in his seat.

"So, I'm given to understand your late father wasn't particularly forthright with you about what exactly it is we do."

"I know about your . . . *our* history. And that we preserve and memorialize that history and the sacrifices our forefathers made for our nation."

"Well, yes and no." Gaines gave him an avuncular smile. "We were founded as a band of brothers who had just won victory over tyranny. We decided to keep alive the memory of what we had done and keep in close contact with our fellow officers. Thus, the Society was founded. Almost immediately, some of the most powerful men in our nascent country tried to abolish us. But we persevered."

"Of course, we also counted among our ranks some of the most powerful men in the country. Founding fathers, war heroes, some of the most influential leaders our nation has ever known. And throughout our history, our members have become presidents, cabinet secretaries, ambassadors, generals, Supreme Court justices . . ." He chuckled. "And, of course, senators."

Gaines leaned forward in his seat, adopting a more confidential, conspiratorial tone. "All of that is publicly known, though very few Americans have any idea we even exist. But what virtually no one knows is that our fight for this country as a cohesive unit did not end with its founding. Since our nation's darkest hour, we have risen to the cause of preserving the union, no matter the cost. And that, Dr. Molyneux, is where you come in."

"I'm afraid I'm not much of a soldier, sir."

"If I'd wanted a soldier, one would be sitting in front of me instead of you. No, Dr. Molyneux . . . Can I call you, 'Patrick'?"

"Sure, sure, that's fine."

"Fantastic. Patrick, we don't need you to be a soldier for us. We have plenty of those. What we need is someone with your particular insight and understanding on certain aspects of our nation's history. That, and a fresh set of eyes."

"I don't understand. The briefing documents said something about an infiltration mission of some sort. How does my background in history come into play?"

Gaines stood and began to pace behind his desk. Slowly, purposefully, hands behind his back with chest held high.

"Once again, we find ourselves at a crossroads in our nation's tumultuous history, Patrick. The Society has staved off threats from within and without over the past two centuries, never faltering when the call of duty comes. From the Revolutionary War to the Civil War to the Cold War, we were always there, doing what was necessary for our great union. And now, our nation is once again on the cusp of another historic milestone. A threat is rising that we must counter at all costs."

"So what can we do about it?"

"What we can do, and what we will do, is whatever is necessary to combat the threat. It won't be easy, and it won't be without sacrifice, but what noble causes ever are?"

"And this Jon Rickner and Chloe Harper?"

"They could have the power to expose our plans and ultimately devastate our nation beyond repair. You will help to ensure that they don't."

"How?"

Gaines sat back down and grinned at Molyneux. "Oh, this part I think will be right up your alley."

# CHAPTER 25
## *Boston, Massachusetts*

Chloe led Jon through the doors and into the soaring glass atrium of the John F. Kennedy Presidential Library and Museum. The distinctive building had been designed by I.M. Pei, the world-famous Harvard-educated Chinese architect. Jackie Kennedy herself had been instrumental in selecting him for the project to honor her husband's legacy. Pei's original design incorporated a truncated pyramid to symbolize how his monumental life and work were cut short. While that idea had been scrapped for the Kennedy project, Pei would revive it decades later for the controversial Louvre Pyramid, made newly famous by *The Da Vinci Code*.

She scanned the spacious chamber. A sweeping staircase traced the far wall, leading up to the secure archives. Surely that was where Bobby Kennedy would have stashed his secrets for his younger brother to find. That is, assuming Ted hadn't already found them. But if he had, why hadn't the truth come out? Why had he held onto the pieces of the puzzle but never done anything with the solution?

*One step at a time, Chloe.*

The trouble was that the library was for researchers only, by appointment only, and after yesterday's trouble at another prominent archive of nationally significant documents, security was sure to be tight. The National Archives and Records Administration oversaw fourteen presidential libraries, including this one, and her fake University of Iowa student ID would surely raise suspicion if used again today, especially after she wasn't accounted for in the aftermath of the National Archives inferno.

"Where to?" Jon asked.

That was the question, wasn't it?

> Where his words live on, the world is now changed.
> Inside is what counts.
> Careful, they're watching.

She had been here once before, about a year ago when she first began investigating her dad's theories. There were two main parts to the facility, as indicated by the official name. So if the library was off limits for the time being, perhaps the museum would hold some clue to Bobby Kennedy's puzzle. If nothing else, perhaps it would jar loose some fragment of knowledge that would give her more insight into what his cryptic clue could mean.

"Let's check out the museum," Chloe said.

"The publicly accessible museum? You think he hid his secret in broad daylight?"

"Why not? From what I read of your exploits in New York, that's exactly what Rockefeller did."

"Well, not exactly . . ." Jon said, but he didn't press the point.

She had to remember that when it came to solving historical mysteries, Jon was the expert. But when it came to JFK, the past year had made her into something of an expert as well. Plus, she had already lost a father and two friends to Kellerman and whoever he was working for. This was her quest.

"Come on," she said, beckoning him toward the museum entrance. "You may even learn something."

"I always do," Jon countered with a grin.

The museum was arranged more or less chronologically, beginning with Kennedy's early life and culminating in his assassination and its aftermath. Their tour began with a short film about JFK's early life, including his upper-crust family upbringing, his collegiate life, his military service in World War II, and his political career. None of the film's content was news to Chloe, but she hoped that it would serve as a refresher to help juice Jon's mystery-solving prowess.

After the film, Chloe and Jon followed the crowd down a flight of stairs and into the museum proper. A zig-zagging array of rooms, the exhibits traced a path through the Kennedy presidency, from the campaign to the assassination. The pair wended their way through the exhibits, passing through the 1960 presidential campaign, the historic Kennedy-Nixon debates—complete with a period television broadcasting reruns of the debates themselves—and JFK's presidential victory. As they scoured an exhibit dedicated to Kennedy's presidential inauguration, Chloe reflected at how much original audio was showcased throughout the museum.

Jon apparently noticed it too.

"Pretty neat, all these original recordings," he said.

"Bobby Kennedy's doing. Especially later on in the museum. And in the library, too."

"Huh. What a great tribute, using the technology of the day to preserve his brother's legacy in such a personal manner."

Indeed, many of the voiceovers in the exhibits were not just preserved audio or video from news broadcasts or major speeches, but from JFK's closest friends and loved ones, sharing what the man was really like. His innermost thoughts at key moments in his life, distilled and shared by the people who knew him best.

This became even more apparent as they entered the next area, a mockup of the Kennedy-era White House. Exhibits here focused on some of the most pivotal moments of JFK's brief presidency. A newly emphasized Peace Corps to engender goodwill across the globe. The Cuban Missile Crisis that brought the planet to the brink of nuclear annihilation. Kennedy's promise to put a man on the moon by the decade's end.

Kennedy presided over a turbulent time, but it was a time endowed with hope. He certainly had his failings as a president and as a man, but there were so many arenas in which Kennedy showed rare discipline, wisdom, and restraint that otherwise could have brought the nation to its knees. He became a symbol of hope amidst some of the country's darkest days. And then, that hope was snuffed out.

But by whom?

"Anything?" she asked as they left a small theater and entered the Space Program room.

"I was about to ask you the same."

"This is useless," she moaned, immediately hating herself for sulking. "It's got to be here somewhere. I'm just not seeing it."

"Okay, let's think about this logically," Jon said, taking her aside while a family conversing in a thick Arkansan drawl *ooh*-ed and *aah*-ed at replicas of Gemini-era rockets across the room. "If Bobby hid something here for his brother to find, then the message he encoded should have been sufficient for him to figure it out."

"It should have been. But he made it so vague. Like he was afraid the bad guys would find the message too." Chloe gestured at the exhibit around them. "And there were so many ways he 'changed the world.' Did he hide it 'inside' that rocket over there? Or maybe in one of those TVs showing the first televised presidential debate? This was a revolutionary era with no shortage of world-changing events, many of which had Kennedy's fingerprints all over them."

"You're right," Jon said with a soft smile that was oddly comforting. "There are too many possibilities. So let's keep looking for something that looks like more of a certainty. Ted couldn't have just started dismantling the exhibits willy-nilly, especially if the people that killed Jack and Bobby were watching him. Maybe something in a later exhibit is more clear-cut."

"Or maybe it's in the library we can't get into."

Jon shook his head. "We'll deal with that if and when we have to. Besides, we haven't even gotten to the assassination section yet. That seems like a prime candidate for hiding the truth about, you know, the assassination."

Chloe brightened. "Yeah. Okay, let's find what we came here for."

They left the space program behind and entered a room dedicated to the various ceremonial and state events hosted by the Kennedys or in honor of the Kennedys. Images around the room showed JFK and the First Lady greeting heads of state, titans of industry, leaders of movements, generals and top ambassadors. Had one of these dignitaries played a role in the president's assassination? Was a foreign power, like the USSR or Cuba, or even one of America's allies, responsible for Kennedy's death?

The next room held even more promise. Modeled after Robert F. Kennedy's office while he served as his brother's attorney general, the room seemed like a prime hiding place. Bobby Kennedy had served not only as his brother's cabinet member but also as one of his closest advisors. At thirty-five, he was the youngest attorney general since 1814, and many derided his appointment as lacking in experience while strong in nepotism. But Robert had led with a strong sense of social justice, which was all the more important as the civil rights movement grew to a head. And even more crucial for Jack Kennedy was how implicitly he trusted his younger brother.

Most of the ersatz office was full of family mementos and typical business fare. Drawings sketched by his children. Bookends, pens, and pencils. The original telephone he had used in his official office. Even his glasses donned the desk at the center of the room.

Two items stood out to Chloe. The first was a copper bust of Winston Churchill sitting on a pedestal against one wall. Robert Kennedy had displayed this bust in his office during his tenure as attorney general. Churchill was another man who had changed the world. Perhaps the clue didn't refer to JFK after all, but rather to another world leader who Bobby revered.

The second item was a toy semi-truck used as evidence against the International Brotherhood of Teamsters in a corruption case. Back when John F. Kennedy was still a senator, the future president was on the Senate Select Committee on Improper Activities in the Labor or Management Field, while Bobby served as the chief counsel to the committee. The Teamsters were another recurring suspect in the rogues' gallery of potential JFK assassination conspirators. Robert even successfully prosecuted the infamous Teamsters President Jimmy Hoffa less than a year after his brother's assassination. Hoffa was a feared powerbroker whose mysterious disappearance in the years after Bobby's assassination had set off its own wave of conspiracy theories. Could the miniature truck hold a secret cargo, hidden by the man who helped bring down the powerful labor union's corrupt leadership?

"Jon, what do you think about . . ." Chloe looked around the room.

Jon was gone.

He was right there just a few seconds ago. How long had she been staring at this exhibit? Where had he gone? Had something happened to him?

"In here!" came a voice from the next room.

Jon.

Chloe let out a deep breath she hadn't realized she was holding and crossed the room. She mentally prepared her arguments for both the truck and the bust.

They would only have one chance. Once they crossed that barrier and entered the office itself, security would no doubt be alerted and their window for successful escape would immediately start to close. There would likely only be time to break into one of the potential hiding places. Chloe was leaning toward the Teamsters truck if only because it would likely be easier to break into than a metal and marble bust. But if she was wrong . . .

"It's perfect," Jon said when Chloe approached.

He stood in front of a rendition of President Kennedy's Oval Office. A replicate of the Resolute desk dominated the center of the room, flanked by video screens showing Martin Luther King Jr. sharing his revolutionary dream with a teeming crowd of men and women gathered on the steps of the Lincoln Memorial. Behind the desk, Kennedy's black office chair sat unoccupied and aging. A rocking chair bearing a Navy seal, gifted to the president on the USS *Kitty Hawk* just months before his assassination, sat to the right of the desk. And to the far left of the room, just a few feet from the gently curving wall, was the object that had drawn Jon's dedicated attention.

A globe.

According to the info card next to Chloe, the globe had been presented to President Kennedy by Admiral Arleigh Burke. An early model of the sort that could be illuminated from within, it was a staple of Kennedy's Oval Office throughout his presidency, used for reference when negotiating world conflicts and for teaching his children when they came to visit.

*The world is now changed.*

*Inside is what matters.*

"He hid it inside the globe?" Chloe asked.

"Seems to fit. It's the kind of unambiguous solution Bobby would have wanted to ensure Ted figured it out."

Chloe immediately resolved to never tell Jon about the toy truck or the Churchill bust. Unless, of course, the globe was empty.

But in that case, they'd have a whole host of other issues breathing down their necks. Ones with guns and handcuffs.

"You want the honor?" Jon said, gesturing toward the globe.

Chloe eyed the waist-high guardrail barring entrance to the Oval Office exhibit. She looked at Jon's long legs, which afforded him a good six inches of extra clearance over her own.

"I think this one's going to be all you," she said, watching as the last tourist meandered into the next area. "I'll stand lookout."

"I won't be long," Jon said, winking as he mounted the guardrail and swung himself over. He was careful to shield his face from the cameras as he trotted to the globe, though they had surely been spotted by other sentinels earlier in the museum. Still, that could buy them just enough time to make their escape.

Of course, that hardly mattered if they were caught red-handed.

Her back to the exhibit, Chloe kept an eye on the two main entrances to her position in the hallway. Straight ahead was the direction they had come from. All the likely red herrings in the exhibits dedicated to the Cuba Missile Crisis, the Space Program, ceremonial and state dinners, and Bobby Kennedy's attorney general office. To her left, the hallway stretched into a series of rooms dedicated to the first family, with particular emphasis on the infectious charisma and high stylings of Jackie Kennedy.

"I have a dream," said the ghost of Dr. Martin Luther King from the television monitors in the Oval Office behind her, "that one day every valley shall be exalted, every hill and mountain shall be made low."

Jackie was such a tragic figure. Really, much of the Kennedy clan could be considered beset with tragedy. But Jackie, the sweetheart ideal of American housewives during her brief tenure as first lady, had shown considerable poise as her unimaginable grief was played out on the world's most public stage.

"The rough places will be made plain," Dr. King continued, "and the crooked places will be made straight."

She had leaned heavily on Bobby Kennedy in the aftermath of the assassination, growing close in mutual mourning, mutual love for the dead president, and mutual fear of those truly responsible. Then another assassin's bullet took him from her, prompting her to remark that "If they're killing Kennedys, then my children are targets." Deciding American soil was no longer safe for her family, she married Greek shipping magnate Aristotle Onassis just months after Bobby's assassination. Then, when Aristotle's son died in a plane crash, Jackie's despondent new husband's health began to decline, dying less than six and a half years after their wedding day.

Forty-six years old and already widowed twice, Jackie returned stateside and became close to Ted, who helped her get through public events as the paparazzi continued to chase her. She would eventually become a book editor in New York, living out her days in whatever semblance of peace she could achieve before succumbing to cancer at the age of sixty-four. If there was any bright side to her early death, it was that she didn't live to see her only surviving son, John F. Kennedy, Jr., die in a plane crash just a few years later.

"With this faith," Dr. King continued, "we will be able to hew out of the mountain of despair a stone of hope."

Chloe stole a glance back at Jon. It looked like he was maneuvering the globe somehow, but his body blocked it from view.

"Hurry," she whispered.

"You mean I'm not supposed to be taking my time in here?" Jon ribbed back. "Why didn't you tell me that in the first place?"

Chloe rolled her eyes and returned her gaze to the hallways and her thoughts to the past. Jackie had, of course, been one suspect that JFK assassination conspiracy buffs would trot out from time to time. Her purported motive was usually cited as revenge for his serial infidelity, ensuring that she got to keep the kids without resorting to a long custody battle with the most powerful man in the free world.

Chloe's father never gave that theory much credit. In fact, Jack Harper believed that, thus far, no one had the story completely right. Not just that the proof hadn't surfaced yet, but that all of the theories were wrong. He was adamant that the truth was either an as-yet-undiscovered combination of several existing theories or that the real culprits were completely off the radar. Though considering how robust the collection of potential conspirators had become in the past half century, Chloe couldn't begin to fathom who was left.

"Oh man."

Chloe spun toward Jon's voice.

"What?" she asked.

Jon wrestled with the globe for a moment more before turning her way. The globe had split in half along the equator. More importantly, Jon was grinning from ear to ear, holding something small and black in his hand.

"You found it?"

"I found something," he said as he started to screw the globe back together.

"What are you doing?" she asked in an urgent stage whisper. "We've got to get out of here."

"I'm buying us some time. A disassembled globe would be an immediate red flag to security that something is wrong. But put back together . . ." He stepped out of the way to admire his work. As far as Chloe could tell, it looked the same as when they arrived.

Jon nodded approvingly at the reassembled globe. "No one knew it was there before, and no one will know it's missing now."

"Wonderful. Now can we please get out of here?"

Jon trotted back over to the guardrail and handed her what he had found.

Chloe studied it, surprised that the technology she recognized from her childhood had been around in the 1960s. Though today's youth might be befuddled by the item, she knew an audio cassette tape when she saw one.

The only trouble in this age of digital music would be finding a tape player to listen to the recording contained within.

When she looked up, Jon had already crossed the guardrail. But while the fact that he was now safely in the museum's public area should have given her some peace of mind, the expression on his face did the complete opposite. He was staring over her shoulder, a mixture of shock, fear, and frustration blanching his countenance.

Chloe turned around to look where Jon was staring, expecting to see a contingent of security guards ready to arrest them.

It was worse.

Staring back at Jon and drawing his sidearm was Kellerman.

# CHAPTER 26
## *Boston, Massachusetts*

For Anthony Kellerman, the next few moments seemed to slow to a crawl.

Turning the corner, he hadn't expected to see his quarry staring back at him. As though Jon had been waiting for him.

Now locked in a staring contest to see whether fight or flight would blink first, Kellerman reached for his weapon, which he had left holstered so as not to draw undue attention.

Though Vance Nicholson hadn't offered him any leads since being shot in Dallas, Kellerman had tracked Jon and Chloe to Boston through the same fake IDs they had used to get to Dallas from Delaware. It was an informed guess on his part that they would come here. Other than Harvard, his birthplace, and a few buildings where he gave speeches or ran campaigns, Boston proper didn't have that much of a connection to JFK, as the family estates were in more exclusive communities across New England. But nothing in Boston screamed the legacy of JFK louder than the John F. Kennedy Presidential Library and Museum. It would have been a perfect place for Robert—a thorn in the Society's side since even before his brother was shot—to have hidden something incriminating about the assassination.

But that was the question Society members had been pondering for half a century: how much did Bobby Kennedy actually know?

Then he saw it. A cassette tape in Chloe's hand. Part of the museum's Oral History Program? Or a completely unknown recording?

"This has gone far enough, Chloe," Kellerman said as he pulled his weapon free. He held it loosely at his side, prepared but not overtly threatening. "No one else has to die today. Give me the tape, the film canister, and the book, and I'll let you both go, no questions asked."

A lie, of course, but he was certain that whatever was on that tape was far more damaging than anything either of them already knew. If they had just retrieved it, they wouldn't yet know what was recorded on it, which limited their damage potential. They would still be dealt with, but priorities were priorities.

"Run!" Jon yelled, dragging Chloe to the right, deeper into the museum.

Stupid. But expected.

Kellerman gave chase. He was loath to actually discharge his weapon within the museum, especially with so many cameras recording his every move and with so many patrons exploring the exhibits lining the hall. The hope was that with their fear of his gun impeding rational thought, Jon and Chloe would make a mistake, allowing him to catch them.

Until then, he would just run them down.

A glittering series of exhibits blew past. Diamond Tiffany bracelets, one-of-a-kind designer dresses, glistening china place settings. The voice of their original owner, Jacqueline Kennedy, echoed through the hall.

The hallway turned to the left, then left again. The theme of the exhibits changed to the assassination. After all this time, with more than half the country believing that there was a conspiracy behind the president's murder, it was astounding to Kellerman that the public didn't press the issue. Even if they had their doubts, the official story of the lone-wolf shooter made people feel safer. Oswald did it alone. Oswald is dead. The world is now safe again.

When it became clear that Cold War paranoia had made Americans less likely to accept the official story, when a whole host of conspiracy junkies began writing books and manifestos purporting to have the unadulterated real story behind JFK's assassination, the Society realized that, eventually, someone might come a little too close to the truth, even if by accident. So steps were taken to discredit many of the theories and their promoters. Some of the more outlandish theories had even been cooked up by the Society to make all conspiracy believers seem loony by association.

But Kellerman's quarry had something in hand that could change all that. Or, it could be nothing. A red herring from the past. Or a trap by Jon Rickner, who had proven himself adept at bluffing his way out of tight spots. Was this entire chase a diversion? Was there a third individual helping them, perhaps leaving the museum by another entrance with something even more substantial?

He was gaining on them. Slowly, but steadily. The agent may have had a few years on Jon and Chloe, but years in the Marines, the US Marshals Service, and the employ of Stanton Gaines had ensured his cardio remained top notch.

The corridor ended, and another jag to the right led them through an exhibit dedicated to Kennedy's legacy. For all he was known for during his short presidency, JFK's death had done far more for this country than anything he had done in life. But the patrons of these halls were far too shortsighted to see that. Let them have their political martyrs, their little saluting JFK Jr., their somber Vice President Johnson taking the oath under unthinkable circumstances. The JFK mythology was far more potent than the truth for achieving the Society's purposes. Especially since their work was far from finished.

The hall ended in a wall. A chunk of the Berlin Wall, no less, emphasizing JFK's solidarity with the divided city—even if the urban legend that his German phrasing led him to claim to be a jelly donut during that historic speech still persisted. Still running full tilt, Jon's head stayed straight for a little too long as he turned, his gaze lingering on the artifact displayed before him. Kellerman chuckled inwardly. It must be killing the young historian to have to fly past all these exhibits. But then, he and Chloe may well have in hand an artifact of more singular historical importance than anything else in here.

Kellerman followed them around the bend to the left, which dumped them back into the soaring glass pavilion near the tour's entrance. His quarry ran up the stairs back toward the lobby. Kellerman followed, taking the stairs two at a time. When he got to the top, he sighted Jon and Chloe again. Unsurprisingly, they had skipped the obligatory gift shop entirely, opting to make a beeline for the exit.

They were almost in his grasp. Once they were outside, with fewer cameras and less tourists, he wouldn't feel nearly as bad about taking the shot. A leg wound perhaps. He still needed to question them. Particularly if there was a third party that had made off with other evidence.

Jon and Chloe darted out the door. So close now. Kellerman booked it to the door, only to be met with a line of nursing-home residents filing into the museum.

He tried the next door, but the horde of febrile retirees plodding in with their walkers and oxygen tanks had clogged up all the doors.

"Excuse me!" He shoved and clawed his way forward, but for all their advanced age and withered musculature, the ancient throng was surprisingly resilient. He peered over their bowed heads to see Jon and

Chloe getting away. Chloe looked over her shoulder at his plight and grinned briefly before returning to her sprint.

"Federal agent, folks! I need everyone to move out of the way, now!"

It took a few more prods and shoves, but he finally broke through the teeming mass of octogenarians, just in time to see Jon and Chloe hop on a bus a hundred yards away. A moment later, the bus roared away from the curb, too far away for Kellerman to reach them. Even with a bullet.

He should have taken the shot when he had the chance. He could deal with the museum patrons. Eyewitnesses were notoriously unreliable, especially in moments of excitement or danger. But the cameras were a different story. And without a building-clearing emergency like back at the Archives, he would have little hope of gaining unfettered access to the security footage after opening fire on civilians in a crowded government museum. If it weren't for all the cameras, he probably would have taken the shot.

Instead, he smelled of prune juice and failure. And Jon and Chloe were in the wind again, this time armed with yet another tidbit of information that had managed to escape the purges.

Frustrated, Kellerman shook his head. Trying to figure out his next move, he turned and looked into the eye of a black half-orb affixed to the ceiling.

Cameras. All those cameras. Perhaps all wasn't lost after all. He'd need to head back to his safe house near the Public Gardens to change his identity and credentials, but a plan was beginning to materialize in his mind.

First, though, he needed to have a serious heart-to-heart with Vance Nicholson.

# CHAPTER 27
## *Cambridge, Massachusetts*

Chloe hadn't seen a Radio Shack in years, but she was glad they had found one. Even if it was in the most unlikely of places.

They had ridden three buses in any direction but back toward the museum, trying to put as much distance between themselves and Kellerman as quickly as possible. But all the while they kept an eye out the window, looking for a store that might hold the tool they needed to reveal what was on their cassette tape.

Apparently this particular Radio Shack had decided that cassette tapes were destined to become the new vinyl, experiencing a new resurgence in popularity as hipsters and audio purists alike tried to return to the age of analog media. Despite the Massachusetts Institute of Technology being on the forefront of innovation, this retail throwback to the 1980s right next to campus had held another revived staple of that era. A brand-new Sony Walkman.

Taking refuge in the colonnade of the Barker Engineering Library, Chloe slid the cassette into the portable cassette player. She handed one of her iPhone earbuds to Jon and placed the other into her own ear. Then, with a silent prayer that the recording hadn't been demagnetized in the half century since its recording, she pressed play.

"Teddy, if you're hearing this from a cassette rather than from me face to face, then something has probably gone wrong."

Chloe recognized the voice as belonging to Robert F. Kennedy. The assassinated senator chuckled awkwardly before continuing.

"In secret, I've been investigating Jack's murder for nearly five years. Oswald was right. He was involved, but he wasn't pulling the strings. And I think I know who is. I've placed a document in a hidden safe in the bow of the *Victura*. The combination is the days of all us brothers' birthdays, oldest to youngest. Once I finish my investigation, I'm going to copy my latest evidence and hide it in there as well. And then I'm going to the Senate floor with what I've discovered. Or the White House, depending on how things go between here and November."

"He's being awfully cryptic," Jon said.

"He's probably afraid he's being spied on." Chloe rewound the tape a few seconds. "Now shush."

"If something happens to me, go to the *Victura*. Hopefully by then I'll have the evidence you will need to bring them down, and, if they get to me before I can publicly denounce them with proof in hand, you can use what I've hidden there to expose and destroy their treasonous machinations.

"Ideally, you'll never hear this tape, and we can laugh about my makeshift spycraft after Jack's killers are brought to justice. But if not . . . God be with you, Teddy."

There was a loud click as the recording ended. Chloe let the tape continue to play, hoping there would be something else on there.

There wasn't.

Chloe sighed and hit stop. "Another clue pointing the way somewhere else."

Jon looked disheartened.

"Of course, that's kind of your world, isn't it?" Chloe asked, afraid she had discouraged him. "Come on, let's listen to it again to figure out that hiding place he mentioned."

"We were so close," Jon said, staring at one of the columns in disbelief.

"We're not giving up yet," Chloe said. "Come on, we can do this."

"The *Victura*," Jon said.

"Yeah, Jack's favorite sailboat. It was an heirloom, used by all the Kennedy brothers over the years. The family bought it in '32, the same year Ted was born."

"Do you know where it is?" Jon asked.

"No, but I'm sure we can find it. Maybe it's anchored at the Kennedy compound in Cape Cod?"

"Not anymore." He sighed. "We were right there."

Chloe finally figured out what he was saying. It would be much harder this time. Security would be on high alert. Not to mention Kellerman. But if that's where the *Victura* was, that was where they had to go.

Back to the very museum they had just fled.

# CHAPTER 28
## Boston, Massachusetts

Jon didn't see any guards. And he prayed they didn't see him.

With his back to the waters of Dorchester Bay, he stared up at the sunlight blaring off the towering glass facade of the John F. Kennedy Presidential Library and Museum. Just a couple of hours ago, he and Chloe had run through that very hall, too blind to the chase to realize that the prize they sought was hidden just yards from their path.

And now they were back. In the sights of both Kellerman and an enraged security force. Preparing to steal yet another artifact the museum didn't know it was in possession of.

Jon and Chloe had walked along the Harborwalk footpath to approach the library's east face. The Harborwalk traced the edge of Columbia Point and allowed them to draw near to their goal without passing through the usual tourist entry points. Indeed, most visitors didn't visit this part of the facility until after concluding their tour of the rest of the site. Which, Jon hoped, would focus the library's security elsewhere.

The *Victura* was permanently dry-docked in the middle of a grassy slope that led from the building to the water. The floor-to-ceiling windows of the eastern part of the library/museum complex looked out on the vessel and the waters beyond, evoking the connection that the so-called "sailing president" felt with the sea.

"He loved the ocean," Chloe said. "And he loved sailing on this boat more than almost anything."

Though all the Kennedy boys sailed this boat over the years, Jon didn't have to ask which brother she was referring to.

"In 1966, Bobby decided to even have JFK's original coffin buried at sea, to prevent it from becoming a political sideshow."

Jon was familiar with the story. The original coffin was chosen out of necessity, shipping the president's body from Dallas to Washington on November 22, 1963 on Air Force One, resting just yards from President

Lyndon B. Johnson as he took the oath of office, the newly widowed Jackie Kennedy at his side. Once in DC, the Kennedy family chose a different coffin to be the final home of the president's body. For the next two years, the original coffin would remain in a vault at the National Archives, before Bobby Kennedy, then the junior senator from New York, would successfully push to dump the coffin deep in the Atlantic.

The secret operation, overseen by none other than Defense Secretary Robert McNamara, saw the coffin transported to Andrews Air Force Base to a C-130 cargo plane, drilled full of holes, weighed down by sandbags, and dumped into the waters off the Delaware coast. The operation had remained secret until a declassified memo surfaced in 1999, detailing the pains taken by the involved parties to ensure the coffin went straight to the bottom and stayed there.

As with all things Kennedy, especially things involving secret operations disposing of evidence and signed off on by the secretary of defense, conspiracists immediately seized on the revelation as further proof of a cover-up. Jon, though, believed that Bobby merely wanted to preserve his brother's memory while also honoring their mutual love of the sea. And while he had recently become a believer in the existence of a conspiracy to assassinate JFK, Jon was not convinced that Bobby Kennedy would have orchestrated a cover-up of the truth. In fact, it seemed as though he was the only one dedicated to revealing it.

Jon led the way up the slope, keeping the *Victura* between them and any eyes that might be observing from within the building. While the worn grass in places intimated that the area was not exactly off-limits to visitors, the location in which Jon would soon be trespassing most certainly was. A low dividing wall to his left separated a triangular concrete plaza from this grassy slope. Thus far, none of the half dozen or so tourists milling about in the plaza had noticed him, content to watch the seagulls and cargo ships cruising into the harbor. He hoped it stayed that way.

The twenty-five-foot sloop was one of only 200 Wianno Senior model sailboats ever built, and surely the most famous of its brethren. When the Kennedys purchased the boat in 1932, a fifteen-year-old JFK christened the vessel *Victura*.

*She who is about to conquer*, in Latin.

Perhaps Bobby had been particularly prescient in his choice of hiding places. If the safe truly contained the evidence they sought, Chloe would finally be able to conquer the forces that had destroyed her father. And America would finally be able to conquer the ghosts of its most controversial crime.

As with the museum's Oval Office exhibit earlier, Chloe had agreed to play lookout while Jon ventured into the belly of the beast. The problem was, there were a lot more angles to watch for out here. And a lot more angles could see what he was doing, cameras or not.

Reaching the hull of the *Victura*, Jon clambered aboard to whispers of good luck from Chloe. Once topside, he dropped low to the deck. If anyone were watching from the upper floors of the library, they would likely still be able to see him. He had to get what he came for and get away from here before someone did.

*Hidden in the bow*, Bobby Kennedy had said. The boat was too small, with too shallow a berth, to offer a full companionway into a lower deck. Instead, the only entry point into the bow was the main hatch beneath the foredeck.

The hatch was secured with a padlock, as he assumed it would be. He unfolded a miniature bolt cutter that he had picked up at an Ace Hardware on the way back here from MIT. With shorter handles and decreased leverage, the bolt cutter wasn't quite as efficient as a full-sized model, but it did the job. After three hard squeezes, the lock gave way. He removed it from the latch and swung open the door leading deeper into the bow.

Crawling inside, his nostrils were immediately filled with the stale scent of must. Clearly no one had been inside the bow in quite some time. Which buoyed his hopes that Bobby Kennedy's secret safe remained undiscovered. Now Jon just had to find it.

The boat's cabin was tiny, not much more than a glorified storage compartment. Whatever accoutrements of seafaring life had once been contained in here—buckets, spare rigging, a picnic basket for wooing a young Jackie Bouvier—were long gone. A man-sized cube of lacquered wood paneling was all that remained. That, and a strong scent of mildew and mold.

There was no sign of a safe.

But then, Bobby had warned his brother it would be hidden.

Jon wriggled a little further inside, endeavoring to tuck his legs into the compartment where they couldn't be seen by security or Kellerman. Despite most of his body being out of sight, he felt incredibly exposed. He was wedged into a dead end, with his only means of escape a blind spot behind him. He was grateful that he had Chloe as a lookout. Even if her last turn in the role had nearly led to Kellerman apprehending them.

"How's it coming in there?" Chloe asked, her voice just loud enough for him to hear.

"Cramped."

"The faster you find it, the sooner you can stretch your legs."

Jon laughed, only to begin coughing as he inhaled a dusty lungful of whatever microbes or spores had been growing down here. He scanned the wood paneling, but came up empty.

*Got to do this the old-fashioned way, then.*

One at a time, he rapped his knuckles upon each panel, listening intently as he did. Halfway through the process, he stopped. This panel sounded different. The one at the very front of the compartment. Deepest into the bow.

He wedged one of the bolt cutter's blades under the bottom of the panel and pulled with all his might. The panel gave slightly before the blade slipped loose.

*Progress.*

Jon shoved the blade back into position, a little further now that the panel had moved somewhat. Then, with one mighty yank, he wrenched the panel free.

Hidden behind it was a flat steel wall safe.

Bingo.

"You all right in there?" Chloe asked. Obviously she had heard his ruckus. Hopefully she was the only one.

"Oh yeah," Jon replied, his fingers already spinning the dial. Thirty numbers on the dial, which fit with the brother's birthdays.

*Jack was born May 29, 1917.* Jon stopped once the pointer hit 29.

*Bobby, November 20, 1925.* Jon spun the dial left until it pointed at 20.

*And Ted was born February 22, 1932.* Right again to 22.

Jon pulled the handle.

It didn't budge.

*Impossible.*

Jon tried the combination again, taking extra care to ensure each number lined up perfectly. Then he pulled the handle again.

Nothing.

"Combo isn't working," Jon said.

"It's not?" Chloe responded, concern tainting her voice. "25-29-20-22?"

"25?" Jon asked.

"Joe Jr."

Jon could kick himself. Born July 25, 1915, Joseph Patrick Kennedy, Jr. was the oldest of the Kennedy boys and had been the heir apparent to the Kennedy fortune and to the political ambitions of family patriarch Joe Sr. When Joe Jr. was killed in England serving in World War II, that mantle of expectation passed to his younger brother, John Fitzgerald Kennedy. But while Jon might have forgotten the brother who had died nearly two decades before his brother moved into the White House, Bobby and Ted surely hadn't.

Joe Jr. was the missing piece of the combination.

"Jon, we've got company. Security guard just leaving the building. Heading our way."

"How long?"

"Twenty seconds. Wrap it up."

Jon tried the combination again, this time using all four brothers' birthdays.

The safe swung open.

Though it was dim inside this little compartment, Jon could see inside the safe well enough to realize it wasn't stuffed full of dossiers, photographs, ballistics reports or other sizable documents that Bobby Kennedy had promised to hide here. Sirhan Sirhan must have gotten to him first.

"Now, Jon."

Jon grabbed the safe's sole contents—a sealed manila envelope—and wriggled his way back out of the compartment. Planting one hand on the deck, he hopped off the boat and down onto the grass beside Chloe.

"Keep walking," he said, trying to appear casual while making good time.

"You get it?"

"I cleaned out the safe. We'll find out what was in it soon enough." He tucked the envelope under his shirt and made a beeline for the Harborwalk, the bushes, and the crowds at the beaches beyond. Just before they slipped out of view, Jon stole a look back at the guard, who was slowing his pace, deciding they weren't worth the effort. Perhaps he assumed they were just a couple of stupid Millennials taking selfies with JFK's sailboat. For once, Jon was grateful for his generation's bad reputation.

Still, they needed to put some distance between themselves and the museum. It wouldn't be long before someone connected the *Victura* selfie-seekers and the museum foot chase from a gun-wielding Kellerman. Jon had a destination in mind for opening Bobby Kennedy's envelope. But, with every step, Jon felt the power of the image emblazoned on the envelope burning into his stomach.

The official seal of the United States Senate.

# CHAPTER 29
## *Washington, DC*

Patrick Molyneux was in historian heaven.

The breadth and quality of original documents in this basement archive were astounding. Thousands of secret missives, military strategies, drafts of important decrees, and wartime journal entries filled the shelves. It was regarded by many as the foremost repository of Revolutionary War historical records in the world.

And yet, despite all this firsthand documentation of this crucial period in the nation's history, it was only part of the story.

Molyneux's conversation with Gaines continued to play in his head. It was as though a veil had been lifted from his understanding of history. Not just of the assassinations of John F. Kennedy and his brother. Of everything since the Revolutionary War.

He now knew that the so-called Kennedy curse had been at least partially strengthened by the Society's efforts. All because one of them had been elected president. John F. Kennedy refused to do what was necessary to ensure the country's future. They had killed his friend and lover Marilyn Monroe to emphasize that they were not to be trifled with. That virtually every president since Reconstruction had kowtowed to their simple but vital demands. The actress and sex icon's death had been officially ruled an accidental drug overdose, but the Society's pointed threats less than a week before her murder left no doubt in the president's mind what had happened. Marilyn was a warning. JFK decided not to heed it.

Johnson had proven to be much more amenable to the Society's demands. Getting the job because your predecessor's brain was forcibly removed from his skull tended to put things in perspective. The Society had helped to push parts of Johnson's civil rights agenda through Congress as thanks for his cooperation, and everyone was happy.

Until it came to light that the late president's brother had been digging around where he shouldn't be. Like his older brother, Robert

F. Kennedy did not listen to reason, so they used an asset from a secret CIA program to remove that problem. And then the last of the brothers, Senator Ted Kennedy, had started sticking his nose where it didn't belong. A spiked drink, a fatal car accident in the tidal channel of Chappaquiddick, and a national scandal later, and Ted became much more compliant. In fact, he had become somewhat of a reluctant ally, mounting a relentless primary challenge to a no-longer-welcome incumbent President Carter in the 1980 election. It was a tactic that the Society hadn't used in nearly seven decades at that point, but it still worked just as well. Carter was out, and Reagan did what was necessary to ensure the Society's demands were met.

All of this Molyneux now knew. But he still couldn't believe it. This was the secret his father had kept all these years. This was the legacy Cyrus Molyneux believed his bookish son couldn't handle. And, as a historian, it flew in the face of everything he thought he knew about his country's past.

And yet, in a twisted sort of way, it made perfect sense.

He studied a map used by General George Washington to chart troop movements during the battle of Lexington. *Washington himself touched this map.* The room was bursting with documents penned and used by founding fathers, colonial generals, and national leaders. A hallowed brotherhood to whom the nation owed an unpayable debt. And now, Patrick Molyneux had the honor of joining that brotherhood in the ongoing fight to protect the nation from its greatest threat.

He would use the next day or so to cement himself here, combing the archives for anything else that might have slipped through the purges, though most of what was here would be older and less likely to present overt problems for the Society than the Kennedy angle Jon Rickner and Chloe Harper were currently chasing. And then, when the time presented itself, he would move into the next phase of his mission.

Molyneux wasn't sure if he could do what Gaines had asked of him. It was so unlike what he'd spent his life doing. He wasn't a CIA agent, a Green Beret, or a Navy SEAL. He was just a passionate student of American history who happened to be born into the right family.

But, according to Gaines, that was exactly why he was perfect for the mission.

And though Molyneux had his doubts about his ability to pull this off, his will to succeed was not in question. He had been given a second chance to prove himself worthy of his family's legacy. Generations of Molyneux ancestors were counting on him to fulfill his destiny and preserve what they had given their lives for.

He would not let them down.

# CHAPTER 30
*Boston, Massachusetts*

Jon gripped the manila envelope tight, excited for and afraid of what might be inside. The truth about the twentieth century's most controversial murder. The most enduring conspiracy theory in American history.

If the American ideals of liberty and justice were a religion, this would be hallowed ground.

A market filled with boutique shops and history-themed books and souvenirs occupied the ground floor. Jon and Chloe had climbed the stairs to the second floor, which was dominated by a massive meeting hall. The balcony where they were seated had an excellent view of the historic gathering place. Rows upon rows of wooden chairs faced a stage that had played host to dozens of influential speeches in the revolutionary birth pangs of what would become the United States—and hundreds more in the following centuries. Above the stage hung a number of large canvases with historic portraits of men who had helped shape the history of Boston and of America. But they were all dominated by George P. A. Healy's gigantic "Webster's Reply to Hayne" that stretched the entire length of the stage and nearly reached the ceiling.

The portrait depicted US Senator Daniel Webster—revered as one of Massachusetts's all-time greatest orators—addressing the United States Senate in a pivotal speech against South Carolina Senator Robert Hayne, defending himself and New England against allegations stemming from a secret plot by delegates from across New England to secede from the Union in the wake of President James Madison's handling of the War of 1812. The 1814 Hartford Convention was not the first conspiracy considering secession from the United States, and it certainly was not the last. Webster's speech defending the American Revolution's roots in New England and pledging eternal allegiance to the Union would prove prescient thirty-one years later when a group of states on the opposite end of the country actually went through with their threat of secession, triggering the bloodiest war in American history.

Here, future founding fathers spouted damnations of tyranny, where revolutionary ideals like "no taxation without representation" became rallying cries. Later, national leaders like Daniel Webster would use the hall for pivotal speeches. And in 1858, a staunchly anti-secessionist senator from Mississippi by the name of Jefferson Davis would use the symbolism of the hall to argue for the strength of the Constitution and the perpetuation of the Union, in spite of the tumultuous conflict raging over slavery and states' rights. Three years later, the South would secede, and a conflicted Davis would become president of the newly founded Confederacy.

Closer to home, John F. Kennedy had used the hall for his last campaign speech in 1960, and Ted Kennedy had used it in 1979 to announce his own bid for the presidency.

Whatever was in this envelope deserved to be revealed in such august surroundings. It was also miles from the JFK Museum and far enough removed from the JFK assassination in historical import that Jon felt safe from Kellerman's reach here.

For now at least.

"Well?" Chloe asked, staring at him expectantly. "Are we going to open it or just stare at the pretty envelope?"

"It *is* a lovely envelope," he said with a playful grin. He handed it to her. "Here. This was your father's quest. You deserve to open it."

Suddenly misty-eyed, Chloe bit her lip. She nodded and accepted the envelope.

"This is for you, Dad," she said after taking a deep breath and looking heavenward. Carefully, she slid a finger beneath the seal and tore open the envelope. She reached in and withdrew two sheets of typewritten paper, each written on the official Senate letterhead of Robert Francis Kennedy.

Dear Teddy,

I'm glad you figured out my codes. I tried to make the clues easy for you to decipher, but harder for our enemies. And enemies we have, dear brother. The same conspirators who cut down Jack are now after me, and, by virtue of association, likely have their eyes on you as well.

The men behind our brother's murder are far more powerful and conniving than I could have ever imagined. They think themselves patriots. They are traitors of the highest order. When rule and law no longer hold sway in the halls of power, the republic is lost. If their crimes go unpunished, I fear that time may soon be upon us.

If they decide that I should join Jack in death, I entrust this quest to you. Discover the truth, the full and whole truth, and expose it to the world. They may be powerful, but their own hubris can be their downfall.

Be careful, though, Teddy. We are the last of the Kennedy brothers, and their machinations will not hesitate to cut you down as well. I pray that my knowledge of their activities remains secret. If I manage to win the presidency this fall, imagine their shock when I come at them full force with all the might of my administration. Previous administrations have kowtowed to their demands, while others, like Jack's, have pushed back— and paid the price. The events of the past five years make me believe President Johnson has acquiesced to their considerable influence. I shall not. And armed from the onset with knowledge of their identity and their past crimes, I will finally snuff out the dark flame that plagues the heart of this great nation.

I served Jack in life as the head of our nation's Justice Department. Since his death, I have worked in secret to bring him justice and to ensure that our nation's justice is restored once and for all. Dr. King's cause is a noble one, but I fear that the Society poses far more danger to even the colored man than do segregation or racism.

I hope to further speak to you about this in person soon, but, regretfully, I must communicate in codes and hidden missives for now. I feel their eyes upon my every move, and have trouble trusting even those in my inner circle. I pray I am wrong and that no harm befalls me, but should another of their unwitting pawns strike me down, you must find their founder's secret to expose the truth.

I apologize for putting you in harm's way, Teddy, but know that this is bigger than either of us. While our brother was assassinated for sticking to the righteous principles upon which our nation was founded, Jack is just one of thousands murdered —directly and in-directly—for the Society's corrupt purposes. Their power, influence, and reach is mighty, but they are not invincible. We must put a stop to them, or I fear our nation will be lost for good.

Your brother,
Bobby

"Wow," Chloe said.

"Wow doesn't begin to cover it."

Something shifted in the envelope. Jon carefully slid out another sheet of paper. It was a small, yellowed scrap of paper with a seal emblazoned across the center.

Jon felt a cold hollow void sink into the pit of his stomach. He knew that symbol. But there was no way *this* could be who Bobby Kennedy was referring to. Jon almost immediately wished it had been the FBI, the CIA, the Cubans, the Soviets, the Mob, or any of the usual suspects in a Kennedy assassination conspiracy. Because down this rabbit hole, this conspiracy could only be much, much worse.

"Is that the Seal of the United States?" Chloe asked.

Jon squirmed. The secret aristocracy that bore this seal had nearly derailed the Constitutional Convention back in the eighteenth century. Allegations of treason and old-world machinations had tainted the group since its inception. But they had proven themselves to be mostly harmless, simply content to record and celebrate history and history makers from the sidelines.

Or so he'd thought.

He'd heard rumors, once. But it was impossible. Unthinkable.

And, according to this secret letter from one US Senator to another, the nightmarish beginnings of a terrifying truth.

"No," he finally responded, tracing the seal with a shaking finger. "This is its evil twin."

# PART TWO
## *WASHINGTON*

"In the councils of government, we must guard against the acquisition of unwarranted influence, whether sought or unsought, by the military-industrial complex. The potential for the disastrous rise of misplaced power exists and will persist."
– Dwight D. Eisenhower

"Painful as the task is to describe the dark side of our affairs, it sometimes becomes a matter of indispensable necessity."
– George Washington

# CHAPTER 31
## Dallas, Texas

Vance Nicholson couldn't stop thinking about Chloe Harper.

He stared at the phone on the draped table. Kellerman had just called to berate him for not doing his part. How he was already in too deep to bail out now. And how if he didn't comply, Kellerman would come see him again, this time with more painful and potentially lethal results.

Vance hadn't left home since getting checked out at Parkland. The same hospital where they took Kennedy. At his age, he couldn't take any chances, particularly having hit the concrete as hard as he did. The heat, he said. It just caused him to faint, and the dart wound was just where he had cut himself shaving. The nurse looked skeptical about the purported shaving wound, but she didn't press it. Far too many real emergencies to attend to. She sent him home and told him to take it easy for a few days, and to stay indoors in the air conditioning as much as possible.

So here he was. Wrestling with a lifetime of guilt. And staring at that damnable phone.

He hadn't wanted to involve Jack Harper. An outspoken critic of the official JFK assassination story, Vance had run a weekend radio program for years, writing a handful of self-published books poking holes in the Warren Commission's findings from a variety of angles. In some regards, his theories had drawn close to the truth. But not close enough. No one's ever had.

Until Anthony Kellerman had come along. He offered a devil's bargain: the truth, for his help. Vance would use his position within the loose-knit community of conspiracy junkies to misdirect and, if necessary, report people who were getting too close to the truth. In return, he would become one of the few people in the world who knew who really killed JFK and why.

Vance told him he would need to think about it. Kellerman told him he'd be back tomorrow for his answer, and that he trusted Vance would choose wisely.

Vance planned to discuss his dilemma over dinner with Beverly. She had always possessed the ability to see through the chaff and offer keen insight. But that night, fate would intervene. His wife was in a car accident on the way home from Bible study. Rear-ended at a red light. No injuries, thankfully, and the damage to her car was minor enough that it didn't even make sense to file an insurance claim. The offending driver apologized profusely and offered her his business card and insurance information, and neither of them called the cops. But once Beverly described the man, he didn't need to call the insurance company to know the cards were fake.

Kellerman. It was an implicit threat against his family. He shouldn't have been surprised. If they would do it to Kennedy, why wouldn't they do it to him?

It jarred him over the edge, just like the agent surely expected it to. When Kellerman visited the next day, Vance gave him the only answer he could.

He wouldn't deny that part of him wanted to know the truth. A big part of him. Ever since he'd been at Dealey back in '63 and seen with his own eyes that the government's story was a lie. But the truth shocked him more than it should have.

Vance had no doubt that the truth Kellerman shared with him was only part of the story. There were questions that remained unanswered, details seemingly missing. But instead of feeling finally relieved at some sense of closure, he only felt more uneasy.

The conspiracy was far bigger than he had anticipated. Far older, too. And unlike his previous beliefs, President Kennedy was neither the beginning nor the end of their plot. In fact, despite his position and the impact of his assassination, JFK was nothing more than a pawn in a far larger game.

And now, Vance was irreparably tied to this vast conspiracy, himself just another pawn to be used up and cast asunder.

It was inevitable that Jack Harper would come calling. He had come across Vance's radar months before. An FBI special agent who would throw away his career at the Bureau to chase down Kennedy assassination theories was the stuff of *National Enquirer* dreams.

Former Special Agent Harper had come to him a week after being let go from the FBI. Already Vance could see the toll losing his job had cost him. The man looked as though he hadn't slept in days, but there remained a steely, if somewhat desperate, determination in his blood-shot eyes.

Vance recognized that determination. He'd once shared it himself.

He had then invited Jack into his home, much as he had done with his daughter just yesterday. Offered him a stiff drink, which he gladly accepted. Vance had given up alcohol four decades earlier after the birth of his son. He broke that streak an hour after Kellerman officially retained his services, locking himself in his office with a bottle of scotch.

Taking a seat opposite Jack, Vance had toasted with his own tumbler of whiskey. To the truth, he said, offering a show of solidarity to the man he was preparing to betray.

Then, for the next two hours, he proceeded to pick the former agent's brain. By Jack's estimation, he was in too deep to give up now. The only way to regain his life was to prove that he wasn't crazy. That he was actually a more dedicated investigator than any of the men who fired him. That his ex-wife and daughter didn't need to be ashamed of him anymore.

Vance offered a few guiding tidbits, but his first priority was discovering what Jack actually knew. At that point, it wasn't much, so Vance pointed him in the wrong direction and sent him on his way.

Apparently, that hadn't stuck.

He had read about Jack's death on a conspiracy theory message board online. Suicide, the authorities said. But Vance knew better. Somewhere along the way, Jack must have discovered something that made him a potential threat to the Society. Vance had hoped that Kellerman would keep him in the loop on that, but then, that wasn't his place. Kellerman had made the nature of their relationship quite clear when he threatened his wife.

Then, about a week after Jack Harper's death, Beverly collapsed coming down the stairs. She wasn't badly injured, but it was then that the doctor found the mass. Stage-four lung cancer. She had never smoked a day in her life. The doctor gave her two months to live.

Always the fighter, Beverly lasted just over three months. But they were hard months. Though her spirit never faded, physically she became a husk of her former self. Weak, bedridden, and withered as the cancer finally took hold. He began to hate himself for allowing his attention to become so fixated on Kellerman and his blackmail that he missed the signs of his wife's declining health. More than that, he had missed out on her final year of life.

Vance was ready to blow the lid on Kellerman and what he now knew about the conspirators and their goals. With his wife at death's door, Kellerman had lost his leverage.

And then, a sympathy card came in the mail. No return address, postmarked from Washington DC's Union Station.

*So sorry about your loss. My condolences to you, your son Rick, his lovely wife Tanya, and your darling grandchildren Ashley, Dylan, and Emily.*

It was signed, simply, "K."

Vance could fill in the rest.

His wife died the next day. Vance was sure Kellerman would show up to the funeral to press his point a little further, but he wasn't there. At least, Vance hadn't seen him. But the point was made. And Vance continued to mislead his fellow conspiracy buffs when he could, and report on them when he couldn't.

But with his wife dead, perhaps partially because of his own negligence, Vance couldn't go on as if nothing had happened. He purchased dozens of drop cloths and covered every piece of furniture that reminded him of Beverly. The dining table, the loveseat in the den, her reading chair by the window. He buried them all under the makeshift funeral shrouds. Their bedroom he locked, vowing to never again enter their shared space and starting instead to sleep on a cot on his office floor. His world was in tatters. But for his son's sake, for his grandchildren's sake, he had to press on.

Which was why this particular bout of guilt would eventually fall to the wayside. Just like every time before. He may have hated what his life had become. He may have despised himself for becoming the enemy he had dedicated his whole life to exposing. But he couldn't put his family—what was left of it anyway—in jeopardy.

At the end of the day, that was all that mattered.

Swallowing the bilious taste in his mouth, he picked up the phone and called Chloe Harper.

# CHAPTER 32
## Boston, Massachusetts

Chloe Harper had tried, unsuccessfully, to get Jon to tell him what the symbol in Robert Kennedy's envelope meant. But he remained tight lipped, telling her that there was someone far better qualified than he to explain the strange turn of events.

It was serious though. She could tell from the way the color drained from his face when he first saw the symbol. The slight quaver in his voice when he talked, which he had done sparingly these past few minutes. When they had thought it was the Mafia, the CIA, the KGB, the FBI, the military, Wall Street, or any combination of the usual suspects in alternate JFK theories, Jon was fine. But now, he seemed terrified.

Who on earth was he afraid of?

They exited Faneuil Hall into a cobblestone plaza facing the famed Quincy Market. A street troupe of break dancers was wowing a crowd of late afternoon tourists while one of their members passed around a bucket for donations.

Carefree and happy. A world away from where she and Jon were right now.

Her phone rang. She plugged her ear with one finger and answered. "Hello?"

"Chloe? It's Vance."

Her eyes went wide. "Vance? You're alive?"

"Well, I seem to be. Just a glancing wound, but apparently I collapsed from shock. That and the heat. Can't be too careful at my age."

Jon steered her away from the shouts and cheers of the dancers and toward their destination. He looked as shocked at her proclamation that Vance was alive as she felt.

"Thank God," she said, pulling her finger out of her ear now that the ambient noise had diminished. "I was afraid he had gotten you."

"Nicked me, the docs said. Some nice lady helped me get to the hospital, and they gave me a clean bill of health. Just have to stay away from the heat. And bullets."

"Did you go to the police?"

"Did you?"

Chloe felt a little guilty. "No."

"Of course you didn't. You already know what I discovered long ago. These guys are above the cops. And at the first whiff of it being connected to a JFK conspiracy theory, you're immediately branded a kook."

She heard the sadness in his voice, a sense of lonely isolation that had only grown worse with his wife's death.

"But you're okay? They guy who shot you, he didn't follow you or threaten you or anything?"

"Honestly, and I don't mean to scare you or anything, but I think he was after the two of you."

She had already inferred that from Kellerman's continuing to shoot at them as they made their escape from Dealey Plaza. Of course, Vance had been unconscious for that little romp.

"Well, we're long gone from Dallas now. Although somehow Kellerman, the guy who shot you down there and tried to kill Jon in DC yesterday, found us up here."

"Where is 'here'?"

"Boston."

Jon twirled his hand in a "wrap it up" motion.

"Boston? Did you find anything?"

"Actually, yes. A document hidden at the JFK Presidential Museum by Bobby Kennedy. A letter written to Ted."

"Really?" Vance asked, sounding impressed. "How incredible! What did it say?"

Good question. "I'm not entirely sure yet," Chloe said. "We're going to Harvard to meet with one of Jon's old professors who he says is an expert in the group that's behind this."

Jon shook his head at her. *What?* she mouthed.

"Hang up," he whispered.

"I've got to go," she said. "I'm so glad you're okay, though."

"Please, keep me posted, Chloe, and let me know if there's any way I can continue to assist you."

"Of course," she said before Jon took the phone and disconnected the line.

She stopped midstride, hands on hips. "What was that for?"

"Kellerman is still in town somewhere, that's not a secure line, and you want to broadcast to the digital ether what we found in the *Victura*?"

Chloe swallowed. He was right. She had let her excitement over hearing Vance, alive and well, distract her from the danger of the mission at hand.

"Sorry. I just couldn't believe he's still alive."

Jon gave a half-hearted smile. "Yeah. Lucky break, that."

There was something in his tone she didn't like. Something like suspicion. But before she could press him on it, he started to descend a staircase into the Government Center MBTA station.

"Come on," he said, motioning for her to follow. "You want answers? This is how we get them."

She followed. Minutes later, while they waited on the platform for the next green-line train toward Park Street Station, she asked if he could give her a hint about what the eagle symbol meant.

Jon smiled and slid out the scrap of parchment with the seal emblazoned upon it.

"You know the story about how Benjamin Franklin felt that the turkey would be a better representative for the nation than the bald eagle? He decried the eagle as a bird of bad moral character, murdering and stealing from other birds to make its living, and generally surrounding its very existence with injustice of the highest order."

"Yeah, I've heard of it."

"Contrary to popular belief, Franklin wasn't referring to the Great Seal of the United States." Jon tapped the symbol. "He was referring to this."

Chloe froze, her breath seemingly sucked away. "So this is bigger than JFK or Cold War politics."

Jon nodded somberly. "Oh yeah. Bigger than anyone ever imagined."

# CHAPTER 33

## *Boston, Massachusetts*

Anthony Kellerman wanted to shoot someone. Just to vent his frustrations. He'd even take emptying a clip into the side of Kennedy's stupid sailboat. But that would solve nothing. Yes, in his haste to change identities so he could return to the library, he had missed Jon and Chloe doubling back on him. While he was at the safe house, gathering his new credentials, they came back for the next piece of the puzzle. And he had had no idea.

It was fascinating, really. For nearly five years, Robert F. Kennedy had secretly investigated the Society and its role in the assassination of his brother. Right under their noses. Five years of potential damage. Five years of secret investigation, first armed with the might of the attorney general's office, then with the weight of RFK's senatorial seat. It was painfully apparent to Anthony Kellerman now, half a century after the Society had orchestrated his murder, that RFK had been a far greater threat, for far longer, than his forebears had realized at the time.

Kellerman was Bill Wright now. FBI. An unmemorable name, easily forgotten. Thus far, no one had recognized him from his chase through the museum. His false nose, glasses, and goatee helped with that effort. Though since he had left, there was a new reason for them to check the surveillance tapes.

"I had no idea this was in here," said Wanda Po, pointing to the open safe door concealed in the inner paneling of the *Victura*. The confluence of her Asian-American heritage and her deep Mississippi drawl made the assistant curator a study in contrasts. As Kellerman had learned long ago, no one is quite what they seem. He reflected on the curious combination briefly before launching into his next volley of questioning.

"No one found it during restorations over the past several decades?"

"We polished the wood, we didn't try to prise it apart. That's kind of the opposite of most restoration work."

Point taken, but he didn't appreciate her lip. Still, no point in antagonizing her. More flies with honey and all that.

"What do you think could have been hidden in there?"

Po gave him a look. "Probably the identities of the real people who killed JFK."

Kellerman willed his face not to betray how unnerving that statement was to him.

"I'm joking, of course," she said, chuckling as though she had just made the funniest and most original joke in the world.

"Of course," Kellerman agreed.

"Honestly, though, I have no idea. Judging by the safe itself, I'd say it's from the 1950s or '60s, but as for when it was installed, and when it was concealed by this paneling, we'll need to thoroughly examine it and then cross reference our findings with documents and records from our archives." Po gave him a collegial grin. "It's all very exciting."

Kellerman didn't share the sentiment. While a newfound discovery in the collection might have delighted the assistant curator, the part of the discovery Po and her team had missed—whatever had been inside that safe—was what concerned him. Back in '68, the Society's agents had cleared Robert Kennedy's office of any and all evidence pointing to potential Society involvement in his brother's assassination. Judging by the freshness of some of that documentation, there shouldn't have been enough time to copy, transmit, and hide the documents anywhere else. Bobby's campaign travels and schedule, coupled with when they raided his office, just didn't fit. The timeline was off.

But what if?

"What about cameras?" Kellerman hadn't wanted to pull that card. If they started looking hard at surveillance footage from the *Victura*, they'd find Jon and Chloe on tape and might try to elevate them to other authorities. They were *his* suspects, and he had to maintain control of them. Bringing in the real FBI would only complicate matters. Plus, once they went down that road, it could only be a matter of time before they found the earlier theft inside the museum itself. And that would lead straight back to Kellerman.

Still, it was his only shot at finding out what they discovered in that safe. Po was clueless, as had they all been before Jon and Chloe broke open the panel and somehow cracked the safe.

"We've looked at the footage, but the angles are all wrong to see faces or what, if anything, they found," Po said. "Of course, you're more than willing to take a look yourself."

Kellerman would take her up on that offer. If the angles truly were bad, maybe it wouldn't matter. But if there was any chance he would need to cover his tracks with either incident, especially with the one that showed him running through exhibit after exhibit, gun waving at his quarry, then he'd have to risk another surveillance footage wipe like the one he did yesterday back at the Archives. Only this time, he'd have to do it with a security supervisor sitting right next to him.

Before he could accept, his phone rang. He excused himself, hopped down from the *Victura*'s deck, and walked toward the water before answering.

"It's me." If the caller ID hadn't given it away, Vance Nicholson's nervous inflection would have. "I made contact."

"Took you long enough. We don't have time for cold feet, Vance."

"I understand, and I'm sorry. It's not easy getting someone to believe you're back from the dead. Besides, if I called them too soon, they'd get suspicious."

Kellerman stifled an inward chuckle. So typical of the modern American culture. Apologizing, then explaining in great detail why they're not really sorry. Still, what mattered were results.

"What did you find out?"

"They found a letter from Bobby Kennedy to Ted. Said it shows who is really responsible for JFK's assassination."

Kellerman felt the ground grow wobbly beneath his feet. "It identified us by name?"

Vance paused. Thinking. "Maybe not. Chloe still didn't seem to understand what was going on."

"What else besides the letter?"

"Nothing that they mentioned."

"No sheaf of documents? No reams of evidence?"

"No, nothing like that."

The ground seemed to stabilize again. It was bad, but not mission critical bad. Not yet.

"Where are they now?" Kellerman asked.

Silence again. He could hear Vance wrestling with his conscience.

"You *do* know, don't you, Vance?"

A pair of muffled grunts, the audible betrayals of a man caught in an impossible choice.

"Let me put it this way," Kellerman said. "I know where your son's family is, so if I can't go see Chloe and Jon, perhaps I'll just go pay your grandchildren a visit."

"Harvard," Vance blurted. "They're going to see one of Jon's old professors at Harvard."

"See, that wasn't so hard was it? Give my regards to Rick and the kids."

Kellerman hung up. Bad angles meant the library wouldn't be focused on the footage. Which meant they probably wouldn't dig too deep into the other footage from the day, especially since Jon had covered his tracks in the Oval Office visit much better than he had out here.

Harvard it was, then. He would give his card to Wanda Po, who was apparently far more interested in the discovery of the safe than of the theft of its contents, and head up to Cambridge.

Armed with a secret letter from Robert F. Kennedy purportedly identifying the masterminds of his brother's assassination, Jon and Chloe had already proven themselves potent adversaries. But playtime was over. It was time to cut off their quest for good before they could become a real threat.

# CHAPTER 34
## *Cambridge, Massachusetts*

Dr. Juliana Bixby hadn't changed much in the half decade or so since Jon had last seen her. Short brown hair with traces of gray, tall and slender, with long bony fingers that had written dozens of peer-reviewed articles and three textbooks longhand. She was a tremendous authority on the American Revolution and the early days of the republic. But, more importantly for his purposes today, she really liked Jon.

"Jon Rickner, as I live and breathe," she said as he entered her office, Chloe at his side. After two decades in New England, her voice was still tinged with the coastal South Carolina accent she had developed in her youth. After earning her undergraduate degree from Clemson and her doctorate from Stanford, she bounced around visiting professorships for a few years before finally landing a tenure-track job at Harvard. By that point she had already authored several award-winning articles and her work had been cited by numerous established voices in the field. Now, more than twenty years later, she still seemed to be at the top of her game.

She'd need to be, if she would be any help in their quest.

"Dr. Bixby," Jon said, grinning as he shook her proffered hand. "How have you been?"

"I can't complain." She gestured to a stack of graduate papers in need of grading. "Not that it would do any good, anyhow." She turned her attention to Chloe. "Who's your friend?"

"Oh, sorry. This is Chloe. Chloe, Dr. Juliana Bixby."

"Please, just call me Dr. B." She leaned in toward Chloe. "He's a real catch this one. Don't let him go."

"Oh, it's not like that," Chloe replied sheepishly. Jon thought she might be blushing, but in the relatively dim light of Dr. Bixby's office, it was difficult to tell.

"Dr. B, I regret that this isn't an entirely social call."

Dr. Bixby's smile disappeared, her demeanor immediately becoming serious.

"Very well. What can I help you with?"

Jon gestured to the door. "Do you mind if I close this? It's kind of a sensitive conversation."

Bixby's countenance became even more curious, but she nodded. Once Jon had shut the door, he and Chloe sat in a pair of seats opposite the professor behind her desk.

He slid the scrap of paper with the eagle symbol out of RFK's secret envelope and placed it upon the desk. Bixby studied it for a moment.

"The Society of the Cincinnati?" she asked. "What's this all about?"

"It's complicated. Can you give me a refresher course in the Society? And bring Chloe up to speed?"

Jon glanced at Chloe and saw she did not even remotely recognize the name. It was understandable. Most people didn't.

"You've stumbled upon something again, haven't you, Jon?" Bixby said, excitement edging into her voice despite the circumstances.

"All in good time, Dr. B.," Jon said with a slight grin.

"Fair enough. Okay then. The Society of the Cincinnati."

The professor leaned back in her chair, slipping into her well-worn lecturer mode. "It was 1782. The American Colonies had defeated the British militarily but had not officially won their independence. This, of course, would be made official in October of the following year by the Treaty of Paris. So the fighting is done, but the United States is still far from becoming the United States. Meanwhile, thousands of officers in the Continental Army, men who left their livelihoods behind in the name of treason against King George, were growing restive. They hadn't been paid in years, and talk of a military coup was growing. The freedoms being drawn up in the Continental Congress were about to be wrenched away by the very men who had fought for them.

"Then, in December, those fears became very real. The so-called Newburgh Addresses, a series of letters drawn up by disgruntled officers proposing a military takeover from the impotent Congress that refused to pay them their due. And the officers behind this movement were heavy hitters, too. Gouverneur Morris, who was a signer of the Articles of Confederation and would go on to sign the US Constitution, was one of the conspiracy's leaders, along with General Horatio Gates—to whom Congress had at one point considered giving control of the entire Continental Army—and his aide-de-camp, Major John Armstrong, who actually penned the addresses and would later serve as a delegate to the Continental Congress, a US senator, and James Madison's secretary of war. According to these letters, if Congress wouldn't fulfill their obligations to the men who had sacrificed everything, the military should rise up and take the reins themselves.

"For years, General George Washington and other key leaders in the Continental Army had been aware of the soldiers' anger and had lobbied Congress over and over, but to little avail. Congress lacked the power to tax at this point, and without a guaranteed source of income, they were loath to promise anything to the men who had just saved them all from King George's executioners. So Washington and his cohort of military officers prodded along the soldiers' sentiment, keeping them encouraged enough to stay on the battlefield, yet frustrated enough to keep the pressure on Congress."

"The Newburgh Addresses changed all that," Jon said. "Now the balancing act became to prevent an outright coup of the embryonic nation. There was a very real conspiracy afoot to take by force what they saw as their rightful reward: control of the country from the foot-dragging delegates who still got to go home to their warm beds at night."

Bixby nodded. "And that's when Washington, Alexander Hamilton, and Henry Knox devised a counter-conspiracy. In order to placate the conspirators and their sympathizers, they laid the groundwork for a new fraternal society for all Continental Army officers. By bringing the treasonous conspirators under their wing and controlling the message, Washington and his cohort hoped to stop the growing insurrection in its tracks. And thus the Society of the Cincinnati was born."

"Why 'the Cincinnati'?" Chloe asked.

Bixby shifted in her seat. "It's not what you probably think. As was common in the Enlightenment era, the founders drew upon the great figures of ancient Greece and Rome for inspiration. Lucius Quintus Cincinnatus was a Roman military leader and farmer in the fifth century before Christ. When invaders came, he left the safety of his estate and led Rome to victory, presiding over the city-state as a dictator during the crisis. While he would certainly have been able to continue ruling after the invasion was repelled, he chose to voluntarily relinquish both his civic and military power, instead returning to life as a private citizen on his farm.

"Having just fought a terrible revolution against a power-hungry monarchy, many Continental Army officers admired Cincinnatus as a legendary ideal. George Washington himself mirrored Cincinnatus to an uncanny degree. Wealthy farmer, left his estate to fight against a distant power for the freedom of his people, then voluntarily returned to private life when many of his followers were encouraging him to establish an American military dictatorship under his rule. A few years later, he would go through the same pattern again, answering the public call for him to lead the young nation as president, then stepping down after two terms against countless calls for him to be president-for-life. Consciously or not, George Washington was the quintessential embodiment of an American Cincinnatus, more than two thousand years after the original had died."

"And so Cincinnati is the Latin plural of Cincinnatus?" Chloe asked.

"Essentially. The Society of the Cincinnati, in keeping with Washington's counter-conspiracy to quell the treasonous plots circulating around the Continental Army, was so named to remind the men of what they had fought for. Not toppling one dictatorship only to install another, but rather to create a new kind of society where freedom reigned over all."

"But the Continental Army officers are long dead now. Why are they still around?"

"Today's membership is comprised of the descendants of those officers. The organization was chartered with six key purposes. First, to perpetuate the memory of their war for independence against British tyranny. Second, to maintain the fraternal bond they had forged with their fellow officers at both the state and national level. Third, to preserve the liberties they had fought for and to forever ensure union and national honor within the new country. Fourth, to provide financial support for the widows and orphans of fellow members. The fifth purpose was to set its members apart as men of honor, which is one reason why the Society commissioned its Diamond Eagle medals for its members. The sixth and final purpose was to secure the pay due the officers by the Continental Congress."

"The Newburgh conspirators' biggest grievance was last on the list?" Chloe asked.

"And the only one no longer in force."

Jon finally chimed in. "The founding members of the Society include about half of a who's who of the nation's founding fathers."

"Seriously?" Chloe asked.

"George Washington, Alexander Hamilton, James Monroe, George Clinton, Henry Knox, Gouverneur Morris, Aaron Burr. Virtually everyone involved in the military side of the struggle for independence. The other half, most notably Thomas Jefferson, John Adams, and Benjamin Franklin, were vehemently against the Society's existence."

"Why?"

"One of the biggest complaints was that the secretive, hereditary nature stank of the very old-world aristocracy they had crossed an ocean and defied the king of the mightiest empire in the world to escape," Jon said. "This wasn't helped by Baron von Steuben and the Marquis de Lafayette being some of the most influential founding members."

"France had a chapter of the Society, too," Bixby said, "for the French officers who had fought with the Continental Army against Britain. King Louis XVI was the patron of the society, with the Cincinnati Eagle the only foreign military medal his officers were allowed to wear. As the French Revolution dawned, they abolished hereditary membership for their chapter, seeking to distance themselves from the growing ire of the populace. But it wasn't enough. Due to their aristocratic moorings and their affiliation with the king, the French chapter was dissolved in 1794 as the Reign of Terror moved into full swing, with numerous members, including their president, meeting their end at the guillotine. So with no method to pass the torch to the next generation, the French chapter died off. The American side wasn't quite as savvy in that regard."

"But they never did take over the country," Chloe said.

"Not in any overt sense, no. The Society these days mainly serves as a social club, promoting fraternal bonds among the descendants of Revolutionary War officers who like dressing up in fancy regalia and remembering the massive sacrifices their ancestors made."

Finally, Chloe asked the question that had been rattling around in Jon's mind since he first saw the Society's seal at Faneuil Hall. "If they're so dedicated to protecting the nation's legacy, why would they kill President Kennedy?"

Members of the Society of the Cincinnati were everywhere in JFK's final days, Jon knew. Admiral Arleigh Burke, who had given him the globe that Bobby Kennedy had hidden the tape in. Henry Cabot Lodge, JFK's ambassador to South Vietnam. Robert S. McNamara, Kennedy's secretary of defense who would go on to lead the charge for the Vietnam

War under Johnson. General William Westmoreland, who would be the commander of US forces in Vietnam from 1964 to 1968. Even John Vernou Bouvier III, Kennedy's father-in-law, was a Society member. They were everywhere. But there was a big difference between their being in his life and orchestrating his murder.

Except one contemporaneous member of the Society of the Cincinnati did stand out. Suspect Number One on their radar since the National Archives.

J. Edgar Hoover.

# CHAPTER 35
## *Washington, DC*

Patrick Molyneux didn't like the way she looked at him. Thinly veiled suspicion. And not in the usual way.

Her name was Amanda. Last name, something that started with T, maybe. He couldn't be bothered to remember. That wasn't why he was here.

Everyone else had been cordial since his arrival. Everyone but her.

As he pulled another volume from the library shelves, he glanced up to find her staring at him. Again.

"Can I help you?" he asked, not bothering to hide his annoyance.

"Just curious about the nature of your research. You know, I have a master's in library sciences and another in American history."

He did know. Amanda had told him twice already. She was either really forgetful, really proud of her credentials, or really nosy.

If it was the latter, they were going to have a problem.

He sighed. His assigned cover story wasn't the strongest, but it was designed to offer him some leeway to adapt if circumstances should so necessitate. "It's kind of broad right now. I've got some ideas, but I'm currently browsing to see if I can find any further connections between my theories and items in the Society's collections."

"Interesting. What are your theories? Maybe I can help."

He gave her his most sympathetic smile. "Unfortunately, I'm not really at the point in my research where I'm comfortable sharing it."

"Huh." She crept closer, arching her neck to get a better look at the book he held. *This woman simply would not be deterred.*

"Look, I appreciate your help, but—"

"You're staying in the Pennsylvania suite aren't you?"

No point in denying it. "I am."

"First time here?"

"It is."

"First time in Washington?"

The question seemed innocent enough, but there was something behind her words that he didn't trust. "It is."

"And you just arrived in Washington today?"

He didn't like the way this was going. Still, she seemed to already know the answer to her question, so lying would only make her more suspicious. "I did."

"Huh."

"Why?"

She shrugged. "Just interesting is all."

"What is?"

She looked at him and must have seen his own suspicion etched across his face. She briefly blanched in panic before quickly regaining her composure. It was a tiny lapse. But it was enough.

"Your accent. It's hard to place."

"It is." Then, in order to not antagonize her further, he added, "I grew up all around. French and American ancestry. Grew up on military bases across the globe."

"French *and* American!" She clapped her hands together like a giddy schoolgirl. "Just like the original Society itself!"

"Yeah," he said. "Just like."

"Well, let me know if you need anything," she said, beaming as she headed for the door. "And good luck with your research."

Molyneux set the book on the table and tried to wrap his mind around the curious encounter. The sudden transformation of her suspicion into effusive congeniality. The strange line of questioning about if he had made any previous visits to the city. And, most bizarre of all, her comment about the timing of his arrival, followed by her momentary seizure of panic.

She knew something. Perhaps not yet enough to be truly dangerous. But enough to know there was something worth fishing for.

Which led Molyneux to a chilling conclusion. Someone had been talking.

# CHAPTER 36
## Cambridge, Massachusetts

Jon was right, Chloe realized. This was far bigger than anything she had expected. If the Kennedy assassinations were orchestrated by a secret society of Revolutionary War officers founded by George Washington, and they were still operating today to hide their secrets and God knew what else . . . that made even the craziest JFK assassination theory she'd come across—and there were some doozies—seem benign by comparison.

Bixby clasped her hands in front of her and leaned forward across the desk. "I'll be honest, that's the very question I've been wondering since you first mentioned Kennedy. Why indeed *would* the nation's oldest and most august hereditary society assassinate a president?"

Chloe figured she'd try her hand. "The Society of the Cincinnati includes military generals, titans of industry, and government leaders, all of whom make regular appearances in JFK conspiracy lore. Perhaps some of the members got together in the 1960s and decided it was in their mutual interest to kill President Kennedy. Bobby, of course, would have been killed as part of the cover up after the fact."

Bixby looked thoughtful. "Perhaps. Or maybe the nation's first conspiracy theory had some truth to it after all."

"Meaning?"

"Meaning maybe the Society of the Cincinnati really *has* been manipulating our nation's history for the past two centuries."

"If that's the case," Jon asked, fully understanding how big that *if* was, "how can we expose them for what they've done? If they're powerful enough to kill a president and a senator and get away with it, what on earth can we do to stop them?"

Bixby thought for a moment. It was a heck of a question, and one that Chloe feared didn't have an answer. And then, the professor thought of one.

"The Society of the Cincinnati considers itself one of the premier keepers of historical records in the country. Primarily, they have gathered perhaps the most extensive private collection of firsthand documents and artifacts from the Revolutionary War, which, of course, was where their members were most active as a unit. Their collections are to memorialize their work on behalf of the country. It stands to reason that, heinous though the acts were, they might have preserved a record of their involvement in the Kennedy brothers' assassinations. After all, assuming the Society is actually behind their murders, then, by some twisted logic, they would believe the regime change they orchestrated by killing JFK to have been in the best interest of the United States.

"Where on earth could we find something like that?" Chloe asked.

"Washington," Jon said.

"I seriously doubt any treasonous records about Society members planning and orchestrating the murder of President Kennedy would be in their publicly accessible collections," Bixby said. "But in want of a better lead, yes, I think the Society's national headquarters would be a good starting point. It holds one of the finest research libraries in the world on the Revolutionary War and its aftermath, along with being a deep repository of Society records. Much of which will be off-limits to non-members like yourself, but I'm sure you'll find a way."

"Thank you so much, Dr. B." Jon said. "We'll be in touch if we find anything else."

Bixby stood to shake their hands. "Always a pleasure, Jon. See that you do, and be careful out there. Chloe, so nice to meet you." She winked at her. "Be good to this one. He's a keeper."

Chloe felt her face grow warm, but she smiled, trying not to make the situation more awkward. "I don't plan on letting him out of my sight." It was true for more reasons than one.

"You see why this wasn't just a five-minute convo in Faneuil Hall or on the subway?" Jon asked when they were back out in the hall.

"I still can't believe it. It's like the worst fever-dream nightmare of every conspiracy theorist, times ten."

"Exactly. It's so outlandish that, without proof, who would ever believe us?"

"Which means we'd still be on the hook for the Archives fire."

Jon opened the door to the stairwell and led the way down. "And the highschooler who Kellerman shot in Dallas, and the 'thefts' at the JFK Library. I mean, you've been on this case for, what, a year now? If someone told you what we just heard, would you believe it?"

"I'd think they were nuts. Too crazy even for 'normal' conspiracy theorists."

"Which is why the only way out of this thing is through," Jon said. "We find proof of the Society's involvement in the Kennedy assassination. Or we go to prison."

*Or end up dead.* Chloe followed Jon out of the building and into the sunlight. Was it really possible? On one level, everything Bixby had said made sense. On another, it was so far down the rabbit hole she feared there was no way back to normalcy. The Society was older than the United States itself. A centuries-old conspiracy of presidents, senators, congressmen, generals, cabinet secretaries, ambassadors, and secret powerbrokers all working in concert to direct American policy from the shadows.

It was unthinkable. But it was also, apparently, true.

Jon grabbed her arm and pulled her into a shadowed alcove against the side of the building.

"What—"

Her words were silenced by Jon's finger on her lips. Was he going to try to kiss her? But then he turned his face from hers, looking over his shoulder while keeping his body close to hers in the alcove. For an archivist, she wasn't expecting such a pronounced musculature. She felt her face growing warm again. She didn't know what he was doing, but part of her wished he *would* kiss her. Bixby's parting words lingered in her mind. Since Jack Harper's shameful ouster from the Bureau, and even more so since his murder, she had avoided romantic entanglements, focusing instead on what was happening with—and what had been done to—her father. But now that she finally had a major breakthrough, she found herself doing something new: letting herself have feelings for someone.

For Jon.

Then she saw the look in his eyes. It was not of romantic attraction but rather of fearful frustration. Something had spooked him. And while she felt her attraction grow by virtue of the way he had leapt into action to protect her from whatever threat he thought he saw, her dreamlike fantasy of the happily-ever-after she'd seen her college friends enjoy in recent years came crashing back to earth.

They were being hunted. And no amount of butterflies would make that cold hard fact go away.

"Come on," he said, stepping out from the alcove and grabbing her hand. He led her in the opposite direction from which they had come, but Chloe was still too frazzled by the mix of emotions she'd just experienced to question why. They exited Harvard's campus through the Porcellian Gate and onto Massachusetts Avenue in Cambridge proper, where all the stores in the immediate vicinity, from Harvard Book Store to John Harvard's Tavern, seemed to include a common theme.

Jon led them down an alley out of view of campus. His palm was sweaty and his eyes continued to dart from side to side in renewed paranoia. What had he seen? Urgency of movement seemed to be paramount, so she didn't question his actions. Something had scared him. And that scared her.

Finally, he stopped. "I need to borrow your phone."

"Okay," she said, handing it over. "Can I ask why?"

"Kellerman was here."

Now it was her turn to be frightened. How had he found them? Again? She felt the blood drain from her face.

"Here? When you pushed us into the alcove?"

"Yeah."

Back in college, before JFK conspiracy theories had consumed her life, Chloe had played a lot of Mario Kart with her friends. One much-maligned feature of the popular racing game series was called rubber-banding, where enemy racers managed to keep up with the player character no matter how fast you went.

Kellerman was proving to be the worst case of rubber-banding she had ever experienced.

"How does he keep finding us?"

"I don't know. But I have a plan to find out."

# CHAPTER 37
## *Washington, DC*

Stanton Gaines had learned firsthand what his Society forebears knew to be true. Presidents are temporary. Congress is forever.

It was what led him to seek his father's former senate seat at the age of thirty-seven. For the next thirty years, he grew his influence on Capitol Hill and beyond, eventually becoming chairman of the Senate Armed Services Committee. Several of his Society brethren held similar posts across both houses of Congress. Intelligence. Foreign Relations. All to steer American policy toward the Society's ends. Defending America against her greatest enemy.

Herself.

The Society of the Cincinnati had been defending the country long before there had been a country to protect. The ideals they fought for were enshrined in the Constitution, and every high public office holder in the land swore an oath to defend that founding document against all enemies. Foreign and domestic.

It was that last part that gave most people trouble. And that, were it not for the vigilance of the Cincinnati, would have been the downfall of the United States while it was still in its infancy. Countless times over the past two centuries the country had found itself on the cusp of destruction from within. And every time, the Cincinnati took the necessary steps to save the nation.

Unfortunately, like a beloved child with a penchant for running into traffic, two centuries of near misses hadn't sufficiently taught their countrymen how to stop putting themselves in these predicaments. They were fast approaching one again.

"Yolanda, please, we've known each other a long while and you know I wouldn't be asking if this weren't a serious issue," Gaines said.

Yolanda Escobar, the US Ambassador to Venezuela, sat in a small lounge just outside his office in the Dwight D. Eisenhower Senate Office Building. He'd always found the moniker curious. Not only was Eisenhower never in the Senate, he had been a real pain in his Vanguard colleagues' backs during his tenure as president. Escobar had President James Talquin's ear, and Gaines hoped he could use her influence to gain a private audience with the big man himself. Gaines and Talquin had never seen eye to eye. Talquin was a moderate Republican, while Gaines was a rare Democratic war hawk. They had clashed on foreign policy multiple times over Talquin's two-year tenure, but Gaines hoped they could come to an understanding. After all, Gaines had helmed the Senate Armed Services Committee for years, and, with a safe senate seat, he had a whole lot of influence to peddle and nothing politically to lose.

"My colleagues and I are of the mind that the time for diplomacy is at an end," he continued. "President Ortega has already all but declared war on the United States. He has blamed us for their oil crisis, for their gun problem. Hell, he even had the stones to blame *us* for their country's drug wars and collapsing economy. Their warships in the Pacific are within a day's cruise of striking distance of Los Angeles, while they have several ships in the Caribbean that could take out Miami, New Orleans, or Houston at a moment's notice. What further proof does the administration need that military force is the only way to deal with these corrupt, drug-running communists?"

Yolanda gave him a tight smile. "The president has made his views on the Venezuelan crisis quite clear. The nation is in the throes of a nascent civil war. Aggressive comments like the ones you mentioned are simply Ortega throwing a bone to the press to appease his followers and take some of the steam away from the rebels. Lord knows our own leaders have done that from time to time."

Gaines knew they had. He and his forebears had often put the words in those leaders' mouths.

"Ten minutes, Yolanda. That's all I ask. Ten minutes alone with President Talquin and I'll be forever in your debt."

The magic words. Yolanda unsuccessfully tried to hide her grin. Favors were worth more than gold on Capitol Hill. And being owed a favor by someone as powerful as Senator Stanton Gaines would be a major coup for an up-and-coming ambassador like Yolanda.

"No promises, but I'll talk to POTUS and see what I can do."

"Thank you, Yolanda. See, you already know how to recognize an opportunity. I envision a long and prosperous political career for you.

Your country is lucky to have a woman of your diligence serving on her behalf."

Having laid on just the right amount of flattery to further encourage her to seal the deal, he showed her to the door. Once he was alone again, he slumped down in his chair and stared at the oil painting hanging on the wall. One of his favorites. It was a nineteenth-century original depicting Washington's winter camp at Valley Forge. The Continental Army was disheartened by the weather, by Congress's foolish obstinacy, by the overwhelming force of the British Army. But they stayed strong, enduring the abuses of friend, foe, and nature alike to do the unthinkable. They left behind everything they knew for a cause they believed in, and, no matter the cost, they were determined to see it through.

Those were the men who founded the Society of the Cincinnati in 1783. Their grandsons answered the call to pull the nation from the brink less than a century later. And, ever since, the United States had relied upon men of honor and fearless determination to quash the forces of destruction at her gates. Men like Stanton Gaines.

He sighed at the realization that he finally had Yolanda Escobar in his pocket, even if she thought the arrangement was flipped. Finally, progress. But Gaines knew better than to put all his eggs in one basket. An audience with the president wasn't an agreement, and, even then, this was Washington. Duplicity and deception were par for the course. Which was why he would keep his backup plan in motion.

One way or another, Stanton Gaines would have his war.

# CHAPTER 38
## *Charlestown, Massachusetts*

Anthony Kellerman was ready this time. Unlike at the National Archives, the Kennedy Library, or Harvard, there was only one way out of this place. Jon and Chloe would not be escaping him again.

He stood outside the exit to the USS *Constitution*, the world's oldest commissioned naval vessel still afloat. Launched in 1797, the *Constitution* was named by George Washington in honor of the young nation's founding document. The heavy frigate was one of the first ships authorized by the Naval Act of 1794, and was a key defender of American shipping lanes during the Quasi-War against French privateers. It later played an integral role in the First Barbary War against the Barbary pirates off the coast of Libya, as well as in the War of 1812, where she defeated five British warships.

Now, the *Constitution* was designated a museum ship, marking the northernmost site on Boston's historic Freedom Trail. Floating in the waters of the Charlestown Navy Yard, "Old Ironsides" had taken up permanent residence at Pier 1, with museum-style exhibits—on board and on the pier itself—and Navy seamen tour guides sharing the rich history of the vessel. It was still seaworthy, too, as the *Constitution*'s crew sailed the ship under its own power around Boston Harbor in 1997 and 2012 to celebrate the 200th anniversary of its launch and its victory over the HMS *Guerriere*, respectively.

Despite the centuries-old vessel serving an exclusively educational mission, the *Constitution* and its adjacent dock remained an active naval facility, complete with heavy military security and a metal detector. But while the Society of the Cincinnati counted among its ranks three current Navy admirals, Kellerman decided he shouldn't press his luck. So he remained armed, waiting outside the sole exit for Jon and Chloe to walk right into his clutches. Which gave him plenty of time to speculate on what was going on inside.

Bobby Kennedy had hidden one clue on a sailing vessel belonging to his brother. It made sense that something else could be hidden in another sailing vessel, this one commissioned by the Cincinnati's President-General George Washington and commanded by founding Society member Captain Silas Talbot. The fact that the frigate had been first used in the Quasi-War, which had strained relations between the French and American branches of the Society, could also be a factor.

The question was, what could be hidden on board? Had Kennedy or some other traitor seeking to expose the Cincinnati secreted some damaging document or clue onto the ship? Had Silas Talbot himself hidden something about what fellow Society member Aaron Burr and his supporters were proposing during the ship's construction? In addition to commanding the vessel during the Quasi-War, Talbot had supervised the construction of the *Constitution* here at the navy yard. He would have had unfettered access. He might have even found it poetic, if he felt that Burr's ideas were a danger to the Constitution for which the frigate was named.

But why hadn't he ever heard of Talbot's views on the subject, if they were that strong? He seemed to be somewhat rank and file within the Society's early membership, despite his being selected personally for the *Constitution* post by George Washington. Though Washington had made his views on Burr's proposals painfully clear.

Kellerman checked his watch. A group of schoolkids wearing matching yellow shirts—surely to help their chaperones keep track of them in a crowd—exited the Pier 1 facility. He distinctly remembered seeing them go in a good half hour after he arrived. It made sense that Jon and Chloe, looking for an opportunity to pry loose some board or access some restricted area of the boat, would spend more time on board than a field trip being shunted from place to place as efficiently as possible.

Even so, he couldn't shake his impatience, nor the other question that nagged at his mind.

Where were Jon and Chloe?

# CHAPTER 39
*Charlestown, Massachusetts*

C hloe and Jon exited the elevator once it reached the top floor. The Constitution Hotel boasted a rooftop bar with fantastic views of East Boston, the Mystic River, and, of course, the USS *Constitution*, from which the hotel drew its name. Jon ordered them both drinks and led her to the balcony.

"Have you ever been down there?" Jon asked as he fished a monocular from his pocket and trained it on the shipyard below.

"To the navy yard?" she asked. "Or the *Constitution*?"

"The *Constitution*."

"No. But this is stupid."

"Is it?" Jon gave her a look that hovered somewhere between amusement and concern.

Frustrated, Chloe composed her thoughts before replying.

"Yes, it absolutely is. Vance put his life on the line for us in Dallas. He took a bullet for us, for crying out loud."

"Yeah, wasn't that a convenient recovery."

Chloe couldn't entertain the idea that Vance Nicholson was a traitor. She just couldn't. But Jon didn't let up.

"Let's look at the facts. Kellerman followed us to Dallas, had time to set up at Dealey Plaza and shoot at us in broad daylight. Yes, he shot Vance instead, but considering how quickly he recovered, it was likely either a glancing blow aimed at you or me that his wild gesticulations got in the way of, or something else like a dart gun designed to knock him out, get us on the run, and maintain his cover. Next, Kellerman finds his way to Boston . . ."

"I never told him we were going to Boston until after we'd already seen Kellerman and the JFK Library," Chloe interjected.

"Fair enough, but once he'd found us in Dallas, he likely could have traced our fake IDs we took to get there and found our next flight to Boston. I think Erik Weisz and Pauline Schmidt's magic has run out.

And once he was in Boston, the JFK Presidential Library would be the most obvious place for us to go for info on the JFK assassination. But Harvard?"

"You went to school there. It was a logical next step."

"In all of Boston, full of both colonial and Kennedy-era history, that's the single most obvious step? I think that's reaching more than a little."

"Still, it doesn't mean Vance is a traitor. He's been nothing but helpful to us . . ."

"And to your dad?" Jon said.

Chloe flinched instinctively, as though he had hit her.

"Sorry," he said, looking genuinely remorseful before turning back to his scouring of the area below. "But none of this adds up to him deserving the benefit of the doubt. It's suspicious at least. We should find out if it's full-on traitorous soon enough."

She took a gulp of her drink and immediately regretted it. Her throat burned, though it likely had less to do with the alcohol and more to do with how upset she was becoming. But no. Her dad had trusted Vance Nicholson, and he'd been nothing but helpful and sympathetic to her and her cause. Sure, he had been a lot more vocal than her dad about the JFK assassination, while Jack Harper was the one who got killed for his investigation. But from what she'd learned in Dr. Bixby's office, her dad had gotten a whole lot closer to the truth than Vance ever had. Despite his well-meaning assistance, Vance's theories simply weren't a threat to the Society of the Cincinnati, just like the thousands of JFK conspiracists with books and radio programs. They were white noise that the Cincinnati didn't bother with since they inadvertently obscured the truth with their wildly divergent theories. But Jack Harper, and Chloe and Jon after him, were threats. They knew more than the Cincinnati was comfortable with. And were learning more all the time.

No, Vance Nicholson wasn't a traitor. He was just fervently wrong about who really killed JFK.

"Bingo," Jon said. He handed her the monocular. "Right there, to the left of the exit area, hiding behind that wall."

Chloe raised the lens to her eye, adjusted the focus, and found the area where visitors exited the USS *Constitution*. Then she followed the path back toward the street.

She felt her stomach drop like someone had knocked her out of an airplane. Not only had she been betrayed, but she had put her trust in the man who had sold out her father and ultimately gotten him killed.

There, waiting for Jon and Chloe to exit the facility where Vance had told him they would be, was Kellerman.

Jon laid a hand on her shoulder. "Do you trust him now?"

# CHAPTER 40
## Dallas, Texas

Vance Nicholson lay atop the painter's drop cloth that covered his couch. He was wrestling with guilt. Guilt was winning.

Two generations of a family, dead because of him. First Jack Harper, now his daughter Chloe. And Jon Rickner, a young man whose contributions to historical knowledge he greatly admired. Vance might as well have pulled the trigger himself.

The couch wasn't comfortable, with the drop cloth bunched in places as he squirmed with inner turmoil. But that was kind of the point. He didn't lie down here to be comfortable. He was lying down because he had to. Remorse had sapped his strength.

He had once been a zealous pursuer of the truth. The lines were clear. People like Jon and Chloe were his allies. People like Kellerman, his enemies. He'd sold his soul to the devil to learn the truth. Armed with the truth he'd sought his whole life, he now became a tool of the very enemy he despised, attacking fellow truth-seekers and getting several of them killed.

Add two more ghosts to the legion that already haunted his nightmares.

His son and his family may have been the only thing worth hanging onto life for, but it didn't make it easy. He would be in Kellerman's back pocket until his dying day. And every time he was forced to choose between his family's lives and his own conscience, another little part of him shriveled up and died.

The house phone rang, jolting him out of his thoughts. He checked the number on the wireless handset on the coffee table next to him.

Blocked. Kellerman.

"We've got a problem," the agent said as soon as Vance answered.

"What's wrong?"

"Your friends never showed."

"Well, you must have missed them," Vance said, with a glimmer of hope that Jon and Chloe were, for the moment at least, safe.

"I didn't miss them. They never showed."

"Look, I told you everything they told me. They were headed to the USS *Constitution* for the next clue."

"And nothing about the Cinncinnati? Or the Vanguard?"

"Nothing."

Kellerman paused. "Seems a little strange, don't you think? Taking a detour from the 1960s to the 1790s without having any inkling of the Society's connection?"

"What do you mean?"

"I mean you're either holding back on me, which is bad, or your cover is blown, which is worse."

"I told you everything. I promise."

A moment of silence. Then, "You know what, I actually believe you. I think you did tell me everything they told you. Which means everything they told you was a lie."

Panic began to rise in Vance's chest. He sat up on the couch.

"Chloe trusts me implicitly. I'm her only ally in this quest besides Jon. They don't know who else to trust, so their paranoia makes me all the more valuable."

"You're not their *only* ally," Kellerman said in a tone that made Vance's skin crawl. "Not anymore."

"Look, let me call them and find out what went wrong. Chloe came to me. I'm like a mentor, a guardian angel, someone she can look to. She trusts me."

Kellerman laughed. "Oh, I'm sure Chloe does trust you. But she's not alone anymore. And Jon Rickner has plenty of reason to be suspicious of someone like you."

"What are you talking about?"

"Isn't it obvious? Between the death of Chloe's dad, your miraculous resurrection, my ability to predict where they're going to be, it was only a matter of time before someone smart and not blinded by her dead father's loyalty saw you for what you really are."

Vance's mouth went dry as he realized what Kellerman was saying. But he dared not speak it, for to do so would be to admit unadulterated failure to the one man who stood between his family and the grave.

Kellerman, meanwhile, had no such compunctions. "They set you up. They suspected you were working with me and they set you up."

"Impossible."

"They were here. Somewhere. Watching to see if I would show. You fed me the bait and I walked right into their trap."

"Not a chance. No way." Vance stood and began to pace the worn carpet of his living room. "Don't blame me for your mistakes. They were there."

"A double agent becomes useless once people realize that he's doubled."

Vance's breathing became panicked. "Please, I can make this right. Just give me a chance."

"Too late for that, I'm afraid." Kellerman's voice was deep and calm now, the complete antithesis of Vance's own feelings. "Say hello to Beverly for me."

The line went dead just as Vance heard a beeping emanate from the kitchen, joined by another from his office and another from the couch he had just been lying on. As the beeping grew louder and more rapid, he realized Kellerman had set up this contingency plan long before. Cleaning his tracks and sending a message all at once.

He could try to run, but what was the point? If he escaped, Kellerman might go after his family, and Vance would have no way to stop him now. No, it was better this way. A fitting punishment for his crimes. To die in the home he'd built with the woman he loved. If there was an afterlife, if his betrayals hadn't condemned him to an eternity apart from his righteous wife, he hoped he would soon be reunited with his bride.

Regardless, he thought, right before the triple waves of flame and overpressure exploded from the bombs and ripped through his body, he'd be free from having to choose between his family and his soul.

Maybe, in death, he'd finally be able to live with himself.

# CHAPTER 41
## Arlington, Virginia

While Chloe took a shower in the bathroom, Jon sat at the foot of the bed, watching the flickering cathode-ray-tube TV and trying to let the day slip away. A previous guest of his hotel room must have absconded with the remote, so he let CNN drone on about North Korea and another scandal involving a White House staffer. Later, he planned to just lie on his bed, stare at the ceiling, and process. Right now, his brain was too full of clashing thoughts and feelings to properly process anything. So the white noise of ivory-tower punditry would have to do the trick.

The Washington Arms Inn didn't live up to its noble name. It was a dingy affair, the sort of place that thought hot water and a working A/C system were optional amenities. The window unit rattled as it blew air into the room that felt roughly the same temperature as the air outside. The comforters that covered the two queen beds were tainted with strange brown stains that Jon preferred to believe were from overturned coffee cups and not from murder blood. It was the kind of place that reminded him of an old *CSI* episode, where a UV wand would light the place up like a body-fluid Christmas tree.

Jon would have preferred to stay at the Hampton up the way, but the Washington Arms took cash and didn't ask questions. With their having exposed the Cincinnati's mole and cutting off contact, they didn't need a credit card bill sending Kellerman an invitation to their new digs. So, disease riddled and interior designed by a B-movie horror director though it may have been, the Washington Arms would have to do for the night.

After watching Kellerman leave the USS *Constitution* in frustration, Jon and Chloe had descended to street level and headed the opposite direction. They bought two Greyhound tickets to DC with cash and found this hotel in which to spend the night.

Tomorrow, they'd be heading across the Potomac to the headquarters of the Society of the Cincinnati in DC proper.

Less than two hundred years ago, they would already be in the nation's capital. For the first half century or so of the country's history, this part of Virginia would have been part of the Federal District, later known as the District of Columbia. In 1790, the district had been formed from land ceded by Maryland and Virginia, a 100-square-mile diamond straddling the mouth of the Potomac River. Unlike previous national capitals in Philadelphia and New York City, Washington was designed to not be dependent on any state. That lesson had been learned the hard way in the Philadelphia Mutiny of 1783, when Continental Army soldiers protesting the same pay issues that had led to the Society of the Cincinnati's founding just a month earlier had stormed Congress demanding their due. Interestingly, it was Cincinnati founders George Washington, Alexander Hamilton, Robert Howe, and William Heath who successfully put down the rebellion. The Executive Council of Pennsylvania, however, had refused to act, demonstrating the need for a federally owned, federally managed home for the national government.

The Federal District was mandated in Article 1, Section 8 of the US Constitution, from its purpose down to the limits of its size. But though splitting the land contribution between two of the largest, wealthiest, and most centrally located of the original thirteen states seemed to be an equitable solution, it wouldn't last.

Alexandria, which, along with Georgetown, was one of the most important and historic towns within the district, was one of the lynchpins in the growing movement in favor of retrocession. Alexandria was a major slave-trading hub, and abolitionists were increasingly troubled by such a practice in the nation's capital. Virginia, a slave state, was not about to give up such a prime market for the trade, so they lobbied Congress to return the land the state had ceded to the federal government in the creation of the District of Columbia. In 1846, Congress granted Virginia's request, restoring all district lands to state control.

Now the District of Columbia comprised only the land on the Maryland side of the Potomac, though the expansion of the federal government had grown to encompass parts of those retroceded lands. Here in Arlington, the Pentagon and Arlington National Cemetery occupied significant chunks of real estate, while other federal agencies had set up shop just outside the Beltway in both states, from Langley and Quantico in Virginia to Bethesda and Fort Meade in Maryland.

Even if Virginia's retrocession hadn't gone through, one hundred square miles was an awfully small chunk of real estate for what was now the largest and most powerful government on the planet. The expansion made sense. After all, as long as the White House, the Capitol Building, and the Supreme Court—the seats of power of the three branches of government—were in the Federal District, the constitutional requirement was satisfied.

"I think I feel dirtier after that shower than before I went in," Chloe said, coming out of the bathroom. She wore a faded Moody Blues T-shirt and a pair of sleeper shorts a size too big. They had visited a second-hand thrift shop down the block to grab a few extra changes of clothes. Jon tried not to laugh at—or get distracted by—Chloe's continual tugging at her shorts to ensure they stayed up.

"Sorry," Jon said. "It's the only way we can stay off their radar."

"And marching right into their headquarters tomorrow will help us to do that how, exactly?" She walked over to her bed, eyed it distrustfully, then eased herself onto the sheets. The springs shrieked in protest. "Thank God I don't roll in my sleep," she chuckled.

"I'll be the judge of that come morning," Jon said, though his bed wasn't any better. "In answer to your question, it's the last place they'd expect us to show up. As far as Kellerman and his allies know, we're still chasing the Kennedy angle. They probably think we're still in New England, chasing down potential leads on Cape Cod, or even going back to the JFK Library. If we play our cards right, they'll never see us coming."

Chloe nodded absent-mindedly before her mouth gaped open. "Oh my God."

Jon followed Chloe's eyes to the TV. On the screen, a suburban home engulfed in flames. Three companies of firefighters were valiantly trying to quell the inferno, but it was clear their efforts were in vain.

Despite the fire twisting the house into a charred nightmare version of itself, Jon recognized it.

He had been there just yesterday. Meeting Vance Nicholson for the first time.

"Vance," Chloe whispered in shock.

Through the CRT scanlines and half-garbled audio of the hotel's outdated television setup, the reporter on screen was detailing the tragedy. Some of the words were lost in static and crossed feeds, but Jon got the bullet point rundown.

Explosions from within the home. Powerful conflagration. No survivors.

The feed switched to an analyst citing guarded conversations with a Dallas County sheriff's deputy—who had asked to remain anonymous because they weren't cleared to speak to the media—speculating that the home's resident, one Vance Nicholson according to property records, had been building explosive devices inside. He was apparently known to local authorities for his "extremist views" on government conspiracies, especially having to do with the JFK assassination.

The screen was once again filled with graphic shots of the once magnificent home burning like a gigantic Victorian torch against the night sky. The reporter's narration over the final footage sent a chill through Jon's bones.

"If this theory pans out, this horrible tragedy may well have saved thousands more from a potential terrorist attack at the hands of this alleged extremist. Back to you, Dan."

The words were couched in conditionals, the sort of legal loopholes the media and politicians alike had used for years to get away with making wild accusations without fully crossing the line into libel or slander. But the sensational allegation was clear as day: Vance Nicholson, the mild-mannered conspiracy theorist who had seen a president get shot as a boy, was a terrorist who got exactly what he deserved.

"We killed him," Chloe said, her voice choking up.

Jon stared at her in disbelief. "What? How on earth do you figure that?"

"That stupid trick you pulled at the USS *Constitution*? It made Kellerman mad, and he took it out on Vance."

He turned on his bed to face her. "First, Vance stopped being our ally the moment he decided to turn on us—and on your father, remember—by betraying us to Kellerman. Second, Kellerman was in Boston with us when Vance died. Those bombs were inside the house already. This was a contingency plan he would have put in place a long time before we exposed Kellerman and Vance at the *Constitution*. I feel bad that Vance is dead, but we didn't kill him. Vance chose to sleep with a viper, and today's the day he finally got bit."

Chloe faced the screen, fighting back tears. CNN had moved on to some other story already, but Jon speculated it was something for her to look at that wasn't him.

Fine, he thought. Let her be angry. But she would get over it. In the past few hours she'd been blindsided by two back-to-back revelations about the only ally she'd had for most of her journey. First, she found out Vance was a traitor. Now, he had been murdered. And at least part of the blame for that she laid at her own feet and those of her newest and last remaining partner in this strange quest: Jon.

What struck him even more than the death was the way it was reported. He'd experienced skepticism before, even with proof in hand. But for Vance to be automatically branded an extremist, a terrorist, just because he had publicly denounced the official version of the JFK assassination? It was all the more proof that, unless they found the smoking gun of the Cincinnati's involvement in the Kennedy assassinations—assuming such evidence still existed—they would be alone and looking over their shoulders for the rest of their lives. Which, considering Kellerman's penchant for tracking them and his clear desire to see them destroyed, would likely not be long at all.

The brazenness of Vance's murder also stood out to Jon. Kellerman had rigged a staged suicide with Chloe's dad. He was a skilled assassin backed by a secret society of untold power. There were any number of ways he could have killed his outed double agent. But he chose to send a message to Jon and Chloe.

*This is what happens to people who mess with us. And you're next on my list.*

Message received. Loud and clear.

Seemingly forgetting about the soiled state of the bedclothes, Chloe wriggled under the covers and faced the wall to sleep.

"Good night," he said. Her only response was a sarcastic huff.

In a run-down motel room, her world was tilting off its axis yet again as the Society of the Cincinnati claimed yet another of her friends, another purported ally in her fight to avenge her father's death. But instead of achieving justice, the body count had increased. Bodies she had put in the path of the Cincinnati.

On some level, he understood her feelings. And he figured that, on some level, she knew that neither of them was responsible for Vance's death. But she needed to process, alone.

Tonight, he would give her that.

But in the morning, they would both have to set aside Vance's betrayal and murder. Because when the sun rose, they would be venturing into the belly of the beast.

And he couldn't do that by himself.

# CHAPTER 42
### *Somerville, Massachusetts*

Dr. Juliana Bixby was drunk, she realized as she slumped down in the back seat of her Uber. No, not *drunk* drunk. More than just tipsy, though.

It had been a good night. Tasha and Bernice had always been her go-to girls when she needed a break. Dinner and wine at PARK, then more drinks at Ryles while the college kids grooved on the dance floor nearby. The youths reminded her of the visit Jon and Chloe had paid her. Yet another reason to drink tonight.

The first was her recent divorce. Not just the divorce, but how quickly Phillip had proposed to the woman he had been having an affair with. They still had mutual friends, so even though she had blocked him on her social media accounts, pictures of the proposal still slipped through via friends of friends. The widely shared images made her sick to her stomach, giving new meaning to the phrase "going viral."

Like the good friends they'd grown to be, Tasha and Bernice helped alleviate much of that stress. That and half a bottle of tequila shared between them. Juliana had helped Bernice through her own nasty divorce five years ago. In March, she would be a bridesmaid in Bernice's wedding. Life went on. No matter how dark things got, there was always another daybreak waiting just around the corner.

This thing with Jon and his friend Chloe, though. That was something else. She always made it a point to include the Society of the Cincinnati in her lectures on the period, but rumors of its darker exploits she kept largely to herself. She'd mentioned it to a few colleagues behind closed doors, even a few eager students during office hours, Jon included. But beyond that, she stuck to the facts. It was pseudo-history, a conspiracy theory concocted out of whole cloth. The irrational tying together of Cold War paranoia and Thomas Jefferson's fears of a new American monarchy.

And then, suddenly, it wasn't.

Bixby couldn't believe how big this could be. Without proof, it was nothing. Less than nothing. Career-destroying. But if Jon could find the evidence he was looking for, it would rewrite the entirety of American history. The Society of the Cincinnati was older than the Constitution itself. The group's long shadow would have tainted the United States from its inception. If their misdeeds were truly exposed and brought into the light, who knew what heights the nation might reach. After, of course, the inevitable backlash of such a revelation.

Heads would roll in Washington. Or maybe not. Things were so entrenched down there that maybe everyone would just slip back into their well-worn roles, growing fat off the public teat while espousing one polarizing paradigm and living out another.

But she could hope.

The Cincinnati would not go easily, though. She worried for Jon and Chloe. They were diving straight into the heart of darkness, and no one, not even Bixby, knew just how deep that hole went.

The Uber driver pulled up to the curb beside her condo. She gave the man a ten-dollar tip and climbed out onto the sidewalk. Thinking about Jon and Chloe, she realized, had sucked the fun out of the night.

She smoothed out her skirt and cracked her neck. Tonight had been a great time and she would focus on her memories with her friends. Jon was fine. He could handle himself. And she couldn't do anything for them right now anyway.

What she could do was take care of herself so she didn't have a raging hangover come morning.

She swiped her gate access card to buzz the main door open. Stopping at the mailboxes just inside, she tried three times to stab her mail key into the lock. When she finally got it on the fourth try, she let out a giggle.

*Maybe I am drunk after all*, she thought, using one arm to brace herself against the wall of mailboxes. She grabbed the bundle of envelopes from within and closed her mailbox door, locking it. The elevator's perpetual "Out of order" sign mocked her again. She sneered at it, then began ascending the stairs, one hand firmly gripping the banister. She would not fall down the stairs as she had in January just after she discovered Phillip's infidelity. A combination of ice caught in the treads of her boots and way too much vodka had sent her tumbling head over heels like a klutz in a bad slapstick movie. The doctors said that, other than some bruising, she was fine. The severity of her inebriation had kept her muscles loose, apparently preventing significantly greater damage.

She didn't feel like testing fate twice.

Once she reached the third-floor landing, she took a moment to breathe. Almost home. She staggered down the hall, bumping from one wall to the next like a drunken pinball and giggling at each impact.

*What would my students think of me now? Or Dean Belkin? Or Phillip?*

She stopped again, just steps from her front door. Character, her father had said, was what you did when no one was watching. She tried to force herself to sober up. She was better than this. It was time to prove it.

Key at the ready, she took the final few steps to her door. She may have locked down the giggling and silliness, but she couldn't stop the slight sway in her gait, nor the way the world bobbed and weaved through her swimming vision. She had made a huge batch of penne and marinara sauce before going out with her friends. That and the two bottles of Gatorade chilling in her fridge was her default hangover prevention kit. She may have overdone it tonight, but tomorrow would be filled with good memories with her friends instead of crippling headaches and nausea.

She didn't notice it at first. When she stepped inside her condo, she locked the door behind her and tossed her keys on the chipped china plate she'd bought for a song at an estate sale in Back Bay years ago. Then she dropped her clutch next to it. Drunk or not, she could do all that blindfolded. Muscle memory from her normal routine took over, so she wasn't really thinking about what she was doing. If she had been, she might have noticed the change sooner.

It wasn't until she walked into her galley kitchen that she realized something was off. She had been running late earlier, so she had just left the pot she'd used to make the pasta soaking in the sink.

Now it was gone.

"I hope you don't mind. I did a little cleaning up while you were out."

Bixby spun around to see a stranger standing at the entrance to the kitchen. Her mind swam at the sight of him.

"I abhor a messy kitchen," he continued. "Don't you? Besides, now that that's all taken care of, we have more time left over for the rest of our evening."

She braced herself on the counter while her alcohol-addled brain tried to process this curious new development. Had Tasha or Bernice set her up with a blind date after their outing? He was kind of handsome, if not exactly her usual type. Close-cropped black hair, deep-brown eyes, strong jaw. She appreciated the gesture, but this was really too much. Right now, all she wanted was to gorge herself on enough pasta and Gatorade to stave off her impending hangover and to pass out in her own bed. Alone.

Then she noticed the gun.

"What's going on here?" she asked, her words coming out garbled and slurred.

"I understand you had a chat with some friends of mine today. I merely want to know what they told you and what you told them."

Kellerman. It was the agent that had been pursuing Jon and Chloe. And now he had broken into her home and was threatening her with a gun.

Her face went hot as rage filled her chest. Perhaps the alcohol was giving her a false sense of bravado in the face of danger. But, gun or not, she refused to be cowed by this bully.

"I have nothing to say to you," she spat, pushing herself off the counter and standing straight as she stared him down. "Get out of my house before I call the police."

Kellerman smiled. "Oh, you have plenty to say to me. The only question is how much pain you want to endure before you tell me what I want to know."

# CHAPTER 43
### *Ramstein-Miesenbach, Germany*

The phone call came at the worst possible moment.

Wayne Wilkins held up a finger and pointed to his cell as he stepped away from the jet idling on the tarmac. The airman waiting by the C-17 Globemaster's stairs tapped at an imaginary watch on his wrist. Wayne nodded and held up his finger once more. *Just one moment.*

This wasn't a call he could take once he was airborne.

Once he was far enough from the warming turbines to hear himself think, he answered the phone. "Tell me you've got some good news."

"Well, you're half right."

The voice belonged to Aida Teshome. Since this call was technically personal in nature, it was one he didn't want to make surrounded by military and CIA personnel on board the waiting plane. Plus, Aida wasn't CIA. She was NSA.

And, for Wayne's money, the best analyst the NSA, and possibly all of the alphabet soup of federal intelligence agencies, had to offer.

They'd met at a cross-agency soirée about eighteen months ago, shortly after Wayne had joined the CIA. The get-together was intended to foster interagency relationships and communication, a key talking point after the intelligence failures in the months leading to 9/11. And while much of Washington remained as entrenched in territorial bureaucracy as ever, Aida and Wayne had hit it off.

She was born and raised in Philadelphia, the only child of Ethiopian immigrants. After double-majoring in applied mathematics and computer science at UC-Berkley, she earned her doctorate in cryptanalysis from Caltech. She was recruited by Google to anticipate and protect the sprawling tech empire from potential cyber threats. Two years into her stint in Silicon Valley, one of the encryption algorithms exposed a Romanian cyberterrorist the NSA had been following. The Romanian was a big fish who had been in the wind since successfully crippling the Denver city utilities system with a ransom-ware attack, and the post mortem on the case brought Aida's code to light. NSA Director Gretl Plessinger called her personally to thank Aida for her inadvertent role in bringing an international fugitive to justice, and offered her a job. Aida had quickly proven her worth, becoming one of the most trusted and skilled analysts in the agency. This also meant she had access to a lot of systems that could help Wayne with his off-the-books work.

"What did you find?" he asked.

"Three things. First, Harper's personnel file is marked Top Secret."

"No problem for you to access."

"Not at all, but that's the issue. There's nothing in there that seems like it would warrant such a classification. It's all fairly pedestrian. His supervisor marked an increasingly erratic attendance record, inattention to his work, misuse of Bureau resources, failure to follow established protocols. All fairly standard."

Wayne frowned. "So why the Top Secret designation?"

"Ding, ding, ding! My thoughts exactly. There's nothing in there that would warrant classification at all, especially now that he's dead."

"Anything on his research? Anything Kennedy-related?"

"Well, yes and no."

"Meaning?"

Aida cleared her throat. "His father apparently offered him a deathbed confession that the old man had played a hand in the cover-up of the JFK assassination early in his own tenure at the Bureau. Ever since, Jack Harper apparently dedicated most of his free time to trying to get to the bottom of what his father had told him. What finally flagged him for his higher-ups was his delving into classified Bureau documents from the '60s, ones that the Warren Commission hadn't included in their report."

Wayne's interest was piqued. "Were any particular documents referenced in his file?"

"Unfortunately, no."

"So what does it say about the nature of his illicit research? Surely there must be something more specific about what he was digging into if they were building a case for termination."

"You would think so, but, as for specifics, there's a whole lot of nothing in his file. But not the natural kind of nothing. The kind where it looks like there may have once been something there, but it's been scrubbed. Missing puzzle pieces you'd never know were supposed to be there unless you were looking close enough."

Sounded like a classic cover-up. And a good reason for Harper's personnel file to be classified Top Secret.

"Anything on this Kellerman fellow?" Wayne asked.

"Nothing yet. Without knowing who he works for or even if he's officially on the government payroll, a surname is way too little to go on, especially considering it may be an alias."

"Of course."

"I'm not giving up though. I've got a search trolling various government databases for sociopathic behaviors in personnel files of all Kellermans between the ages of thirty and fifty actively employed by the federal government or military within the past ten years. Cross-referencing with both Kennedy assassinations as well as all the usual suspects in conspiracy lore. It may take a while, though, and still may come up empty, so if you can offer any other tidbits on the guy, that'd be a huge help."

"I can check in with my contact to see if he's learned anything else."

"That would be lovely."

Her voice had a slight lilt that Wayne had always found charming. Though they had quickly realized that theirs was a platonic attraction, he considered her a close friend and confidant, both in person and in the field. Of course, he wouldn't have reached out with this to someone he didn't trust implicitly.

"There's one other thing," Aida said.

The airman by the plane waved and stabbed at his wrist once more, indicating that Wayne's time was up. He wouldn't be the only passenger on the Globemaster, and the Air Force had a schedule to keep.

"I've got to go," Wayne said.

"Just, be careful, all right? We still don't know the half of this, and I already don't like the way this smells."

Wayne grinned. "You know me. I'm a paragon of caution and restraint."

Aida laughed in his ear and hung up.

He was at an impasse. He could either miss his flight and try to call Jon now or he could wait until he was on the ground stateside. He considered what Aida had told him. The choice was obvious.

He pocketed the phone and made a beeline for the waiting plane. He would have to skip his briefing at Langley. His supervisors would have to take a rain check. Jon had stumbled onto something far bigger than a Serbian bombmaker, and it couldn't wait.

A phone call couldn't help Jon now.

# CHAPTER 44
## *Washington, DC*

Chloe noticed the statue first.

"Is that George Washington?"

Jon grinned. "It sure is. The perfect statue for this place."

She looked at the bronze figure in front of the gray stone wall. "Why's that?"

"It's a reproduction of a famous statue Jean-Antoine Houdon did about two centuries ago. The original is in the Virginia statehouse, and it was actually completed during Washington's lifetime based on a life mask and his actual measurements. One of the cool things about this representation, though, is that most scholars believe Houdon intentionally depicted him as Cincinnatus."

She studied the statue. It certainly was different than other representations she had seen of Washington. He was dressed in contemporary military attire, looking regal with walking stick and sword. His left hand rested on a strange pillar-like object of some sort.

"It's a fasces," Jon said, apparently reading her thoughts. "A bundle of rods wrapped around an axe. In 1920s Italy it inspired the name of the nascent Fascist movement. But when this statue was carved, the fasces harkened to an older age when it served as a symbol of imperial power in ancient Rome. It's intrinsically tied to the Cincinnatus mythos."

George Washington as the American Cincinnatus indeed. And what a perfect place for it.

Chloe stared up at the palatial edifice of Anderson House, simultaneously struck with awe and fear. Twin gates off Massachusetts Avenue opened into a marble courtyard, flanked on either side by the magnificent wings of the three-story mansion. The massive Beaux-Arts building was just over a century old and sat in the middle of Embassy Row in the capital city of the United States, but it felt like more like an old-world manor house than something belonging in Washington.

Once she stepped inside, that feeling was multiplied tenfold. The atrium stretched left and right for dozens of yards. Italianate splendor mixed with solid walls of gray marble and dim lighting gave an impression somewhere between a Renaissance palace, a medieval castle, and a Victorian mansion.

It had been built in the first years of the twentieth century by a wealthy ambassador named Larz Anderson. Anderson's family was inextricably tied to some of the most important events in the nation's history, though most people had never heard of him or his heritage. He was one of the first prolific collectors of automobiles, hobnobbed with presidents and kings, and threw parties that would make Jay Gatsby jealous. But his most significant passion was, like his fortune and influence, inherited.

His membership in the Society of the Cincinnati.

After his death, he willed the house to form a new national headquarters for the Society in the capital of the country it had helped found. And now, nearly a century later, it housed both the Society's headquarters and its extensive archives.

At least, the parts of its archives they would publicly admit to.

"Welcome," said a curly-haired woman standing behind a counter to their right. According to her name badge, the woman's name was Erica DeHart. She was in her late forties and gave off an air balanced between hospitable and knowledgeable. The perfect tour guide.

"Is this your first visit?" DeHart asked.

"It is," Chloe responded. "For both of us."

She turned to where she expected Jon to be, but he was still looking around the entryway, seemingly scouring the room for clues. Or, knowing him, perhaps just taking in the historical architecture and rich furnishings.

"We'll be starting our next tour in about five minutes," DeHart said before inviting them to sign the guestbook.

Chloe couldn't help herself. She signed for both Pauline Schmidt and Erik Weisz to thumb her nose at her father's killers. If Kellerman or his allies ever read through these guestbooks to see who might've been snooping, they'd find the two historical magicians who were about to pull off their greatest trick yet: bringing down the most powerful secret society in American history.

Either that, or they'd soon be as dead as their illusionist namesakes.

"Tour in five minutes," she told Jon once she'd finished at the desk.

"I've got a feeling the smoking gun won't be here," Jon said. His tone said that he was disappointed but not surprised. "There's no way they'd conduct full tours of this place if a powder keg like a dossier about how they killed Kennedy were here. Even if it was locked in an impenetrable vault behind two false doors in a secure, 'authorized personnel only' area."

"Why not?"

"Because I wouldn't store something like that here. And they've given this much more thought than I have. Besides, the Cincinnati was already more than a century old by the time Anderson House was built, decades older than that by the time it became their new headquarters. And if this really goes back to Washington . . ."

"But this was their headquarters during the Kennedy assassinations," Chloe argued.

"True enough," Jon conceded. "Of course, there's always the possibility that we're chasing ghosts. That whatever documentation they may have made at the time has been since purged or destroyed."

*That* was a sentiment she didn't even dare to entertain. The proof they sought was everything. If it didn't exist, Kellerman and the Cincinnati would prove unstoppable, and she and Jon would end up in prison or dead.

Just like her dad. And, traitor though he was, just like Vance.

"It's got to still exist. You heard Dr. Bixby. Recording and preserving history is one of their key tenets. And we'll learn something here. Even if the proof isn't here, the Society and its history is."

"Agreed," Jon said. "We'll keep our eyes open during the tour, then see what we can find down in the Society's public archives."

Chloe caught movement out of the corner of her eye. The camera, nestled into the corner just beside them. Had it always been pointing directly toward them? Or had their whispered mention of Kennedy attracted unwanted attention? Perhaps some facial recognition software Kellerman had been using to help track their movements had been triggered by their arrival here? She stared at the lens, subconsciously hoping to see who was watching her on the other side.

"What are you looking at?" Jon asked.

"Nothing," she lied. "Just around."

It was paranoia, plain and simple. Yes, there clearly were bad men out to get them. Powerful, well-connected men, at that. But it didn't mean there was danger and deception behind every camera, in every stranger's face. The camera hadn't moved to focus on them. They were standing near the entryway, next to a three-hundred-year-old Russian armoire, festooned with hand-laid gold leaf and other priceless ornamentation. It was a logical place for a security camera to focus its gaze. The perceived movement, meanwhile, was likely fatigue combined with self-fulling expectations, unfamiliar surroundings, and a trick of the light. All of which were tools magicians had used against their audiences since the days of Schmidt and Houdini.

If they were going to finish this, she had to get her mind out of the cheap seats and start controlling the show for once.

DeHart's voice cut through Chloe's thoughts. "Anyone for the house tour, please gather over here."

They entered the east stair hall and joined a small group at the base of a red velvet-lined marble staircase, along which was an array of portraits. All the presidents-general of the Society of the Cincinnati, from George Washington and Alexander Hamilton all the way to the present day. Though for most of its history presidents-general ruled for life, a recent change had reduced modern Cincinnati leaders' tenure to three years apiece. Was this change to keep things fresh, switching out management regularly and giving more members a chance to reach that high office? Or was it push-back against the allegations levied by Thomas Jefferson and a host of others over the centuries that the Society of the Cincinnati was a secret New World monarchy. Most military dictators appointed themselves supreme leader for life, and it appeared that the Society's hierarchy had historically positioned themselves in a similar fashion. Not just in its early years, but all the way through the advent of the Cold War. In fact, the first three-year tenure didn't start until 1953, when the seventeenth president-general took over.

His four immediate predecessors all died within a three-year span.

Chloe found it interesting that all this happened right around the Korean War. And it didn't stop until Eisenhower moved into the White House.

Something had shifted in the organization. A rapid-fire succession of Cincinnati leaders succumbing to the grave, followed by a major change that had persisted to this day. And then, a decade later, they assassinate the president of the United States.

Was all this just a horrible bout of Cold War intrigue gone horribly awry? Or was something even darker going on? Chloe felt as though the more she learned, the less she understood. Like some sort of conspiracy hydra, every question answered sprouted two new mysteries.

DeHart led them through the opulent home, illustrating each magnificent room with history about the Andersons and the Society. It wasn't until they reached the serving pantry upstairs that Chloe realized something was wrong.

The room stretched for more than twenty feet. The walls were lined with glass-door cabinets above tiled countertops displaying dozens of pieces of eighteenth- and nineteenth-century porcelain, many of which were painted with the same Society eagle symbol that Bobby Kennedy had hidden in the *Victura* safe.

DeHart was sharing about the history of the room, about the lavish dinners the Andersons would host for not only Society of the Cincinnati gatherings but also for elite visitors like the Vanderbilts and the du Ponts, military leaders like General John J. Pershing, and US presidents like William Howard Taft and Calvin Coolidge.

Chloe felt it again. The preternatural sensation of being watched. She whirled around just in time to see a figure disappear into the shadows of a chamber adjoining the pantry. She tried to follow, but DeHart called her back, warning her that the area was for Anderson House staff only.

Chloe lingered in the doorway for a moment, but she could see that DeHart was right. Storage boxes were stacked in one corner, while a rack of computer servers hummed against the other wall. Nowhere obvious for someone to hide. But opposite where she stood, a metal door secured with a key card lock mocked her brief pursuit.

It wasn't her imagination this time.

Someone in Anderson House was watching them.

# CHAPTER 45
## *Washington, DC*

Stanton Gaines could feel his plans crumbling beneath his feet. He came here with high hopes. But the impassive face of President James Talquin refused to be moved by any of his arguments.

When he was a boy, Gaines had dreamed of occupying this office. From its iconic rounded walls to the historic Resolute desk to the Presidential Seal woven into the carpet, the Oval Office commanded a majesty and awe commensurate with the power vested in its occupant.

But then Gaines grew up and realized how temporary and tenuous was the power of a president. The Twenty-Second Amendment limited a president's tenure to two terms, but political realities shortened it even further. It was commonly said on Capitol Hill that a president's first term goal was to secure re-election, while his second term goal—assuming he was re-elected—was to secure his legacy. Effectively, presidents had only one term to fully enact their desired changes. True change introduced political instability, and most politicians were loath to risk such a fate without an appropriate catalyst.

A mass shooting, to push gun control. A stock market crash, to enact tax reform and corporate regulations.

Or a terror attack, to launch a war.

Even beyond term limits, being elected by the entire country was a beast. Between the liberal yuppies of California and New York, the redneck conservatives of the Deep South, and the demographic tossed salad of swing states like Florida and Ohio, it was impossible to please everyone. And while the past few decades had been favorable to incumbent presidents' re-election chances, control of Congress steadily swung toward the opposing party.

Even for the highest office in the land, the support of Congress could not be overstated.

Barack Obama had learned this the hard way. Frustrated with a gridlocked Congress that became increasingly opposed to his agenda, he wielded his presidential pen to enact executive orders in lieu of legislation. But as soon as he was out of office, his successor overturned many of those orders with his own presidential powers.

It was how the founders had intended it. Checks and balances. Executive orders for when expediency precluded a slower-moving Congress from acting in time. But that slower-moving Congress held the real, lasting power. Laws were harder to pass, but they were also harder to overturn.

That stronger, more lasting power of action was one element that drew Stanton Gaines to refocus his vision from the White House to the Capitol building. Congress held the power to declare war, to ratify treaties, to pass constitutional amendments, and to impeach presidents. It held the nation's purse strings. It approved or rejected presidential nominees and Supreme Court candidates.

And it had no term limits. Despite perennial cries from the disaffected who wanted a constitutional amendment requiring regular turnover of new faces in the House and Senate, any attempt to actually make something happen to that effect had been immediately strangled in the crib.

That was perhaps the greatest thing about being in Congress. Despite a historically low overall approval rating hovering in the low teens, the incumbent re-election rate was over 95%. People may hate the ineptitude of Congress as a whole, but they still tended to support their own representative or senator. It was the other guys, those bigoted Republicans or those socialist Democrats, who were causing all the problems. All an aspiring powerbroker had to do was secure a "safe" congressional seat and avoid major scandals, and a lifetime of national and international influence was open to them.

So while half a dozen occupants of the White House had come and gone in the past three decades, Stanton Gaines continued to wield power as the top-ranking Democrat on the Senate Armed Services Committee. The second-ranking Republican on the committee was also a like-minded member of the Cincinnati, as were high-ranking members of both parties across other key committees in both houses of Congress. Not only were they able to further their agenda through official channels, but they could also use their positions to influence matters outside the public eye.

At present, neither avenue was working for Gaines.

"Surely you see the threat posed to us," Gaines argued. "Ortega has threatened American shipping lanes in the Atlantic and Caribbean. He's even threatened to attack us directly."

Talquin sighed as though he was speaking to a recalcitrant child. "I have made my policies toward Venezuela and any other nation abundantly clear. Threats are not acts of war. If he sinks one of our ships or brings his warplanes toward Galveston or Miami, then that's another story. But, come on, Stanton, his country's on the cusp of civil war, and he's got to cast the blame somewhere."

It was all Gaines could do not to laugh at the irony. Between the emboldening of far-left and far-right activists, an increase in hate crimes across the political and social spectrum, and public discourse soaked in vitriol and ingrained distrust, their own country was coming apart at the seams. The clickbait-obsessed media and troll-fueled netherworld of social media was heaping fuel on the fire, with no sign of abating. But the president was more worried about cutting some slack for a foreign leader whose own nation was about to be set aflame by the turmoil within.

If only he could make Talquin see.

"Mr. President, with all due respect, I think you're making a terrible mistake here. Do the American people have to suffer another Pearl Harbor, another 9/11, for us to see how real the danger is here?"

Talquin leaned in, his stoic expression matching his stony tone. "Or another Gulf of Tonkin incident, Senator?"

Gaines did his best not to recoil at the comment. So that was how it was going to be. Talquin knew more than he was letting on. He was trying to puff his chest, show he knew what cards Gaines held.

Talquin knew nothing. If he had any idea, he would have Gaines arrested for treason. For, as far as the Justice Department was concerned, the Cincinnati's Plan B was a textbook definition of that capital charge.

Conjecture and rumor. Gaines's allies never fully revealed themselves to outsiders. Not even presidents who cooperated with their agenda and eventually were granted honorary membership in the Society of the Cincinnati got anything approaching the full picture. They were pawns. Willing or unwilling, the result was the same. Without the Cincinnati's vigilance, the nation would crumble.

Gaines would not let that happen on his watch.

"If you like, Mr. President," he said, refusing to be cowed by Talquin's blind jab. "The fact remains that a foreign power continues to publicly threaten us, and no amount of diplomacy is helping deescalate the situation. They are not a nuclear power, and there is no doubt that we could win this war without significant loss of American life. But only if we take the appropriate actions before it's too late."

Talquin's smile was condescending to the extreme. He folded his hands and leaned forward across his desk, sighing in exasperation. "See, that's the great thing about a government that takes its security seriously," he said. "We have tens of thousands of assets in the CIA, DIA, NSA, Homeland Security, and the Coast Guard, alongside the FBI, local authorities, and a host of other agencies and divisions, constantly watching for threats to American interests. No offense, Senator, but my daily intelligence briefing is a little more complete and accurate than yours."

No doubt it was. But the alphabet soup of Washington intelligence agencies looked at singular threats, named terror groups and movements, and hostile foreign powers. What was coming didn't have a name, nor was it easily defined. But when it came, it would not be as an outside invader but, rather, as a dam breaking from within, unleashing a tsunami of civil war and chaos upon the United States.

And then, Venezuela, North Korea, Russia, Iran, and all of America's enemies and jilted allies would descend upon the writhing carcass of this once-great nation and cheer as the world's brightest beacon of freedom collapsed into darkness.

It was a possibility beyond the imagination of security consultants concerned about the next crazed lunatic with an automatic rifle, the next true believer with a bomb strapped to his chest and a lust for martyrdom.

But for Gaines, it was the most consistently dangerous scenario of all. And when he and his cohort were the only ones watching for it, the task fell to them when the danger reared its head again.

It always had. And like those who had held his post before him, Stanton Gaines would not falter in his defense of the nation his forebears had given their life and livelihoods to create.

Talquin wasn't having it. "Venezuela may be fractious, but they are flush with natural resources and have a sizable military force and millions of able-bodied citizens who have been inculcated to hate the United States. An unwarranted invasion would raise the ire not only of their potent populace but of countless other Latin American countries who we need as allies. Could we defeat Venezuela militarily? Sure. But if their neighbors unite against us, or even if they withdraw their support for our presence in the region, we'd have a new Vietnam on our hands. Or worse. Not to mention the fact that the American public has no appetite for another half-baked war, much less one that will result in a bloody, drawn-out conflict and send oil prices skyrocketing once again."

The president stood, smoothing his suit. "Now, if you'll excuse me, I have a meeting with the secretary of the Treasury in ten minutes. Thank you for your thoughts, Senator, and know that I have taken them under advisement."

Miffed at being so quickly rebuffed, Gaines stood and shook the president's hand. He wasn't surprised. This meeting was a formality, a last-ditch effort to avoid what was to come.

Gaines was silent as he left the Oval Office and walked out of the White House. It wasn't until he was alone inside his waiting limo that he pulled out his phone. There was still an hour drive before he reached his destination, but this was a call that couldn't wait.

"How'd it go?" the man on the other end answered.

"About as well as you expected," Gaines said.

"I told you it was a waste of time."

"I had to try. What we're about to do isn't to be taken lightly."

"It never is. But it seems necessary now."

Gaines swallowed. He decided not to mention Talquin's apparent suspicions. After tomorrow, the president's resistance would be swept away by a torrent of public fury.

"I agree. Move ahead with Operation Broken Serpent."

"Yes, sir," the man said before disconnecting.

So it was done. Within forty-eight hours, the country would be at war with Venezuela. And, once again, at great and terrible cost, the Society of the Cincinnati would have saved the United States from itself.

# CHAPTER 46
*Washington, DC*

Jon's senses were on high alert as the tour group entered the grand ballroom of Anderson House. With its soaring ceiling, ornate woodwork, and lavish decor, it would not have been out of place in the villa of an Italian count. Indeed, the architects had designed the building based on the noble houses of nineteenth-century England and Italy.

Yet, throughout, the accents were what gave the building its unique character. A giant golden Buddha, sitting atop a green marble pedestal. A wooden black Madonna from a Romanian monastery. An impossibly detailed bowl depicting a scene of ocean life, hand-crafted from blue glass and gold filigree by a Japanese artisan. Between Larz's service as a US Ambassador and the family's personal travels across the globe, the Andersons were quite the collectors of art from far-flung lands. This curious mash-up of Western European architecture and Eastern art pieces seemed to represent Larz Anderson himself. And if Jon could understand the man who built the house and brought the Society to his home, perhaps he could figure out where the Cincinnati might hide their secrets.

Exiting the dining room led to a sweeping arc of a musicians' balcony that overlooked the palatial ballroom. Over the past century, it would have provided performers, servants, and spectators alike a grand view of the stately soirées and ceremonies held below. A pair of smaller curtained balconies overlooked the far end of the ballroom, directly above two sets of double doors flanking a grand fireplace. A magnificent crystal chandelier hung overhead, while oil paintings and gilded ornamentation adorned the walls. The marble staircase Erica DeHart was leading them down from the right-hand side of the musicians' balcony was worn by the shoes of thousands of visitors, the way the front steps of cathedrals or historic government buildings were. This was once a home, yes. But it had always been designed as a place of gathering.

"This is where the Andersons would host receptions and events for Society members as well as friends from Washington's elite," DeHart told the tour group. "Of course, there was a lot of overlap between those two groups."

DeHart gave her group a knowing grin, but Jon didn't find her attempt at levity funny. The fact that a centuries-old secret society had an uncanny amount of sway in Washington ceased to be cause for a nudge and a wink when they were actively gunning for you. Being female, DeHart obviously wasn't a member of the Society of the Cincinnati. But it didn't mean she wasn't related to one. A member who could potentially be in league with Kellerman.

She led the group toward the back of the house and into the Winter Garden. A walled outer garden filled with sculptures, a dormant fountain, and plenty of dead greenery beckoned from beyond the row of glass doors and floor-to-ceiling windows. But in this sunlit corridor between the outer garden and the ballroom, the Winter Garden came to life.

DeHart pointed to a black-and-white photograph hanging on the wall. Jon recognized the room as this very Winter Garden, though, in the photograph, it lived up to its name. Vines climbed trellises over the doorways, and expansive plants that looked like they hailed from more tropical climes than Washington grew from planters and pots along the floors and tables.

"Looks so different now," Chloe whispered.

And she was right. The glass-lined hallway was almost entirely free of plant life, its space now dedicated to preserving mementos of the past. More of Larz Anderson's far-eastern art collection decorated the tables, while a handful of pleasant pastorals and framed period paintings hung on what little wall space was available in the window-and doorway-heavy corridor. Some of the walls even displayed hand-painted murals that had surely been inspired by the Andersons' journeys overseas. It was an unexpected mishmash of cultures across centuries and continents, but, somehow, it worked.

"As much as the Andersons loved the finer things of high society, they also relished the outdoors. From their travels overseas and across the country, to their Sunday drives across the greater Washington area to some of their favorite landmarks, the endless bounds and life-filled bounty of nature called to them. But since winters in DC can be harsh, they built this indoor garden to utilize the natural heat and sunlight captured during the day, allowing them to bask in the vibrancy of their beloved nature 365 days a year."

Jon tried to imagine what this room would feel like back then. Right in between the ballroom and the walled garden outside. Green and full of life, even in the dead of winter.

*Too* full of life, in fact. Especially of the human variety. This was a magnificent set of rooms, patterned after the great houses of Europe and their gilded-age counterparts at Biltmore and The Breakers. But any world-rocking secrets about the Society of the Cincinnati killing JFK would be hidden far from this well-trafficked area. Jon was ready for the tour to move along.

Thankfully, that's exactly what it did. DeHart led the group back across the ballroom. Passing into another passage, they walked through a darkened room filled with Eastern-European art. The left and right walls were lined with medieval choir stalls purloined from ruined Old World cathedrals, their ancient wood blackened with age and conflict. Exiting at the other end of the choir room, up another staircase. This was the grandest he had yet seen. A wide stairway stopped at a landing before splitting into two smaller stairs on either side continuing to the next floor. A huge painting of a Venetian gala dominated the wall of the landing. According to DeHart's narration, the grand staircase and the giant wall of the landing were built so large because Larz had fallen in love with the painting while traveling abroad and needed a place to display it. The painting had more square footage than Jon's bedroom. Yet another grandiose nod to Larz Anderson's larger-than-life persona.

Jon felt the hair on the back of his neck tingle. His instincts had saved his life on several continents over the years, and he trusted them today. But when he turned around, no one was there. No flash of someone darting behind cover. No marble-and-shoe echo of a hastily beaten retreat.

"What?" Chloe asked from two steps above him.

"I thought . . ." No. It wouldn't do to worry her. Or to make the rest of the tour think he was nuts.

"Someone was following us?" Chloe asked, her voice guarded and hushed.

Jon slowly nodded, keeping eye contact with her. She nodded back, a knowing expression on her face.

She'd sensed it too. Earlier perhaps, since she hadn't stopped when he did just now.

Someone was watching them. Someone who had eluded them on separate occasions. Someone who knew this place better than they did, and apparently was able to explore the house at their leisure.

Kellerman's allies already knew they were here.

They had come too far to give up now, though. If their ruse was exposed, leaving now would only give their stalker a chance to act even sooner. And Jon had no intention of leaving Anderson House without answers.

He and Chloe hurried up the stairs to the next room, where the rest of the tour was waiting. DeHart introduced the chamber as the Key Room, so named for the distinctive, twisting pattern of black-and-white tiles set into the floor, an architectural design dating to ancient Greece. Three masterful murals covered three of the walls, each depicting a different scene in American history.

The Anderson family was intrinsically tied to each.

One was of George Washington, the Marquis de Lafayette, and Richard Clough Anderson at the founding of the Society of the Cincinnati in the closing days of the Revolutionary War. The next illustrated the Confederate attack on Fort Sumter that had ignited the Civil War. The Union commander of Fort Sumter that day was none other than Larz's great-uncle. The third mural was of Larz's war, the Spanish-American War, during which the founder of Anderson House did not see battle, spending most of the conflict in the suburbs of Washington, DC. Despite his receiving a captain's commission, Larz was in the military all of eleven months before resigning his post and moving on to something else, much as he had with most of his professional exploits. And yet, by including his war alongside those of his more famous forebears, he clearly sought to be seen as equally great. Indeed, in the elaborate friezes and motifs carved and painted into the room's ceiling, two cartouches stood out: one bore the initials of Richard Clough Anderson, the other those of Larz Anderson.

*Big shoes to fill*, Jon thought.

DeHart led them through another series of rooms in the north wing of the house before crossing the upper gallery to the south wing. She stopped in the middle of the corridor and pointed to a non-descript panel in the wall.

"Now here's an interesting tidbit. Isabel Anderson had a terrible fear of dying in a fire, so during this house's construction, she had the builders install an escape tunnel right here."

"Seriously?" said a gray-haired black man in the tour group. "A real-life secret passage?"

"Quite seriously." She pointed to an oval decoration carved in the wood, one of several in on the molding next to the panel. On closer inspection, this particular oval had a deep groove cut all the way around it. A button. "Thankfully, the house never caught on fire, so she never had to use it. But just knowing she had it available calmed her nerves."

"Where does it go?" Jon asked.

"Supposedly to the far side of the house."

"Supposedly?"

"To my knowledge, it hasn't been opened in quite some time."

"And you haven't tried it? You're not curious?"

She gave him the patient smile of an exasperated teacher to a particularly difficult student. "That's not my decision to make."

DeHart shepherded the tour to the far wing, sharing more information about the house, the Society, and the Anderson family.

"Larz Anderson's love of international art was served well by his foreign postings in the diplomatic circuit," she said. "He served as US Minister to Belgium, then Ambassador to Japan under President William Howard Taft. His first diplomatic posting, however, was to the Court of St. James, where he served as second secretary of America's United Kingdom delegation. His boss while there was US Ambassador to the United Kingdom, Robert Todd Lincoln—Abraham Lincoln's oldest and only surviving child."

Amid *oohs* and *ahhs* from the rest of the tour group, the mention of yet another assassinated president made Jon ponder a far darker question. As connected as the Anderson family had been to key moments in American history and to the Society of the Cincinnati, was Larz's role in the more treasonous side of the organization's purported activities more active than his *bon vivant* lifestyle would betray?

The tour finally circled back around to the entrance, where DeHart offered concluding remarks and thanked everyone for visiting. Most of the tourgoers applauded their guide. Jon clapped, but he was less than impressed.

DeHart's tour had given him no hint as to where any secret JFK documents might be.

Which left only one option.

"Can you direct us to the library?" Jon asked once the rest of the tour group had filtered back outside. "We wanted to do some research about the Society."

DeHart frowned. "Unfortunately, access to the archives is by appointment only. And we don't do same-day appointments."

"Please," Chloe asked. "We flew all the way here from Idaho. Can't you make an exception just this once."

DeHart appeared sympathetic as she thought about it for a moment. "Wait here. We've got a new archivist who might have an open slot. But no promises."

She left the room. Jon remained silent, not wanting to jinx whatever good vibes Chloe had given DeHart.

He glanced at his companion. She smiled at him, an innocent but blissfully attractive grin that stirred something long dormant in his chest. She was beautiful, no doubt, but her confidence, gumption, and intelligence set her leagues apart. He hadn't exactly been active in the dating game for quite some time, laser-focused on finishing his doctorate and still trying to put back together the emotional pieces his brother's death had left shattered. But not only had she managed to rekindle his love of adventuring, questing after some grand historical mystery, she had more than held her own throughout this cross-country journey.

"What?" she asked. Jon blushed as he realized he had been staring.

"Nothing." He turned to stare at a portrait of Larz Anderson hanging nearby, though his thoughts didn't leave Chloe. He was deluding himself. She had reached out to him only because she believed he could help finish her father's final case and bring his killer to justice. Thus far, they had certainly made some significant headway in that department, but they still had a relentless assassin on their tail and had made enemies of the oldest and best-connected secret society in the country. Even entertaining thoughts of romantic attraction right now was futile at best. And it could be the sort of distraction that got them both killed.

He turned his attention to the hallway down which DeHart had disappeared. Hopefully she would let them in, though without an appointment or legitimate academic credentials, there was little chance

of the archivist allowing them unsupervised access to the priceless manuscripts and artifacts housed within. He could try using his National
Archives employment as an in, but that would tip off Kellerman as well
as create more issues for them if investigators had already realized that
Jon was neither among the dead nor among the accounted-for living in
the aftermath of the blaze.

Was it really just yesterday morning that Chloe and Kellerman had
walked into his life and sent him on this crazy cross-country adventure?
It seemed like weeks. Yet for all they had discovered, it seemed like behind every answer there were only more questions.

There. The feeling again. Jon spun around. No one. But they were
free from the tour group's supervision now. He could investigate. It was
time to unveil their mystery stalker.

"Good news," DeHart said, returning.

Jon cursed her timing, but held out hope for her report.

"We have an opening after all. Please bear in mind, though, that the
archives and the house will be closing for the night in an hour."

"We'll work fast," Chloe said. "Thank you."

Half distracted by the stalker who had once again evaded his grasp,
Jon mumbled his thanks and followed as DeHart led them into the basement. Seated at a table stacked with thick old tomes wrapped in clear
plastic and what looked to be an original battle plan for the Siege of
Yorktown, a thirty-something man with a strong academic vibe rose to
greet them.

"Welcome," he said. "I'm Dr. Patrick Molyneux."

# CHAPTER 47
## *Washington, DC*

Patrick Molyneux smiled at his guests, much in the same way he imagined a cat might at a naive mouse. Everything had been building up to this moment. Everything that came before was preparation. Now was action. Now he found out if he was worthy of his father's legacy after all.

Jon and Chloe introduced themselves in turn as he shook their hands. False names, both of them. It made Molyneux's chest swell with power. He knew far more about each of them than they could ever suspect. And virtually everything he would tell them would be a lie. Or, at least, truth tainted enough with deception to spur them on toward his own ends.

"We're doing some research for a grad school paper," Jon said. "And we were hoping to get to use your archives."

"The American Revolution Institute is always happy to help young academics better understand our country's origins," Molyneux said. "What is the intended subject of your paper?"

"It's complicated," Chloe said.

"The best papers often are. Try me. I've been in academia for years, and I'm sure I can help you sort out an approach for your paper and the best resources we have for you."

Jon hesitated. Molyneux knew that they had taken the tour of Anderson House in the hopes of finding some great secret that would help them to bring Chloe's father's killer to justice. Molyneux knew his forefathers hadn't been foolish enough to leave an Achilles' heel for the world to see. But let them hope. Chloe had found something at the National Archives, and something else in Boston. Now it was Molyneux's job to find out exactly what that was, and snuff out the threat.

"We're looking for information about any potential connection the Society of the Cincinnati might have to . . . illicit matters in the nation's past," Jon said, his voice just above a whisper. "Not in its early days. More recent. Like during the Cold War."

Molyneux forced himself not to laugh at the irony. The only person who could hear Jon's hushed words was the one he should have been hiding them from.

"The Cold War?" Molyneux asked, his tone striking just the right balance so that he could feign complete ignorance or co-conspire along with them, depending on their next words.

"Yeah," Chloe said, echoing Jon's low volume. "I know it sounds weird, but even any rumors or old stories you might be able to offer could be incredibly helpful."

Time to reel them in.

Molyneux shot a suspicious glance at the door. Not that anyone would be watching, but rather to gain their trust as a valued ally surrounded on all sides by potential enemies. Jon and Chloe both followed his eyes to the door. No one was there, but the impact was made.

"I must say I'm surprised at your query." He leaned back in his chair, steepling his fingers. "I know our early days were clouded by suspicion, but I think history has borne out that we are hardly the sinister tyrants Thomas Jefferson and his ilk feared us to be. May I ask where you came across the idea that the Society of the Cincinnati was involved in illicit matters during the Cold War, or indeed at any time in the past two centuries?"

"A friend," Jon said. Cagey. Molyneux liked it. Normally he would have relished the intellectual challenge of sparring with someone like Dr. Jonathan Rickner. But this wasn't a fair fight. For the most part, Molyneux already had all the answers, and Jon didn't even realize what he was dealing with.

Molyneux leaned forward again, his voice conspiratorially low. "Trust me, this isn't a rabbit hole you want to be diving down blindly." Another glance at the door, then back to Jon and Chloe. He could see the tension on their faces. Worried about the assassin who had driven them here, looking for a life raft in this storm they were caught in.

"Fair enough," Jon said. "Can you help us learn more? Maybe find some firsthand documents here in the Society's archives?"

And there it was. Molyneux was in.

"I'll do what I can. Why don't you start by telling me what you already know? What led you here in the first place?"

"We found something," Chloe said. "Something tying the Society of the Cincinnati to Kennedy's assassination. Both Kennedys, actually."

Jon eyed Chloe for speaking so frankly, but the damage was done. So someone, perhaps Bobby Kennedy, perhaps an associate, had left a trail of clues leading from the National Archives to JFK's presidential library. But what could have implicated the Vanguard in their deaths? They were careful, using proxies hiding behind proxies whenever decisive action had to be taken. They were the puppet masters, enshrouded in the darkened rafters where neither the audience nor the actors could see them.

Then Molyneux realized the flaw in his fears. Chloe had said the Society was implicated by this purported evidence, not the Vanguard.

"That's incredible," he said, again adopting the role of interested ally. "Can I see it?"

"We left it in a safe place," Jon said, his defense sliding back into place after Chloe's outburst.

"I suppose that's understandable. But what is this evidence? I must admit, I'm fascinated."

"If the Society of the Cincinnati were to have a secret archive of any more recent exploits, would they keep them here? Or perhaps somewhere else?" Jon asked, not rising to the bait.

So he wouldn't be as trusting as Molyneux might have hoped. Unfortunate, but not unexpected.

Time for a little misdirection.

Molyneux dropped his voice to a conspiratorial whisper. "To be honest, I've been working to figure out the same thing. I've run across rumors of a few Cincinnati members who may have been active during the Cold War, committing acts of treason and sullying our name as a whole. And, yes, I've even heard whispers of these individuals being in some way connected to the JFK assassination. Now, if some clever researcher were to discover and expose their misdeeds, it could be a very ugly black eye for the Society, especially in light of those fears from our nation's early days.

"However, if that researcher were smart enough to see those individuals' actions as just that, and not on behalf of some great conspiracy to control the world or whatever . . ." He leaned forward with a collegial grin. "Especially if that discovery were made with the assistance of a Society researcher."

Chloe's eyes lit up. Jon's were more cautious, leery of such a fortuitous coincidence. But Molyneux could see the hope burning behind the wall of doubt.

"Will you help us?" Chloe asked, her voice just a notch away from desperation.

"Honestly, I was hoping we could help each other. We seem to be on a mutual quest, after all."

Jon wasn't as ecstatic about the prospect of their partnership. "See, here's the problem with that theory. Those lone wolves who weren't working with anyone somehow still have hired killers protecting their dirty little secret."

Molyneux feigned shock. "Killers?"

"You saw on the news about the fire at the National Archives? Or the explosion at that house in Dallas? We've been shot at in three states by the guy behind both of those. And for some reason, he doesn't want us to find out who killed Kennedy. He wasn't even alive when Kennedy was shot, so what reason would he have to cover it up if no organization was behind it?"

"Perhaps a son or grandson? Family legacy is a powerful motivator, as most members of this esteemed organization recognize."

He saw a shift in Chloe's expression. She and Jon knew the importance of family legacy. It was, after all, the whole reason they had embarked on this fool's errand.

"Besides," Molyneux continued, "I said that the Cincinnati was not behind any Cold War intrigue. But our ranks have included some of the most powerful men in the world over the years, from presidents like Washington and Reagan, to titans of industry like Rockefeller and du Pont, to generals, cabinet members, agency heads, members of Congress, and even foreign leaders like Winston Churchill. Just because our hands are clean in the matter doesn't mean that some other organization—the CIA or the FBI, perhaps—didn't ultimately have a role in the assassinations, and . . ."

He could see the gears turning in Jon's head, deciding whether or not to trust him. But Molyneux saw his eyes flicker at the mention of the FBI.

"All right," Jon said finally, eliciting a relieved exhalation from Chloe beside him. "We're in."

"Great," Molyneux said. "But we definitely need to keep this between the three of us for now. If some federal agency is covering their tracks, we don't want any word of our theories getting out before we've armed ourselves with the smoking gun. Their spies are everywhere."

He looked at his watch. 3:55 p.m. Perfect.

"The library is closing in five minutes, so we don't have much time." He screwed up his face, pretending to just now come up with a plan. "I have an idea about where to start, though."

"J. Edgar Hoover?" Chloe asked.

Molyneux beamed. And his smile was genuine.

*Bump, set, spike.* But he'd give them a little something extra to spin their wheels.

"You read my mind. But here's the thing. It's a little-known fact outside of the Society of the Cincinnati, but Hoover was obsessed with founding member Pierre L'Enfant. He felt that L'Enfant had disguised some hidden truth in one or several of his works, ones that would lead him to even greater power. If he is indeed our culprit, that could explain why the Cincinnati's name came up during your . . . friend's research."

Jon furrowed his brow, nodding slightly, as though something that hadn't made sense before finally did.

Molyneux adjusted some of the manuscripts on the table before him. "Let me see what I can dig up after hours in the archives here. You go get all the evidence you have, and we'll meet up tomorrow morning to see what we can discover together. How about 8:00 a.m. at the main entrance to the Library of Congress?"

Jon and Chloe agreed. Molyneux thanked them and again urged caution moving forward. After he showed them out, he breathed a sigh of relief. The trap was set, and the clock was ticking. And if there was one thing Jon and Chloe didn't have, it was the luxury of time.

The hair on the back of Molyneux's neck stood up. He spun around just in time to see a shadowy figure disappear through a darkened doorway at the end of the hall.

# CHAPTER 48
*Little Rock, Arkansas*

Rafael Vargas could already smell the salty surf of his new beachfront mansion. The cheering masses greeting him as he strolled down Paseo de los Proceros. He would be a millionaire several times over, and a national hero to boot. He just had to keep his nerves in check for the next twenty-four hours. And then, everything would change.

The honk of an angry motorist jarred him back to his present mission. Vargas waved in apology as he steered the rental van back into his own lane. Little Rock was a far cry from the Venezuelan coast of his daydreams, but it was a necessary step to make his dreams a reality.

It was crazy to think that he was so close to the final stage of his mission. Up to now, everything had been planning. It was easy to distance himself then. Everything was talk, research, training. Hypothetical. But now it was real. Now he had to find out what kind of man he really was.

Vargas was first approached at UC-Berkley, where he was working on his doctorate in chemical engineering. The man didn't give his name at first. Common enough for a spook, Vargas assumed. But his opening line intrigued him.

*Do you want to do your country a great service?*

"I'm Venezuelan," Vargas spat in reply. "*Not* American."

"As am I. Come, we have much to talk about."

Against his better judgment, Vargas followed him to an out-of-the-way Cuban café. The man bought them both coffee, and they took a seat at a booth at the far end of the room.

"Caracas has been following your political activities since you got to California," the man said.

At that, Vargas immediately regretted following this stranger here. He wanted to be anywhere but here. What did the Venezuelan government want with him?

"What do you mean?" was all he could muster in reply.

"You are a proud Venezuelan living in a hostile land. Yet you do not let yourself be intimidated by their hatred toward our homeland. You thrive on it, letting it spur you on to even greater things."

Vargas sat silently, confused and unsure what to say. He was the president and founder of the Students for a Stronger Venezuela and the Anti-Neocolonialism Student Coalition, both born out of a mildly popular bilingual blog he had been writing since his undergrad days at Universidad Central in Caracas.

"This is the greater thing your trials have prepared you for, Rafael. Let me ask you, do you love Venezuela as much as you say on social media, on your blogs, and at your rallies?"

"Even more," Vargas replied.

"And if you were given the opportunity to do your country a great service, one you would be handsomely rewarded for afterward, would you do it?"

"Without hesitation."

The man smiled and pulled out a badge. Vargas recognized it immediately.

The *Servicio Bolivariano de Inteligencia Nacional*. Venezuela's premier spy agency.

Vargas's father had been an agent, until eight years ago, when a bomb detonated by US-backed rebels blew up a hotel bar where he was enjoying a cocktail.

Vargas had never forgiven the Americans for their role in stealing away his father before his time. He had become radicalized at home, then taken that fervor with him into the heart of the beast.

Gifted in math and science, he wanted to use his natural abilities to help build Venezuela into a global powerhouse. For the time being, the United States had some of the best universities in the world, and to get the best training, he would have to go there. But even this wasn't antithetical to his ethos. How beautifully ironic that he would learn the secrets from his greatest enemy to educate himself and better his homeland. All the while, he would take full advantage of the freedoms enjoyed by Americans to share his message with a much broader and more international audience.

But, apparently, moving as far away from home as he did had helped to attract the attention of his government.

The man introduced himself as Pablo Arocha, officially a consular paper pusher out of LA, unofficially Venezuela's head spy in California. He had never known Vargas's father personally, but he had heard good things about him through friends of friends in the service.

And now, he was offering him an opportunity to act on his rage. To make a difference in the lives of all Venezuelans. To change the world for the better.

Vargas was fascinated as Arocha laid out his plan. It was audacious. Insanely audacious. But it could work. And if it did work, he would finally succeed in his dream.

Bringing America to its knees.

Over the next two months, Vargas pored over maps, charts, diagrams, and schematics. He traveled back home to Venezuela for special-ops training with the type of equipment that was illegal in virtually every nation on earth. And now, the time had come. He was ready. Or, at least, he was trained. He would find out if he was truly ready soon enough.

Vargas pulled into the Handy Dandy Self-Storage lot, punched a code into the keypad by the entrance, and drove through the gate. He backed up to the unit Arocha had specified and got out. The lot was empty, but he still looked around before unlocking the padlock and rolling up the door. You couldn't be too careful. Especially now.

Everything had to be perfect for the next twenty-four hours. If it was, he would be living the high life, celebrated across Venezuela for his heroism. If not, he'd be dead.

He stepped inside and let his eyes adjust to the dark space. Heavy blankets covered several boxes at the rear of the unit. Atop one of them, a sealed envelope bearing Vargas's name beckoned to him. He opened it and slid out its contents.

A burner cell phone, a pair of ID cards in a false name, and two keycards that would help him gain access for the attack.

He pocketed the items, and then pulled back the blankets on the boxes, one at a time.

There it was. Simple, but effective. Incredibly effective, considering tomorrow's target.

He felt a shiver of fear crawl down his spine, but something else crawl back up. Pride? Excitement?

Before, it was just talk. But now, he was taking possession of the weapon that he would use to change the world.

A new era was dawning. And this time, the soon-to-be-crippled United States of America would not be calling the shots.

# CHAPTER 49
## Washington, DC

Rush hour was just starting as Chloe and Jon exited the now-closed Anderson House. Chloe shook her head. That tour had been for nothing. If only they had headed straight to the library instead of wasting two hours touring the old mansion, they might have answers already. Instead, they had to cool their heels for sixteen hours, waiting for their morning meeting with Molyneux. But he had given them a clue. Maybe they could find something out themselves during that time. Maybe by 8:00 a.m. they'd have already found the proof they sought.

Jon had mentioned that J. Edgar Hoover was a member of the Society of the Cincinnati after they'd thrown Kellerman off their scent in Boston. But Molyneux's mention of lone wolf conspirators had changed how she looked at it all.

"I don't like it," Jon said.

"What, Dr. Molyneux?"

"Something about him unnerved me. But no, he's not the problem. His theory is."

"About J. Edgar?"

"About individual members striking out on their own with assassinations and other treasonous acts during the Cold War. Yes Hoover was both a member of the Cincinnati as well as the head of the FBI, and he certainly did plenty of salacious and illegal things during his tenure. But if Bobby Kennedy suspected Hoover, he would have fingered him directly, rather than the Society of the Cincinnati as a whole. Hoover certainly may have been a player, but I don't think it was just him, or even just the FBI. He was a known player with his own agenda. Yet Bobby focused on the Cincinnati."

"But what about the Pierre L'Enfant angle? Hoover himself may have been the one who dragged the Cincinnati's name into it. If he truly was obsessed with the work of one of the Society's founding members, couldn't that explain the connection?"

Jon didn't answer, appearing deep in thought, wrestling with some unspoken objection. Reaching the street, Chloe stared at the litany of century-old mansions repurposed into the modern Embassy Row. Directly across the street was the Embassy of India. Within a few minutes' walk in either direction along Massachusetts Avenue were the embassies of Greece, South Korea, Ireland, Romania, Indonesia, Spain, Chad, Great Britain, Sudan, Morocco, Italy, Sri Lanka, Kenya, Haiti, Mexico, Kyrgyzstan, Japan, Turkey, Belize, and countless other nations.

A little further down the street, Chloe knew, the former Iranian Embassy sat dormant as a testament to the failures of American foreign policy. In the '50s, the CIA had ousted a democratically elected leader in Iran and installed a puppet dictator, and it had worked for a couple of decades. Then the Islamic Revolution happened, and a year-long hostage crisis later, the United States had itself a new enemy.

"The Society's headquarters, right here amid all these foreign nations' American headquarters," Chloe observed aloud. "Almost as though they're their own geopolitical power."

"Or puppet master," Jon rejoined, walking toward the nearest Metro station.

"What are you thinking?"

"Dr. B's theory that the original conspiracy theory may have been true. That the Society of the Cincinnati really has been wielding some sort of power from the shadows."

"And killing President Kennedy somehow furthered their diabolical agenda?"

Jon shrugged. "I didn't say it was a *good* theory."

She smiled at him. Something about his sense of humor, his mind, his *energy* made her want to throw her arms around him and never let go. A line from the movie *Speed*, one of her favorites growing up, flashed into her mind. At the end of the action-packed flick, Keanu Reeves's character tells Sandra Bullock's that relationships based on intense experiences never work. And while they share their first kiss just moments later, sure enough, Keanu's character didn't make it into the sequel.

With all that was at stake right now, risking it all for some schoolgirl crush was the epitome of foolishness. And after turning her back on her father when he needed her the most, she was done being a fool.

"The Hoover angle has been explored to bits by JFK conspiracy theorists over the years," Jon said. "But Pierre L'Enfant is something new.

The man was a highly influential engineer and designer, but that's the problem. He was *too* influential."

"How so?"

"He was the creator of the L'Enfant Plan, for one."

"The design for DC? *That* L'Enfant?"

"The same."

The plan, Chloe knew, was the original layout for the capital city of the new nation. A few elements were changed before implementation, but most of downtown Washington still bore his fingerprints. From street layouts to park locations to the sites of the White House and the US Capitol building, the L'Enfant Plan was the blueprint from which the District of Columbia was built. Every once in a while, his name popped up in conspiracy lore because of one section of the plan where an arrangement of streets and parks formed what looked like four-fifths of an inverted pentagram. But his involvement with the Society of the Cincinnati rarely came up.

Which was strange since, as with the capital city itself, L'Enfant's fingerprints were all over the legacy and symbolism of the Society.

"He designed the Society eagle, the Society flag, even the artistry of the Society's original charter," Jon said. "He served on Washington's staff during the Revolutionary War, and was one of the founding members of the Cincinnati. But he outlived Washington by a quarter century. Like his fellow founding members, the Marquis de Lafayette and Baron von Steuben, L'Enfant was an aristocrat in his homeland, used to having influence on the political leaders of the day. If we combine Dr. Bixby's theory with Molyneux's, perhaps there could be something to this after all."

Jon had a point. But he was also right that L'Enfant's impact on the city was almost too big.

"So where do we start? He designed Washington, DC, but we'd need to find someplace more localized. A building or something."

"Well, there's L'Enfant Plaza, but that was just named in his honor in the twentieth century. Freedom Plaza is right on Pennsylvania Avenue and is full of L'Enfant symbols drawn from his plan for the capital city, but that's relatively new, too. I think he's buried in Arlington, but the cemetery wasn't founded until well after his death, so it's not his original burial site."

Chloe felt a hand grab her arm. Instinctively she swatted it away as she turned and backed up. A young Asian man wearing an open North

Face jacket with Beats headphones hanging around his neck held up his hands in defense.

"Sorry to startle you," he said, panting slightly. "I just had to catch up before you got on the train."

"I think you've got us confused with someone else," Jon said, stepping between them.

"Hey, man, I'm just the delivery guy." He handed an envelope to Jon and gave him a thumbs up. "Mission accomplished. I'm out, bro."

"What was that all about?" Chloe asked.

Jon held up the envelope. "Let's find out." He tore open the seal to reveal a single folded sheet of paper.

> Dear "Erik" and "Pauline,"
>
> I know what you're after, and I think I can help. Something big and awful is going to happen soon, and I need your help to stop it. Meet me at Jefferson Memorial tonight at midnight. I wish I could have spoken with you earlier, but their spies are everywhere and I think we're both being watched. Be careful, and come alone tonight. Don't trust the Frenchman.
>
> A friend

"'A friend'?" Chloe said once she finished reading.

Jon grunted. "'Don't trust the Frenchman.' Dr. Molyneux? Or Pierre L'Enfant?"

Chloe remembered the sense that she was being watched in Anderson House. Was that their mysterious "friend"? Or one of the spies the letter mentioned?

"What do we do?" she asked.

Jon shrugged. "We go."

"Seriously? We have no idea who this person is. It could be a trap."

"Of course it could be. But thus far, Kellerman has been much more brazen about his attacks. He could have had that guy deliver a mail bomb instead of a letter. Or just shoot us on the street or drag us into a building and kill us there. This strikes me as something different."

"'Something big and awful,'" Chloe read aloud.

Without further insight, the Pierre L'Enfant clue seemed like a dead end. Maybe Molyneux's research would be able to provide more context in the morning, but at least this was a way to potentially make some progress before dawn.

Or to potentially not live to see dawn.

"Look, if this letter is to be believed, time is not on our side," Jon said. "I don't want to be sitting on our thumbs until morning, and we need all the help we can get. We have a known physical place at a specific time, which is a whole lot more concrete than the complete life history and body of work of a famous designer from two centuries ago."

Chloe nodded. "Then we go."

It could be a trap. But they were running out of options.

# CHAPTER 50
## College Park, Maryland

tanton Gaines sifted through yet another box of Cold War documents. Nothing. Which was both good and bad.

They called it Archives II. The College Park facility of the National Archives was a modern building of glass and steel just a stone's throw from the University of Maryland. The environment was less urban and the architecture less classical than its DC counterpart, but the repository of firsthand artifacts and media was top-notch. Which was why Gaines himself had come.

He needed to be sure there were no more potential weaknesses. No forgotten or hidden documents that could implicate the Vanguard or the Cincinnati. Before yesterday, he was sure. Then Chloe Harper and Jon Rickner happened. And since then, everything had spiraled out of control.

It was time to stop the bleeding.

"Here's another one, Senator," said the junior archivist helping him, her arms laden with yet another box of documents.

He smiled and thanked her. She'd introduced herself as Jenny. She was pretty. Young, and probably new to the job. Maybe even a little starstruck at working alongside a high-ranking senator. This kind of access wasn't usually extended to outsiders, even if they were a sitting government official. He had Jenny's boss's boss's boss to thank for that.

Carolyn Rovetta was the first female Archivist of the United States, and Gaines had been instrumental in getting her there. He had called in a few favors to get her the support she needed to win the job. And, in return, he had unfettered access to the National Archives collection.

It was a move he and his group's inner leadership had decided was necessary. The 1992 JFK Records Act threatened to dump thousands of previously classified documents into the public sphere twenty-five years down the line. But Congress underestimated the power of the then-young Internet. Social media, fake news, and a truly World Wide Web were beyond the understanding of his counterparts more than two decades ago. People were more connected to their devices than they were to each other, and information traveled at the speed of light. What was it Mark Twain had said? *A lie can travel halfway around the world while the truth is putting on its shoes.* Unfortunately, a truth of the magnitude that Gaines and his forefathers had covered up could travel even faster.

So he helped groom Rovetta for the job, and when she became the nation's top archivist four years ago, he cashed in on the favor, sending his underlings to scour the collections for anything that could potentially expose them. In summer 2017, just months before the deadline Congress had set for the documents' release, Gaines's men completed their work, scrubbing all potentially problematic records from the Archives forever.

Apparently, they'd missed something.

His right jacket pocket buzzed. His main cell phone was in his left jacket pocket. Which meant this call was about Society business.

He excused himself and stepped into the hall, closing the door behind him.

"Tell me some good news."

"The professor spilled her beans," Kellerman said.

"Of course she did. What did you learn?"

"Bobby Kennedy all but identified us as the masterminds behind his brother's assassination."

Gaines felt the blood drain from his face. He measured his next words carefully.

"What, exactly, did Bobby leave behind?"

"Not much," Kellerman said. "A voice recording and a couple of sheets of paper. All addressed specifically to his brother, Ted."

Gaines knew Ted well. They had been colleagues in the Senate together for decades. Both Democrats, though the two hadn't seen eye to eye on as many subjects as the shared party would suggest. Still, if Ted Kennedy had known that Gaines represented the men who were behind both of his brothers' assassinations, he had never shown it. Chappaquiddick had brought him to heel, but even that wouldn't have been able to quell his fury at shaking hands and sitting on committees with the leader of the group that had murdered his brothers.

"He never got the messages, did he?"

"Ted?" Kellerman asked. "No. He never even knew they existed. They were found in what Jon and Chloe believed to be Bobby's original hiding places."

"You said their discoveries all but implicated us."

"The Society seal was with his letter to Ted. He doesn't mention the Society or the Vanguard by name in the letter, probably because he wasn't sure exactly how the Cincinnati fit into what he had discovered. But he did fear his own death at the Vanguard's hands, which was why he hid this stuff in the first place. There's good news, though. He planned to copy the evidence once his investigation was complete and hide it in Boston with the letter. But there wasn't anything there."

"He died before he could copy it," Gaines said, at last seeing the silver lining.

"Which means that the purges we did in '68 got it all."

That seemed to be the case once more. The night Bobby Kennedy was in California, being shot by the Vanguard's latest patsy, two teams of blackmailed FBI agents raided the senator's home in New York and office in Washington, taking with them boxes of research that were eventually given to Gaines's father, Bradley. The elder Gaines carefully read through each document, and once he was satisfied that the threat had died with Bobby Kennedy, he hid them away. A fascinating and turbulent chapter in the Vanguard's history had come to a close, and, as they had for nearly two centuries by that point, they maintained their commitment to preserving the memory of their exploits.

In retrospect, it seemed Bradley Gaines's closing the book on Bobby Kennedy was a little premature. But now that the final pieces of his research had been unveiled, and revealed to be insubstantial, Stanton Gaines found himself puzzled.

If Bobby Kennedy's trail was at an end, what on earth were Jon and Chloe doing in Washington?

"Get to DC as fast as you can," Gaines told Kellerman. "I have a feeling we'll be needing all hands on deck shortly."

Kellerman assented and hung up. Gaines checked his watch. He had time. Not much, but it'd have to do.

He was eager to get back to sifting through the documents, but he felt relieved knowing that Chloe Harper's big discovery was a dead end. But first, he had a phone call to make.

Jon and Chloe had threatened their plans long enough. It was time to find out what kind of soldier Patrick Molyneux really was.

# CHAPTER 51
## Washington, DC

It was a curious choice of setting for a secret meeting. Jon stood at the water's edge, watching the moon play across the light waves in the Tidal Basin. Behind him, Chloe stared up at the neoclassical dome of the Jefferson Memorial.

Waiting.

Jon checked his watch. 11:54. He started climbing the wide marble stairs to the dome. They were early. But he didn't want to miss their mysterious "friend" and what he or she might have to share.

Unlike the Lincoln Memorial, which stood opposite the Washington Monument across the oft-photographed reflecting pool, the Jefferson Memorial was set apart from the cluster of museums, government buildings, and monuments that was the National Mall. Abraham Lincoln hadn't even been born when Pierre L'Enfant designed the federal city, but his monument still managed to find a place in the heart of those plans. Thomas Jefferson, meanwhile, was exiled to the far reaches of the city, perched on a placid peninsula surrounded by wooded parkland and waterfront views.

Jon reached the top of the stairs and stepped into the hallowed space of the memorial itself. The walls were etched with the timeless words of the Enlightenment-era thinker, a towering bronze statue of whom stood atop a pedestal at the center of the pavilion. Overhead, the domed roof terminated in an open oculus to the starry sky, evoking comparisons to the ancient Pantheon in Rome.

Jon found the setting fitting. A lover of learning and nature, Jefferson would have appreciated the more contemplative site for his memorial. He likely would have hated the modern political powermongers that had arisen in Washington, the lobbyist culture, the overreaching government that, in many ways, made the tyranny of King George look tame by comparison.

But, if Jon's most recent working theory was true, Jefferson also would have hated that his fears had come true. The Society of the Cincinnati had become the powerful secret aristocracy he had warned against from the onset, even going so far as to kill a sitting president. Jefferson had been against the Cincinnati from the onset, adamant that their hereditary and secretive nature, coupled with its founders' conflicts with Congress and cherished role in winning the American Revolution, would inevitably lead to their desire to wield power themselves, if not overtly, then from the shadows.

Apparently, Jefferson was right.

"Someone's coming," Chloe said, stepping back from the moonlight and into the shadows.

A long-haired figure in a dark sweat suit approached by a footpath alongside the Tidal Basin. A late-night power walker? Or their expected guest?

The figure hesitated at the base of the monument, looking around to see if anyone had followed. In the moonlight, Jon was able to see her face. Late forties, a pleasant face aged by worry.

The woman started climbing the steps. Chloe began to step out to meet her, but Jon caught her arm. She turned to face him, a question on her face.

"We don't know if she's being watched," Jon said by way of reply. "Let's stay in the shadows here and let her come to us."

Chloe nodded and stepped back with Jon. Thirty seconds later, their visitor arrived atop the monument.

"Erik?" she called in a stage whisper. "Pauline?"

"We're here," Jon said, remaining in shadow. "Who are you?"

"You can call me Isabel. I'm sorry, but I'm new to this whole cloak-and-dagger bit. But I'm here to help you."

Chloe stepped forward. "Why do you think you can help us? Help us with what?"

"You want the truth about Kennedy, right?"

Jon felt a lump in his throat. They were the words he had been expecting, but now it was real. The secret note from the Asian delivery guy wasn't a fluke. It was either a step toward the answers they sought or a dive over the precipice.

Or both.

"We do," Jon said.

"Well, you should start by knowing that this didn't start with Jack Kennedy. Or end with Bobby."

"Pierre L'Enfant?" Chloe hazarded.

"What about him?"

Chloe looked confused in the shadowed moonlight. Jon was, too, but he remained silent to let their mysterious host fill in the blanks.

"L'Enfant didn't have anything to do with the Vanguard."

"What is the Vanguard?"

The woman sighed deeply. "Y'all really don't know much yet, do you? Well, I'll make this quick."

Jon's ears perked up. Finally, some answers.

"The Vanguard is the shadow side to the Society of the Cincinnati. All of the Society's earliest detractors' deepest fears come true, and then some. As legend tells it, they felt that, since they had given their lives and livelihoods to create the nation, they and their descendants deserved to be justly compensated by the nation that owed its existence to their sacrifice."

"The sixth part of the Society's charter," Jon said.

"Exactly. Even though Congress reneged multiple times on their promises to pay the Continental Army officers before finally agreeing to a half measure significantly less than their prior offers, the Society of the Cincinnati as a whole considered that debt paid in full. The Vanguard, it seems, feels differently.

"Aaron Burr is considered the spiritual father of the group. In 1804, while still serving as vice president of the United States, Burr killed Alexander Hamilton, then president-general of the Society, in a duel. Publicly, it was the inevitable conclusion to a long and bitter rivalry between the two men. Burr had ousted Hamilton's father-in-law from his Senate seat, and then Hamilton's support for Morgan Lewis in the New York gubernatorial race led to Burr's defeat. Society records, however, show that the rift was less about political feuding and more about divergent beliefs in the role the Society should play in determining the future of America.

"After the duel, Burr lost his position as vice president and much of his direct influence in the Society. Burr traveled west and began drumming up support for a treasonous plot to create an autonomous nation in what is today the Midwest. In 1807, he would be arrested and eventually acquitted of the charges, but his most lasting legacy was the wave of secret support for Burr's beliefs within the Society. Those who felt the larger Society of the Cincinnati wasn't doing enough to fulfill the sixth purpose of the charter—with steadily mounting interest."

"The Vanguard," Chloe said.

"Exactly. But it wouldn't be until the final days of the Civil War that the Vanguard finally coalesced into its current form. A secret society within a secret society."

"What happened to cause that shift?" Chloe asked.

"The nation was finally about to be reunited, but, as Reconstruction showed us, it wasn't an easy path back to one nation. When the South seceded, it took away the bulk of the nation's agriculture. Food, textiles, the raw materials that were not only processed in northern factories and consumed by the American populace, but also some of the key goods in the country's international trade. Tobacco, sugar cane, cotton, dozens of cash crops that simply weren't as tenable in the colder, shorter growing seasons of the north."

Acid began crawling up Jon's throat as his mind lit upon a theory. It was impossible. At least, it would have been until a few days ago.

"In the mid-1800s, agriculture was the backbone of the economy. A United States without the South would have been weak, and thus unable to provide the Vanguard their due. Plus, the membership would have been split, as several of the Cincinnati's chapters were in Confederate states. The only way to seal the deal and prevent the breakout of another treasury-draining conflict was treasonous, but, to their minds, necessary for their goals. They felt the nation needed a martyr to mourn together, a common villain to hate, and a new Southern-based leader to rally behind."

He looked at Chloe to see if she comprehended what the woman seemed to be saying. The shock and fear in her eyes told her she did. And, seconds later, the mysterious woman confirmed it.

"So, at a secret meeting in a Philadelphia mansion in early 1865," she said, "the Vanguard finally acted on their treasonous ambitions and plotted the assassination of Abraham Lincoln."

# CHAPTER 52
## *Washington, DC*

"So they killed Lincoln *and* they killed Kennedy?" Jon asked.

"If rumors are to be believed, yes," Isabel said. "And I understand you have additional reason to believe the latter assassination to be their handiwork."

Jon shook his head in disbelief. He had heard the long string of coincidences between the two men's assassinations that had begun to circulate not long after Kennedy's death. Lincoln was first elected to Congress in 1846, Kennedy in 1946. Lincoln was first elected to the presidency in 1860, Kennedy in 1960. They were both president during turbulent periods dealing with civil rights. They were both succeeded by men named Johnson. Both of their assassins were killed before they could stand trial. And so on. As a whole, it was interesting and perhaps a bit eerie, but nothing more. Coincidences happen.

This was on a whole other level.

"But why?" Chloe asked. "What could they have gained by killing Kennedy? There was no threat to the American economy then."

Isabel smiled grimly. "By that point, the Vanguard had long moved past surviving. Their greed had grown in the decades since Lincoln's murder, and they found other, more direct methods of securing their due."

It clicked. "The military-industrial complex," Jon said.

Isabel nodded. "The Vanguard doesn't make up the whole of the military-industrial complex, of course. But they represent a solid core of the unholy alliance. And they have their fingers in enough pies to make sure they continue getting their ancestors' long-due payments."

"Like what?" Chloe asked. "False flag operations?"

"Dozens of them. To be sure, some wars were legitimate conflicts that simply doubled to suit the Vanguard's needs. But others were concocted out of whole cloth, duping the nation into war to unite them in whatever way possible."

"The Indian Wars of the 1870s were launched under Society member Ulysses S. Grant," Jon leapt in. "The Spanish-American War was launched by William McKinley, the Philippine-American War by Teddy Roosevelt, World War I by Woodrow Wilson, World War II by FDR, the Korean War by Truman. All Society members. All successful distractions from troubles at home."

"Virtually every president from Reconstruction through the first decade of the Cold War was a member of the Society of the Cincinnati. Most of them were honorary members, granted membership because of their contributions in military or public service. But it's the one who broke the trend that makes things really interesting."

"Eisenhower," Chloe guessed as the puzzle began to take shape.

Isabel nodded. "Dwight D. Eisenhower was the first top-ranking general since Ulysses S. Grant to become Commander-in-Chief. But when he ascended to the Oval Office, one of his first acts was to get the United States out of the Korean War. Sure, thousands of American troops are still stationed in South Korea and in the DMZ even to this day, but the ongoing conflict was no longer on anyone's mind. And despite an array of nations falling to Communist hands across Eastern Europe, Asia, and even Latin America on his watch, no more major wars were launched during his tenure."

"And then, his farewell address."

"Exactly. As a final parting salvo against the Vanguard's influence in foreign affairs, Eisenhower warned against the pernicious influence of what he called the 'military-industrial complex.' In the decades since, pundits have taken that to be an admonition against defense contractors and war profiteers who grow fat off America's military conflicts. But, in truth, he was warning us against the group behind the curtain, whose members undoubtedly have a hand in some of those contractors but whose motives are far more deep-seated than simple greed."

Jon tried his hand at extrapolating this into existing conspiracy lore. "So Kennedy stood in the way of the Vanguard's plan for a war with Cuba by hamstringing the air support for the Bay of Pigs invasion. And then again with launching a full-on war in Vietnam. He pushed back and dragged his heels until they had finally had enough."

"Marilyn Monroe was a warning . . ." Chloe said, absentmindedly, her eyes glazing over as the enormity of their enemy began to take shape.

She had a point. There were plenty of theories that whoever killed JFK killed his longtime mistress to show how serious they were—and how powerful.

"But he didn't take the hint," she continued, "so they killed him and got someone who would."

Isabel nodded in somber resignation. "On November 24, 1963, before Kennedy was even in the ground, President Johnson pledged to join 'the battle against communism' with 'strength and determination.' But the nation was not prepared to commit another generation of its youth to another war in Asia, the third in as many decades. So the Vanguard and their puppets needed to present a clear and compelling reason why the Vietnamese were our enemies."

"The Gulf of Tonkin Incident," Chloe said. The word "incident" was a bit of a euphemism, as it described an attack against the USS *Maddox* in August 1964 by three North Vietnamese torpedo boats while patrolling the eponymous body of water. The *Maddox* was damaged by a single bullet hole and no American sailors were harmed, but the event, which saw the death of four North Vietnamese sailors and the wounding of six more, was all the cause Congress needed to pass the Gulf of Tonkin Resolution, essentially freeing Johnson's hands to command the military into any Asian nation suffering from "Communist aggression."

"Almost from the onset, detractors called the incident a false flag attack," Jon agreed. "Certainly it wasn't serious enough to warrant a full-on war. But Johnson was cleared to combat the forces of communism in yet another Cold War proxy battle with the Soviet Union—the very same Soviet Union to whom Lee Harvey Oswald had supposedly pledged his undying support."

"Only this time," Isabel said, "the Vanguard's plans backfired. The Vietnam War was ugly on both sides, and it was televised. The worst parts of what our military was doing ended up on the covers of magazines and on the nightly news. Not good PR for the Vanguard's war machine. Nixon ran on a platform of getting us out of Vietnam, but once he was in the Oval Office, Vanguard representatives made it clear how that was not an option. Eventually, they would see that the Vietnam War had become a drag on the nation overall. They greenlit a phased tactical withdrawal, a big deal since it would result in a rare defeat for the American military. Of course, by the time Nixon was finished getting America out of Vietnam, his star—and, by association, the star of his successor, Gerald Ford—had crashed to earth, giving the anti-Washington crowd a new bone to pick.

"Which is why the Vanguard tapped a likeable, down-to-earth Washington outsider—a God-fearing peanut farmer of all things!—to follow Ford into the White House. Then, when his brand of leadership proved unfit for the global challenges the United States was facing in Iran, Latin America, and the Soviet Union, they tapped a different Washington outsider, this one already famous for a different type of leadership, to helm the nation. Ronald Reagan was the first US president to be granted an honorary Society membership in a generation, and it's clear why. The 1980s were an era dominated by the final confrontations of the United States and the Soviet Union, and, despite a number of crises at home, most of the public's attention stayed focused on a resurgent Moscow until we finally emerged victorious. Lots of money was poured into American defense during the Soviet Union's last hurrah, and the Vanguard made a killing. Then George H. W. Bush presided over the final collapse of the USSR and took us to war in Desert Storm, and he is, to date, the last US president to be made an honorary member of the Society."

"So the Vanguard is done getting us into wars?" Chloe asked.

"No more than they were during the '60s and '70s. They're just keeping more of a low profile now."

"The Internet," Jon said.

"Bingo. Nowadays, all world news stories are available 24/7 in the hands and pockets of every American. Conferring an honorary membership in a centuries-old secret society upon a sitting president now would draw a lot more attention than it did before the digital age."

"So how do we stop them?" Chloe asked. "If they've been subverting foreign policy for more than two centuries, killing presidents, attacking American ships, starting wars, and bending the most powerful men in the world to their whim, what on earth can *we* do?"

"As you probably know, the Society of the Cincinnati considers itself one of the premier keepers of historical records in the country. Primarily, they have gathered the most extensive private collection of firsthand documents and artifacts from the Revolutionary War, which, of course, was where their members were most active as a unit. Their collections are to memorialize their work on behalf of the country. It stands to reason that, being a part of the larger Society, the Vanguard would also keep records of their work."

"They'd really preserve documents that would prove their treason?" Jon asked. "Murdering Kennedy and Lincoln, starting the Vietnam War and God knows whatever other conflicts?"

Isabel looked thoughtful. "Maybe. Maybe not. But there is one document I know exists."

"About the Kennedy assassination?" Chloe asked.

Isabel chuckled. "Not quite."

"What then?"

"There's another reason I came to you. Something urgent.

"I work at Anderson House as a tour guide, and, as you can probably surmise, I was following you during your tour with Erica. I know of your interest in the Cincinnati's darker side, and it's rearing its head again."

"What do you mean?" Jon asked, hoping she'd loop back around to the document she mentioned moments ago.

"My husband is a member of the Society of the Cincinnati. Proud member, like his father, and his grandfather, and . . . Well, you know how it works. The other night he came home from a Society gathering, furious. He wouldn't tell me what about, but after a few glasses of scotch loosened his tongue, I found out why."

"Why?" Chloe asked.

"They're doing it again. The Vanguard. Planning another attack of some sort. Another false flag impetus for another war."

"When? Where?" Jon asked.

"No idea where. But soon. Tomorrow, the next day, I don't know for sure. Imminent was the word he used. Imminent and unstoppable."

Which meant the pieces were already in play. And no one outside of the circle had any idea of the target, the timing, or the type of attack. Which usually meant people were going to die.

"Why are you coming to us with this?" he asked.

The woman smiled. "Because I know who you are, Jonathan Rickner."

Jon staggered back as though hit. "How?"

"I'm a historian. My husband is the eighth-generation member of a society that predates America itself. After what you did in New York, how it rewrote the history books, how could I not know who you were? Don't worry, your secret's safe with me, 'Erik.' But when I saw you walk into Anderson House today, I knew it was a sign."

"A sign?" Jon said, fighting to temper the skepticism in his voice.

"Molyneux, the archivist with the vaguely French accent, just showed up yesterday. I don't trust him. Didn't before, and definitely didn't after you showed up. I think he's a plant."

Jon raised an eyebrow. "Why do you think that?"

"Call it a hunch. He starts working in the archives right before you show up asking about the Society's role in the Kennedy assassinations? Right before this attack is supposed to be happening?"

He didn't know what to think about that. Had Molyneux been playing them? If so, to what end? Or was this woman simply seeing ghosts where there were none? Or, worse, was she herself an operative in league with Kellerman, trying to manipulate them away from the truth?

"So how can you help us?" Chloe asked.

"Anderson House has a secret," the woman said. "If legend is to be believed."

"What secret?" Jon asked.

"In the Key Room, you saw the portrait of Larz Anderson's great-grandfather, Richard Clough Anderson?"

"The Fort Sumter guy or the Revolutionary War guy?"

"Revolutionary War. Society legend holds that George Washington was worried that the Society of the Cincinnati would be taken over by the very forces that the Continental Congress had warned against. Men like Aaron Burr and the founders of the Vanguard."

"Interesting," he said. "But how is that supposed to help us?"

"He supposedly committed those fears to parchment. Detailed who he thought was suspect, the dangers of what they might do, and even, apparently, rumored plans for a breakaway sect—along with the location of that sect's headquarters."

That got Jon's attention.

"And these papers are somewhere in the Society's archives?"

The woman frowned. "Sadly, no. Apparently he sent them out of the country."

"Out of the country?" Chloe asked. "Why would he do that?"

"Because his friend and fellow Cincinnatus was removed from the plague that was creeping into the American chapters of the Society. The French chapter had already been abolished, its members murdered and scattered to the wind. No chance of a Vanguard-like takeover threat there. So he sent his papers about the nascent proto-Vanguard to Gilbert du Motier, the Marquis de Lafayette, at his estate in France."

It made sense. And Lafayette was one of the few leading Cincinnati who even Thomas Jefferson trusted. In fact, the two men had coauthored the Declaration of the Rights of Man and of the Citizen, perhaps the most fundamental document of the French Revolution. Jefferson was the US Minister to France during the build-up to the revolution, so the men's closeness was not unexpected. But this twist did present a new problem.

"So the papers are in France now?" Jon said, feeling defeated. If a terror attack was imminent, a trip across the Atlantic would eat into time they didn't have. But, even worse, the Vanguard was wise to their aliases now, making air travel a non-starter.

"Not according to the legend. After the storming of the Bastille during the French Revolution, the Marquis de Lafayette sent George Washington the key to the infamous prison, saying that this symbol of French freedom was a testament to the ideals of liberty triumphing over tyranny that the American president had helped to become reality. Washington responded in kind and included a key with his so-called Lafayette Confession, along with instructions for his friend to follow after his death."

"What did those instructions say?" Chloe asked.

"We don't know for sure. But apparently after he had followed them, Lafayette entrusted the key to another American Cincinnatus, believing that if a conspiracy took hold of the American chapter of the Society, the noble members within their ranks should be the ones to bring it down."

"Who?" Jon asked. "Alexander Hamilton? Henry Knox?"

"None other than Lafayette's own aide-de-camp. Richard Clough Anderson."

"How do you know this isn't just some urban legend, spun out of two hundred years of superstition and boys' club drinks?"

"Because I've seen a picture of it. A young Larz Anderson, long before Anderson House was built, holding the key during his brief tenure in the Army. Legend says he hid it in the house sometime before he opened it to the public in 1905. But it's never been found."

"What does it open?" Chloe asked. A very good question Jon was ashamed he hadn't thought of first.

The woman shrugged. "I don't know exactly. But wherever it is, it may hold the answers you seek."

The origins of the Vanguard. And, perhaps, the way to bring them down.

"So how are we supposed to even search for it?" Jon asked. "They don't let tourists go wandering about in Anderson House during the day. And I doubt they take kindly to breaking and entering."

At that, the woman smiled. She reached into her sweatpants pocket and pulled out a set of modern keys.

"Who said you have to break in?"

# CHAPTER 53
*Washington, DC*

Chloe was still processing what the woman had told them back at the Jefferson Memorial as she and Jon walked north past the endless columns of the Bureau of Printing and Engraving's western entrance.

"Do you think she's for real?" Chloe asked.

"It sounds too outlandish for her to make up. So, at the very least, I think she believes in the legend."

"It smells like a trap to me."

"Still?" Jon asked. "Why?"

"Sure, they didn't kill us at the Memorial, because that would be too public, raise too many questions. But on their own turf, when we're breaking into the Society's headquarters in the dead of night?"

"True. But if she just wanted to get us in the house so they could kill us, why go to all the trouble of the convoluted story? Why not just give us another key and tell us the proof of the Vanguard's orchestrating the Kennedy assassination is hidden in one particular room? Then they'd know exactly where we'd be going in the house. Plus, the clearer directions would ensure we'd go straight there instead of making a detour somewhere to investigate Lafayette or Anderson's history."

Even with the present ruse, if that was what it was, they were not making a detour. At this late hour, public transportation within the city was closed for the night. Unlike many US cities of its size and import, Washington was not a nighttime city, with many of its businesses closed by seven, and even its shopping and restaurant districts typically shuttering by nine. So the demand simply wasn't there for late-night subway service. Taxis and ride-sharing services left witnesses and a digital paper trail. So they were hoofing it back to Embassy Row.

"Probably to sell it to us better," Chloe said. "If the answers came too easily, we wouldn't trust them. If the need was so great and the proof was just sitting there behind a door to which she just happened to have the key, we'd wonder why she hadn't exposed them herself."

Even as she argued her points, she could hear how hollow her arguments were beginning to sound. But in her experience, paranoia wasn't always irrational. The past year had taught her the dangers of trusting the wrong person. Too many people she cared about had died. That lesson was even more pronounced in the past twenty-four hours with their betrayal by and the subsequent murder of Vance Nicholson.

"The same could be said for Dr. Molyneux," Jon argued. "He was cagey when we first mentioned the Kennedy connection, and only when we pushed did he open up. Like he wanted it to be our idea."

"He was scared. Talking about the Kennedy assassinations in the Society's headquarters is not a pleasant experience, I'm sure."

She wasn't sure why she continued to play devil's advocate for Molyneux. In truth, she didn't trust him further than she could throw him, but the circle of people who were not out to get her was shrinking by the hour, and, increasingly irrational though it seemed, some part of her needed the bookish young researcher not to be in league with the murderous Kellerman.

They reached the Mall, and Chloe welcomed the distraction. She marveled at the long expanse of parkland, dotted with monuments and memorials to men and women who either helped define what America meant, or laid down their lives to preserve it. Turning west toward the Washington Monument, she stared up at the towering obelisk. Upon its completion in 1888, it was the tallest manmade structure in the world, a 555-foot spire stabbing into the night sky. The very next year, the opening of the Eiffel Tower bumped the monument down to second place. Unlike many memorials to great Americans throughout the city, Washington's was not dominated by the image of the man for whom it was named. In fact, other than his timeless words inscribed upon and within the obelisk, George was curiously absent from the edifice.

It was not originally designed to be so. Architect Robert Mills's original 1836 plans for the Washington Monument were much more grandiose, with the obelisk at the center of a massive neoclassical temple filled with statues of dozens of Revolutionary War heroes as well as the signers of the Declaration of Independence. And foremost among those statues would be Washington himself, at the helm of a six-horse chariot, surveying the federal city from atop the colonnaded temple's portico. Initial estimates for the proposed structure were prohibitively expensive, exceeding half a billion dollars in today's currency. So the temple was scrapped, while the construction moved forward with the obelisk, which, half a century and plenty of controversy later, would become one of the most iconic structures in the nation's capital, and, eventually, the world.

"We've got L'Enfant on one side, and Lafayette on the other," Jon said as they circumnavigated the hilltop monument. "Dr. Molyneux's claim that 'their spies are everywhere' and Isabel's warning not to trust the Frenchman. Either Molyneux's working with Kellerman, or Isabel is. With time increasingly at a premium, I'm going to take my chances on Isabel's theory tonight. If we're wrong and we survive whatever trap she has planned, we can still catch up with Molyneux after dawn. Though you're welcome to go back to the hotel to catch a few winks if you'd rather."

"Not on your life," she countered. "My dad started this quest, and I dragged you into it. If you think I'm going to bail now that things are getting interesting, I've got a bridge to sell you."

Jon grinned at her. "What, you didn't find Bobby Kennedy's codes and hidden messages interesting?"

"Meh. It was okay, I guess." She slow-shoved his shoulder, a playful gesture she regretted almost as soon as she'd done it. Then she caught a look in his eyes. It was fleeting, but for a brief moment he let down his guard. She was glad she had acted on her impulse after all. She smiled contentedly to herself as she turned away, happy to feel his gaze still lingering on her.

The Washington Monument marked the midpoint of the National Mall. Now on the western side, she could see the Lincoln Memorial at the end of its long reflecting pool. She couldn't make out details from this distance, but she had visited the site before. Another secular temple, like Jefferson's, but this one exuding more power and sorrow. The martyred president sitting in massive stone effigy, frozen in eternal contemplation atop his throne-like chair. But what struck Chloe now was not the beauty of the site nor the majesty of its construction.

It was what the marble president was forced to look at in perpetuity.

The expanse between the Lincoln Memorial and the Washington Monument was primarily divided into two purposes. The Lincoln Reflecting Pool, the grassy fields, and the pedestrian-friendly wooded paths along the periphery offered natural beauty to visitors. But the area was also home to three massive memorials for three deadly conflicts.

The World War II Memorial, with state-by-state representations of America's sacrifices, terraced walkways, and a gorgeous fountain, hugged the base of the Washington Monument's central hill. The Korean War Monument, at the southwest of the plaza, was haunted by stainless steel soldiers buried knee-deep in juniper bushes and featured a sand-blasted mural rife with symbolism. But it was the memorial directly in Chloe and Jon's path toward Anderson House that resonated the most strongly.

The Vietnam War Memorial.

A massive black granite wall, known simply as "The Wall," stretched along the somber site. Etched into the wall were the names of more than 58,000 Americans killed in the Vietnam War. Several years ago, Chloe had accompanied her college roommate Nan on a pilgrimage to the site. Nan's grandfather had perished in the Tet Offensive in 1967, and once she found his name on the wall, Nan used a pencil and paper to get a rubbing of his name from the memorial. At the time, Chloe had been moved by the gesture, accompanied by dozens of others making rubbings of their own lost loved ones' names. Though she hadn't been alive during Vietnam, it now seemed like such a pointless, horrible war. America had lost not only the war, but also much of the international good will it had built up post-World War II. Television made the horrors of Agent Orange, carpet bombing, revenge-fueled slaughters of civilian villages, and a host of other wartime atrocities much more accessible to an angry populace at home. Not only that, but millions of soldiers who were drafted against their will had survived the bloody conflict only to have hippies and peaceniks spit and curse at them when they finally arrived home. An ugly chapter all around, but one she thought, until recently, that America had fought because of an ill-placed but well-intentioned fear of the Domino Theory of global communism.

She now knew differently.

Nan's grandfather and tens of thousands more, not to mention the millions of Vietnamese, Cambodians, and Laotians killed on both sides of the escalating conflict, dead because of the Vanguard's twisted aims.

And they were about to do it again.

No, she was definitely not sitting this one out.

Jon pulled his phone from his pocket.

"What are you doing?" she asked.

"Calling Dr. Bixby. See if she has any insight into Lafayette or Richard Clough Anderson."

He put his phone to his ear, listening. After a moment, he made a face, tapped at his phone, and put it back to his ear.

"No answer?" she asked.

"Going straight to voicemail."

"It is one in the morning."

"Yeah, but it should at least ring."

"Unless she's got it on some do-not-disturb setting to keep eager former students from waking her up in the middle of the night," Chloe said with a smirk.

"*Touché.*"

They reached Constitution Avenue on the north side of the Mall and headed up 21st Street.

"How much farther?"

"Just the other side of George Washington University," Jon said, pointing ahead. "Maybe another mile and a half?"

"Good. My feet are getting tired."

"Miles to go before we sleep, my dear. Miles to go before we sleep."

Chloe grinned in the darkness at his slip. *My dear.* Maybe there was something there after all. But whether they lived to find out would be another story.

# CHAPTER 54
*Washington, DC*

Amanda Taylor, recently known as "Isabel," simultaneously felt as though a weight had been lifted from her shoulders and that a target was freshly painted on her back. The Vanguard was not a group to be crossed lightly. But her husband's concerns about recent activities had forced her to act.

They were going to attack our own people yet again. Another terror attack, another false flag operation. Whatever it took to secure their twisted agenda.

If they found out, they would come for her. Maybe even for her husband. Her children were likely safe, since the Vanguard usually just punished the perpetrators unless they wanted leverage. But she had no leverage to give.

She had wrestled with what it would mean to turn actively on the Vanguard. To rat them out to an outsider. She thought of going to the FBI, Homeland Security, even Metro PD. But anyone who might be able to prevent whatever was coming would not believe her crazy-sounding tale. And all she had to offer as evidence was the word of her husband, who would himself be upset at her airing the Society's dirty laundry.

Then Jon Rickner came through the doors of Anderson House. She saw her solution.

She prayed her faith in him hadn't been ill placed.

While he and his female companion headed northeast after leaving the Jefferson Memorial, Amanda headed west along the Tidal Basin Loop Trail. She crossed the Inlet Bridge, which spanned the channel that allowed the tidal waters of the Potomac to fill the nineteenth-century man-made pond, and continued to trace the edge of the Tidal Basin. The city's famous cherry blossom trees were planted all along the path.

The area's first cherry blossom trees had been planted further down the trail more than a century before in a ceremony between First Lady Helen Herron Taft and the wife of the ambassador from Japan. As the trees' springtime explosion of color grew in popularity, more trees were planted and the path Amanda walked was plotted, all with an eye toward observing Japanese customs for ideal viewing of the trees. The path also boasted several of the city's most memorable memorials, including ones to Jefferson, Franklin Delano Roosevelt, and Martin Luther King, Jr. She loved walking the loop trail, a beautiful commingling of nature and history that both stirred and quietened her spirit.

In the early springtime, the entire loop exploded with cherry blossoms, a magical event that transformed simple trees into otherworldly pink clouds. Now, though, the iconic blooms had withered and fallen to the earth, blown away to parts unknown. In their stead, craggy branches loomed overhead, clawing at the moonlit night.

Amanda shivered as a cold breeze blew off the pond's waters, swaying the skeletal branches like grasping hands. She wasn't given to irrational fears. But she was ready to get back to her car, her home, and her bed.

After crossing the Vanguard, even her worst nightmares no longer felt irrational.

≈≈≈≈≈

Moonlight was Molyneux's best friend and worst enemy tonight as he strode silently along the Tidal Basin Loop Trail. He didn't know who Amanda had just met with, but he had a pretty good guess. She was married to a Society officer who was a vocal opponent of the Vanguard's plans. A potential source of the leaks on Operation Broken Serpent. He would report that to Senator Gaines once he finished here.

It was intoxicating, this sense of power. Amanda had haunted his movements in Anderson House, and, presumably, those of Jon and Chloe. But now Molyneux had the upper hand. He could stalk her with impunity, choosing his moment to strike.

He couldn't wait too long, though. God only knew what Jon and Chloe were doing now. And with the Vanguard's plans set to go into motion the next day, he didn't have time to waste.

The wooded path along the Tidal Basin's shore was empty, save for the presence of a few transients sleeping under tattered blankets. The shade of a cherry blossom tree hanging over the path shielded her position from the moon's glare. Molyneux surveyed the area one last time and made his move.

Quickening his stealthy approach into a run, he tackled Amanda from behind, knocking the wind out of her as they fell to the ground as one. She tried to scream, but Molyneux clapped his hand around her mouth and muffled her cries. He flipped her over, straddling her and pinning her arms with his legs.

A shock of recognition jolted through her face as she saw him. And then she saw the knife, glinting in the pale moonlight reflecting off the nearby water.

"This is very simple, Amanda," Molyneux said in what he hoped was a threatening whisper. "You tell me everything you just told Chloe Harper and Jon Rickner, and I do mean everything, and you'll live to see your husband tonight."

Her eyes flashed with even greater fear at the mention of Jon's name. Clearly, Molyneux's theory had been spot on.

Amanda thrashed underneath him, twisting her head about to find some sort of savior, a fellow late-night walker who could come to her rescue.

Keeping one hand over her mouth, he slapped her face with his other. And then again. And again. For the first four or five slaps, his violence spurred her toward greater effort to escape. But when she realized that help was not on its way and that she could not overpower him, her struggles weakened after each successive impact. When she had finally calmed down, shuddering and whimpering on the cold concrete, Molyneux spoke again.

"One chance. You scream, you'll be dead before your voice reaches the water. Understand?"

Amanda nodded tremblingly, and Molyneux withdrew his hand from her mouth.

"I just told them that I thought Larz Anderson might have hidden something at the house."

That was news to him. "What?"

"A key."

"A key to what?"

"I don't know."

Wrong answer. He pressed the tip of the knife to her throat, just hard enough to release a thin trickle of blood. "A key to what?" he repeated through gritted teeth.

"I don't know. I don't know," Amanda pleaded. "Something having to do with Washington and Lafayette. Just rumors among the Anderson House staff, that's all."

The Lafayette Confession. He'd overheard his father talking about it years ago. But it was just a legend, twentieth-century anti-Vanguard propaganda retconning the Cincinnati's founding leader as a staunch opposer of their cause.

Unless it wasn't.

"What else did you tell them?" Molyneux pressed. "Be specific."

"Nothing. I gave them my keys to get into Anderson House. Nothing more."

"Your keys? Why your keys? They could get in tomorrow during visiting hours just fine."

Amanda said nothing. But she didn't have to.

"What's so urgent that they felt the need to find this legendary key in the middle of the night, Amanda?"

"Please, just let me go."

Molyneux smiled. "What did your husband tell you?"

"Nothing, honest. Leave him out of this."

"He's already in this. He brought himself into this when he started spouting off secrets to non-Cincinnati like you. He's the reason you're here now, bleeding from a neck wound in the middle of an abandoned park. So don't try to protect him now. He should have thought about that before he put your life in danger."

He had hoped his words would make her turn on her husband. Instead, they only strengthened her resolve. No matter. Her reactions had said enough already. Greg Taylor didn't know anything concrete about the Vanguard's plans for tomorrow, but he would be dealt with regardless. There was no room for error.

That included right now.

"Fine." Molyneux clamped his hand around her mouth again and plunged the knife into the side of her neck until it hit vertebrae. Her eyes grew wide as she screamed against his hand. It was no use. She was losing blood at an alarming rate, and within moments her heart didn't have enough to pump.

Though his brother and father had killed on the battlefield, that was from a distance at the other end of a gun barrel. They had never really talked about the experience, but he doubted they had ever seen the life fade from a person's eyes as the soul vacated the body.

Now, Molyneux had.

He worried that he would be traumatized beyond belief, reduced to a quivering mess by a paralyzing cocktail of shock, revulsion, and remorse. To take a fellow human's life, particularly like this, was not the natural order of things. It was supposed to do horrible things to a killer's psyche. Shame and horror should have flooded his being.

He felt none of that. Instead, a completely unexpected feeling surged through him.

Power.

He stood and surveyed his victim. Her body had stopped twitching, wallowing in a shallow pool of her own blood. He looked around again. No one. He had done it. Still, it was a little too simple.

He dragged her body to the water's edge and tossed it into the Tidal Basin. The blood trail would make it obvious where she had died, but separating the victim from the crime scene would help. He hadn't been in DC long enough to understand how the pond's titular tides worked, but he hoped that her body would find its way into the Potomac before dawn. That would really create some separation.

But not enough confusion. One victim meant a relatively clear-cut investigation. An investigation that could potentially lead back to Anderson House and the Society of the Cincinnati. And now was not the time to draw attention to either.

He walked up the path and found a bearded transient sleeping in the shadow of the FDR Memorial. Creeping up on his slumbering prey, Molyneux sprang upon the man. The man's eyes popped open as Molyneux's knife—still wet with Amanda's clotting blood—plunged into his chest and punctured his heart. Within seconds, he was dead.

The double murder of two seeming strangers would throw investigators for a loop. Were both murders random? Was there a connection between the victims? Was there a serial killer on the loose in Washington? The potential headlines were numerous. But increasingly few led to the Society's doorstep.

Though by tomorrow night, even a grisly double murder would be drowned out by what was to come.

He stood, taking the knife with him. He had a feeling he would be needing it again before the night was over.

He left the trail, retreating to a trash can in which he had hidden a backpack an hour earlier. The pack held several gallon-size Ziploc bags, a roll of plastic drawstring trash bags, and a change of clothes. In the shade of a cluster of elms, he changed out of his blood-soaked sweat suit and into a plaid flannel shirt, a pair of jeans, and a new set of sneakers.

The bloodied clothes went into the Ziploc bags, then into a nested set of four trash bags. After cinching the drawstrings tight, he placed his clothes into the backpack and started for the nearest road.

As he began his nighttime journey toward Anderson House, he realized the gravity of what had just transpired. Patrick Molyneux, itinerant professor of history and once-shunned son, had killed in defense of his country. He had sought out and slain the enemies of the United States, and was preparing to do so again.

In death, it seemed, Cyrus Molyneux knew his son better than he'd let on.

Patrick Molyneux was a Cincinnatus after all.

# CHAPTER 55
*Washington, DC*

M assachusetts Avenue had changed since Chloe had last visited Anderson House. While the street had been busy with early rush-hour traffic when they'd exited the headquarters of the Society of the Cincinnati that afternoon, now it was desolate. The windows of the Beaux-Arts embassies that lined the street were dark now. It was the perfect hour for a break-in.

She and Jon walked into the dual-entranced drive in front of Anderson House. She sized up the setting with new eyes now. No longer entranced by the palatial architecture or the imposing entryway, she looked for security cameras, tripwires, anything that could impede their progress—or land them in jail.

The high stone wall between the entrances to the street would help cover their entry. Though, according to "Isabel," their entry wouldn't be all that unusual. As Erica DeHart, their tour guide that afternoon, had relayed toward the end of the tour, Society members were able to stay in designated quarters within the mansion accessible through a separate entrance. So though they were alone out here, they might not be alone inside.

Which presented another serious wrinkle.

*One step at a time.*

"You ready?" Jon asked.

"Let's do it."

Chloe used Isabel's keys to unlock the door and the deadbolt, then swung open the heavy door. Immediately, a dull but persistent beeping began. Jon darted inside and punched in the alarm code their pseudonymous benefactor had given them. The beeping ceased as the alarm panel turned green.

They were in.

Chloe looked around the atrium. The lights were dimmed, giving the spacious and lavishly appointed interior more of a somber, ecclesiastical vibe compared to their previous visit. Which was fitting, because they'd need divine intervention if they were going to find a long-lost key hidden within this massive home.

"Let's split up," she said. "We can cover more ground."

"Works for me. Do you have a floor preference?"

She thought for a moment. He had been the one to discover Bobby Kennedy's note within the globe at the JFK museum. He had found the tape in the *Victura*. And he had recognized the Society of the Cincinnati's seal at first glance. Yes, his prowess with puzzles and historical obscurities was the reason she had sought him out in the first place, but she wanted to solve something. She knew it was selfish, but this was her quest. Her father had given up his career and, unwittingly, his life in pursuit of this quest. She owed it to him to finish it. And in order to do that, she needed to make a discovery of her own.

"I'll take this floor," she said, thinking about Larz Anderson's study stuffed to the brim with books and artifacts. "You take upstairs. If we don't find anything, we meet back down here and tackle the archives together."

"Sounds good. I'll start with the *Key* Room." He winked and pretended to jab her in the ribs with his elbow before leaving the room. She kicked herself for not thinking of that room, relinquishing it to him. But no, that was far too obvious. Jon's corny tone showed even he knew that. Unless it wasn't, and Washington's key actually was hidden beneath the patterned tilework that gave the room its name.

She sighed. It was too late to change her mind now. If the key was hidden up there, at least they'd have their prize and be out of here sooner. Even if Jon got to tick yet another score in the win column.

Crossing the grand ballroom, she entered Larz Anderson's study. DeHart had pointed it out during their tour, but because of time constraints they were only able to poke their heads in for an all-too-brief moment. Now Chloe could explore it at her leisure.

Built-in bookshelves lined the walls to the ceiling, each stuffed with thick leather-bound tomes original to Anderson's collection. Marble busts of past Society presidents-general stared down at her from their perches along the shelves, while a portrait of Larz Anderson himself, robed in his resplendent Society finest and bedecked with honorary medals garnered from across the globe, hung over the fireplace. At the center of the room sat a massive wooden desk. It was the sort of furniture piece you purchased to impress guests, built in a time when such works were designed to last several lifetimes.

She had picked the wrong room. It was a perfect hiding place for Anderson's secrets. A place that exuded power, the throne room of the little kingdom of the mansion he'd built. Perhaps he would show off Lafayette's key to prestigious guests here, extracting it from its hiding place beforehand and regaling them with the proof of how much the lauded general had trusted his great-grandfather.

But there were far too many places to hide it. She could tell from a pair of historical photos on a side table that the room hadn't changed much in the century since Anderson had died. The portrait was different, and a few pieces of furniture had been moved to make the room more easily navigable for larger tour groups, but the desk, the bookshelves, and most of the books looked to be untouched.

Anderson could have hidden the key in a hollowed-out section in any one of the hundreds upon hundreds of books lining the shelves. In a hidden compartment in the desk. Behind a specially built hidey-hole concealed within the bookshelves themselves. To properly search the room would take hours. And if Society members really did stay the night inside Anderson House as guests, time was not a luxury she could afford to fritter away flipping through each book, scouring each inch of the shelves, or tugging and prodding for secret latches in the desk.

But it was the best she had.

Pushing from her mind the resurgent suspicion that Isabel had, in fact, led them into a trap, Chloe started with the desk. Tugging at each drawer confirmed her fears. They were all locked. Of course they were. Anyone who had business with whatever the Society stored in the desk drawers would have the keys to open them.

Her hand bumped against the bulge in her pocket. Isabel's keyring. Maybe Chloe had the necessary keys after all.

She dug in her pocket and sifted through the keys, trying each small one she found. The first one didn't fit, while the second one wouldn't turn in the lock. The third one, however, slid into place and unlocked the drawer.

She was in.

Casting a cautious glance toward the closed study door, she slid open the drawer. She removed a stack of blank Society letterhead from within and began to feel around inside. The wood inside was surprisingly smooth for such an old and well-used piece of furniture. She tapped and pushed and rubbed the bottom, back, and sides of the drawer, but nothing yielded to her efforts.

She moved on to the next drawer. And then the next.

Nothing.

She slumped down into the chair behind the desk, trying not to let a sense of defeat creep in.

*Think, Chloe. Think.*

Seated in the chair, she looked around the study, trying to envision the space through Larz Anderson's eyes a century ago. She hoped something would jump out at her as a prime potential hiding place. But nothing did.

Brute force it was, then.

Starting with the shelf immediately to the desk's right, she traced her fingers along the molding, looking for any seams that might betray the presence of a secret opening. Failing to find anything there, she started pulling books from the shelf. She opened each one, flipped through it to see if any pages were glued together and hollowed out to create a hidden compartment, and stacked it on the desk. Once she had emptied a shelf, she studied the back and sides of the woodwork to see if any seams or latches were concealed there. Again, nothing.

She replaced the books on the shelf and started on the next, stacking secret-less tomes atop the desk and scouring the bookcase for anything anomalous.

After completing the process for three shelves, she sighed. She was getting nowhere. Maybe the Washington key was nothing but a legend after all.

Chloe replaced the last books on the shelf and crossed the study to the door. No sounds from the other side. She had claimed the entire floor for searching, not just this one room. Besides, the study, with its library full of potential hiding places, was taunting her now. She had to try something else. If both she and Jon turned up nothing elsewhere in the house, they could tag-team the rest of the shelves together.

Despite having been in the room multiple times over the past twelve hours, the sheer scale and spectacle of the grand ballroom still staggered her. The study, imposing and impressive as it was, paled in comparison to this aristocratic great hall. That the Society of the Cincinnati had chosen such a regal setting for their national headquarters wouldn't have done much to quell Thomas Jefferson's fears of the Cincinnati as a secret aristocracy working to rule from the shadows. Despite the clashing viewpoints within the Society on their ultimate role in post-Revolution America, she wondered how much influence the Vanguard would have had in choosing Anderson House for the Society's permanent home.

Had Larz Anderson, in his blue-blooded braggadocio, shown the key to the wrong person all those years ago? Had the Vanguard already intercepted Washington's key? Was all this for naught? And, for that matter, what did the key even unlock?

Approaching footsteps shook her from her thoughts. Somewhere toward the front of the mansion. Possibly upstairs, though it was hard to tell. Sound echoed strangely in this cavernous space. If it was upstairs, she hoped Jon heard it too. If it wasn't . . .

She retreated to the Winter Garden, hiding from whoever was walking through the house at this hour. She didn't know the exact numbers of Society members who swore allegiance to the Vanguard, but for them to hold such sway over American foreign policy for so long, they had to be a sizable chunk at least. Which meant that, just going by the law of averages, there was a good chance that at least one or two of Anderson House's guests belonged to the Vanguard. Perhaps even more, considering how their leadership couldn't have been too thrilled by their recent discoveries or their escape from Kellerman. If something big were going down as Isabel had claimed, the Vanguard would likely be descending on the capital.

Which led her to one obvious conclusion. There were better than even odds that those footsteps belonged to a Vanguard member. Perhaps even Kellerman himself. And whoever it was, they were hunting her and Jon.

She looked at the walls of glass behind her. The greenhouse-like design let plenty of sunlight in for plants in the winter. But escaping that way would be dangerous, noisy, and likely set off the alarm.

The footsteps were drawing nearer, now echoing more clearly in the ballroom.

Perhaps one of Isabel's keys would open the door to the walled garden outside, but even finding the right key would make too much noise. Not to mention that she couldn't leave Jon in the lurch. This was their only chance. If they were discovered in the house in the middle of the night, they would be barred from the house and possibly wind up in jail. The Vanguard would win. And Kellerman would be able to orchestrate their deaths long before they could tell anyone what they knew. Which, at the moment, wasn't backed up by enough evidence to even convince a third-rate radio journalist, much less a court of law.

The footsteps moved away. It wouldn't hurt to at least know if the key worked. She reached into her pocket.

And then she saw it.

The mural on the wall of the Winter Garden. Painted roadways tracing all over the Washington area. DeHart had told the tour group about the Sunday drives Larz Anderson would take with his wife. A handful of landmarks were easily recognizable on the map, but one stood out.

High on the wall, at the end of a long and winding road, stood Mount Vernon.

George Washington's ancestral home.

Could it be?

Chloe tapped her fingers against the wall below the painted representation of the homestead of the original American Cincinnatus. The masonry beneath was solid. Stretching on tiptoes, she tapped against Mount Vernon itself.

It felt different.

Hollow.

"Hey."

She spun around at the whispered greeting, fearing the worst. But it wasn't a murder-minded Kellerman or an armed security guard. It was Jon.

"Did you hear the footsteps?" she whispered back.

"Was I that loud?" he asked. "I guess sound does carry in here."

"Wait, so that was you?" She felt her face flush. Of course it was him. She should have known, but her paranoia, coupled with her frustration over her lack of success in the study, had gotten the better of her.

"Only footsteps I've heard have been my own. I came down here looking for you. No luck so far upstairs. How about you?"

Chloe pointed her chin at the mural. "I think it's hidden behind there."

"Behind the map?"

"Behind Mount Vernon."

Jon's eyes grew wide with realization. "Washington's home."

"Tap it. It's hollow."

Jon did. "Wow. You got a knife?"

"It's beautiful, though. I don't want to destroy the painting."

"I don't want to die."

She laughed. "Good point. You're taller. Here," she said, handing him Isabel's keys, "use one of these."

"Sorry, Larz," Jon said before stabbing one of the keys into the mural. He sawed with the key's teeth around the edge of the hole in the masonry. Then he plunged his hand inside.

When he withdrew it, he held a tarnished old iron key.

"Way to go, Chloe," he said with a grin as they both sighed in relief. They still didn't know what the key opened, but at least they were done skulking around the enemy's headquarters.

They left the shelter of the Winter Garden and reentered the ballroom, heading toward the front door. Then a trio of sounds froze her in place.

The rattle of keys in a lock.

The creaking of a door opening.

And the incessant chirping of an alarm panel in need of deactivation.

A fourth sound quickly joined the chorus. Voices.

Someone was coming in the front door.

She turned and retreated to the Winter Garden, gesturing for Jon to unlock the back door. But, just as he did so, she sighted a figure, perched like a devilish gargoyle atop the stone wall outside, staring down at him. As the gargoyle hopped down into the outer garden, Chloe recognized the Frenchman.

What she didn't recognize was the malicious grin on Patrick Molyneux's face. Nor the bloodstained knife gleaming in the moonlight.

Behind her, the voices grew louder as Anderson House's newest late-night guests walked deeper into the mansion.

They were trapped.

# CHAPTER 56
## *Parkers Crossroads, Tennessee*

Rafael Vargas knew what the flashing lights meant. In Venezuela, they meant trouble. Here, tonight, it could be disastrous.

Back in Caracas, and especially in the countryside outside the city, a bribe could get you out of trouble if the amount was right and the cop was amenable. It was an open secret. More than a few officers made a nice supplemental income from pulling over unassuming tourists on drummed up charges and shaking them down. But in the US, bribery of a law enforcement officer was frowned upon. And his cargo made his predicament all the more dire.

A flashlight blazed in his rearview mirror as the trooper stepped out of the vehicle and started a slow, measured walk toward the Venezuelan's van. Vargas tried to figure out why he had been pulled over. He had been careful to set the cruise control just under the speed limit. He had signaled every lane change, used his high and low beams at the appropriate times, and made sure not to swerve. Had he broken some other traffic law he wasn't aware of? Or had someone witnessed his loading up the van at the storage unit in Little Rock?

He tensed up as the flashlight-wielding officer grew closer. Vargas had a gun in the center console. Using it would be a last resort. This stretch of I-40 wasn't particularly busy at this late hour, but killing a Tennessee state trooper could still draw attention. And that was something he needed to avoid.

He had done nothing wrong. This had to be racial profiling. Though his van and the trooper's car were parked on the side of a dark stretch of highway, Vargas had passed beneath several high lampposts shortly before he saw the lights and sirens kick on behind him. Plenty of opportunity for a trooper hiding in a dark patch to see his Hispanic complexion through the floodlit windshield and target him.

So it would be a balancing act. Cooperate, then play the race card if needed. And if that didn't work . . .

Suddenly, the flashlight halted its advance.

"Get out of the vehicle with your hands up," the trooper shouted.

Not good. He had a decision to make. The trooper was yards from his own vehicle. Vargas would have the advantage of surprise if he just took off. There was an exit for State Road 22 half a mile ahead. He might be able to lose the trooper in the backroads. But the trooper would call for backup. And they knew these roads far better than he did. Plus, Vargas was on a deadline. He couldn't be wasting time running around rural Tennessee, getting lost and likely getting caught in the process.

He'd have to take his chances with the trooper.

But not without taking necessary precautions.

He took the pistol from its hiding place and tucked it into the back of his pants, covering it with his shirt.

"I'm coming out!" he shouted as he eased open the door, careful to keep his hands in view.

"Slowly," the trooper urged.

Feet on the ground, Vargas blinked into the flashlight's beam. "What's this about, Officer?"

"Anyone else in the vehicle with you, sir?"

"No, sir, just me. Did I do something wrong? I was going the speed limit."

"Anything in the vehicle I should know about, sir? Anything illegal I might find if I search it?"

They knew. Time to take this to the next level.

"Is this because I'm Hispanic?" Vargas asked, indignant. "Just because I'm not white like you doesn't mean I'm a drug runner or whatever you're blaming me for. What's your badge number?"

The trooper shone his flashlight on his own face for a moment, illuminating a set of decidedly Central American features.

"White like me, huh?" he countered.

There went the race card.

"No, Officer, there's nothing illegal in my van. It's a rental anyway."

"And what brings you to our beautiful corner of Tennessee this time of night?"

"Just passing through."

"Uh huh," the trooper said, unimpressed. "License and rental agreement, please."

Time to find out just how good Arocha's fake IDs were. Vargas handed over the Missouri license he'd retrieved from the storage unit.

Out of state so it wasn't overly familiar, but not from so far away that it invited questions, the spymaster had explained.

The trooper looked over the license. "Mr. Echevarria?"

Vargas nodded.

The trooper stepped toward his car. "Wait right here, please."

If the officer ran his license against whatever database he had access to through his car, there was no guarantee there would even be a record of it. He couldn't let him call this in. "Officer, I'm in a bit of a hurry. Can't you tell me why you stopped me in the first place?"

"I-40's become a significant drug-running corridor, with Memphis as one of its hubs. Anonymous white cargo van, middle of the night. You do the math. Stay right there."

The trooper retreated to his car. Vargas felt the weight of his pistol in the small of his back.

*Now. Take the shot. Before it's too late.*

The trooper was typing something into his computer. If that license came up empty, Vargas's mission was over. And when the van was searched after he'd been tossed in the back of the cop car, he'd be looking at a substantial sentence in an American prison.

He took a step toward the trooper's vehicle, lifting up his shirt and preparing to withdraw his weapon. Then a pair of headlights from an oncoming car lit him up. As soon as the car zoomed past, the lights of a semi-truck illuminated him. He dropped his shirt, hiding the gun once more. *No witnesses.*

Just as the semi passed, the trooper climbed out of his car and approached Vargas, flashlight once again at the ready. He handed back the false ID.

"Everything check out all right?" Vargas said, immediately cursing himself for sounding too eager and hopeful. A truly innocent man would have known the check would come back clean.

"Seems to. Mind if I take a look inside your van before you go, though?"

"Actually, yes. My boss is rather particular about allowing anyone, law enforcement or not, to search our property without a warrant."

"Oh, well we can certainly arrange a warrant. My sergeant is the son-in-law of the on-call judge tonight. No problem there. It might take a few hours, and with you being in a hurry and all . . ."

Vargas caught his drift. Either let the trooper search the van now, or be detained for hours waiting for the warrant to come through, then let the trooper search the van anyway, this time with much more of a paper trail.

So be it.

"Fine, if it'll get me out of here sooner. Just don't let my boss know I showed you, okay?"

"Sure, sure," the trooper mumbled as he approached the van's back doors.

Vargas looked behind him down the stretch of dark highway. No more headlights.

The trooper opened the back doors and peered into the cabin. He lifted a blanket and froze.

"What the—"

The blast from Vargas's gun cut the trooper's words short. His gray matter splattered across the inside of the van's cabin, the man slumped forward into the van. Vargas lifted the man's legs and slid the rest of him inside.

Slamming the doors shut, Vargas ran to the trooper's vehicle. He reached inside, flipped off the headlights and the emergency strobes. Then he shot the computer's screen and hard drive, as well as the center console, hoping to destroy the dashcam video that had surely recorded the murder. After popping the patrol vehicle's gas cap cover, he returned to the van to grab a hose, a handkerchief, and a lighter. He siphoned a little gas from the van's recently-filled tank and soaked the handkerchief in fuel. Returning to the trooper's car, he stuffed the volatile handkerchief into the gas tank, leaving a short wick dangling from the opening.

Sitting back in the car, he shifted to neutral and turned the wheel to the right. Then he got back out of the car, flicked open the lighter, and set flame to the handkerchief.

He ran to the rear of the car and gave it a mighty shove. The vehicle began to roll, its front wheels angling down the slope that led to the woods below.

He had done all he could. He raced back to the van and drove back onto the highway. Moments later, a fireball erupted from the trees behind him. Within seconds, the trooper's car would be engulfed in flames, the heat destroying all evidence of what had happened.

Vargas sighed. This was not how he wanted this trip to go. He had a dead state trooper rotting in the back of the van, and had left a police vehicle ablaze on the side of the highway. Arocha would be furious. But, all things considered, Vargas did as well as could be expected.

The operation had claimed its first victim. It would not be the last.

Before he reached his destination, he would have to stop somewhere to dump the body and sponge down the van's cabin, but, right now, his top priority was to put as much road behind him as possible.

So he drove onward into the night.

His destiny awaited.

# CHAPTER 57
## *Washington, DC*

Jon grabbed Chloe's arm and tugged. There had to be another exit.

Through the glass, he saw Molyneux pull his own set of keys from his pocket. The Frenchman advanced toward the door to the Winter Garden. And the voices from the entryway grew louder.

Everyone was converging on their position in the ballroom. The study was a dead end. And the rest of the exit points converged in the entry chambers where the voices were.

There was only one option. Jon didn't like it. But it would buy them more time.

Up.

He ran across the polished marble, cringing as his and Chloe's footfalls echoed in the cavernous space. They raced up the stairs and darted into the second-floor gallery just as they heard a door open and a new set of footsteps enter the house.

Molyneux was inside.

Below, voices drifted indiscriminately. Jon tried to ascertain the speakers' location and direction to no avail. They could be staying downstairs, or they could be taking any of the three staircases that he knew of toward their position. And with Molyneux surely not far behind, there was only one option Jon could think of.

Hide.

He beckoned to Chloe as he ran down the gallery, away from the staircases leading to the entrance hall and the grand ballroom. He had been so busy scouring the building for potential Kennedy assassination evidence during their tour earlier that he had failed to search for exits in case of an emergency. It was not a mistake he would make again.

Assuming they were able to escape to have a next time, that was.

The gallery emptied into the grand stair hall, the imposing painting of the Venetian gala appearing more haunting in the crepuscular gloom. *Should I chance it?* he thought. Odds weren't great that they wouldn't run into Molyneux or the other visitors at the bottom, but he didn't like their chances if they simply hid. Who knew how long the visitors would be loitering about, or even what their purpose here was? And Molyneux, Jon had no doubt, would be relentless in his pursuit.

He started toward the staircase, then slid to a halt as the visitors below came into view as they began to ascend the staircase. Chloe crashed into him, not expecting the sudden stop. He felt himself tumbling forward from the impact but managed to snag the handrail and arrest his fall before he went careening down the staircase.

Jon shot a thumb back toward the Key Room, and Chloe led their retreat from the stairs.

The Key Room held no closets or cabinets that could hide two full-grown adults. The French drawing room held an eighteenth-century Nordic sea chest that could have accommodated one of them, but it was locked tight. The English drawing room held an armoire, but it, too, was secured.

They were running out of time.

Then Jon saw it.

A set of full-length curtains against the far wall. It felt a bit clichéd, hiding behind the curtains, but it was their only option.

Jon and Chloe ran to the wall just as the pitch and echo of the visitors' voices changed. The newcomers were now on the second floor. They slipped through the curtains of the English drawing room, now hidden from view.

And then he realized he had made a terrible mistake.

He felt it first. The space was wrong. Not the tight seclusion that he should have felt but a gaping openness that left him feeling even more exposed than before. Turning around, he realized he had chosen one of the worst hiding spots in the house. Rather than a closet or a sheltered alcove, they now stood on one of the small balconies flanking the fireplace overlooking the ballroom. Chloe's face reflected the shock and horror he felt.

The visitors were in the Key Room now, blocking their only egress to a stairwell, an exit, or freedom.

Their backs exposed to the open ballroom, they had no option but to hunker down, stay quiet, and pray.

# CHAPTER 58
*Washington, DC*

"**D**o you know how hard it was for me to shake my security detail?"

Stanton Gaines gave his guest a sympathetic smile.

"You're not the only one with a security detail in this town," he said. "But I wouldn't have called you in the middle of the night if it weren't important."

In truth, his guest had precipitated this meeting. This wasn't the first time Gaines or his Vanguard forebears had used the history and opulence of Anderson House to woo allies, though the late-night meeting stank more of skullduggery than he liked. Still, waiting until morning was not an option. This was not the time for cold feet. Which was why Gaines had to seal the deal before tomorrow's events went forward.

"Dale, I understand why you might have reservations. But let's be honest with each other. We both know that this is the best course for our nation."

"Is it?" His guest chewed at his lip. Unbecoming of a man of such high office, but Gaines had to work with what he had.

"Do you see these paintings?" Gaines gestured around the Key Room to the depiction of Larz Anderson's ancestors. "The Revolutionary War. The War of 1812. The Civil War. Every time armed conflict came to our shores, the Cincinnati stood strong to defend our homeland. And every time we emerged victorious. But the cost was heavy. Brother against brother. Father against son. The very fabric of our nation nearly rent asunder. Yet we persevered because of strategic sacrifices made by unsung American heroes. And behind the curtain, we made the hard choices that pulled the country back from the breaking point time and time again."

"Like attacking our own people?"

Gaines shook his head. He had already had this discussion with his guest weeks ago. But he understood. Unlike the Vanguard, the man before him was a neophyte when it came to comprehending what it really took to keep the American Empire alive and thriving.

"An unfortunate but necessary sacrifice, ultimately for the better good. When the lives of millions hang in the balance, a few dozen deaths seems like a pittance, doesn't it?"

His guest's countenance shifted as resignation set in. The way of the world wasn't pretty, but it didn't change what had to be done.

"None of this will be traced back to me?"

Gaines grinned. "Of course not. This isn't our first rodeo. And all of this is news to you, isn't it?"

The man nodded. He fancied himself a scholar of American history, and the fact that the actions of the Vanguard had eluded his understanding before Gaines had approached him stood as a testament to how well kept their secrets were.

"So, can we count on your support?" Gaines asked, offering his hand. "This afternoon, then in Venezuela, and beyond?"

After the briefest of hesitations, the man accepted the handshake. "You can."

Gaines gripped tight the hand that would soon launch his war. "Glad to hear it, Mr. Vice President."

# CHAPTER 59
## *Washington, DC*

Patrick Molyneux slunk from behind the display he had used to hide himself. The room had once served as Larz Anderson's billiard room, but it now played host to a number of exhibits about Larz's wife, Isabel. According to the array of display cases and placards scattered throughout the room, she was just as much a world traveler as her husband, though she had used her travels to actually create something.

A Boston heiress who could trace her ancestry to the Massachusetts Bay Colony, Isabel largely fit the stereotypical image of a Gilded Age socialite. Born from the marital merger of two illustrious shipping dynasties, she inherited a multi-million-dollar fortune from her grandfather when she was only five years old, while her father—Commodore George H. Perkins—was a celebrated Civil War hero, the commander of the USS *Cayuga* gunboat critical to the Union blockades of Confederate supply routes. Her marriage to Larz Anderson, also the child of a Civil War hero, joined her family with a noble pre-Revolution lineage rivaling that of her own. While she enjoyed all the prestige and grandeur attendant on an upbringing and marriage of such high status, she was not content to simply sit on her laurels.

During World War I, she volunteered with the Red Cross, first in Washington, then overseas in France and Belgium. After caring for the war-wounded in Europe, she returned home to find America in the throes of the Spanish Flu epidemic. But rather than retreating to the safety of her family estates, she continued to care for the sick and needy throughout the epidemic. For her efforts, she was awarded medals by three countries. But even then, she wasn't content to simply be a *bon vivant*, hosting social functions and living the high life.

She became an author.

Though she wasn't particularly well-known, she drew on her frequent travels with Larz to pen several travelogues. She was even more prolific with her children's stories, despite she and Larz never having any children of their own. And she showed a particular penchant for family history. She wrote a definitive biography on the Weld family dynasty, focusing on her shipping magnate maternal great-grandfather, the father of the grandfather who had willed her a fortune when she was but a child.

But the work that most interested Molyneux was the papers she had collected and edited from her father-in-law, Nicholas Longworth Anderson. Larz's father had been in Philadelphia in 1865 when the Vanguard was forged in the flames of treason, plotting the death of President Lincoln. As Vanguard lore held it, the men who had called the meeting had misjudged his loyalties, as it was Nicholas who first leaked to the greater Society of the Cincinnati what the newly christened Vanguard was plotting. But despite his concerns, he had committed nothing of the Vanguard to paper. As soon as he had arrived at Anderson House, Molyneux had scoured the collected works Isabel had assembled, but nothing had hinted at what had transpired at that fateful meeting, nor of his fellow attendees' role in the infamous events that followed.

But that didn't mean Nicholas hadn't passed down something in secret. Something that, like hereditary membership in the Society itself, was passed from father to son.

Something that Larz had then hidden within the wall of the Winter Garden.

He had seen Jon and Chloe staring with wonder at something in their hands, then noticed the hole in the wallpaper overhead as he opened the door. It didn't take a rocket scientist to figure out. But was it really related to the legendary Lafayette Confession penned by George Washington himself? Jon had quickly palmed the item, but it seemed too small to be the infamous letters themselves.

Which meant another clue. And Molyneux was still one step behind.

Time to fix that imbalance.

The voices overhead moved toward the east wing of the house now. Which meant a window of opportunity was opening. Neither Molyneux nor his quarry dared be spotted by Senator Gaines or his guest. Molyneux because he knew the import of the meeting and didn't want to ruin his chance to prove himself to the Vanguard leader, Jon and Chloe because they were here illegally. Now that the coast was clearing, the two thieves would try to make their escape. Molyneux would have to ensure he was there to ensnare them when they made their attempt.

Careful to soften his footfalls, he bounded up the stairs in the great stair hall. Reaching the top, he peered into the gallery to his left to ensure that Gaines and Vice President Dale Finney were out of view. Satisfied, Molyneux advanced toward the chambers where he had seen Jon and Chloe take refuge.

He hoped they hadn't managed to slip away already.

The Key Room held no hiding places large enough. He tested a sizable sea chest in the French drawing room, confirming that it was securely locked. Then, as he entered the next room, he saw the curtains. It would be a cliché, but things only became clichéd because—for a time at least—they worked.

Silently, he lowered himself to the floor, squinting through the gap between curtain and floor. No shoes betrayed their presence on the other side.

But he wasn't through searching yet.

He stood. Walking softly, heel to toe, he crept further into the next room. Crossing to the armoire, he gave its doors a gentle tug to confirm that they were still locked.

Which left only one other hiding spot.

Dropping to the ground once more, he confirmed two pairs of feet on the balcony just beyond the curtains.

He perked up his ears, straining for any sound of Gaines and Finney. Their conversation had drifted far enough to the other side of the house that Molyneux could scarcely hear it. Perfect. His next move could upset the delicate balance Gaines was trying to achieve if Finney were to see it. Being complicit in innocent people's deaths was more easily stomached if you didn't have to witness their executions firsthand.

And while Molyneux had little doubt that Jon and Chloe were sure they were doing the right thing, their actions could threaten the future of the country. Which meant, innocent or not, their deaths would be an unfortunate but necessary casualty of war. Just like everyone else who would die in the march to Caracas in the coming months.

Molyneux unsheathed his knife and advanced toward his targets' hiding place.

# CHAPTER 60
## *Washington, DC*

Chloe was still reeling from shock at hearing the vice president discussing what could only be described as treason. Attacking Americans? A necessary sacrifice? Despite what she had learned of her nation's history over the past year as she dug into her father's quixotic quest, she was sickened at the very thought of what the men had been discussing.

Some sort of false flag attack on American citizens.

And while she and Jon now knew when the Vanguard planned to move forward with the attack, it did them little good.

It was happening this afternoon. It was still a long time before dawn, but the realization that it wasn't a matter of days or weeks but mere hours before the Vanguard's plans came to fruition sent shivers down her spine. For centuries, this mystery had lain unsolved. She and Jon now had half a day.

She had a hunch where to head next. But first, they had to escape Anderson House.

Once the voices drifted away from the west wing, Chloe started to leave their exposed alcove, but Jon put his hand on her shoulder.

"Not yet," he whispered, and tapped his ear. She listened. The noise was faint. But, despite the echo-prone ballroom enveloping them on both sides, above, below, and behind, through the curtains she could just make out the faintest pattern of sounds.

Footsteps.

With the retreat of Vice President Finney and the Vanguard spokesman to the other side of the mansion, there was little doubt who would be sneaking through this suite of rooms.

Jon raised his finger to his lips. She held her breath. If Molyneux suspected they were behind the curtain, it was all over. Their only hope was that he would overlook the curtains as they had the first time.

But the footsteps kept coming.

Jon motioned for her to stand back against the rail, to the side of the balcony. Jon did the same on the opposite side. It wasn't much of a strategy, Chloe conceded, but if Molyneux only did a cursory look through a parted curtain, perhaps he would miss them.

The curtains tore open. In the same moment, a knife-wielding arm plunged through the now-empty center of the balcony.

It was exactly what Jon had been planning for.

In one fluid motion, he grabbed Molyneux's extended arm and, using the would-be assassin's momentum against him, yanked him through the balcony and over the ledge.

"Run!" Jon urged her. She didn't need to be told twice.

They darted through the curtains and into the English drawing room, through the French drawing room and the Key Room until they reached the great stair hall.

They had to get downstairs. But, assuming he hadn't broken both his legs in the fall, Molyneux could easily be at the bottom of those stairs by the time they reached them. They had to do the unexpected.

The east stair hall would be their best bet. It was the longest route to get downstairs, but it was closest to the front door. By the time they got down to Molyneux's level, it was just a quick dash to freedom.

Jon must have had the same thought, as he abandoned the great stair hall and ran into the gallery, retracing the path of their earlier flight from Molyneux's grasp. The far end of the gallery, the longest room in the sprawling estate, emptied into the east stair hall, which in turn abutted the entrance hall.

They were almost out of here.

And then they stopped short.

Voices. Coming right for them.

Trapped again.

Then she remembered. Isabel Anderson's secret escape route.

Chloe turned to the wall Erica DeHart had pointed out on their tour. She found the hidden button and pressed it with her thumb.

A click, and the adjacent wall panel creaked inward a few inches.

Chloe led the charge inside, Jon quickly catching on to what she was doing. DeHart might not have known where exactly the secret passage ended up, but they were about to find out.

Jon closed the door behind them and clicked on a penlight. A tight wooden spiral staircase greeted them a few steps inside. The staircase emptied into a low narrow passage heading toward the east wing. Chloe and Jon had to stoop, walking bowed over while keeping a wary eye out for rotten timbers underfoot.

*Isabel Anderson may have had an undue fear of burning to death in her home, but she clearly didn't suffer from claustrophobia.*

After nearly a century of disuse, the passageway was clotted with cobwebs hanging from every rafter, with dust piled along the edges of the path. Eventually, the passage terminated at another stairwell, down which Chloe led the way.

At the bottom was a dead end.

"Did they seal it up?" Chloe whispered, panic setting in. "DeHart would have mentioned if they did, right?"

Jon pointed at the wall. Chloe followed his eyes to a small lever set between two joists. Feeling sheepish, she pulled down on the lever.

As with the entrance in the gallery, the wall panel cracked open, re-vealing a darkened room beyond. Simply judging by the shapes of shad-ows in the room, she didn't recognize it from their tour.

Suddenly, the lights flicked on. Jon was standing by the wall switch he had just flipped, and the rest of the room came into focus. It was a bedroom, simply but tastefully appointed for guests. A heavy oaken dresser was set against the wall to their right, while straight ahead was a small writing desk, atop which sat a short stack of papers and folders. A full-size bed, neatly made, sat against the left wall. And just beyond the foot of the bed, a door.

"This must be one of the guestrooms for visiting members of the Society," Jon said. To confirm this, he pointed at a small metal placard affixed on the wall between the writing desk and the door.

> The Pennsylvania Chapter of the Society of the Cincin-nati welcomes you to Anderson House. Thank you for representing our historic brotherhood on your visit to our nation's capital.

Neat trivia, but Chloe just wanted to get out of here. Molyneux, wounded or not, would be all the more determined to kill them after Jon outmaneuvered him on the balcony. The duplicitous historian had proven he had both the means and will to murder them in order to further his own ends. Which, it now seemed, were in line with those of the Vanguard.

"Come on," Chloe said. "Molyneux will figure out where we went before long."

Jon reached for the doorknob, but stopped as he heard Chloe gasp.

Her eyes were fixed on the pile of papers on the desk. One name stared up at her.

Her own.

She stepped closer to the desk and sifted through the papers. Three typed dossiers—one each for Jon, Vance, and her—were at the top of the stack, while below that were a handful of handwritten notes scrawled on yellow notebook paper.

"This is Molyneux's room," she said as a chill went through her.

"Take them," Jon said, pointing to the notes.

"He'll be furious."

"If he survived that fall, I'm sure he's already furious. But that might give us a leg up on him. Or, at the very least, make him think we know more than we do."

She grabbed the papers, tucking them into one of the folders for easier carrying.

Jon cracked open the door and peered into the darkened hall. Judging the coast to be clear, he beckoned her to follow.

Wall sconces provided dim illumination for the corridor, from which more guestrooms stemmed. A long series of Turkish-style rugs covered the center of the tiled hallway, while the wood-panel walls were hung with paintings of Revolutionary War battles. The sacrifices made by these men's ancestors.

Jon ran down the hall toward the stairwell beckoning at the end. Chloe rushed alongside, careful to keep her feet on the padded carpet to soften her hurried steps. They reached the stairwell, dashed downstairs, and, to the left, was one of the most beautiful sights she had ever seen.

An exit door.

Jon shoved through the crash bar and raced into the cool air of night. Streetlights wore diaphanous halos as fog had rolled in off the Potomac since they'd entered Anderson House. The mist would, she hoped, obscure their escape from anyone watching from the mansion.

The Metro trains and the Metrobus system had finished service for the night, so their options for transport to their next destination were limited. An Uber would immediately be tagged to Jon or Chloe's name, alerting the Vanguard to their destination. The alternative wasn't perfect, but it would at least operate on a no-name basis.

After jogging a few blocks to Dupont Circle, they hailed a cab and gave him their destination. The driver, a beleaguered Sikh who looked like he was on his third double shift in a row, raised an eyebrow, as though they were joking. Jon flashed a hundred-dollar bill to show they were quite serious and had the money to pay for the long journey. Thus placated, the man started driving.

As the dark city streets rolled past, Chloe thought of the centuries-old key in Jon's pocket, and of Molyneux's dossiers on her lap. The Vanguard would be coming for them full force now. She just hoped she and Jon found what they sought before they did.

# CHAPTER 61
*Washington, DC*

Patrick Molyneux's arms felt as if they were on fire. He had managed to catch the railing on the way over the balcony, but his grip had slipped and he had to grab the brass balustrade at the base of the balcony to arrest his fall. His knife had tumbled from his grasp, spearing itself into the upholstery of a wingback chair original to the house that had been set by the fireplace for an upcoming event. A purist historian and lover of all things Cincinnati, Gaines would be furious at the damage to the chair. But, at present, there were far greater things for him to be furious about.

Like how Jon and Chloe were on the run. Again.

He had thought he could succeed where Kellerman had failed. Kellerman had tried brute force, while Gaines felt that Molyneux could try subterfuge. But thanks to Amanda Taylor's meddling, not only had he lost Jon and Chloe's trust, he had also fallen another step behind. They were in possession of yet another hidden clue, left behind by the enemies of the Vanguard. The enemies of America.

Whatever they had found in the National Archives had set them on a path that the Vanguard hadn't foreseen. A series of clues, apparently hidden away by some of the nation's unsung powerbrokers over the past century or two, leading straight to the Vanguard's doorstep.

What an asset having their confidence would have been. He could have followed the trail with them, destroying the evidence and them in one fell swoop. Instead, he was forced to play catch-up, perpetually running behind. After Taylor's betrayal, Molyneux had no choice but to show his hand. And he had come up short.

He managed to claw his way up the twisting balustrade and swing himself over the balcony railing. He could only imagine Gaines's face if he and Vice President Finney had seen him dangling there.

It was a miracle that they hadn't. In fact, it was a miracle he hadn't broken both his legs—or his neck—in the fall. At most, he may have sprained his shoulder as he snagged the railing. He'd survived worse. His pride hurt most of all.

He'd gotten overconfident after interrogating and killing Taylor without a hitch. He had to remember that he was new to this game. Gaines had recruited him for his cunning. He had to use his brain, not his balls.

It was time to redeem himself.

He had no doubt that Jon and Chloe had long since left the house, but he wasn't sure about Gaines and Finney. Still listening for any sign of their presence, Molyneux made his way downstairs to the Winter Garden.

There. About two-thirds of the way up the wall, toward the top of the mural depicting the Andersons' favorite routes for their Sunday drive. A hole had been torn in the wallpaper, exposing a small recess within the wall itself. Molyneux reached up to see if they had accidentally left anything behind. They hadn't.

He bent the torn wallpaper back into place and studied the damaged image the pieces made. He recognized the place. Any true student of Revolution-era American history would.

He smiled. Jon and Chloe may have eluded his grasp with their prize, but he knew exactly where they were going. Unlike this rush job, he'd be prepared. No more outsized bravado, no more recklessness. He would use his talents to finally put an end to this.

And this time he would have help.

# CHAPTER 62
### *Alexandria, Virginia*

Kellerman had been waiting for this call for hours. When it finally came, he was pacing the streets of Old Town Alexandria. The numerous restaurants and shops that lined King Street were shuttered for the night, while the bars were offering last calls to the few patrons who remained. The trolleys that ferried tourists around the historic city were tucked away in an unseen depot, and those visitors who staggered out of the bars after one too many were forced to contend with the uneven stonework of the cobbled streets.

Yet another reason why Kellerman was a teetotaler. For more than a decade, since his father died of a cirrhotic liver at the age of fifty-nine, Kellerman had abstained from all alcohol. And the universe had rewarded him. Not only had he inherited his father's membership in the Society of the Cincinnati, but he had quickly risen through the ranks of the Vanguard, using his Special Forces training and fervor for the cause to become the favorite enforcer of the group's current leader. But that favorite-son status was in danger of faltering as Stanton Gaines had relieved him of duty—temporarily, he had said—so another Vanguard member could try a different approach.

So Kellerman had been forced to fume on the sidelines while this newcomer could throw his hat into the ring. While his pride was bruised—it had, after all, been his repeated failure to capture or kill Jon and Chloe that had led to this unwanted downtime—he ultimately supported any steps that furthered the Vanguard's mission. He couldn't let his hubris come before the national interest. Yet another lesson from his active-duty days in the Marines.

This wasn't personal for him. It was so much more.

He had left the cobbles and drunken tourists of King Street behind when the call came. The water of the Potomac lapped at the concrete barrier below as he meandered along the parks and marinas lining the shore. While he was in Virginia, the water line just feet away marked DC territory. In fact, less than two centuries ago, Alexandria had formed the historic heart of the Federal District, long before construction had begun on the capital city of Washington. Though it was miles from his sprawling estate downriver, George Washington had called Alexandria home long before he became a general, a president, and a legend.

*And, currently, a major thorn in my side.*

The Lafayette Confession was the name given to a rumored letter penned by Washington a few years before his death and sent overseas to his friend Gilbert du Motier, the Marquis de Lafayette. The contents were unknown, but legend held that it exposed some weakness in the Society of the Cincinnati. It was common knowledge among Vanguard members that Washington had sought to dissolve the Society of the Cincinnati less than a year after its formation, fearful of its power to become the very aristocratic powerbrokers they had just defeated. But upon the Society's next meeting, he was stymied by his friend Pierre L'Enfant, who delivered a set of diamond eagles and other regalia he had designed and had made in France for President-General Washington and the rest of the membership. Despite this grand gesture, Washington pushed ahead with his concerns, and, surprisingly, the Society relented, removing its hereditary continuance.

Washington was placated. Then, once the accompanying fervor in Congress had died down, the Society promptly reinstated the hereditary provision, which had remained intact for more than two centuries, allowing new generations to honor the sacrifices of their progenitors through word and deed.

But if Washington's confession to Lafayette was as dangerous as it was rumored, it could cast an unwelcome spotlight on the darker side of the Society at the worst possible time. Which was why Jon and Chloe had to be stopped.

Kellerman stopped pacing when the phone buzzed in his pocket.

"They escaped again."

Gaines's words elicited a clash of emotions. Frustration and fury that they had again eluded the Vanguard's grasp. A smidge of fear that they could actually derail Gaines's plans and threaten the nation's future. And prideful vindication that this newcomer hadn't succeeded where Kellerman had failed.

"What do you need from me?"

"We know where they're going," Gaines said. "I'm going to text you an address. Dr. Patrick Molyneux will be there waiting for you. Pick him up and head to Mount Vernon. Our young interlopers found an old key hidden in the Winter Garden at Anderson House."

Kellerman knew the connection. Richard Clough Anderson, Lafayette's aide-de-camp, founding Cincinnatus, and a member of the inaugural Electoral College that elevated the Society's president-general to the highest office in the land, was Larz Anderson's great-grandfather. If Larz had hidden something of that import in his palatial home, it may well have been handed down from father to son, tracing its origins back to Lafayette himself.

The dreaded Lafayette Confession might finally be within reach.

For both the Vanguard and its enemies.

"Get to Mount Vernon and put an end to this," Gaines continued, anger seeping into his normally staid voice. "I want them dead before sunrise, and everything they have found secured."

"Understood." Kellerman hung up, looking downriver toward Washington's ancestral estate.

Tonight, Jon and Chloe would finally receive their due. Since their first meeting at the National Archives, Kellerman had been chasing from behind. But now, he would finally be one step ahead.

And that would make all the difference.

# CHAPTER 63
## *Mount Vernon, Virginia*

It was darker than his last visit a decade before, but George Washington's timeless estate was just as Jon remembered it. The land had first belonged to George's great-grandfather, John Washington, who came into possession of the land in 1674. While the 500-acre homestead was originally passed down to George's older half-brother, Lawrence, upon his death in 1752, Lawrence named his widow, Anne Fairfax, and half-brother as heirs to the estate. After Anne's death in 1761, George Washington became the full owner of his childhood home.

George had been managing the estate for some years before he came into his full ownership, and it still bore his fingerprints more than two centuries later. The Palladian mansion overlooking the Potomac had more than doubled in size under George's tenure. He also oversaw improvements to the numerous outbuildings, orchards, and other facilities across the plantation, spending more than four hundred days of his eight-year presidency at Mount Vernon.

He was, in so many ways, the true embodiment of the legendary farmer-turned-leader, Lucius Quinctus Cincinnatus.

Jon and Chloe had left the cab at the front entrance, telling the driver that a friend of theirs who lived nearby would pick them up from there. A lie, but hopefully one that would keep him from suspecting foul play and calling the authorities.

Bypassing the closed visitor center, they had walked through fields and wooded paths toward the mansion at the heart of the estate. A long bowling green stretched ahead, and, in the distance, the two-and-a-half-story building George Washington had called home materialized from the mist, whitewashed and gleaming spectrally in the moonlight. The mansion was flanked by two smaller buildings, a kitchen to one side, a servants' hall to the other. Colonnaded walkways connected both to the central home, covered to allow movement to and from the outer wings during inclement weather.

That was the problem with Mount Vernon. It was almost too big. Beyond the main three-building home, the estate spanned a distillery, stables, workshops, staff quarters, barns, and a gristmill, not to mention acres of gardens, orchards, woods, and farmland. Far too many buildings original to Washington's time. Far too many doors—both obvious and hidden—that their key might unlock.

And they had only hours to find the right one.

Jon's initial thought was that it would be something in the main house. While the basement had been made famous in the second National Treasure film and its depiction of a Masonic entrance to a hidden tunnel, the real basement held no such secret. But the two stories above, or the cupola that comprised the half-floor above that, might hold a cabinet or hidden compartment where Washington's confession could have been hidden away for the past two-hundred years.

Of course, that would necessitate breaking into the historic home of the nation's first president. A home surely guarded by a state-of-the-art security system. And they didn't have an inside source to provide them with a key or the entry code this time.

They approached the *cour d'honneur*, the three-sided courtyard formed by the main mansion and its connected wings. Yet another throwback to Old World aristocracy, the *cour d'honneur*, French for "court of honor," had its roots in the country houses and palaces of sixteenth- and seventeenth-century European nobility. Perhaps its most famous example was the Palace of Versailles, built by Louis XIV, the so-called Sun King of seventeenth-century France, and hailed as a key exhibit in the lavish decadence that led to the French Revolution. While Washington's home was far more modest and not built with tax dollars stolen from a kingdom, the aristocratic connection was impossible to ignore, particularly in light of why they had come tonight.

Jon and Chloe crept through the brick courtyard and tried the door. Locked, of course.

But there were other entrances.

Jon led the way to the left, around the north side of the house. Once they reached the front piazza, Chloe gasped.

"Beautiful, isn't it," Jon said.

"It's gorgeous. No wonder Washington liked to spend his days here."

As much money and effort as he had spent on the mansion and the surrounding estate, one of Mount Vernon's most spectacular treasures was completely natural. From the wide porch at the rear of the home, an unbroken slope of grass stretched downhill to the moonlit waters of the Potomac. A gentle cooling breeze wafted up from the river, and Jon imagined George and Martha, along with their adopted son George Washington Parke Custis and their many guests over the years, enjoying the view as drafts of fresh air provided natural air conditioning for the summer heat. Modern visitors were clearly invited to partake in this historic pastime, as several rocking chairs sat on the piazza, waiting for a new generation of guests to take a load off and relish the estate's natural splendor.

Despite being primo waterfront real estate, the land across the Potomac remained largely as Washington would have seen it. Interestingly, development across the river had been stymied by President Kennedy himself. In 1961, Kennedy had established the National Park Service's Piscataway Park on the Maryland shore, preserving Washington's view for generations to come.

Chloe smiled thoughtfully. "A glass of lemonade on a cool summer evening and I'm in heaven."

Jon turned from the bucolic scene and faced the east door of the mansion. Trying the doorknob, he was stymied again.

*Of all the times people accidentally forget to lock their doors these days, why couldn't this be one of them?*

He peered into the window to the left of the door. As was common with homes of the period, the front and back doors opened into a central passageway, forming a hub for the rest of the house. While George Washington had expanded the home both vertically and horizontally, this hallway and the rooms to either side were the original core of the mansion, dating back to 1734, when Augustine Washington had moved his family, including young George Washington, to Mount Vernon, then called Little Hunting Creek Plantation. The passageway, like others of its ilk, also served an important purpose for the period—ventilation. Opening the front and back doors during certain periods of the day allowed breezes to flow through the home and keep it cool in the days before air conditioning. The cupola overhead, Jon remembered from his tour, had a similar effect, allowing rising hot air to flow out of the house and drawing in more cool air from below.

What caught his attention, however, was a display case hung on the wall just inside the passageway. It was hard to see from this angle, but returning here on his current mission reminded him of its contents.

A massive, nineteen-ounce cast-iron key.

The key held tremendous symbolic importance for George Washington. The building it opened was once among the most infamous in the western world. The Bastille prison in Paris, which gave its name to France's day of independence, Bastille Day, was a powerful symbol of the injustices wrought upon the populace by the French aristocracy.

The storming of the Bastille on July 14, 1789, was a turning point in the French Revolution, a monumental symbolic and tactical victory by *Garde National*. The very next day, command of the *Garde National* was given to the man who had named the peasant military force and inspired millions with his Jefferson-esque Declaration of the Rights of Man and of the Citizen. An aristocrat with significant experience leading revolutions to throw off the shackles of tyranny.

Gilbert du Motier. The Marquis de Lafayette.

Lafayette was given the key to the Bastille in honor of his contribution to the burgeoning French Revolution. He, in turn, sent it to his old friend overseas, who had led him throughout the American Revolution, which provided a heavy dose of inspiration for its French counterpart a few years later.

General George Washington, who had by then become President Washington. And, until the day he died, would be President-General George Washington, leader of the Society of the Cincinnati.

For the duration of his public life, Washington would take the key with him and display it at functions and in his offices as a point of pride for the good he and his revolutionary friends had done both here and overseas. A new day had come, and Cincinnati like himself and Lafayette had been instrumental in its dawning.

"It's not here," Jon said.

Chloe stared at him in bewilderment. "What do you mean it's not here?"

"So much of this place has been restored. Most of the furnishings are from the period, but aren't original to the house. Even during his lifetime, Washington made much of his home and estate open to the public, insofar as the visitors were sober and sound of mind."

"So?"

"So think about what Isabel said. These papers were sent overseas to Lafayette, with instructions to be followed after his death."

"Washington was dead when the papers were hidden here," Chloe said, realization dawning on her face.

"Exactly. Which meant there would be one important new hiding place. One that would remain undisturbed until the right time came."

"His tomb."

Jon led the way south, through a small village's worth of workshops, storehouses, and slave quarters. Upon the death of the nation's first president in 1799, Congress passed a joint resolution to inter Washington's body in a massive marble mausoleum beneath the Capitol's rotunda, which was still under construction. A year later, the House passed a $200,000 appropriations bill for the construction of the 100-foot-square pyramid—nearly $4 million in today's money. By that point, though, Washington had already been buried at Mount Vernon, and the final measure failed to pass in the Senate.

"In 1824," Jon said, "Lafayette finally undertook his long-planned grand tour of the United States, with a special stop at Mount Vernon where he had been Washington's guest numerous times. History records Lafayette paying his respects at the tomb of his old friend during that visit. It would have been the perfect opportunity to hide the letters."

The landscape changed from the utilitarian workspaces of a bustling plantation to the secluded woodland and gardens of a reflective American aristocrat. Past a fruit orchard, twin gray obelisks appeared from the fog to the right. They turned and approached the structures.

The obelisks were memorials to two prominent Washington family members who outlived the former president. Bushrod Washington, George's nephew, inherited Mount Vernon after Martha Washington's death in 1802. Bushrod's most famous claim to fame was serving more than thirty years as an associate justice in the Supreme Court, appointed to that high office by John Adams. The other obelisk was dedicated to John Augustine Washington II, Bushrod's nephew, who was raised at Mount Vernon and inherited the estate following the Supreme Court justice's death. The lines immediately below John's name stood out.

Lt. Col. CSA
1820–1861

An early casualty of the American Civil War, Jon realized. And the fact that this Washington fought for the Confederacy just illustrated how very divisive that war—like the one his more famous great-grand-uncle had fought in—really was.

Brother against brother, father against son.

"Did you hear that?" Chloe whispered at his side.

Jon listened, but heard nothing but the wind that sent ghostly tendrils of mist spinning through the air. He shook his head. Whether or not someone or something was out there, they needed to hurry.

Across the tomb's courtyard was the wide brick-faced Washington family vault. Overhead, a stone tablet had been set into the brickwork, inscribed with a simple legend.

> Within this Enclosure Rest the remains of Gen.l George Washington

This being the family vault, George was, of course, not the only Washington family member interred within. In addition to the men honored on the obelisks and their wives, several other family members who had lived on the property claimed this tomb as their final resting place.

But the most famous pair of Washingtons resided in two marble sarcophagi rising from the floor of the vault.

George and Martha Washington.

Jon squinted through the wrought-iron gate that barred entry into the mausoleum. Unable to see much of anything in the dim, fog-diffused moonlight, he clicked on his penlight and scoured the interior of the tomb for a keyhole. Chloe, meanwhile, felt along the exterior of the tomb.

The first sarcophagus he saw, positioned closest to the entrance, read, simply, "Washington." To the left, closer to an inner vault, the second read "Martha, Consort of Washington."

Jon was shocked. "Consort" usually referred to the spouse of royalty, as in "queen consort." Again with the notions of aristocracy that seemed to permeate many of the founding fathers' thinking, one which the Society of the Cincinnati and the Vanguard seemed to have taken to heart. Despite the surprising inscription, Jon could see nothing more of interest—like a keyhole—in either sarcophagus.

"There it is again," Chloe whispered, her voice tense.

That time, Jon *had* heard it.

Further north, back toward the house, or possibly beyond. The breeze carried the distant sounds to his ears, but they were unmistakable.

Voices.

They weren't alone.

# CHAPTER 64
## *Mount Vernon, Virginia*

Anthony Kellerman was getting close. He could smell it.

By his estimates, Jon and Chloe couldn't have had more than a half-hour head start on him, even with his having to pick up the Vanguard's newest member from a strategic halfway point near the Pentagon. Even if they had known exactly where to go on the property, they wouldn't have been able to leave the property in time. No cars were parked by the roadside or the entrance to Mount Vernon when Kellerman arrived. They would have to call for another cab or ridesharing service, and Gaines had his sources at the NSA actively monitoring those channels.

No, Jon and Chloe were still here. And they were about to see their string of luck run out.

"Do you think it's real?" Patrick Molyneux asked as they climbed up the gentle slope of the bowling green stretching toward the mansion in the distance.

"No, it's probably just an apparition." Kellerman rolled his eyes. This guy was supposedly a professional historian, with a doctorate in American history. Why on earth was he doubting the existence of the Mount Vernon mansion?

"Not the house, genius. The Lafayette Confession."

*Ah. That.*

"Could be. That possibility is all that matters right now. Jon and Chloe may already have something that could be damaging to the Vanguard, and, thus, dangerous to the nation. They are seeking even more. The fact of the matter is, Confession or not, they've become a threat. We have to stop them."

Despite his dismissal of Molyneux's query, Kellerman had himself pondered the existence of the fabled letters. How could the father of the country, the man who had embodied the American Cincinnatus so perfectly, betray his brothers-in-arms so easily? He had twice left his aristocratic existence here on his idyllic Virginia manor to serve his countrymen—first as a general on the front lines of a brutal war to create the nation, then as president to lead it for its first eight years. He had presided over the 1787 convention that penned the US Constitution, and won the presidency with 100% of the Electoral College votes, the only president in history to do so. And he did it twice. Just like Cincinnatus, there were those who called for him to become king over the new nation, so admired was he by his fellow man. And just like that Roman farmer, Washington emphatically refused. He was urged to run for a third term, an election he surely would have won. But he turned them down, choosing instead to retire from public life in 1797 and setting a precedent for two-term presidencies, which would only be broken thirty-one presidencies later by Franklin Delano Roosevelt.

Perhaps that was his problem. He was *too* much like the original Cincinnatus, content to let other men steward the nation he had brought to life.

The southern secession and the Civil War proved the folly in such a mindset. It was a mistake the Vanguard had vowed never to repeat.

They cut a swath through the gray miasma that had settled low over the property, nearing the 11,000-square-foot colonial manse that Washington had called home. The fog would cover their approach, but it would also inhibit their ability to see their quarry. Thankfully, Kellerman had been at this a while, honing his Special Forces skills to slight movements and other anomalies in worse conditions than these.

He remembered an early Marines mission in Myanmar, the rain a horizontal torrent on the moonless night. His team was infiltrating a dockyard warehouse used by an extremist group to house stores of a weaponized nerve agent. The warm summer rain rendered useless the infrared heat signatures the surveillance plane high overhead attempted to gather, forcing them to rely on their own faculties to recon and clear the area. As his point man was making his stealthy approach to the entrance, Kellerman caught sight of the slightest irregular shift in movement in the wind-slapped palm fronds at the edge of the clearing. Reacting on instinct, he shot at the anomaly. A terrorist fell forward from the foliage, a Type 69 RPG tumbling from his shoulder. A rocket propelled grenade could have killed their entire unit. Instead, the mission carried on. The nerve gas was secured, and the unit exfiltrated with no casualties.

Kellerman received his first bronze star for his actions that night.

"So in how many cities have these guys eluded you in now?" Molyneux prodded once they reached the house.

"Too many. But I had an asset go bad. And we didn't realize the threat they posed until it was too late."

"A heck of a string of bad luck, if you ask me. How long have you been doing this?"

Kellerman stopped and looked the bookish historian up and down. "About a decade longer than you. Marines Special Forces before that."

Molyneux grunted dismissively.

Kellerman had promised himself not to let pride get the better of him, but this newbie needed to be put in his place. "How about you, hotshot? Gaines got them to come straight to you. You had a friendly conversation with them. And they still got the better of you."

"Yeah, but I'm new. I just started a couple of days ago."

*You don't get training wheels or mulligans in the Vanguard, you fool.* Kellerman wanted to slap the amateur, but he restrained himself. The mission was all that mattered. Better to let the affront slide than to kick up unneeded animosity between them. Once tomorrow was over, Gaines could deal with him appropriately.

"Maybe it's time you hung up your hat, huh?" Molyneux pressed.

*Or I could kick his teeth in now.*

The guy seemed to have a Napoleon complex. The new kid on the block, coming on board at a pivotal moment in time, Molyneux clearly felt like he had something to prove. And as the veteran alpha wolf of the Vanguard's enforcement wing, Kellerman was the perfect target for him to test out his aggression. It didn't help that Kellerman had given him a sizable target with his own recent failures to capture or kill them. But this was not the time for playground antics. The rookie had to be put in his place, or Jon and Chloe could escape again.

"Do you have anything positive to contribute to this mission?" Kellerman asked, repressed anger seething in his hushed voice. "Because the fate of the country is at stake here, and I don't have time to babysit."

Molyneux's cheeks reddened in the pale moonlight. "I have just as much right to be here as you do, Anthony. My great-great-great-great-great-great-grandfather fought alongside Washington, Knox, Hamilton, Burr, and all the rest, just like yours."

He definitely felt like he had something to prove. The problem was, this wasn't the time to be testing his mettle for the first time. Molyneux was making Kellerman doubt the reasoning behind hereditary membership after all. In most things, Kellerman believed in meritocracy, which was why he had worked so hard to become so invaluable to the Vanguard.

Still, family was a bond that couldn't be earned by just anyone. It made certain people forever set apart from the rest. An elite group of caretakers in whose veins ran the blood of men who had already risen to the challenge for their nation. It gave a higher sense of purpose, a destiny, to your duty.

Regardless, ancestry could only get you so far. If Molyneux wanted to get anywhere with the Vanguard—or survive the evening without Kellerman's boot down his throat—he would need to cull the smart talk and up his game. It irked Kellerman that Continental Army Lieutenant Denis Molyneux was able to carry his Cincinnati lineage to today, while founding President-General George Washington—who sired no sons of his own—was not. Though he had adopted Martha's grandson, George Washington "Washy" Parke Custis, adoption didn't count for the Cincinnati's inheritance rules.

Washy, who had British royal blood in his veins through his birth mother, Eleanor Calvert, grew up at Mount Vernon and eventually inherited a plantation in what is today Arlington, Virginia. There he built the Greek Revival mansion known as Arlington House, which served as much as a shrine to his adoptive father as it was a home. Upon his death in 1857, Arlington House and the surrounding plantation were inherited by his daughter, Mary Anna Custis, and her husband, Robert E. Lee. Following the Confederacy's defeat in the Civil War, the United States government confiscated the property, repurposing the estate as a sprawling cemetery for Union soldiers. Today, the nation's military continue to be interred there, while Arlington House, now a memorial to Robert E. Lee, overlooked the Arlington National Cemetery that was once George Washington Parke Custis's estate.

So much lost from that ugly, ugly war. While pundits and bloggers argued about the true cause of the Civil War, they missed the most important lesson from the conflict.

It must never be allowed to happen again.

"There," Molyneux whispered, pointing south past a collection of outbuildings.

Kellerman looked. In the distance, the narrow beam of a flashlight diffused through the fog ever so briefly before being extinguished.

It was enough.

He put a finger to his lips, signaling silence to the smart-mouthed rookie. Recognizing that the dynamic of their hunt had just changed, Molyneux's face grew serious as he nodded.

*Maybe he'd prove a valuable agent yet.*

Kellerman gripped his pistol and began to move.

# CHAPTER 65
## *Mount Vernon, Virginia*

The distant voices had increased the urgency Chloe felt, but it had failed to produce results. She hadn't been able to find anything resembling a keyhole along the exterior, and, judging from Jon's frustrated huffing, he hadn't found anything either.

"I can't see anything inside," Jon said, confirming her suspicions. Even if he had spied a keyhole within, the iron gate was double-padlocked, a protection against vandals and thieves.

Maybe Jon was wrong. Maybe Washington, through Lafayette, had hidden his papers elsewhere on the property.

Or maybe there was nothing to find at all.

Nearby, the brickwork bore the hand-etched initials of Civil War soldiers from both the Union and the Confederacy who had paid their respects to the resting place of the father of the nation. Mount Vernon had been declared neutral territory, a historic site right at the dividing line between North and South. In fact, the waters of the Potomac at the east edge of the property formed the boundary line between the Confederacy's Virginia and the Union's Maryland. But instead of the site becoming a casualty of the bloodiest war the nation had ever seen, both sides recognized the important role that General Washington had played in their shared heritage and chose to honor that throughout the conflict.

Today, she wondered, how many would be willing to put aside personal feelings for the better of the country. Recent years had seen violent assaults on historic sites and memorials to great men from the nation's past. While the monuments to Confederate leaders like Robert E. Lee had taken the brunt of the attacks, it had since bled over to founding fathers like Washington, Jefferson, and Hamilton because they had owned slaves. While that practice was universally recognized as reprehensible today, vilifying men to whom the nation literally owed its existence for engaging in a common practice was both disingenuous and unhistori-

cal. As with the Bible, history had to be viewed through a proper con-
textual lens, not whatever "enlightened" retrospective magnifying glass
happened to be *en vogue*. If you looked hard enough, practically everyone worth celebrating from history had a skeleton or two that could be
condemned by modern revisionist tribunals. Ironically, so did the members of those very self-appointed populist tribunals, whose whole legacy
would likely be derided by the next generation of historians.

No, she didn't trust for a minute that the bulk of her technolo-
gy-obsessed peers felt even an inkling of the respect and reverence for
history and its makers held by the young soldiers who made their wartime pilgrimage here to Mount Vernon. If, God forbid, the country were
to one day descend into a second Civil War, countless irreplaceable historic treasures would undoubtedly be lost to the fires of blind, self-as-
sured rage.

Yet another reason to get to the bottom of what Washington and
Lafayette had hidden. And how it fit in with the Vanguard's current
treasonous plans.

Then she saw it. Proof that they were looking in the wrong place.

"It's not here," she said definitively.

"What do you mean it's not here? There's got to be something."

"There is. Just not here." She pointed to the sign posted to the far
left of the tomb. According to the sign, George and Martha Washington had been reinterred here upon completion of the new vault in 1831.
More than three decades after the general's death, the couple's remains
had been moved from the older family vault, which was located elsewhere on the property. Despite instructions for the new vault being
included in George's will, right down to the location and the building
material, the Washingtons' bodies moldered in the old vault, which his
will considered "in need of repairs" and "improperly positioned."

"Of course," Jon said, slapping his forehead. "That fits with the timeline. Lafayette visited in 1824, seven years before this tomb was built."

"And since Richard Clough Anderson, the only man with whom
Lafayette shared his secret, died in 1826, the hiding place wouldn't have
been moved," Chloe added.

Jon led the way back to the path from which they had come and
pointed to a signpost. "Didn't see it on the way in."

*Old Tomb.* An arrow pointing into the woods to the east of the path.

Neither of them had been looking for it, as for nearly two centuries it had been the larger and far grander new tomb and its surrounding memorial plaza where visitors had come to pay their respects. Perhaps that was what Washington meant by "improperly positioned." The new tomb was a magnificent edifice, not nearly as extravagant as the neoclassical mausoleum of future Chief Executive Ulysses S. Grant, but more fitting with the colonial plantation life Washington so adored. Its larger size and attendant plaza were more in line with the stature of the American Cincinnatus and the legacy he left behind.

*Though it seemed his bones were not all that had been interred in that first ancestral vault.*

They followed the sign, taking a side path into the woods before a short flight of stairs culminated in a small brick patio overhung with trees. At the southern end of the patio, a crumbling brick edifice huddled in the shifting shadows.

The original Washington family vault.

It was squat, just barely taller than Jon, though the weathered wooden door to the tomb only came up to her shoulder. The door was secured with a rusty padlock, a modern convenience prematurely decayed in this forgotten memorial. Even the bricks of the surrounding patio were faded with the years. It was as though, with no presidential remains to command interest any longer, this tomb had all but faded from history. This wasn't helped by the location. Chloe understood what Washington had meant in his will when he said the vault was "improperly located." Though twenty-two members of the Washington family had been interred here prior to the construction of the new tomb—including George's older brother Lawrence, who died in 1752—the site was isolated, hidden within a tangle of forest and vines at the edge of the wooded bluffs that dropped precipitously toward the banks of the Potomac below. The patio could hold a fraction of the visitors that the new tomb's plaza could, and the new vault itself could easily accommodate many more generations of Washingtons. In fact, judging by what she could tell of the exterior, this tomb was likely already at or near capacity before it was emptied.

She started feeling her way along the exterior of the tomb again, searching for something keyhole shaped. Almost immediately, her finger slipped into a hole to the right of the door. Upon closer examination, though, it was simply a divot where a chunk of ancient mortar had crumbled away.

*As a mason, you'd think Washington would do a better job with brick-work,* she mused. Despite his prominence as one of the young nation's most prominent Freemasons, he was not himself a practitioner of the trade that had given the masons its name. By the American Revolution, however, most Freemasons were not stone masons, but, rather, came from a number of trades and professions. Washington himself, she remembered, had been offered the post of Grand Master in 1783 by the newly formed Grand Lodge in Alexandria. Washington turned the offer down, instead becoming the inaugural president-general of the Society of the Cincinnati that same year.

A crash startled her from her reflection. She looked toward its source and saw Jon, a purloined stone in hand, attempting to break the lock.

"Whoever is out there is going to hear," she whispered with fearful urgency.

"It's in here. It's got to be. As a good friend of Washington's, Lafayette would have been able to gain access to the interior, probably even allowed to spend some time alone within. As good a time as any to hide the letters."

She couldn't argue with his logic. Still, every percussive impact felt like a sonar beacon calling to whoever else had come to Mount Vernon tonight. She hadn't seen signs of night watchmen, but that didn't mean they weren't elsewhere, prowling the sprawling property.

With one final blow, Jon slammed the rock into the lock, breaking loose not the lock itself but rather the latch that the lock secured. The whole assemblage fell to the ground in a burst of splinters, clattering on the brick pavers.

Smiling at her, he creaked open the door, flicked on his penlight, and stepped inside. Chloe was right behind.

Though the front and back of the tomb were brick, the remainder of the tomb was a barrel vault of cracked stone. Measuring twelve feet in length, seven feet wide, and only just tall enough at the apex for Jon to stand upright, Chloe again wondered how twenty-two coffins had fit within the space. While the centuries had etched broken veins in the stone, a quick survey proved what she had suspected—no hiding places there.

Which left one obvious option.

High on the back wall, just below the arch's peak, Jon's flashlight beam illuminated a familiar symbol, stamped into a brick.

*Bingo.*

Jon took out his knife and dug away at the mortar holding it in place. The old cement crumbled away easily. As though it had been designed to—one day—dissolve away, revealing its secrets to those enlightened enough to seek them.

Having cut a trough in the surrounding mortar, Jon wiggled the brick, easing it from its perch and placing it on the vault floor. His light returning to the void left behind, they immediately spied what had been hidden behind.

A keyhole.

"You found the key," he said. "Would you like to do the honors?"

"Absolutely." She took the key and slid it into the keyhole. It took some effort, the centuries having taken their toll on the locking mechanism, but she finally got it to turn. The hinges of the small iron door audibly protested, being nearly fused together by almost two centuries of disuse. On the third hard tug, it swiveled open.

"Flashlight," she said, holding out her hand. Jon passed it to her, and she pointed the beam inside the narrow aperture. Amid the dingy reflection of timeworn iron, a yellowed envelope lay in the center of the forgotten safe.

The Lafayette Confession.

She grabbed it and shut the safe door. Jon was at the ready with the brick he had removed, sliding it back into place and kicking at the crumbled mortar on the floor to disperse it. It wouldn't take the staff long to find the loose brick once they investigated the broken lock, but there was no sense in broadcasting it to them.

"Come on," he said as she slid the letter inside a jacket pocket. "Let's get out of here before those night watchmen show up."

She clicked off the penlight and led the way across the low vault, opening the tomb door. When she stepped outside, she froze.

At first, she tried to tell herself her mind was playing tricks on her, that the thickening fog and the shadow-scratched moonlight was conjuring ghosts from the night air. But she had no such luck.

Waiting on the brick patio and blocking their exit were her current two least favorite people in the world. Kellerman and Molyneux, both with pistols pointed her way, both wearing a look of vengeance and victory.

Kellerman grinned at her. "Did you really think we wouldn't find you?"

# CHAPTER 66
## *Mount Vernon, Virginia*

Jon was inches from exiting the tomb when Chloe froze at Keller-man's words. He halted, then slunk back into the shadows, scrambling for a plan.

The brick. It wasn't much of a weapon, but it could work in a pinch. As quietly as he could, he extracted Lafayette's brick from the wall once more and hefted it as he crept back to the tomb's entrance. But before he stepped outside, he realized the plan wasn't going to work.

Kellerman wasn't alone. Jon could hear Molyneux's voice now, too. He might be able to clobber one of them before he shot Chloe or himself, but he only had one brick. He was outnumbered and outgunned.

Still, he couldn't leave her out there alone. While he was a loose end, she had what they really wanted—the envelope hidden in Washington's tomb. It might be a losing proposition, but if he could hide the brick until just the right moment . . .

His phone buzzed in his pocket. The vibration seemed to echo in the barrel-vaulted chamber. He hoped it was just in his head, fear magnifying every potential betrayal of his presence.

It wasn't.

"I hear you in there, Jon," Kellerman called, his tone mocking. "Does your girlfriend here know you're getting booty call texts this late at night?"

Jon checked the screen, sure it wasn't a booty call and praying it wasn't a drunk text. It was neither.

*On your move.*

He turned the phone back to sleep mode and slid it back into his pocket. Holding the brick behind his back in a pitcher's grip, he stepped from the tomb and into the pale moonlight. Kellerman stood straight ahead, his pistol aimed casually at Chloe. Molyneux stood to the left, blocking the closest exit from the small brick plaza, white-knuckle gripping his gun with both hands.

"Thanks for joining our little party," Kellerman said, clearly in charge. "You've taken quite a few things that rightly belong to us. And we'd like them back now."

"I'm sure I have no idea what you're talking about," Chloe countered, her face set hard.

"Cute. But acting tough when you've already lost just stinks of bad sportsmanship. You've had quite a busy forty-eight hours. Vandalism, breaking and entering, theft of property from several federal institutions and well-connected private entities. You're both looking at quite a lot of prison time. Give us what you took from the National Archives, the JFK museum exhibit, from the *Victura*, from Anderson House—"

"And from my room," Molyneux interjected.

Kellerman smiled mirthlessly, pained to have to humor the junior agent. "As well as whatever reason you just desecrated the tomb of the founder of our country, and we can make the charges go away."

Both of their faces bore moon-shadowed smirks of predestined victory.

Jon knew the folly of assuming victory prematurely. As Yogi Berra had once rightly quipped, it ain't over 'til it's over.

"We know all about the Vanguard and your war profiteering," Jon said. "Your presidential assassinations and your false flag attacks, all so you can make a quick buck by riding your great-great-granddaddy's coattails."

Kellerman's reaction was not what he was expecting.

"War profiteering?" Kellerman laughed. "Is that what you think this is about? I thought you were smarter than that. After all you've managed to dig up, and you actually think we're trying to start global conflicts for fun and profit?" His demeanor turned serious, glaring and accusatory. "You know *nothing*."

Was Kellerman screwing with them, trying to throw them off course? Or was there really more to the equation that they weren't seeing? Jon would have to unpack that later. For now, he had two guns pointed at his head.

Time for a different strategy.

"You've got us," Jon said. "We're just two hyped-up millennials who love urban exploration. Abandoned sailboats, abandoned tombs, fancy mansions after everyone's gone home . . . Well, not everyone." He fixed Molyneux with a stare. "Does Vice President Finney know that his treasonous conversation was overheard earlier tonight? Or is that yet another of your screwups, Patrick?"

His gun still trained on Chloe and Jon, Kellerman glared ice daggers at Molyneux.

Exactly as Jon had planned.

Jon whipped the brick forward, hitting Kellerman in the shoulder as he crashed into Chloe, dodging the reflexive shot fired by the assassin. Molyneux froze for a moment, caught off guard by Jon's sudden assault, then leveled his weapon at them.

Another gunshot tore through the still night air.

Molyneux collapsed to the ground, screaming as he clutched his bleeding leg. He stared accusingly at Kellerman, whose eyes went wide.

Another shot pierced the air, this one slicing harmlessly through Kellerman's jacket and pinging off the low brick wall at the back of the plaza.

The assassin reached for a hostage, but Jon and Chloe were already on the move.

Leaping over the prone Molyneux, Jon led the way up the short set of stairs and south down the path, away from Washington's mansion.

Kellerman started to pursue, yelling, "Get up, you fool!" to his fallen comrade. But, as Jon looked behind him, another gunshot sent the agent scrambling back into cover.

They had a window for escape, Jon knew, but it was about to slam shut. The shooter who had stymied the Vanguard's shakedown attempt had another role to play shortly, and once he moved to do so, Kellerman would be free to pursue them.

Jon and Chloe ran full-tilt down the path, wading through the thick fog as though the hounds of hell nipped at their heels. The weather would help to occlude their escape, but it also made seeing where they were going at this speed difficult. They may have had a head start, but breaking an ankle with an ill-placed step, or slamming into a tree or signpost, would give Kellerman more than enough time to catch up.

A fourth shot rang out, likely in response to Kellerman trying to chase them again. The shooter would need to be on the move now. Jon hoped it would be enough.

The path split, the right a flatter, more meandering path to the pioneer farm. To the left, a steep descent down unevenly spaced dirt terraces separated by massive unfinished timbers. It was treacherous, but there was really only one option.

Jon plunged down the left path, Chloe breathing heavily at his side. His lungs burned from the effort, gulping down the cool moist air as he bounded down the makeshift stairs. The thick trees surrounding the path merged their branches overhead, crowding out the moonlight and casting the fog-drenched path in shadow.

Another gunshot sounded from behind. A different caliber than the last one. Kellerman was back in the hunt at last.

Through the trees ahead, Jon could see moonlight reflecting off the mist-shrouded waters of the Potomac. The wharf had been used in Washington's day not only for large-scale fishing but also for sending the produce of the plantation to markets along the eastern seaboard. Now, as it had been in the centuries since the plantation fell into disuse, the wharf was primarily used for receiving visitors to Mount Vernon. While the river cruise boats and ferries that would dock in the morning were absent tonight, the pier that received them beckoned in the distance.

They were almost there.

Behind them, Kellerman fired a pair of shots in their direction. A bush to their left shook as shards of leaves exploded into the air. The fog and the chase must have been impairing their pursuer's aim. But their luck wouldn't hold forever.

Racing down one last section of timbered stairs, Jon and Chloe reached the river. A number of reconstructed farm buildings dotted the hillside to the right, while the river's waves lapped at the embankment to their left. Straight ahead was a wooden pier, at the end of which was an octagonal, open-air structure that dated to 1880, when the Mount Vernon Ladies' Association commissioned the construction of a new wharf to replace the earlier structure that had stood at the site.

Dirt exploded to Jon's right as another of Kellerman's bullets buried itself in the ground. He was getting closer.

"Come on," Jon urged between gasps, rushing down the wooden planks of the pier. He felt exposed, nowhere to hide and nothing between him and Kellerman's bullet beyond the gray miasma that floated atop the Potomac. The brick pillars of the building at the end of the wharf promised some shelter, but it was still a dead end.

"Now what?" Chloe asked once they reached the building, their backs pressed against a pair of pillars between them and Kellerman. "We can't hide here forever. He's bound to search here before morning."

Over the pounding of blood in his ears, Jon heard the roar of an engine. As the sound grew louder, a go-fast boat appeared through the mist, heading straight for the wharf.

"Are you kidding me?" Chloe's eyes were wide with panic. "We can't just jump in the water! If this envelope gets wet . . ."

Jon smiled and put his hand on her arm. "It's fine, Chloe. He's on our side."

Popularized during the Prohibition era, go-fast boats had become synonymous with smuggling. From rum-running in the 1920s to smuggling drugs ashore in the present day, the boats' combination of high speed and low radar profile made them valuable tools for quick infiltrations. Or, in this case, exfiltrations. Also known as "cigarette boats," the modern version had become popular with offshore powerboat racers in the 1960s, though their speedier incarnations were still the go-to method for many drug smugglers.

Tonight, this particular boat would be smuggling something far more valuable than bricks of cocaine or heroin.

The boat pulled up alongside the far side of the wharf, slowing but not stopping. Jon ran across the building and out the other side, a resigned Chloe following right behind. A pair of bullets splintered the brick pillar to their right, blasting a shard of hardened clay into Jon's forearm. He grunted, but refused to let Kellerman know he'd scored any sort of hit. They leapt into the boat, another fusillade of shots chasing after them as the driver gunned the engine, steering them into the depths of the fog-drenched river.

The last sound Jon heard before they rounded a bend in the river, leaving behind Mount Vernon for good, was a howling scream, born of Kellerman's bottomless frustration at being outmaneuvered once again.

It was music to his ears.

# CHAPTER 67
*Charles County, Maryland*

C hloe was still trying to piece together the events of the past few
minutes.

Jon had told her he had reached out to a trusted friend while
she was in the airport bathroom before their flight from Dallas to Boston,
but he didn't elaborate. At the time, she didn't think too much of it. Then he
had received a call from his friend before they broke into Anderson House
earlier that night, but her thoughts had quickly shifted to the task at hand
as soon as they'd arrived at the mansion. A flurry of text messages had followed in the back of the cab taking them to Mount Vernon, and again she
hadn't pressed. Part of her was afraid that his "friend" might've been a significant other. His caginess certainly seemed to indicate it was something like
that. But she couldn't have been more wrong.

As their savior continued to steer them down the wide serpentine
swath of the Potomac, Jon turned to her and grinned.

"Chloe, this is Wayne Wilkins. Wayne, Chloe Harper."

Wayne gave her a friendly smile and extended his hand in welcome,
keeping one hand on the wheel. "It's a pleasure to meet you."

"And you didn't think to let me in on your plans?" Chloe asked,
giving Jon a half-serious scowl.

Jon gave her an apologetic grimace. "Sorry. When I first called him,
I didn't want to expose him to some cute girl I'd just met and some old
conspiracy theorist who, as it so happened, was feeding our info to the
enemy. Then things at Anderson House kind of took over, and once we
got to Mount Vernon, I wanted to keep everything as close to the vest
as possible. I had hoped that we wouldn't even need Wayne's support,
but if we did, I didn't want any accidental betrayal of that. I'm sorry. I
should have trusted you enough to clue you in."

In her elation at learning that he hadn't been texting some undis-
closed lover while they risked life and limb together, she skipped right
over anger and settled in relief.

Then something else clicked.

"Wait," she said. "You're Wayne Wilkins. I know that name."

Jon shrugged sheepishly. "Considering how thoroughly you seem to have researched me, I'd be surprised if you didn't come across his name at some point."

Then she remembered. "You were there. In New York two years ago."

Wayne clicked his tongue. "Officially, no. Unofficially, Jon and I may have helped each other out a time or two."

"So you're a civilian now?"

"Not exactly. But if I told you exactly what I do and who I work for, I'd have to kill you. And considering how we just met and how you seemingly just escaped from death's grasp, I'd say that'd be a real shame."

"But do you work for a federal agency or institution? Someone with teeth?"

"You could say that."

"Good. Because we've got a big problem."

"One step at a time, Chloe," Jon admonished. "Let's see what President Washington had to say."

In all the excitement with Kellerman and Molyneux, she had all but forgotten about the envelope inside her jacket pocket. She pulled it out and examined it, Jon drawing close alongside to shine his penlight on their prize.

Her first thought was that the envelope felt too new to date from the 1700s or even from 1824. She flipped it over and saw an embossed eagle in the paper above the flap.

But it wasn't the Society eagle. Nor was it the Great Seal of the United States, nor that of the Office of the President. It was almost identical to the Great Seal, though it bore a key difference. Beneath the eagle was a single star, representing the creation of its unique institution as the one high body that could rule on legal matters throughout the nation.

The Supreme Court of the United States.

"What in the world?" Jon mused aloud, clearly coming to the same conclusions as she had. "Why is Washington's 220-year-old confession inside an envelope from the Supreme Court?"

Chloe didn't know, but she didn't think they'd like the answer. Carefully, she pried loose the adhesive and removed a single sheet of yellowed paper from the envelope.

> To whomever finds this, looking for the confessions of George Washington: I have taken them. I have seen firsthand the perils that the Vanguard pose to our nation and its future. But they are too powerful, holding sway in Washington, DC, as well as with Hearst and other publications of note. This traitorous cabal did not hesitate to kill President Lincoln, so I fear they would not take issue with killing a Supreme Court Justice. Thus, my need for caution.
>
> I have entrusted President Washington's letters, as well as my own findings about the Society's misdeeds, to my son, Charles. Secrets of this heightened gravity must be entrusted to those closest to me: my family. If you have found this letter and earnestly believe that the time has finally come for the truth to come to light, seek out my son and he shall aid you in your quest. And godspeed to you and Charles both.
>
> If the reader of this unsent missive supports the so-called Vanguard, know that you will find no answers from Charles. My son understands the stakes and will not be threatened into compliance. You may have staked your claim on my hometown more than a century ago, but you will not turn this great nation into your own permanent kingdom. America is stronger

and better than you. In the end, the truth will out, and you will fall.

Most Sincerely,
William Howard Taft
Chief Justice of the United States, formerly President
of the United States

June 18, 1922

"So close, yet so far," Chloe said, disheartened.

Jon sounded less disappointed. "With Taft and Larz Anderson being such good friends, I guess it's not all that surprising that the blue-blooded braggart would share his family secret with his most powerful pal in Washington. The question is, why did Anderson let him take the papers, only to hide the key in the Winter Garden?"

"Maybe he wanted the Vanguard to fail after all. But with all the purpose that the Society gave to his life, he couldn't bring himself to reveal the confessions himself, instead allowing Taft to have them and washing his hands of the matter."

"Trying to have his cake and eat it too," Jon quipped. "Wayne, we need to get to Ohio, ASAP."

"Ohio?" Chloe asked. "What part?"

"Taft's hometown. Cincinnati."

She was floored. She had been thinking about the Society's name as the plural of Cincinnatus for so long that she'd all but forgotten the far more common usage of the word. The coincidence was too much to ignore.

"The Vanguard's secret archives," she said. "The records of all their assassinations and false flag attacks, all the wars they've started. It's got to be there."

"*Something* is there," Jon said. "Or, at least, it was a century ago."

Wayne dialed back on the throttle, quieting the motor to chime in on the conversation. "I can get us on a jet to get there by daybreak."

"You're coming too?" Chloe asked.

"Jon said an attack is imminent, right? And if the vice president is involved, we may be looking at an assassination attempt."

"Right, so?"

"So it's going to be a little tricky snooping around unnoticed in Cincinnati in the morning. The president is coming to town."

# PART THREE
*TAFT*

"The means of defense against foreign danger have been always the instruments of tyranny at home."
– James Madison

"The trouble with me is I like to talk too much."
– William Howard Taft

# CHAPTER 68
## *Cincinnati, Ohio*

The eastern horizon was ablaze with dawn's early light as Rafael Vargas drove into Cincinnati. He had swapped license plates in Tennessee shortly after dumping the trooper's body in the woods. In a matter of minutes, he would be done with the van for good. And by this afternoon, a missing trooper would be the least of anyone's worries.

Today was the culmination of a long and deadly saga orchestrated by the United States itself. His own anger with the global tyrant was strong, born from the effects of a crippled Venezuelan economy that had seen his father gunned down by American-made weapons in the hands of drug lords who had seized upon the failed war on drugs to create and thrive from economies of fear. But his countrymen had even more at stake, and he fought for them as well. His homeland had been brought to the brink of another civil war by the domineering influence of American aggression, a cycle that had seen Washington topple leaders across Latin America for more than a century. They had mercilessly imposed their will in Nicaragua, in El Salvador, in Panama, in Chile, in Mexico, in Venezuela, and beyond.

The United States continued to flex its muscles in honor of the two-century-old Monroe Doctrine. The policy was established in 1823 by President James Monroe, seeking to end the colonization of the Americas by European powers. As leader of the expanding United States that was not only expanding in size and population but also commercially on a global scale, Monroe called for Europe to assert itself in its own sphere of influence—specifically, Asia, Africa, and the Middle East—and leave the Western Hemisphere alone. This, of course, paved the way for the US to establish its own brand of dominance in the sphere of influence it had claimed, a policy that ramped up significantly during the Cold War, when many of the troubled economies and broken governments of Latin America had turned to socialism as a potential cure for their ills. Socialism being anathema to Washington's war on the Soviet brand of militant leftism, millions of Central and South Americans quickly learned the ill effects of falling afoul of the United States.

Vargas's GPS told him he had arrived at his destination. He parked the van in the garage beneath the building, unloaded his shrouded cargo onto a waiting handcart, and pushed it into the elevator.

Moments later, when he reached his destination, he was amazed at how preset everything was. Holes had been drilled in the floor to properly align his attack. The setting was at once open for maximum effect while also providing sufficient hiding places to obscure his presence until the moment arrived. Arocha had thought of everything. Even the method of attack would be unexpected. For Vargas, it was all proof of how the universe was smiling upon their venture.

Today, Venezuela would push back. With his actions this afternoon, the balance would finally be tipped in Latin America's favor, toppling Washington from its throne and recapturing the pride that dwelled within the heart of every Venezuelan. In a Venezuela without the United States, the possibilities were endless. The nation would be free to pursue its own destiny, free from self-serving drug wars, free from anti-socialist coups, free from military interventions to protect American stock prices, free from the pernicious influence of unbridled hubris and avarice.

After two-hundred years of dominance in the Western Hemisphere, the United States was about to discover how very vulnerable it was.

# CHAPTER 69
*Hebron, Kentucky*

Jon could see the verdant diamond of Great American Ball Park, where the Cincinnati Reds played, as well as the dazzling digital displays of the Jumbotron at the Bengals' Paul Brown Field, as the private plane made its final approach.

Wayne had called in some favor to arrange the last-minute flight out of Maryland Airport 2W5, a single-runway airfield east of the tiny coastal community of Indian Head. The town's claim to fame was the Indian Head Naval Surface Warfare Center, where the Navy had worked since 1890 to develop new and more efficient propellants for guns and rockets. It was Major Carla Yancy, the second-in-command of the center, whom Wayne had called for the favor. Yancy picked up the disheveled trio at the docks, gave them a ride to the airport, and chartered the flight—complete with emergency after-hours flight authorization.

The city of Cincinnati had been founded in 1788 and christened "Losantiville" by an overly clever surveyor by the name of John Filson. Filson had called it "the city opposite mouth of the Licking River," using the French "ville" for city, the Greek "anti" for opposite, the Latin "os" for mouth, and the leading "L" to represent the Licking River. The Licking River was a tributary of the greater Ohio River on the Kentucky side, but the city's rise to prominence was due to its location at the confluence of the Ohio, the Miami, and the Greater Miami Rivers. The town's nod to the less-important waterway would not last.

In 1800, Arthur St. Clair, first governor of the Northwest Territory and former president of the Continental Congress, traveled to Losantiville and saw the potential of the burgeoning settlement's strategic placement. He renamed it in honor of the Society of the Cincinnati, of which he was a founding member. In decades that followed, Cincinnati grew to become one of the most important and prosperous cities in the region. Many historians considered it to be the first truly American city, as its eastern rivals such as New York, Boston, and Philadelphia had been founded under British rule.

Jon and Chloe had tried to nap during the flight, anticipating hitting the ground running. His efforts had been hit or miss, but he had managed to grab a few winks in transit. By the sound of her snoring, Chloe had been more successful in her slumbering.

Wayne, meanwhile, had been busy.

"Thirty-four calls to eleven different agencies," he said, hanging up his phone as he saw Chloe stirring to life. "Not a one of them thinks what we have is actionable to get the president to change his schedule for the day."

Chloe protested, "But the vice president . . ."

"That's one heck of an accusation for someone to follow on faith. They don't know you as a trusted source, so the tie is definitely going to the VP. Plus, even you didn't hear either of them say, specifically, that they're going to kill the president. Not to mention specifics on time, location, or anything like that."

"So it's useless?"

"Do you see me giving up?" Wayne countered. "The Secret Service gets thousands of threats every day, and while they vet all of them, they don't change the president's itinerary for anything but serious, specific, and credible threats. If they took as gospel every threat that came in, he'd never come out of the White House bunker."

He turned a tablet computer toward them. "I did, however, find out some info on your friends. Patrick Molyneux, PhD in American History from the University of Chicago six years ago. Top of his class. He's published a handful of papers in peer-reviewed journals, but has hopped from university to university every year since graduation."

"Brilliant mind, but restless," Jon said, knowing the feeling all too well.

"Something like that." Wayne tapped the screen. "A last name wasn't much to go on via conventional methods, but I tapped into the Society of the Cincinnati's hereditary records. Three Kellermans in the Society, but only one of them matches the age range you described."

He spun the tablet around again. Kellerman's face stared back at them. "Anthony Kellerman. High school quarterback, then straight into the Marines after graduation. He excelled there, eventually being tapped for their elite Force Recon division. Dozens of black operations across the globe before retiring from the unit and working for Vanguard Solutions, a domestic security consultancy group based out of DC"

"Seriously?" Chloe said. "They're brazen enough to name their cover operations after their top-secret secret society?"

"Why not?" Jon asked. "Had you heard of either one before last night?"

Chloe shook her head.

"People can't put pieces together if they don't know they even exist," Wayne said, returning his attention to the tablet. "Neither one has a criminal history beyond a handful of parking tickets and minor traffic violations. Both single, never married, no living family beyond Kellerman's mom, who is dealing with late-stage Alzheimer's at a Florida nursing home."

"So no real leverage there," Chloe said. Her statement gave Jon pause. That she thought of the enemy's family as potential leverage over their foe revealed how personal this had become for her. But then, this had started with Kellerman stealing family from her. He understood all too well. When your loved ones were involved, all bets were off.

"I'm guessing Vanguard Solutions is the group's cover to pay its enforcers," Wayne continued. "And probably how they launder money to finance their operations. Skimming corporate and government tills, using blackmail to fund bribes."

Jon saw a potential lead there. "Who's on the company's board? Any high-level government officials?"

Wayne shook his head. "That's a black hole. It's a private company, and it seems to be a shell at that. In fact, are you familiar with matryoshka dolls?"

Jon was indeed familiar with the famous Russian nesting dolls, one of the nation's most recognized historic handicrafts.

"It's like that," Wayne continued. "Shell after shell after shell. Each one less revealing than the last."

Chloe's face fell. "So that's a dead end."

"For now. I've got my guy working on it still. But we can't count on him finding anything to prevent whatever they've got planned today."

Wayne unzipped his carry-on and handed Jon a pistol. "Can I trust you both not to shoot yourselves in the foot?"

Chloe held out her hand, and Jon handed over the gun. In a series of smooth, quick motions, Chloe dismantled the pistol, then reassembled it. Jon raised his eyebrows.

Chloe caught his expression and gave him a sheepish grin. "My dad was an FBI agent for decades. Of course he showed me how to handle a weapon."

"Good to know." Jon took back the pistol, checked to make sure the safety was on, then stood, twirled the weapon like a gunslinger, and aimed down the sights at the far end of the plane. "Bang."

Wayne chuckled. "You two are adorable."

Jon ignored the comment. "How are we going to get these through the airport?"

"Private terminal. Yancy sorted us all out."

"Seriously, who are you?" Chloe asked.

Wayne just smiled. "I'm your guardian angel. Your very well-connected guardian angel."

The plane leveled out and descended to the tarmac below. It was Jon's least favorite part of the flight, part of him always sure that one wheel would rip off with the impact and send the plane twisting and tumbling down the runway, breaking apart piece by piece until nothing was left but a smoldering ruin of steel and bone. But, as with every one of the numerous flights Jon had taken in his life, the pilot stuck the landing, the plane remaining intact.

"Nervous?" Chloe asked, sensing the tension that had arisen, then flooded out of him upon landing.

"Just not my favorite part of traveling."

"Me neither. But now is."

"Taxiing to the gate?" Jon asked.

"No. Arriving somewhere new."

They had discussed their plans while waiting for the plane back in Maryland, but now it was time to put them into action. He and Chloe would endeavor to discover where Charles Phelps Taft II had hidden the Washington letters his more famous father had purloined from the Mount Vernon tomb, hopefully finding a weakness that could finally bring down the Vanguard. Meanwhile, Wayne would use every connection he had to try to prevent an attack on the president.

Jon envied Wayne. The agent had connections throughout the government, and had recently gained the ear of the president himself. His task was clear-cut, if still difficult. Jon and Chloe's, meanwhile, was amorphous, a needle in a city-sized haystack.

Though he had an idea where to start looking.

Once the plane had pulled into the shelter of a private hangar, the trio disembarked and took a golf-cart shuttle to a taxi stand servicing airport arrivals.

"Be safe out there, you guys," Wayne said as he got into his cab. "I won't be able to have your backs this time."

"You too. And godspeed, my friend." Jon had a strange feeling that he might never see him again. The odds were stacked against them on both fronts, and time was not in their favor. But they had to try.

As Wayne's taxi drove off toward the city, Jon and Chloe climbed into the next waiting vehicle. He checked his watch. Just past ten in the morning. The president took the stage at three. Which meant they had to hurry.

If they didn't find a way to finish this in the next five hours, the Vanguard would win. And America would never be the same again.

# CHAPTER 70
### *30,000 feet above West Virginia*

Anthony Kellerman's fingers dug into the cushioned armrest of his seat. The Gulfstream may have been a cushy ride, but its armrests made for lousy stress relievers.

He had already torn through three neck pillows and dug holes in two seats, but none of it was quelling his rage at being outmaneuvered yet again.

Who could have guessed Jon would have brought along his special agent pal to provide overwatch with a sniper rifle in hand? Wayne Wilkins, who Kellerman had since traced to Jon's exploits in New York two years earlier, was a force to be reckoned with on the battlefield. It had worked in his favor in Mount Vernon. But it would prove to be useless where they were going next.

Unfortunately, injuring Patrick Molyneux and facilitating Jon and Chloe's escape wasn't the end of Wilkins's meddling. Not only had he reportedly arranged transport to Cincinnati for them and tagged along for the ride, he had also been tied to a series of recent queries by an NSA analyst about him and Molyneux, as well as about Vanguard Solutions. Exactly the sort of questions that could be very bad for the Vanguard if today's mission went sour.

Which meant it was all the more imperative for Kellerman to ensure it didn't.

In a matter of hours, whatever Jon and Chloe had already found would be lost beneath the media onslaught that would follow the assassination of President Talquin. If they had already found anything that could stand on its own, they would have gone to the authorities. They were still chasing leads, looking for something substantive to stop the Vanguard's plans.

Kellerman drew little relief from the apparent fact that Jon and Chloe had thus far found nothing actionable. That they had come to Cincinnati based on what they had discovered meant they were on a track the Vanguard did not want them on. Which was why Kellerman and Molyneux were heading there themselves. To regain their honor by killing their foes. And to preserve the legacy of the Vanguard.

Molyneux had said little on the flight thus far, nursing his leg wound and grumbling to himself in the corner. Though the wound was superficial, the itinerant professor had been shocked into silence by being shot.

*At least now I know how to shut him up in the future.*

Kellerman had assured Gaines that both of them would be prepared for action once they landed. But, unlike before, they were playing on their home turf now. It was late in the fourth, with the game on the line. But Kellerman had snagged a ringer. And that would make all the difference.

This time they weren't playing from behind. This time, the Vanguard held all the cards.

He only hoped it would be enough.

When Gaines had presented his plans for the trap, Kellerman had initially been skeptical. But the more he considered it, the more it seemed perfect.

Growing up in the mountains of Colorado, his father had taken him hunting from a young age. One of Kellerman's most vivid early memories was felling his first deer at age seven. The day before, he had spotted a deer and chased after it, his rifle in hand. The ruckus spooked the deer, which darted away into the woods. Then his father taught him how to use the deer's own natural instincts against it. Using stealth, camouflage, and pheromones to lure the animal into position, young Anthony Kellerman waited until the right moment, then delivered the kill shot.

Decades later, Kellerman still claimed that night's feast of venison was the tastiest meal he had ever eaten.

So it would be today. Jon and Chloe had been thorns in his side for far too long. Which would make the bloody conclusion to their cross-country dance so much more worth savoring.

One way or another, Jon and Chloe would be dead by nightfall.

# CHAPTER 71
## Cincinnati, Ohio

After spending the night exploring George Washington's grand estate, Jon found William Howard Taft's childhood home to be somewhat meager by comparison. The house itself was a sizable mansion that was far from humble, even if its grandeur paled against the aristocratic manor house at Mount Vernon. But unlike the rural sprawl of Washington's colonial plantation, Taft's home was built in historic Mount Auburn, an upper-class community overlooking downtown Cincinnati. Built a mile north of the bustling downtown area, the suburban Mount Auburn enjoyed a cooler, more sedate setting than Cincinnati proper while offering picturesque views of the city and the Ohio River beyond. By contemporary standards of the district, the Greek Revival house was smaller than many of its well-heeled neighbors, but its occupants went on to greatness few of them would ever know.

The future president's father, Alphonso Taft, had moved the family to the house in 1851, having established his law practice in Cincinnati a decade earlier. Six years later, Alphonso's seventh child and third to survive infancy was born in this very house. Though schoolchildren today knew William Howard Taft because of a rumor that his girth had gotten him stuck in a bathtub, he had a far greater claim to fame. Taft was the only man to ever serve as both president of the United States and chief justice of the Supreme Court.

And apparently he and his family also held the key to bringing down the Vanguard once and for all.

The Taft political dynasty was one of the longest-running in the country, though it didn't have the modern-day name recognition that the Kennedy or Bush clans did. Tracing their American roots to Robert Taft, Sr., who had immigrated to the Massachusetts colony from England in the mid-1600s, the Taft family built up a legacy of public service across New England from the beginning of the United States. A cousin

310

of Alphonso Taft, Ezra Taft Benson, had been one of the first apostles in the Church of Jesus Christ of Latter-Day Saints, while his great-grandson, also named Ezra Taft Benson, had been the Mormon church's thirteenth president, as well as Eisenhower's Secretary of Agriculture.

But the real dynasty began with Alphonso. A Vermont native, Alphonso Taft set a tradition of Tafts at Yale, getting his undergrad from the university before earning his law degree there as well. In 1832, he co-founded the infamous Skull and Bones secret society that dominated conspiracy headlines during the 2004 presidential election, as both George W. Bush and John Kerry were Bonesmen. Taft would go on to become a successful lawyer in Cincinnati, serving as an Ohio Superior Court justice before accepting a post as the first president of the Cincinnati Bar Association. He made a few unsuccessful forays for elected office as well, first in 1856 for a US House seat, then in 1875 for the governorship of Ohio. But the pinnacle of his career was serving in Ulysses S. Grant's cabinet, first as secretary of war—a post his son would later hold under Teddy Roosevelt—and then as attorney general.

And though Alphonso Taft's descendants had gone on to become senators, governors, ambassadors, and cabinet members, they all paled in comparison to the gregarious third surviving son of the dynasty's founder.

"William Howard Taft was really born here, huh?" Chloe asked.

"Sure enough. The National Park Service even restored it to how it would have looked when he lived here."

They entered the visitor's center and were immediately greeted by a park ranger. A tall forty-something black woman with a close-cropped haircut, Ranger Grosh invited them to sign into the guestbook and look around the exhibits and bookstore until the next tour, which was slated to begin in five minutes.

"So why here?" Chloe asked once Grosh had stepped away.

In truth, Jon didn't have anything solid to go on. Just a series of hunches that he prayed played out. But he wasn't about to tell Chloe that.

"Taft specifically mentioned his hometown in the letter he left in Washington's tomb," he said. "He also mentioned his son. While Taft had two sons, the oldest, Robert, became a US Senator and spent much of his career in Washington, following in his father's footsteps in that regard. But Charles, his youngest, stayed in Cincinnati, getting heavily involved in local politics starting in the 1920s and serving as the mayor during the 1950s. Other than a stint serving in a pair of directorial roles under FDR during World War II, he was a Cincinnati man through and through."

"So what does Charles have to do with this place?"

Jon pointed to a nearby diorama of a life-sized animatronic of Charlie Taft sitting on a riverbank surrounded by fishing gear and the back end of a classic AMC Matador. "Everything. It was his passion project for the last few decades of his life. Reacquiring the home, getting it designated as a national historic landmark, and restoring it to its original state. He apparently even managed to track down a lot of the original furniture before his death in 1983."

"And you think Charles maybe, what, hid Washington's confession in the baseboards or something?"

He caught her snark, but chalked it up to the same frustration he was feeling. "It wouldn't be the first time we found something hidden in a wall in the past twenty-four hours. I don't know what President Taft had him hide or what instructions he gave him, but with my Internet searches on the way over turning up nothing else, I figure this is as good a place to start as any."

Chloe conceded the point. It wasn't as if she had any better ideas. At this stage, they were shooting in the dark and praying for a lucky break. It was an awful time to run out of concrete leads. The Vanguard planned to kill the president in a matter of hours, and it wouldn't be long before Kellerman and Molyneux tracked them to Cincinnati. And even if he and Chloe were able to elude the killers for the next few hours, it would only get worse from there. Once Vice President Finney became the Vanguard's man in the White House, the architects of yet another presidential assassination would have near-unlimited resources to hunt down and destroy both of them.

Which meant Jon was praying more than ever that there was something to his hunch.

Ranger Grosh came back into the room. "The tour is about to begin. Follow me, please."

They were joined on the tour by a pair of other couples, a family of five, and a greasy-haired hippie guy filming everything with a camcorder. Jon shook his head and smiled. *Talk about a blast from the past.*

Grosh led the group across the grounds from the visitor center into what was once the kitchen of the Taft family home. Everyone took their seats in front of a widescreen television set against one wall, and Grosh queued up the welcome video, which was rife with information about the home, the life and legacy of William Howard Taft, and the restoration of the home to its nineteenth-century appearance. Once the video was completed, Grosh took the group on the tour of the home.

The three-story mansion was large, especially by mid-1800s standards. Long and narrow, it cut a curious profile, but the interior was filled with historical delights. The majority of rooms, including the dining room, a handful of bedrooms, a nursery, a library, and a family room were stocked with original or period furniture, including the very crib William Howard Taft slept in as a baby. Several other rooms held exhibits showcasing the home's history, the Taft family, and the political legacy of William Howard Taft. One exhibit was filled with campaign materials from his 1908 presidential run, including a ticket to the Republican National Convention that year and the Bible he swore on when taking the Oath of Office. Another charted his public fallout with Teddy Roosevelt that cost the party the White House in 1912. Still another was dedicated to what he had considered his greatest legacy—his tenure as chief justice of the United States.

Knowing what he did now of the Vanguard's pernicious influence, Jon surmised that the sweeping changes to the Supreme Court Taft was able to orchestrate was not the only reason he preferred the latter role. The lifelong appointment was free from decisions about foreign policy or war. He was finally able to effect nationwide change without enduring threats from the Vanguard's agents.

Of course, if they had had any idea what Taft had stolen from Washington's grave and hidden in its place, even retirement would not have protected him from their wrath.

"Anything screaming 'secret hiding place' to you?" Chloe asked.

"No, not yet. You?"

"Afraid not."

Jon was trying not to grow despondent. After all this time, following clues across the country and through the centuries, the trail was finally growing cold. At the eleventh hour, their quest was on the cusp of coming up short. He racked his brain to think of where else Charles might have hidden his father's evidence against the Vanguard.

The problem was that the elder Taft had died more than half a century before his son. In fact, Taft may well have expected Charles to

reveal his findings publicly when he found the right time and opportunity. But such an opportunity never came. Perhaps it was fear of the
Vanguard's retaliation. Perhaps it was fear of the Cold War fallout that
the revelations might wreak on national security. One way or another,
Charles buried the secret. And unlike Bobby Kennedy or George Washington, he hadn't provided much of a road map to finding it.

Grosh conducted the tour upstairs to the top floor. After walking
through a few more rooms, Jon stopped short.

The room was a combination library/home office Alphonso Taft
had built for himself. Glass-fronted bookshelves stuffed with century-old tomes filled one corner of the room, while a gas-powered lamp
sat on a table in the office's center. An ornate fireplace—one of many
Jon had seen in the tour thus far—would have provided warmth for
the room in the days before central heating. But what drew his eye was
almost tucked out of sight.

In the far corner of the room, at the far corner of the house, was an
antique desk. The sheen of its varnished wood may have faded with the
years, but its handmade craftsmanship was still ageless as the day it was
built. Like many such desks, it was a full-size cabinet, rife with drawers
for paper, pens, ink, and letters. But this particular piece of furniture
featured a design element Jon had never seen before.

"The Temple of Solomon," he whispered to himself. Though apparently not quietly enough.

"You recognize it," Grosh said, smiling. "This desk is not only original to the home, but is also a custom-made piece commissioned by Alphonso Taft himself. His grandson, Charles, managed to track it down
years later, forgotten in a storage closet of a law office downtown. And,
as you can see, its design is certainly unique."

The bottom half of the desk was fairly standard for the time. A series
of wide drawers was capped by a retractable writing surface which was currently pulled out, displaying half a dozen replica memos written in Alphonso's hand. Above that pullout tabletop, though, everything changed.

The top half of the desk was modeled after the legendary Temple
of Solomon in Jerusalem. Though the temple had been destroyed by a
Babylonian invasion in the sixth century BC, the iconography of the
magnificent edifice lived on. Architecture throughout the world echoed
the temple's design, while Freemasonry, Kaballah, and Mormonism had
co-opted numerous thematic elements for their rituals and symbolism.

But this was the first time Jon had encountered a piece of furniture inspired by the temple's architecture.

A set of miniature stairs led to a wide, U-shaped temple floor. Four wooden pillars, patterned after those built from the cedars of Lebanon in biblical times, spanned the width of the tiny plaza, while half-pillars were set into a mirror that formed the back wall of the temple. Two pairs of small drawers flanked the stairs, while two larger drawers were set into a sweeping, wing-like motif serving as the temple's pediment carved overhead.

"What's particularly interesting about this desk is something we just discovered a week ago," Grosh said in a stage whisper. "Not only is this desk modeled after Solomon's Temple, but it has hidden compartments."

Jon was floored. *Could this be it?*

"Cool!" exclaimed a towheaded eight-year-old boy from the family of five.

"Was anything inside?" Chloe asked.

Grosh chuckled. "That's the funny thing. We haven't figured out how to open it up yet. Some of the historians on staff here have tried to figure out the mechanism, but no luck yet."

"Can I try?" asked the little boy again.

"I'm afraid not, buddy. This is a very old and very special desk. Only people who have had years and years of training handling old things are allowed to touch things like this."

"But I've got plenty of experience with old things!" the boy protested. "I'm around my mom all the time!"

Even Jon had to laugh at that. The boy's mother turned beet red and placed her hand on the boys shoulder as the group's laughter subsided.

Grosh bent over a little and spoke in a tone that only a fellow mother could. "This desk is much much older than your mom is, believe me. But maybe one day, when you're older, you might want to go to college to become a historian and get to deal with cool old things like this all the time!"

The boy started to argue, but a quick shoulder squeeze from his mother made him think better of it.

"And on that note, let's proceed to the next room."

Jon placed a hand on Chloe's arm as the group filtered out the door. "Are you thinking what I'm thinking?"

"Of course I am," she said. "Where do you think I've been the past two days?"

*Touché*, Jon thought. But if a fleet of historians who had dedicated their careers to studying the Taft family hadn't been able to figure out how to get into the secret compartment, how could he and Chloe expect to do so in a matter of minutes?

Grosh ducked back into the room. "Let's stick together, please."

Jon sighed, and he and Chloe followed Grosh into the hall. So close, yet so far. But now that they had an idea where to look, they would seek an opportunity to get back into the office and try to ferret out the desk's secrets.

They got their chance ten minutes later.

"This concludes our tour," Grosh said once the group was gathered back by the staircase. "For the next fifteen minutes, feel free to explore the house and return to any of the exhibits we've passed through. Take as many pictures and videos as you like. But please remember—" she looked at the towheaded boy "—no touching."

"I won't, I won't," the boy said defeatedly, eliciting another smile from both his parents and Grosh.

"Come on," Chloe said. She headed back toward the office by way of an adjoining room to make their destination not quite as obvious to Grosh or the rest of the group. A few moments later, they were back in the office.

"Any ideas?" Jon asked once they were standing in front of Alphonso Taft's desk.

"I thought you were the puzzle guy," Chloe said with a smirk.

Jon grinned. "I just figured my prowess might've been rubbing off on you."

She squared her shoulders and studied the desk. "Okay, let's look at what we know. The desk's original owner was Alphonso Taft. His son discovered the Lafayette Confession in Washington's tomb years after Alphonso was dead, and his grandson rediscovered the desk decades after *his* death."

Jon nodded. "So Alphonso Taft was long dead and buried by the time Charlie came into possession of the desk . . ."

"At which time he had also received the Lafayette Confession from his father and instructions to do what he could to bring down the Vanguard."

"Obviously that didn't pan out how President Taft might have hoped, but, assuming Charlie was still trying to fulfill his father's wishes, he would have hidden the papers somewhere that would have survived."

"But why hide them in a hidden compartment no one can figure out how to get into?"

Jon looked close at the desk's features, paying close attention to the joints where the miniature stairs came together. Then he noticed something in the mirror at the back of the replica temple.

"Maybe it just has to be the right people."

Chloe raised an eyebrow. "What are you talking about?"

"Look here." Jon pointed to the reflection of the backsides of the little wooden pillars. He curled his finger around one of the pillars and pointed to a tiny geared dial. The number 7 was carved into the dial. He rolled the dial to one side, and it clicked beneath his finger. Now the number 8 was visible.

"They all have them," Chloe said, pointing to similar numbers on all four pillars at the front of the temple. The numerals had been carved in reverse, but in the mirror they appeared normally.

"They all have two of them," Jon clarified, pointing to another set of dials at the base of each pillar.

"Eight dials, ten digits apiece, that's a hundred million combinations."

The rest went unsaid. They didn't have time to try a hundred combinations, much less a hundred million.

"One thing that's been bothering me. Taft never left clues like Kennedy or Washington did. Which means the answer has to be obvious if you know what you're looking for."

"It doesn't seem so obvious to me," Chloe said.

"Eight digits, broken up into two sets of four digits. Those sets are also broken up into halves of the temple."

"A date?"

"Exactly what I was thinking." He tapped each dial in turn. "Two dials for the month, two dials for the day, four digits for the year."

"But what day?"

"My first thought was that it would be something important to Alphonso Taft. The date he moved to Cincinnati, his anniversary, the birthday of one of his children. Heck, with all the esoteric symbolism of this desk, maybe even the day he founded Skull and Bones at Yale."

"The historians here would have already tried those though," Chloe said.

"Assuming they discovered the dials, yeah I'm sure they would have. But what if the dials were programmable? What if there are gears inside that Charlie Taft was able to manipulate to create a new date that opens the secret compartment?"

"A date that Alphonso wouldn't have known about. One important to his son instead."

Jon shook his head, running into another dead end in his thinking. "But then, the staff here would have tried those dates too. His birthday, the date he graduated law school, when he passed the bar, when he was elected president, when he became chief justice."

"What about when Roosevelt was shot during the 1912 campaign? October 12."

"Good idea. It's not an obvious Taft milestone. But it might have been a major demonstration of the Vanguard's abuse of power, one that personally impacted Taft."

He dialed 1-0-1-2 on the top row, and 1-9-1-2 on the second.

"Nothing happened," Chloe said.

"Really? I thought something seemed amiss."

She ignored his sarcasm. Then she gasped. Jon turned to see her eyes twinkling with revelation.

"What?"

"A date that wouldn't be easily guessed, but would be obvious to those seeking Washington's papers."

*Light bulb.*

"Taft's letter," he said, pulling it from his pocket. He slid the letter from the envelope and unfolded the paper.

Chloe tapped the bottom of the page. "June 18, 1922. The day Taft thumbed his nose at the Vanguard and hid this letter right under their noses."

"Let's try it."

Voices of others from the tour group drew nearer. The library was undoubtedly one of the more interesting rooms in the house, so chances were high that they would not have the space to themselves for much longer.

"Let's tag team it," Jon said, working the dials on the left side of the desk. Chloe started turning the ones to the right.

0 6 1 8
1 9 2 2

As Chloe slid the last "2" into place, an audible click emanated from the center of the desk.

"Did you see that?" she asked.

He had. The click had coincided with a momentary shift in the stairs of the tabletop temple. He prodded at them with a finger. They retracted slightly. With the code-triggered lock deactivated, the stairs were now movable. He slid them back beneath the temple floor, revealing a hidden compartment.

Eager, they both dropped down and spied inside. A flat shape with a small bulge along one side was tucked within the chamber.

Voices now. Coming straight for them.

Jon grabbed the package and shoved it under his shirt. He tried to tug the stairs back into place, but they weren't budging. Perhaps it was a safeguard to prevent someone from getting their hand trapped inside without activating a different mechanism to release the catch. They didn't have time to figure out another mechanism. The voices were in the next room now, and they were unlikely to stay there for long.

He grabbed Chloe's hand and led her out of the room through the side door. Away from the voices. No sooner were they clear of the door than the voice of the towheaded boy from earlier exclaimed how the desk didn't have stairs anymore.

The jig was up.

Jon made a beeline for the staircase, keeping his pace purposefully brisk without breaking into a suspicious run. At the bottom, he almost collided with Ranger Grosh.

"Whoa, careful there," she said.

"I'm so sorry," Chloe said. "I just realized that we're late for a lunch date with my mom. Completely slipped my mind, and she's going to be livid after the last time if we keep her waiting much longer. What's the quickest way out of here?"

"Right through those doors. Follow the sidewalk back to the visitor's center and the parking lot."

"Thanks so much."

Jon just offered a sheepish grin as they headed toward the exit. Yet again, he was glad they had used aliases to sign the guestbook. Another historic site left a little different than they had found it. Something changed, something stolen. But what, exactly, they had pinched from the depths of Alphonso Taft's secret compartment was the big question.

They bypassed the visitor's center and turned left when they reached the road, walking south along Auburn Avenue until they entered Hopkins Park. Jon looked behind him and stopped against a stone retaining wall within the block-sized urban park.

"As good a place as any," he said, pulling the envelope from under his shirt. He opened the envelope and slid out the contents. A small metal gear-like device tumbled out first, while a small folded stack of ancient parchment required a little more coaxing to leave the envelope.

Gingerly, he unfolded the document, knowing that every historian he'd ever studied under and every one of his coworkers at the National Archives would gasp in horror if they knew he was handling an original letter from George Washington in the middle of a city park.

"The Lafayette Confession," Chloe said in breathy amazement as she read the opening lines.

Addressed to his friend and comrade-in-arms the Marquis de Lafayette, the three-page missive outlined Washington's fears for the young nation he had helped found and his concerns about the Society he had helped survive the charges of treason levied against it in its early years. What was even more profound was that Washington was the president-general of the Society of the Cincinnati even as he wrote these apocalyptic words. Jon was particularly astonished at how prescient the man was. Washington may not have lived to see the dawn of the nineteenth century, but he foresaw "elements within the Society" taking it upon themselves to "exercise undue influence on Congress and the presidency, and thus, the nation itself." He even specifically mentioned "threats and coercions upon the Person and Office of the President of these United States," though he hadn't specifically foreseen those rogue elements actually murdering presidents. Presidents being murdered in broad daylight, particularly by agents of the very group sworn to protect the memory of the union's bloody creation, was practically unthinkable in those days. Thanks to the Vanguard's machinations over the following centuries, it no longer was.

The letter closed with a veiled reference to a separate set of instructions Washington had given Lafayette, to be executed posthumously in the event of Washington's death. Jon could take a pretty good guess as to what those instructions were, having seen their faithful fulfillment firsthand. What Lafayette hadn't been counting on was his old friend's remains being moved to a new location just a few years after he'd completed Washington's final request.

It was damning stuff, particularly coming from the man who had for two hundred years served as the embodiment of the American Cincinnatus and the foremost hero of the greater Society. But it was more than two centuries old, predating Aaron Burr's revelation of his true colors a few years later and the formal creation of the Vanguard in 1865. Though it offered a fascinating historical perspective and would likely create some public relations fallout for the modern Society of the Cincinnati, its release to the public would do little to temper the Vanguard's ambitions.

But that wasn't all that was in the envelope.

A final yellowed sheet of paper was stuck inside. Jon tugged it free. The text appeared to have been created by an electronic typewriter, which would fit with the 1970s origin of the envelope. He read the typewritten words.

> Here are the prophetic words of George Washington, revealing the treachery of the Society of the Cincinnati decades before their words became deeds. Despite all my resistance, their nefarious off-shoot, the so-called Vanguard, have descended upon our beloved city of Cincinnati in ways even my father could not have predicted. I tried to root them out, but I failed. I have located a forgotten path to their lair—the epicenter of their power and the key to their destruction. I pray that you are strong enough of mind and will to finish what I could not. As for me, I must take this secret to my grave.

The letter was unsigned, but its author was clear enough.
Charlie Taft.

"What the heck, man?" Chloe exclaimed. "Why on earth would he go on about how important it is for us to bring down the Vanguard, then leave us hanging like that? Like, he preserves a letter of Washington excoriating the Society of the Cincinnati, but protects the Vanguard 'lair' he despises so much? It doesn't make any sense."

But it did.

Jon chuckled.

"Something funny I missed?" Chloe asked, still angry.

"It's brilliant," he said, stuffing the envelope with its original contents.

"What is?"

"Come on. We've got another cab to catch."

# CHAPTER 72
## Cincinnati, Ohio

Wayne Wilkins cracked his neck in frustration as he got the cold shoulder from yet another hotel attendant. No doubt there were plenty of tourists and looky-loos here at the Cincinnatian Hotel that had seen the president's motorcade sneak into the parking garage earlier this morning. Perhaps the historic four-star hotel had already received plenty of threats or concerns about the president's safety, and they were growing weary with the number of crazies coming out of the woodwork.

But Wayne wasn't crying wolf, nor was he just some random citizen. He had met with the president on multiple occasions over the past year, including twice alone in the Oval Office. Technically, he was CIA, but he also led a small team of elite operatives that worked under the radar at the president's behest. Since the team's first mission in Dubai a year earlier, Wayne had earned President Talquin's respect and trust.

That mattered little today. Wayne wasn't a Secret Service agent. And they were calling the shots here.

He understood their dilemma. The goal of the Secret Service's protection arm was to ensure the president was difficult to get to. Plenty of people wanted to hurt him, and, through obfuscation, vigilance, and show of force, they were tasked with making sure those who would harm the president were unable to do so.

It didn't help Wayne, though.

*I should have gotten his cell number the last time we spoke at the White House.*

The president was upstairs, no doubt, going over his speech, liaising with his staff and cabinet members back in Washington on any number of priorities that demanded his attention. There was a good reason why most presidents seemed to age far more than the average person during their tenure. The weight of the world on their shoulders. And a perpetual target on their back.

Wayne felt he owed Talquin. Not only as an American seeking to prevent untold havoc on the nation's psyche and political process, but also at a personal level. Politics aside, Talquin had seen some nugget of greatness in Wayne and elevated him to his personal fixer for matters of national security. More even than his regular missions for the CIA, his work with the Reapers—the unofficial name he had bestowed upon his group at the conclusion of their first mission together—had proven to be some of the most challenging but rewarding of his already impressive career.

*A close second, perhaps, to whenever Jon Rickner crosses my path*, Wayne thought with a sly grin.

But none of that would matter if Talquin was assassinated today. And if the Reapers were to pass on to the next man to take his place in the Oval Office, Wayne would disband the group immediately. As much as he loved the difference he was able to make on the world stage through his small but effective team, he would not use it to serve the whims of the man who had conspired to murder the president to further his own political ambitions.

Which was another reason to see this through. If he failed, a traitor would sit in the Oval Office. If Vice President Dale Finney started his presidential career complicit in a treasonous assassination, Wayne didn't want to imagine how deeply into the darkness the corrupting influence of the power of the highest office in the land would take him.

"Excuse me, sir?"

Wayne was wrenched from his thoughts by a stocky blond man with a chiseled jaw set firm in a no-nonsense grimace. His standard-issue suit and tie, coupled with the radio tucked into one ear, immediately betrayed him as a Secret Service agent.

*Finally, we're getting somewhere.*

The man identified himself as Agent Schrute, flashing his ID and asking Wayne to follow him. Schrute led Wayne to a bank of elevators. When one opened, he motioned for Wayne to enter, then followed him inside, sliding a security card into the keypad panel. He held out his palm, refusing entry to an elderly couple laden with bags.

"Catch the next one," he told them as the doors slid shut.

Wayne felt off as soon as the elevator started moving. He glanced over at the keypad panel and was surprised to see that, instead of moving upward toward whichever floor the president was on, they were going down instead.

The elevator stopped at a subbasement level and the doors slid open. Another agent, this one taller and black but with the same hard-set demeanor, joined them as they stepped out. The newcomer didn't give his name. Wayne was liking this less and less.

The elevator bank emptied into a concrete block hallway. A door at the far end read "Authorized Personnel Only," while the sounds of car engines and protesting brake pads emanated from beyond. *The parking garage?* The lot was valet only, though Wayne assumed hotel management made exceptions for the president. Still, where were the agents taking him? It was far too early for the president to have loaded up for the trip to Fountain Square, where he would be giving his speech this afternoon. Perhaps he was working from inside the Beast, fielding calls from world leaders and congressional allies before his big rally. A part of Wayne got excited. He had visited Talquin's Oval Office numerous times, but he had never been inside the armored presidential SUV.

His excitement quickly dissolved as Shrute turned left down a side corridor, swiping his keycard at a door that read "Security Office Annex" and leading them inside.

A secretarial desk sat empty to the right of the entryway. Following the agents' lead, Wayne walked past a pair of agents studying a bank of security monitors. The screens flipped through views of the lobby, parking garage, guest hallways, stairwells, and hotel exterior, each from a dozen different angles. Finally, Schrute opened a door and ushered Wayne inside. Neither he nor his silent colleague followed him inside.

The president was not in the room. Instead, another besuited man, this one in his late fifties, stood behind a small conference table. Despite the gray that permeated his hair and his age-lined face, he projected a similar strength as his colleagues outside, coupled with an air of experience that left Wayne with the immediate understanding that this guy had the grease to get him an audience with the president.

Or to get him kicked out of the hotel entirely.

"Thank you for coming, Mr. Wilkins," the man said, offering his hand. "I'm Special Agent in Charge Ian Hardwick. Please, sit down."

Wayne took a seat opposite his host, who also sat.

Hardwick's demeanor was professional, but with an undercurrent of irritation. This wasn't how he wanted to spend his day. There were bigger priorities upstairs. The biggest of all, from the Secret Service's perspective. Still, Wayne had been persistent, and, in all likelihood, it had been the combination of his calls on the plane ride from Maryland and his showing up in person at the president's hotel that had gotten the attention of Talquin's protection team. He sensed that this meeting was a formality, ticking off the box to show that they had done their due diligence to determine that Wayne's allegations were sufficiently baseless to not concern themselves with.

"I understand that you believe there to be some imminent threat against POTUS's safety," Hardwick began. "Please elaborate."

Wayne could hear the annoyance and suspicion dripping from Hardwick's voice. As though this completely unknown threat at the eleventh hour was an affront to the weeks of preparation his agents had done for today's event. Still, Wayne had been given an audience. He wouldn't let it go to waste.

"An attack will be made on the president today. I don't know the nature of the attack, but I have good reason to believe that it will be done at his rally this afternoon."

"What's your source on this?"

"An overheard conversation last night."

"You've got to give me more than that."

Wayne shrugged. "You know how this works as well as I. Source is confidential. Trusted. But confidential."

"And you have no more specifics about the alleged attack itself. Not whether it will be a rooftop sniper, a gunman in the crowd, a suicide bomber, or a whole assault team?"

Wayne frowned and slowly shook his head.

Now it was Hardwick's turn to shrug. "Not much we can do with that, is there?" It wasn't a question. "We've received a dozen more-detailed threats since breakfast, Mr. Wilkins. None of them panned out, but we at least had something to check. See, that's the thing about the Secret Service. We're very, very good at what we do. No matter who sits in the Oval Office, more than half the world, and nearly half the country, hates him. And despite that, the Secret Service is the reason no one has managed to even fire a shot at a sitting president in nearly forty years. We've vetted the route from here to the rally site, the site itself, and his exit route. We've checked everyone he'll be sharing the stage with, and the people who set up the stage itself. The resources of the Cincinnati Police Department, the Hamilton County Sheriff's Office, and the Ohio State Highway Patrol, not to mention extra support from neighboring counties in Ohio and Kentucky, are at our disposal today, and believe me when I say that we're covering every conceivable angle. So unless you have something concrete we should check out . . ."

"The vice president is involved," Wayne blurted.

Hardwick raised an eyebrow. "Excuse me?"

*In for a penny . . .*

"Vice President Finney was overheard plotting the aftermath of the attack," Wayne said. "He plans to use the president's murder as a catalyst to launch a war against Venezuela."

Hardwick's professional veneer melted away. The barely concealed condescension that once lay just under the surface cracked a bit too, leaving a quickly hardening core of pity. "Thank you for your time, Mr. Wilkins. I'll have one of my agents escort you out."

Wayne admitted that it was probably one of the craziest theories Hardwick had heard recently, and he heard all of them. But he wouldn't be dismissed that easily.

"Do you know who I am?"

Hardwick gave a barely perceptible nod. "I've been apprised."

"Then you know that the president trusts me."

"In certain matters, in the past, yes."

"I know it sounds crazy, but—"

The senior agent steepled his fingers and leaned forward on his elbows. "No, Mr. Wilkins. It doesn't just *sound* crazy. And if you want to remain in POTUS's favor, I highly recommend you go get some rest, perhaps some professional help. I don't know who your 'trusted source' is in all of this, but you seriously need to revisit your vetting process."

Wayne felt his window rapidly slamming shut. "Just let me speak with the president. That's all I ask."

"He doesn't have the time or the energy to deal with your wild conspiracies about his number two. He has a country to lead, a world to engage with, and a speech to deliver. And believe me, I'm doing you a favor by *not* giving you an audience with him or passing along your theory. You would be drummed out of government service forever with talk like that."

"Please, Agent Hardwick. I know it isn't much to go on, but the president's life, and *your* job may depend on you taking this information seriously."

Hardwick's expression hardened, the pity replaced by stony anger.

"You have two options at this point, Mr. Wilkins. Neither of them involve you talking to POTUS. You either leave this hotel of your own accord and do not attempt to interfere with Secret Service business for the remainder of the day, or you will be remanded to our custody until the president has left Cincinnati tonight. Your pick."

Wayne stood, tamping down his rising fury and frustration. No sense in giving Hardwick any extra reason to detain him. "I'll be going then. Sorry to have wasted your time."

"Thank you for your concerns, Mr. Wilkins," Hardwick said, his professional demeanor returning. "Rest assured, the president's safety is in good hands."

*Yes it is*, Wayne thought as he exited the room. *Mine.*

# CHAPTER 73
## *Cincinnati, Ohio*

C hloe realized their mistake only moments after arriving.
Cincinnati's Spring Grove Cemetery was one of the largest
cemeteries in the nation. Founded in 1845, the 733-acre property had been designed as a peaceful final resting place and arboretum
by Prussian-born landscape architect Adolph Strauch. Strauch had lent
his talents to the creation of a number of non-funereal parks within the
city, including the hilltop Eden Park that played host to the Cincinnati
Art Museum. Unlike many cemeteries of the era, Spring Grove was an
expansive realm of rolling hills, sparkling ponds, manicured gardens,
and memorable monuments. One of its most famous memorials, high
on a hill deep within the property, was a sculpture garden dedicated to
John Chapman, the pioneer missionary and naturalist immortalized in
American folklore as Johnny Appleseed.

It was also home to a who's who of Cincinnati's most influential.
William Proctor and James Gamble of Proctor & Gamble fame were
both buried here. So was Salmon P. Chase, who served as governor of
Ohio, US senator, secretary of the treasury, and chief justice of the US
Supreme Court. As secretary of the treasury, Chase had been responsible for finalizing the language "In God we trust" which now appeared
on all US currency, and was the name behind the Chase finance and
banking empire.

One name on the map that shocked Chloe was Nicholas Longworth
Anderson. The Longworths were an institution in Cincinnati, one of the
first families of the city, with a political powerhouse dynasty that traced its
roots to colonial New England just as the Tafts did. But while Nicholas's
mother was a Longworth, his father was an Anderson. His grandfather was
Lafayette's aide-de-camp and holder of the key to Washington's vault, Richard Clough Anderson. And his son was none other than Larz Anderson.

*Scary how connected everything is,* she thought. Especially when they
hadn't been looking for an Anderson presence here in Cincinnati. In

fact, the tomb they'd come here to find was much newer than that of Richard, Nicholas, or Larz.

Armed with a guide map of the area procured from the visitor's center at the entrance to the site, she discovered that Spring Grove Cemetery was far larger than she had anticipated.

"We should have kept the cab," Jon said, echoing her thoughts.

Keeping to the marked roads cross-cutting the sprawling property, they followed the map toward the Taft family plot. Alphonso was buried here, as was his second wife—William Howard's mother—and numerous other descendants. After Alphonso uprooted his family from Vermont in the 1830s, Cincinnati became the new stomping ground of the Taft dynasty, and, with the exception of President Taft himself, most of Alphonso's most prominent descendants were buried here at Spring Grove.

When they finally reached their destination, Chloe was unimpressed. En route, they had passed somber mausoleums, gothic lakeside tombs, and reflective gravesites stocked with fresh flowers and stone benches for the bereaved. The Taft plot was nothing of the sort. It was a rather small plot, with weathered stone markers crammed together. It was still well kept, with headstones and markers intact and legible. It just wasn't as grand as she was expecting from a family of such prominence.

"It's not here," Jon said.

"What are you talking about? This is the Taft family plot. I thought you said Charlie was buried here."

"He's supposed to be. Let me see the map."

Chloe handed it over, double-checking the names and dates on the cenotaphs. Sure enough. No Charlie.

"There's another plot. Completely missed it the first time." Jon stabbed his finger at a point on the map. "Over here."

She could understand how they had missed it. The map, though informative, highlighted dozens upon dozens of famous graves and family plots in tiny font running down the side of the paper, each linked to a grid designation on the cartograph itself. They had simply found the first Taft—the most important one for starting a burial legacy—and stopped looking.

As it turned out, Charles Phelps Taft II, the first son of the city, once hailed by *Fortune* magazine as "Mr. Cincinnati," was not buried with the rest of his family.

When they finally reached Charlie's plot, they realized why.

The grave backed up to one of Spring Grove's twelve ponds. Unlike the crammed plot his grandfather had founded, Charlie's site was spacious, surrounded by wide expanses of grass and a clear view of the sky.

"You think he literally took the secret to his grave," Chloe said.

"I do. It's the only thing that makes sense."

"I agree, it makes sense. But what doesn't is how he would safeguard it from visitors or groundskeepers who might just stumble across it. Or, alternatively, I can't imagine him wanting to be disinterred to get to his secret."

Jon was silent as he circumnavigated the gravestone. While the front held the traditional elements such as his name and dates of birth and death, the reverse held a humorous epitaph.

Gone Fishin'

Beneath the words was a bronze relief of a fisherman in a boat, his line cast in an arc into the waters before him. She flashed back to the animatronic Charlie Taft sitting by the water's edge in the visitor's center at President Taft's childhood home. The man did love to fish.

"Cute," she said.

"Maybe more than just cute. It could be a clue."

She studied the epitaph and the fisherman.

Jon turned to the lake. "Maybe Charlie chose this location because of the water. Maybe he stuck his proof in a waterproof bag and sank it in the lake. And if we want to find it, we have to 'go fishing' like he did."

"What about during droughts?"

"These ponds are artificial in the first place. I'm sure the groundskeepers are tasked with keeping the ponds at a certain level. A level that Charlie would have been familiar with before sinking his secret." Jon started pacing the edge of the lake. "Maybe there's a line or something that it's tied to. Fishing."

He moved back to her side, tapping the end of the fishing pole and following it down into the grass. His finger pointed at the ground, he continued the imaginary line, tracing it back to the water's edge.

Chloe, meanwhile, followed the fishing pole in the opposite direction, down to where it was gripped by a bronze fisherman.

"Before you start digging around in the mud over there," Chloe said, "I've got a theory."

"What's that?" Jon walked back over to her.

Just above the fisherman's hands, a small, shallow hole beckoned.

"The little gear thingy from the envelope," she said. "You still have it?"

"Yeah, of course." He opened the old manila envelope and handed her the item.

Upon closer inspection, it was more than just a gear. A tiny handle stretched outward from one of the sides.

A Lilliputian fishing reel.

She slotted the gear into the hole. It fit perfectly.

"No way," Jon said from over her shoulder. "Chloe, you're a genius."

She blushed at his compliment, but focused on the task at hand. Ever so gently, she turned the reel by the handle. Despite its diminutive size, it was surprisingly strong, and it turned the gear with ease. After four revolutions, she felt the reel lock into place. For the briefest of moments, she heard a soft grating sound, like a stone being dragged over concrete. But it was gone as soon as she heard it, making her wonder if she'd simply imagined it.

"I'd like to retract that statement," Jon said. "You're a *freaking* genius."

He touched the side of the headstone. Behind the marble facade, a metal drawer was concealed vertically within the stone, which Jon slid out to the left.

"Something in there. But that's all you."

Chloe stood and peered into the hidden compartment. A manila envelope, a twin of the one Jon held, had been concealed within Charlie Taft's gravestone. She grabbed it and brought it into the light of day for the first time in nearly forty years.

This one was not as thick as the one from Alphonso Taft's desk, but there was definitely something inside. She opened it to reveal a single sheet of paper, this one handwritten.

> My father's fury has become my own. The Vanguard believe themselves impervious, but their hubris and slavish devotion to preserving a record of their own treasonous exploits will be their own undoing. Since the early twentieth century, they have used the bowels of our great city to house their archives, which is not

only their greatest point of pride but also can prove their undoing. Expose the archives, you expose the Vanguard's deeds. Expose the Vanguard's deeds and they will wither and burn into oblivion.

"The Vanguard archives!" Chloe exclaimed. "They're here in Cincinnati after all."

"It would seem so," Jon said, apparently keeping pace with her reading. "A perfect place for them. Symbolic in name, more out of the public spotlight, and even more centrally located within the growing nation."

But there was more to the letter.

> Go to the river's edge, at the southern edge of the city. Find the statue dedicated to the mother group's ideal, and follow the line of the law inland for 350 yards. From there, head east 120 yards until you reach a fork in the path. A ramp leading down to the right will lead to a blocked door into the city's bedrock. Head through that door, then straight, left, right, straight, straight, right, straight, left, straight, left, a journey of just under an hour if you keep your wits about you and your path well-lit. After approximately 100 yards following that final juncture, you will find a service door on your left. Through that door is a brief hallway at the end of which you will discover the entrance to the archives.
>
> In my younger days, I trailed a pair of chatty Vanguard agents on this path, but I lingered too long before following them through the service door. Regrettably, I never figured out how to open the final door, and the agents never reappeared, leading me to believe there is another entrance somewhere, though that too has eluded my grasp.
>
> May you succeed where I have failed. God be with you.
>
> Charles P. Taft II

She shook her head in confusion. "The statue dedicated to the mother group's ideal?"

Jon grinned, beckoning for her to follow. "Cincinnatus. It's an old-fashioned treasure hunt now, Chloe. And X finally marks the spot."

# CHAPTER 74
## Cincinnati, Ohio

Patrick Molyneux felt a thrill tingle through his body as he stepped into the opulent lobby of a nondescript office building. Overhead, an early 1900s crown-molding ceiling crested to a dome in the center of the lobby. From the apex of the dome hung an expertly crafted chandelier of Tiffany glass and gleaming Italian silver, its lights refracted into a thousand stars glinting across the room. A three-terraced fountain taller than Molyneux spouted just beyond the chandelier, the crystal-clear water cascading to a pool in the floor itself.

Anthony Kellerman led the way across the room, navigating around clusters of armchairs and couches for guests to use while waiting for appointments. He nodded to the security officer behind the counter, who picked up a phone and dialed a number from memory. Molyneux wanted to stop and see what the man called ahead, but Kellerman kept moving deeper into the building.

Kellerman had chastised Molyneux on the way here for his actions in DC. His hubris and irrationality could get them both killed and could destroy everything the Vanguard had worked for. Valor was earned, not demanded. But the next few hours could be Molyneux's chance to prove himself worthy of the Vanguard's charge. Molyneux had apologized, though he still bore some resentment for Kellerman's babysitting comments back at Mount Vernon. He had let the thrill of the kill, something he had never thought he'd experience, twist his brain with primordial hormones. Gaines had brought him on board for his mind. He wouldn't let caveman emotions cloud his judgment again.

A series of placards bearing the name and floor of a few dozen tenants was affixed to the wall next to the elevator bank. Molyneux expected their short-term destination would be the elevator, but Kellerman turned to the right, curling around the bank and pushing through a service door. The door led to a short hallway which terminated in yet another door.

Kellerman pushed a button to the left of the door. The black eye of a surveillance camera above the portal let them know they were being watched.

"Who's your friend?" asked a disembodied voice. Molyneux noted the small speaker mounted just beneath the button.

"New recruit," Kellerman responded. He glanced back at Molyneux. "He plays his cards right, you might be seeing a lot more of him."

Molyneux raised an eyebrow, unsure of Kellerman's meaning. But before he could ponder the statement further, the door buzzed open and they were on the move again.

The next corridor was wider and more utilitarian, lit only by a series of flickering fluorescent lights. Strips of black rubber had been glued to the baseboards as though to protect the walls from damage.

But why?

Kellerman turned right at a T-junction, stopping before the doors of a freight elevator. He slipped a keycard into a wall panel and punched in a series of numbers.

The doors rumbled open.

"After you," Kellerman said with a sweep of his arm. Molyneux stepped inside the car. Kellerman followed him in. He slid his keycard into another slot, punched in another series of numbers, and pressed the single floor button available.

The doors slid shut and the elevator began to move.

"Where, exactly, are we going?" Molyneux asked.

Kellerman gave him a rare smile. "The end of the line for Chloe Harper and Jon Rickner. And paradise for someone like you."

The elevator slowed to a stop, and Molyneux's stomach clenched in anticipation. What awaited him below?

His answer came when the doors slid open. He stepped out of the elevator, mouth agape.

"Is this what I think it is?" he asked, incredulous.

"It sure is," Kellerman said. He elbowed Molyneux. "Quit your gawking now. We've got work to do. And I still have to go get the most important part."

"Are you sure about this? Gaines didn't clear your change to the plan."

Kellerman shook his head. "He doesn't have to. All he cares about are results. And results are exactly what we are going to deliver."

# CHAPTER 75
*Cincinnati, Ohio*

Wayne found himself wishing, for just one moment, that he was a civilian. Not armed with the knowledge of an impending attack on the president, not tasked with the duty to do whatever it took to stop it. For just one moment, here in this bustling city square, Wayne wished he could shed all his professional burdens and just be a tourist for once.

Fountain Square was one of the most famous sites in all of Cincinnati. Built atop what was once an ancient Indian mound, the square had been constructed in 1871 as a gathering place for Reconstruction-era Cincinnatians. The site drew its name from the towering bronze and granite fountain that stood at its heart. The Tyler Davidson Fountain, christened by its German artisans as *The Genius of Water*, stood forty-three feet tall and featured four tiered faces, each displaying practical uses of water. Agrarian, familial, industrial, and community themes featured throughout, while four "pleasures of water" drinking fountains featured naked young boys playing with animals at each of the compass points. Unlike the religious and mythological subjects of traditional European sculpture, this iconic fountain was commissioned to focus on the works of mankind.

Wayne was here to prevent one of those works from coming to fruition.

Office buildings, including the national headquarters of Fifth Third Bank, bordered the square, while the street-level floors played host to a variety of boutique shops, restaurants, tourist information booths, and ice-cream parlors. Throngs of crowds milled about the square, from office workers on a late lunch break to tourists snapping photos of the fountain. But one major addition to the plaza's structure wrenched Wayne's attention from the fantasies of carefree tourism.

An elevated stage had been erected at the southwest corner of the plaza. The P&G Music Stage was often used to showcase musical artists in free concerts sponsored by the city. The sprawling plaza was more than large enough to accommodate hundreds of concertgoers, and the steady stream of foot traffic through Fountain Square ensured many more would get to enjoy the performances.

Very soon, that foot traffic would cease as law enforcement and security personnel closed the area to pedestrians and blocked off traffic on adjacent streets in preparation for a special guest to take the stage.

The president of the United States.

Wayne checked his watch. Less than two hours until Talquin's rally was scheduled to begin. And if Wayne failed to figure out how the Vanguard planned to kill the president, it would be just a little longer before Talquin's funeral. And the launching of yet another bloody war built upon a monstrous lie.

He scanned the plaza and sighted a Cincinnati police officer standing near the stage. Technicians were setting up the president's podium under the watchful eye of a Secret Service agent. SAC Hardwick had already shown the Secret Service weren't amenable to his claims of a secret assassination plot. So Wayne would give the locals a try.

He approached the CPD officer, wearing his best disarming grin. Today, all of these men and women in uniform would be on high alert, which meant Wayne had to quickly show himself to not be a threat but an ally in their protection preparation. In a situation where logistical leaks could lead to the death of the chief executive, playing the curious tourist would get him nowhere. Only perceived power would be respected today. So he went for the quickest, most direct way he could think of.

"Wayne Wilkins, CIA," he said, brandishing his CIA ID as he approached the officer. "We received a tip about an assassination attempt on POTUS today."

The officer looked surprised at the boldness of his statement—and the horror the words implied. She studied his ID for a moment before looking at Wayne. She had short sandy hair and her eyes were shrouded in sunglasses. Officer M. Rostova—according to her name plate—was of medium height and build, but she carried the demeanor of someone twice her size. Wayne immediately sized her up as being ambitious but tough, which meant she could either be eager to help the CIA or decide to shut him down in a hurry.

"What sort of tip?" she asked.

"A credible one. Source is classified, I'm afraid. What can you tell me about your security here?"

She gave him a disappointed look. Already she was seeing through his ruse. If he really needed to know what the security details were here, he would have been on the preapproved list, and would be speaking with the higher-ups at the Secret Service, instead of with a rank-and-file Cincinnati police officer.

"Agent Wilkins, with all due respect, we're keeping things on a need-to-know basis for security purposes today. If you feel you have a need to know, please share your concerns with my supervisors or with the Secret Service."

Time for a different tack.

"I understand that's how things normally go. But despite post-9/11 reforms between our nation's federal agencies, the Secret Service has rebuffed our tip because they can't source it themselves. There's still a lot of dick-measuring contests going on between the powers-that-be in Washington. And unfortunately, I'm not willing to let the president die because of interagency politics."

Rostova's stony expression softened just a smidge. Wayne could see she wasn't buying it yet, but he had made a dent.

"Listen, this isn't the Secret Service's first rodeo. Nor is it ours. We've swept the plaza for bombs. There's a twenty-block no-fly-zone in force for drones or any other aircraft. We've just cleared every window with a line of sight to the stage. And in just a moment, we'll be emptying the plaza before we let people back in after passing through a security check. Hundreds of law enforcement and security personnel will be on site for the duration of the president's speech. This place is locked down. So unless you have something more concrete to offer . . ."

Wayne noticed one of the Secret Service agents he had previously questioned heading his way. Clearly he had outstayed his welcome. He thanked Officer Rostova for her time and headed south out of the plaza, crossing to the other side of the road before heading east up Fifth Street. A glance behind told him that the Secret Service was glad to see him go and would not be pursuing, this time.

Still, he was no closer to stopping the attack on the president. He trusted Jon implicitly, and Chloe had also heard the unthinkable conversation between the Vanguard leader and the vice president. Perhaps the Vanguard was just overconfident? But it had been a long while since a president had actually been shot. These days, the majority of assassination attempts were half-hearted efforts by crazed fence-hoppers and kamikaze pilots crashing on the White House lawn, more often than not when the president was not even in the same city as the would-be attackers. Perhaps the new breed of Secret Service had gotten soft? Or maybe there was a security hole the Vanguard knew to exploit?

Four sitting US presidents had been killed in the century between the Civil War and the Civil Rights Act. Teddy Roosevelt and Ronald Reagan had also been shot, but they hadn't succumbed to their wounds. But as Wayne knew far too well, death was always just a heartbeat away.

Suddenly, something Officer Rostova had said clicked into place.

He'd almost missed it.

Because every assassinated president had been felled by a bullet, that was the most commonly recognized threat. A resurgence of global terrorism in recent decades had also brought bombs and suicide vests to the forefront of security considerations. But there was another devastating weapon that had been the ruin of nations for centuries. One that, if used correctly, could achieve everything that the Vanguard was planning.

All that time securing Fountain Square was for naught. He had been looking in the wrong place for the assassin. They all were.

# CHAPTER 76
## *Cincinnati, Ohio*

A cool breeze rolled off the Ohio River and across Sawyer Point Park as Jon and Chloe arrived. The park stretched along the northern bank of the river, forming the southern boundary not only of Cincinnati but also of the state of Ohio. Across the wide expanse of flowing water was Kentucky. And in the Vanguard's earliest days, that would have meant everything.

Jon saw the flags first. A quartet of banners flapped softly in the light wind, their poles stabbing into the blue sky at each corner of a small plaza. Three of the flags had obvious purposes and could be found all over the city. The flags of the United States, the State of Ohio, and the City of Cincinnati all waved proudly overhead. But the fourth sent chills down Jon's spine.

Its design was patterned after the star-spangled banner itself, though the stripes were blue and white instead of red and white. And on a blue field where fifty stars representing fifty states should have been, thirteen white stars encircled a bald eagle.

The flag of the Society of the Cincinnati.

At the center of the plaza, a ten-foot bronze statue of a man stood atop a pink granite rock. Affixed to the base was a plaque.

> Lucius Quinctius Cincinnatus
> Circa 458 BC
>
> The legendary Roman is seen here after he had defeated the Aequians and rescued the trapped Roman Army. With one hand he returns the fasces, symbol of power as appointed Dictator of Rome, his other hand holds the plow, as he resumes the life of a citizen and farmer.
>
> Our city was named in 1790 by Governor Arthur St. Clair, member of the Society of the Cincinnati, an Or-

der of Revolutionary War officers whose first president
was George Washington.

Given to the City, to honor the volunteer spirit of the
Citizen-Soldier-Cincinnatus, by members and friends
of the Cincinnatus Association.

"I'd say we're in the right spot," Jon said.

"I can't believe this is here in the middle of everything," Chloe said. "Right under everyone's noses."

"Remember that, today, the Society of the Cincinnati goes largely under the radar. It isn't like two hundred years ago when their very existence threatened to undermine the Constitutional Convention. And for the few who are aware of their presence, they are largely viewed as an entirely benign historical society, not unlike Daughters of the American Revolution or groups like that."

"But the Vanguard . . ."

"Is a whole different animal. No one knows they exist, and those who do aren't talking about it. The 'mother group,' as Charlie Taft called it, has been at war with the Vanguard since its inception. It's just a war they've had to fight on their own, since the Vanguard is made up entirely of their own membership."

"Not good PR if the Society were to go public with it."

Jon laughed. "No, not so much."

The statue held a formidable presence. In his right hand, he held out the fasces, a smaller version of the same symbol of ancient imperial power the bronze Washington had leaned on in front of Anderson House. Cincinnatus's other hand was on a plow, half buried in the earth behind him. But though his heart was clearly with the land he wished to farm, his eyes faced forward. His expression was expectant, ready for someone to relieve him of the burden of ruling so that he could return to the agrarian life he loved.

Jon suddenly felt a deep sense of sorrow for George Washington. The archetypal founding father was more like Cincinnatus than anyone could have imagined. And even though he officially retired from public life at the end of the Revolutionary War and then again when he left the presidency in 1797, he never truly could shake the burden of being the leader of a secret aristocracy that he feared would one day be the nation's undoing.

"Wait a minute, though," Chloe said. "Look at the bottom of the plaque. It says '1984.' Charlie Taft died in 1983."

"He did," Jon said. "But this plaza was commissioned years before that. In fact, the statue itself was finished in 1982, even though it wasn't installed until after Charlie's death. As 'Mr. Cincinnati,' he would have had a great number of friends who would share information with him about the city's plans for the plaza. He may have even been able to provide input to help tailor the plans."

"Good point," she conceded, returning her gaze to the statue.

Jon looked across the river. It made perfect sense. In 1865, when the newly formalized Vanguard was planning their first presidential assassination, the land beyond was Confederate territory. Kentucky had seceded in 1861 after a failed attempt to declare neutrality in the all-consuming Civil War. Just like at Mount Vernon and Washington DC, a sliver of water was all that separated Union-controlled Cincinnati from the Confederacy. From this vantage on the border between North and South, Cincinnatians would have seen and heard the horrors of the war. Nowhere was the brother-against-brother aspect of the conflict more prevalent than in border states, where divided loyalties had rent families asunder with lethal regularity.

Kellerman's words at Mount Vernon still niggled at him. The more Jon thought about it, the more he started to believe that Amanda Taylor's theory about the Vanguard's mission was shortsighted and incomplete. There was something big they were missing. And, somehow, the Civil War stood at the heart of it all.

"That's the fasces, huh?" Chloe asked, pointing to the bundle of rods held by the bronze Cincinnatus. "So if we follow that inland . . ."

She walked around behind the statue, keeping her eye on the fasces and what lay beyond. The axe within the bundle pointed away from the river, toward some waypoint charted by Charlie Taft. Closing one eye, she sighted down the straight lines of the rods and pointed.

"That way."

The trick was maintaining the straight course. The paths, tunnels, and other features of Sawyer Point Park made walking in a direct line for a significant distance all but impossible. They paced it off and ballparked the distance as well as they could. The waypoint was tucked under a warren of highway overpasses as I-471 and US 50 met just west of the Daniel Carter Beard Bridge to Kentucky. They turned west, pacing off the next section of the trip, continuing underneath US 50, before popping back into the daylight and entering the warren of downtown streets. They hit the turning point in the middle of a crosswalk, which seemed like confirmation they were on the right path. Turning north, the street began to rise as they moved further away from the river.

"Okay, so where is this door?" Chloe asked, slowing as they neared the end of the third leg of their journey.

It was a good question. There were a handful of doors in the area, and allowing for margin of error in both their measurements and in Charlie Taft's, it was all but impossible to be sure which one.

He glanced to the left. A smile lit up his face. "That one."

All along this area, the rolling hills had been streamlined in areas to aid in city planning. The towering cliffs of the historic Mount Adams neighborhood a stone's throw to the east was a testament to what happened when civil engineering fell second behind preserving the natural beauty. Incredible vistas, but devilishly difficult to navigate the steep, narrow, curving streets. In downtown Cincinnati, in the creation of what was to be the gateway from the great cities of the East Coast to the untapped potential of the American frontier, a more aggressive approach was sometimes needed.

While office buildings and parking garages lined much of the street, the natural rock face of the rising hill to the left had been sheared off to pave the way for this road. A cordoned-off service road led down from street level to a forgotten door set into the bedrock.

They slipped through the blockade and down the cracked bare asphalt of the path down below the street. The door was once painted white, but the paint had been largely chipped away over the years, exposing the bare metal beneath. A plastic sign affixed to the door read "Authorized Entry Only. Property of Cincinnati Public Works." A broken padlock hung from a rusty hook on the jamb. Clearly they weren't the first to illegally pass through this out-of-the-way entrance.

Suddenly it dawned on him where they were headed. Pieces from Cincinnati's history began to click into place like never before.

"The Cincinnati subway," he said.

Chloe looked confused. "I didn't know Cincinnati had a subway system."

Jon just grinned. "They don't."

He lifted the padlock from its hasp and tossed it to the ground. Better to not get accidentally locked in, though, if his hunch was right, there would likely be other exits from the subterranean labyrinth.

"Look," Chloe said, placing a hand on his chest before he could open the door. "I just want you to know, however this turns out, I really, *really* appreciate all of your help. There's no way I could have gotten this far on my own."

He gave her a soft smile. They had been through a lot in the past forty-eight hours. And ever since his brother had died, he thought he'd never find an adventuring partner again. He had sunk himself into finishing his doctorate, only to be blackballed by every university he'd pursued employment with. After Michael's death, he'd felt that he would never again find the close companionship nor the affinity for exploring he'd shared with his brother. Thinking about Chloe, particularly about a future in which they successfully stopped the Vanguard today, made him think he might've been wrong on both counts. Maybe, just maybe, he would find something even greater with her.

"The pleasure is all mine, Miss Harper. But we *are* going to finish this. Here. Now. Together."

They had to.

Neither he and Chloe nor Wayne could fail in their tasks. If Wayne succeeded and they failed, even an attempted presidential assassination could spur the Vanguard's war with Venezuela. If Wayne failed and they succeeded, their find would be swallowed up by the coverage of the assassination and quickly dismissed as the fake news ramblings of conspiracy nuts, especially with the Vanguard's man in the White House.

He checked his watch. Less than an hour until the president's rally was scheduled to begin. As they descended into the forgotten bowels of the city, he offered a silent prayer for victory on both fronts in this final stretch of their mission.

Wayne aboveground to prevent an assassination, Jon and Chloe underground to prevent a war.

# CHAPTER 77
## Cincinnati, Ohio

*Line of sight.*

    For Wayne Wilkins, those three words had triggered memories of the battlefield. Years earlier, entrenched against an insurgent Taliban in the rugged mountains of Afghanistan, then-US Army Sergeant Wayne Wilkins's squad had been pinned down by a pair of snipers perched on a bluff. A Taliban force fifty men strong was advancing on their position, and the marksmen were covering their only avenue of escape.

Wayne was himself an expert sharpshooter, but from his position he couldn't leave cover to get a line of sight on the snipers without their blowing his head off. So he had one of the men under his command prepare to fire a weapon that had first been used in Mehmet the Conqueror's 1453 Siege of Constantinople, the decisive battle that had effectively removed the last stronghold of Christendom from the Ottoman Empire.

The mortar.

Unlike most modern projectile weapons, the ballistic mortar fired shells in an arc that was not reliant on having a line of sight. And, if the Vanguard's assassin was, in fact, armed with one, those in Fountain Square could soon share the same fate as the Taliban snipers.

Total annihilation.

He unlocked his phone and dialed a number.

"Rick's Fish Market," chimed Aida Teshome.

"Aida, it's Wayne."

"Agent Wilkins, how can I help?"

Backed into a corner armed with nothing but a hunch and a host of burning bridges with the Secret Service, he had few other options. Aida was already in the loop with the mission, such that it was. She was the obvious choice for what he needed now.

"I need you to pull any satellites we have over Cincinnati right now. Ours, NSA, anything you can get your hands on."

"Chinese and Russian, too?"

Wayne stopped midstride. "You can do that?"

"What do you think they pay me the big bucks for? Of course, if I were to officially confirm that, I'd have to kill you."

He grinned. A woman after his own heart. "Whatever you can get your hands on."

"Since you're calling me directly and the CIA has no jurisdiction in downtown Cincinnati, I'm assuming this is strictly off-the-record."

"If I'm right, official protocols will hardly matter."

"And if you're wrong?" Aida asked, her normal chipper tone momentarily faltering.

"Then we'll have a whole lot more trouble than some unfiled paperwork."

Wayne could hear her typing. His last words hung heavy in the dead air between them. He looked around, trying to get his bearings after walking on autopilot after leaving Fountain Square.

Aida came back on with words he did not want to hear. "Got no real-time coverage in the area. I can try a redirect, but that will take at least thirty minutes. And that's only if it doesn't raise enough eyebrows above my paygrade to get it stopped."

Wayne covered the mouthpiece before uttering a stifled curse. Then he had a thought.

"Hang on, what's the most recent coverage you have of the area? Specifically within a three mile radius of Fountain Square."

"Fountain Square? Where the president is speaking? What's this about, Wayne?"

"A hunch."

"I hope it's a good one. My butt's on the line here too, you know."

"I do. And I appreciate it. And you know I wouldn't ask you for this if it wasn't important."

"Really? No comment about my butt? That was a softball there. Men today are always afraid to take a hint."

Wayne laughed. "Aida, you get me what I need here and I'll take you and your butt out to any restaurant you want. My treat."

"Well hopefully this doesn't get you fired, because you'll need that salary. I'm an expensive date."

"Of that I have no doubt."

Aida's tone became more serious. "Okay, the last coverage of that particular area was about four hours ago. What am I looking for?"

"A mortar emplacement."

She was silent a moment. "A what?"

"You heard me."

"In downtown Cincinnati?"

"Please just look, Aida."

She sighed. She knew him well enough to know his hunches were rarely wrong, especially when he believed in them enough to ask for help. But he was less sure about today's hunch than most. He just didn't have the luxury of evaluating its validity much further. One way or another, within less than two hours, it would be painfully clear whether he was right or not. But by then it would be too late.

"I may have something. *May*. Barnett Tower. A half-built high-rise about a mile northeast of Fountain Square. Funding ran out a year ago when the construction company declared Chapter 11 and the lead tenant pulled out of the deal. The property's been tied up in litigation ever since."

It seemed like a possible site for the assassin. Isolated. Close enough to Fountain Square to mount the attack on the president. Far enough away to evade the Secret Service's security precautions.

But it was far from the smoking gun he'd hoped for.

Aida wasn't finished. "This morning, traffic cams snagged a van going into the complex. It doesn't look like anyone flagged it, since no traffic laws were broken and nobody was looking for the van or at the high-rise."

"And no workers or deliveries or anything like that were scheduled for today?"

"Nothing I can find."

"The van still there?"

A pause as Aida scrubbed through the footage. "No record of it leaving."

"Druggies?" Wayne offered as potential explanation, playing devil's advocate to his own theory. "Urban explorers?"

"They hop the fence. This was a utility van, not the Mystery Machine."

"And there's nothing else that looks suspicious in the search area?"

"Downtown real estate is at a premium. There's nothing that has been abandoned that long. Rooftops are clear."

"But a half-finished exterior wall, or a glass-free bay window could be a primo firing spot for a mortar."

"This is your theory," she said. "But yeah, it could work."

Plus, Wayne realized, the fixed target of the P&G Music Stage, along with the length of time that Barnett Tower had been empty, would have afforded the Vanguard and their patsy assassin ample time to measure the trajectory needed for a direct hit.

"Give me the address."

When she did, he looked at the street corner directly ahead of him and turned north. In the distance, the concrete and steel husk of a forsaken skyscraper peeked into view between a pair of glass-fronted office towers.

It was near enough to the assassination site for the authorities to snag the assassin afterward, to give the nation an external villain to focus their hate upon. Just like Lee Harvey Oswald. Only this time, the connection between the assassin and a foreign power would be more clear-cut. *A common enemy had attacked the United States. It was time for the United States to unite as a nation once more.*

"I'm only a few blocks away. Call the Secret Service, local PD, anyone you can get ahold of."

"I'll try, but I imagine they may be stretched a little thin."

Wayne kicked himself. Of course they were. Dealing with credible threats and securing a motorcade route and the most popular and highly-trafficked plaza in town for the president's speech.

"Do what you can, at least. Thanks for all your help, Aida. I'm headed to the site now."

"What are you going to do?"

"Whatever I can."

The streets were already bled of traffic, the result of roadblocks being set up around downtown. No taxis were to be found. So he set off at a jog, heading north toward the last-ditch culmination of his half-baked hunch.

He checked his watch mid-stride and quickened his pace.

The president was already on the move.

# CHAPTER 78
## Cincinnati, Ohio

C hloe flicked on the flashlight they had used at Mount Vernon and took in their new surroundings. They had stepped from the sunlight of downtown Cincinnati into a netherworld of graffiti-spackled shadows. A long gray tunnel stretched from the entrance to a cavernous space out of her worst nightmares. Urban explorers and homeless drug addicts had spray-painted tags along the half-finished walls, while cracked concrete pillars held the weight of the city overhead at bay.

"So this is the subway, huh?" she asked.

"It was supposed to be. It started out over a century ago with the city planners looking to repurpose the Erie Canal that ran through the city. Around the turn of the twentieth century, the canal was littered with trash and no longer used for regular transit. Fearing a public health concern from the sewage floating through the middle of the city, the plan was to drain the canal and use the bed as the base for a new subway system, mirroring those already established in cities like Boston and New York. Construction began on the subway project, which was designed to be a loop around the city, with stops throughout downtown and on up into nearby communities that have since become part of Cincinnati."

"But something went wrong."

"Actually, a lot of things went wrong. World War I began to sap the raw materials, sending supply costs skyrocketing. Political infighting and shifting priorities at City Hall stymied progress as well. Then the one-two punch of the Great Depression and World War II killed the project for good. They finished about half of the planned route, with construction halting midway through downtown. Every few years someone will float the idea of resurrecting the subway, but nothing substantial has ever come from it."

"I can't believe they would just leave all of this for more than a century."

Jon smiled knowingly. "You wouldn't believe the stuff hidden beneath most major cities, forsaken and forgotten by the advent of progress. But Charlie Taft leading us here makes me wonder . . ."

"What?"

"If the Vanguard's headquarters is hidden down here, perhaps their presence predates even the beginning of the subway. With the city's name and history so closely tied to the Society of the Cincinnati, plus it's being a blank slate around the turn of the nineteenth century—unlike the old colonial east-coast cities—would have made it prime territory for carving out their home. Especially right here on the border between the Union and the Confederacy."

She shook her head in disbelief. It made perfect sense. A vanguard was the first group to take action in a military conflict. She had assumed that the name simply referred to their continuing mission to take those first steps that no one knew about. Presidential assassinations, false flag attacks, whatever it took to initiate the conflicts and wars they believed were all that held the United States from collapse. But perhaps it was geographic, too. Here in their parent group's namesake city, the newly formalized Vanguard would have been on the verge of enemy territory. And though Kentucky was no longer at war with Ohio, the location remained in remembrance of the horrors wrought by a divided nation.

"And if the Vanguard were down here first, they would have the clout to somehow disrupt and derail the subway project before the workers discovered their subterranean headquarters," she said.

"That's what I'm thinking. And, being mayor during the fifties, when suburbia was blowing up and mass transit became a potential solution to the city's transportation needs, Charlie Taft might have discovered the real reason why previous efforts to finish the subway fell apart."

"Leading him to look down here in the first place."

Jon nodded almost imperceptibly in the near darkness. Her flashlight beam cut through the inky blackness, catching motes of dust and dirt floating ahead.

"So what is this place now?" she asked, noting the graffiti tags along the walls and pillars.

"An urban explorer's dream. But the city's pretty serious about keeping people out of here. They open it up for a guided tour one day per year. Other than that, it's strictly off limits."

Increased policing of the area would explain why she had yet to see homeless people living down here. But unlike abandoned stations or areas in subways in New York or London, there was no power down here. No light fixtures had been added, nor had the electrical wiring been completed. This wasn't just a forgotten part of a working subway system. Long before it reached the point of operation, this labyrinth had been forsaken altogether.

They followed Charlie Taft's instructions through the maze of gray stone and shifting shadows. They were only navigating a short chunk of the larger system, but the area they were exploring was even less finished than much of the rest, sending them through a warren of service hallways, crumbling construction, and rugged stairways. It was tense going. Every intersection brought them one step closer to their final destination. But it also brought them to another site of potential conflict. A fellow lawbreaker, a policeman, or even a Vanguard spy might be around any corner, not to mention wild dogs or rodents of unusual size.

"That's it," she said as they paced off the final step of Taft's directions. She shone the flashlight beam ahead on a gray service door on the left-hand wall in the distance. When they approached, Jon audibly sighed.

"An actual lock," he said. Unlike the door on Washington's tomb or on the entrance to these mass transit catacombs, this door featured a pin tumbler lock. Not as easily smashed with a rock. Thankfully, Chloe came prepared.

"Is that what I think it is?" Jon asked as Chloe fished a lock-picking kit from her pocket and set to work on the lock.

"It started as a hobby, just to see if I could. Then it became a plea for attention. My dad was so consumed with his work, and then with his JFK conspiracy hunting. I would crack locks and break into places just to get a rise out of him. It wasn't until I got collared for B&E that he took any notice. And even then, once the charges were dismissed, he went back into his tunnel vision."

"I'm sorry you had to go through that, Chloe. I know what it's like having a dad who won't give you the time of day. With mine, it was grief that sent him into his safe place of academia. There just wasn't enough room in that safe place for me or my brother."

She could hear the genuine compassion in his voice. Not pity nor condemnation. True understanding. He had been there. He may have dealt with the pain differently, but he got where she was coming from. He had lived it. She felt her face grow warm thinking about it. Yet another reason to make sure they made it through this alive. Perhaps once this was all over, they could find some normalcy together.

"Got it," she said as the final tumbler locked into place. She pocketed her tools and tried the knob.

The door swung open, revealing yet another service hallway. Unlike previous ones, endless darkness did not beckon beyond the end of this one. Instead, it seemed to terminate in something large and reflective.

She entered the hallway, playing her flashlight around in anticipation of security cameras or booby traps. She saw neither. But what she did see at the end of the tunnel took her breath away.

# CHAPTER 79
## *Cincinnati, Ohio*

Senator Stanton Gaines trudged out of the airport terminal to the waiting town car. He desperately wanted to be anywhere but Cincinnati today. It was too close to the impending attack. And though he would be steering foreign policy once Vice President Finney was in the Oval Office this evening, he didn't want any conspiracy theorist to catch wind of his presence here today. He didn't broadcast his membership in the Society of the Cincinnati, but it wasn't a secret either. Society membership records were generally available upon request, and Gaines had touted his family's long-running military service during several of his political campaigns.

Still, despite his distaste for being so close when the nation's course violently pivoted once again, it was necessary.

He still remembered his father's recounting of the events surrounding the JFK assassination. How Lee Harvey Oswald had been approached by a Vanguard proxy. How the proxy had offered to pay off Oswald's gambling debts and ensure he never saw a prison cell if he would take a few shots at Texas Governor John Connally while he rode in the president's motorcade. How a pair of ex-CIA sharpshooters had fired the fatal bullets, one from an adjacent building, another from the grassy knoll. How the proxy's promise was fulfilled when Jack Ruby, recently diagnosed with lung cancer, had been paid to do what millions of Americans wanted to do: murder Oswald.

He thought of how closely that plot mirrored the one moving forward today. And how overconfidence and a host of armchair conspiracy detectives had nearly cost the Vanguard everything.

In fact, he thought of little else these days.

At the end of the day, the nation had its martyr in Kennedy and its common enemy with the communist Vietcong. But Vietnam had proved an ugly and unconventional war. Grisly details were broadcast daily to millions of living rooms, and the countercultural protesters proved to be more formidable and influential than anyone could have imagined. Still, the Vanguard stuck to the old playbook they had run for more than a century.

Afraid of losing re-election in 1972, Richard Nixon moved to fulfill his 1968 campaign promise to pull out of Vietnam. But the Vanguard had stepped in and changed his mind, offering him a controversial but effective plan for ensuring electoral victory. Then, in 1973, when newly re-elected President Nixon decided he didn't need the Vanguard anymore, he tried to pull the plug on the war once more. So the Vanguard used back channels to send details of the "foolproof" reelection plan they'd baited Nixon into using to FBI Associate Director Mark Felt. Decades later, Felt would be revealed to be "Deep Throat," the informant responsible for exposing the Watergate scandal and helping to bring down the Nixon administration. As a final step, the Vanguard successfully bribed Rose Mary Woods, Nixon's secretary, to erase an incriminating eighteen-minute conversation between the president and his chief of staff specifically mentioning how it had been Bradley Gaines's idea for the Watergate break-in three days earlier.

By the end of the whole affair, Vietnam had blown up in their faces. The nation was sick of war, the presidency had been dishonored, and public distrust of Washington was sky high. But once the United States finally withdrew from Vietnam, more enemies had arisen, as OPEC-led oil crises hit Americans in the pocketbook and the Soviet Union geared up for one last push for world domination.

The Vanguard had their next set of enemies to rally the American populace against. There was always one available if you looked hard enough. Forty years ago it was Moscow. Fifteen years ago it was Iraq. Tomorrow, it would be Venezuela. And the Vanguard would always be there to foster that enmity and point American heads in the right direction.

Except for this one little wrinkle that had now arisen.

Even though it had been his great-grandfather who headed the Vanguard in 1912, Gaines felt personally slighted that William Howard Taft had betrayed them. Taft had run politically afoul of his friend, fellow honorary Society member and presidential predecessor, Teddy Roosevelt. After declining to run for a third term in 1908, Teddy Roosevelt had turned the reins of the Republican Party over to Taft, who handily beat perennial Democratic candidate William Jennings Bryan. Then, after Taft's first term was up, Roosevelt went back on his promise not to run again and threw his hat into the race as a third-party candidate, threatening to split the Republican vote.

Gaines's great-grandfather consulted with Roosevelt, urging him to withdraw from the race, but Roosevelt would not bend. Then, in an event that would forever immortalize the toughness of the famed Rough Rider, Milwaukee saloon keeper and Vanguard patsy John Frammang Schrank would shoot Roosevelt at a campaign rally on October 14, 1912. The bullet hit Roosevelt square in the chest, but the impact was weakened by passing through a copy of his speech and a steel eyeglasses case in his pocket. Not only did Roosevelt not die or withdraw from the race, he stood at the podium and delivered his entire ninety-minute speech, quipping to the crowd, "Ladies and gentlemen, I don't know whether you fully understand that I have just been shot, but it takes more than that to kill a Bull Moose."

Roosevelt would go on to win 27.4% of the popular vote, while Taft won 23.2%. The split allowed Woodrow Wilson to sweep into an Electoral College landslide with a mere 41.8% of the popular vote, bringing into power the first Democratic president since Grover Cleveland, and only the second since before the Civil War. Wilson would go on to win not only a second term in 1916 but also his own honorary membership in the Society of the Cincinnati.

No matter what, Democrat or Republican, the Vanguard always got its way. The day that failed to happen would be the day the United States destroyed itself once and for all.

Taft returned to lawyering after his reelection defeat, but years after he left the Oval Office, Gaines's great-grandfather helped Taft to achieve his lifelong goal of becoming a judge. And not just any judge, but chief justice of the United States of America. Following his appointment by Wilson to the post, Taft would institute sweeping changes to the nation's highest court, clearing a monumental backlog of unheard cases, establishing a process for the nine-justice body to select the cases they wanted to hear, and laying the groundwork for the construction of a separate building dedicated to the work of the court. And though Taft would die five years before the United States Supreme Court Building was completed on the east end of the National Mall in DC, the neoclassical temple of justice was as much a monument to him as it was to any who had served on the high court.

And now, after all the Vanguard had done for Taft, after all Gaines's family had done for him, it appeared that he was threatening from beyond the grave to destroy all they had worked for.

That would not stand.

Not today. Not ever.

Today was the day that the Vanguard would once again take the distasteful but necessary actions needed to pull the nation back from the precipice of self-destruction. The United States was at its most divided since 1861, but this time the populace was divided along so many lines—political, social, racial, ethnic, gender, religious, ideological, income class, generational—that a new civil war would quickly devolve into anarchy. There was far too much iconoclastic anger in twenty-first-century America, and the advent of social media and the instant propagation of ideas on the Internet had allowed every grievance and counter-grievance to spread like wildfire.

It was time to harness that power to give the nation a common enemy to rally against. A Venezuelan assassin sent by his government to destroy our way of life. This time they wouldn't make the same mistakes they had made with Oswald. Talquin's assassination would be airtight, and the trail from Rafael Vargas to Caracas would be clear and unassailable.

Unfortunately, today was also the day that the Vanguard was fighting its greatest threat of exposure since 1968. Jon Rickner and Chloe Harper were closer than anyone had any right to be at discovering the Vanguard's Achilles' heel, building off forgotten secrets hidden by Bobby Kennedy, George Washington, and William Howard Taft.

It was imperative that the Vanguard succeed on two fronts today. But if they did succeed, one battle might never need be fought again. Jon and Chloe were eating up a trail of bread crumbs hidden long ago, and once they were dead, the trail would be forever lost, removing any chance of another similar threat.

Talquin's assassination would help ensure America's survival tomorrow. But the deaths of Jon Rickner and Chloe Harper would ensure the Vanguard's survival forever.

"Right here is fine," Gaines told his driver. He grabbed his briefcase as the car pulled up to the curb. "This shouldn't take more than an hour. I'll call when I'm ready for pickup."

The driver signaled his understanding, and Gaines stepped out of the car. The senator brushed the wrinkles from his pants and jacket before shaking his head at his actions. He wasn't going into a committee meeting or a donor luncheon. This may have been far more important, but immaculate appearances mattered little where he was going.

His forefathers in both his Gaines bloodline and the Vanguard hadn't shrunk from getting their hands dirty in times of need. Indeed, that was exactly what had earned the Society's founders a free nation of their own and an influence that still continued today. They left their lives of luxury and learning for a corpse-strewn battlefield in defense of the land they loved.

Gaines would be no less of a man than those who had gone before him.

He pulled the pistol from his briefcase and slid it into his jacket pocket. It was time to get his hands dirty.

# CHAPTER 80
## *Cincinnati, Ohio*

Jon did not expect to see this in the middle of the abandoned Cincinnati subway.

The short hallway behind the service door terminated in a massive bank-vault door.

"So this is why Charlie Taft couldn't follow the Vanguard agent any further," Chloe said.

"It would seem so."

Was this really it? Were the Vanguard's secret archives really behind this formidable steel portal?

A metal handle, wrapped in faded leather, jutted from the right side of the door. Above the handle was a series of eight dials. Jon stepped closer as Chloe aimed her flashlight beam on the dials.

"Alphanumeric," he said, his heart sinking. "A through Z, then 0 through 9."

"Thirty-six possible settings, times eight dials, that's got to be a billion possibilities."

"Almost three trillion, actually."

Chloe poked him in the ribs. "Nerd."

He couldn't help but chuckle. "Everything we know about the Vanguard is that they are intentional. They don't make decisions willy-nilly. Everything has a purpose."

"Including the combination to this door?"

"I don't see why not. They're not some maniacal villains trying to control the world for profit and power. They truly feel that they're fulfilling a higher purpose, that what they're doing is the only thing keeping the United States united. So, yeah, for safeguarding their greatest secrets, I think they'd choose something that held meaning to them."

"Eight characters," Chloe said. "How about 'VANGUARD'?"

"Worth a try." Jon set the dials while Chloe held the light. The handle wouldn't budge.

"Taft hid Washington's confession with an eight-digit code. Why not a date?"

Jon set the dials to 05131783. The date the Society of the Cincinnati was founded. He tried the handle.

Nothing.

"You said they do everything for a reason," Chloe said. "The dials have both numbers and letters on them, so maybe the combination does too."

She had a point. "Maybe a name of a key founder, along with a year," he said.

Washington was too long, Lafayette, L'Enfant, and Von Steuben weren't native-born. But General Henry Knox might work.

"Knox. Four letters. Enough to fit a date afterward."

Chloe agreed. "1783 is already in there. Let's just change the first four and see if it works."

It didn't.

"Hang on, we're going about this wrong," she said.

"What do you mean?"

"This isn't the Society of the Cincinnati's vault. This is the Vanguard's."

"Right, but they hail from the same lineage."

"Sure, but they've forged their own ideological paths since the Civil War. So maybe something more important to them in particular, rather than to the greater Society."

That was it. "Not something more important. Someone."

Chloe realized it too. "Aaron Burr."

Jon spun the first four dials again. BURR1783 did not work.

Then they tried BURR1865, the year the Vanguard was officially formed as such, when it met in secret to plot its most audacious act of treason yet—the assassination of Abraham Lincoln.

The handle remained fixed in place.

"What are we missing?" Chloe whispered to herself, her face scrunched in thought.

Jon wondered the same thing. BURR1865 seemed like the perfect code for the Vanguard, incorporating both their ideological founder and the moment when those ideas became world-shaking actions.

Unless they counted an earlier act as their first pivot point toward their own destiny.

In 1804, while Aaron Burr was still serving as Vice President of the United States, he engaged Alexander Hamilton in a duel. In those days, turning down a duel once you had been challenged was a mark of cowardice. The preponderance of dueling was such that it had been outlawed in New York, so Hamilton and Burr had to travel to New Jersey, where Hamilton's own son had been killed in a duel just three years earlier. In a letter to his wife shortly before the duel, Hamilton confessed that he planned for his shot to miss his opponent. Burr had no such compunctions.

Hamilton's shot missed as planned. Burr's shot was fatal.

His slaying of an American icon effectively ended Burr's political career. But killing the sitting president-general of the Society of the Cincinnati would have cemented his ideological break with the organization, a moment the Vanguard, who believed they alone were fulfilling the charges of the society's charter, would have revered.

Jon set the dials again.

B U R R 1 8 0 4

The handle swiveled downward in his hand.

He grinned at Chloe, her wide-eyed look of excited anticipation mirroring his own feelings.

"Come on," he said. "Let's finish this."

He eased the heavy door open and stepped inside.

Inside, overhead lighting from a series of LED bulbs set into ceiling panels provided museum-quality controlled illumination. But even at first glance, he knew they'd hit the motherlode. Row after row of shelves stuffed to the brim with binders and bound manuscripts. Dozens of file cabinets, including several of the flat file variety for storing maps and charts.

The Vanguard's archives, at last.

Chloe rushed to the first row of binders, running a finger along the spines. "Watergate? They were involved in Watergate?"

Jon looked around in amazement. The chamber seemed to stretch far beyond these initial rows. "Considering the size of this place, I'd imagine there's less that they weren't involved in. Between all the international conflicts they've started and all the scandals they whipped up to keep their elected puppets in line, it seems like they've had quite the impact on our history."

He raced along another row, scanning the binders and section headers. Andrew Johnson—Impeachment Trial. Teapot Dome. Gulf of

Tonkin. World War I—Lend-Lease. Operation Northwoods. Economic—Black Friday, 1929.

*Good God, they were behind the stock market crash that started the Great
Depression?* Jon felt a shiver run through him. These guys were ridic-
ulously powerful. For most of the nation's history, the Vanguard had
been orchestrating disasters and recoveries, wars and economic crashes,
scandals and assassinations.

And here was proof of every treasonous offense, meticulously recorded by their own hand.

Even more chilling was the fact that many of the subjects on these
shelves were not connected to any wars or military conflicts. Not even
remotely. No war, no war profiteering.

Which meant Kellerman hadn't been lying. There was far more at stake
here than the military-industrial complex. Amanda Taylor had it all wrong.
And as a theory began to take shape in Jon's mind, he recoiled at the depths
of the Vanguard's villainy, and the twisted genius of their plans.

"I found it!" Chloe shrieked from two rows over. "JFK!"

Jon jogged out of the aisle and headed toward hers. He stopped
mid-stride, noticing a folder atop a conference table. "Operation Broken Serpent" was typewritten on a label across its front.

He flipped it open. Inside was a dossier on a Venezuelan national
named Rafael Vargas, a surveyor's map of downtown Cincinnati, a trajectory diagram, photographs of Vargas training at some sort of military
camp in a foreign country, official-looking documents from the president's office in Caracas, and more.

"Chloe, come here and look at this."

When she arrived, he stepped aside to let her browse through the
folder's contents.

"I've never heard of this guy," she said before turning to the map of
Cincinnati. "Oh."

"Yeah. It hasn't happened yet. This is what they're trying to do today."

"Why on earth would they just leave it lying around here? I mean, I
know this place is super secret and secure and all, but it seems careless
to have it out in the open."

The vault door slammed shut and Jon spun around. In front of the
now-closed exit was the last person he wanted to see. Anthony Kellerman, gloating, his pistol aimed straight at them.

"Not a mistake," Kellerman said. "But before you die, I just wanted you to see what you failed to prevent."

"I'll kill you," Jon said through gritted teeth.

Kellerman laughed. "I don't think it's you who will be doing the killing today. But hey, good try and all that. But as the depths of your failure sinks in, you should know that it's not only *your* life you've forfeited by coming up against us."

Movement drew Jon's attention to the shadows to Kellerman's left. Emerging from the stacks was Patrick Molyneux. And with the business end of Molyneux's pistol pressed against her blood-encrusted temple, a dirty gag in her mouth, her hands zip-tied in front of her, was a hollow-eyed figure Jon scarcely recognized.

Dr. Joanna Bixby.

# CHAPTER 81
## Cincinnati, Ohio

Wayne Wilkins stared up at the towering husk of the half-finished thirty-story building. The shell of Barnett Tower would become the new Texas Book Depository. A site made forever infamous by its role in the murder of a president.

Unless Wayne could get to the assassin first.

He ducked through the same gate that the traffic cameras had indicated the van had used that morning. Closing it behind him, he took in his new surroundings. Landscaping had not begun before funding ran out, so the lot was a wasteland of dirt and resurgent scrub grass. A faded traffic cone lay abandoned on its side. A rusting I-beam leaned against a trash barrel overflowing with refuse. McDonald's wrappers, red plastic cups, and other assorted litter was scattered about the place, left by uninvited visitors taking advantage of the litigious property's de facto hospitality.

The building had been constructed for Forbes 500 tenants to conduct billion-dollar transactions. Instead, it served as a weather-beaten playground for the bottom-dwellers of the city.

His CIA-issue pistol drawn, he approached the building. As he stepped into the shadows beneath the building, he caught sight of the van. He sidestepped discarded beer bottles and shards of broken glass, crossing the parking garage that provided part of the building's foundation. The van was white, but it was caked with the dust that covered everything in the lot. He tried the doors. Locked. But it was still here. Which meant its driver was too.

A set of parallel trails in the dust led from the rear of the van deeper into the garage. Wayne followed them, realizing that they were either drag marks or wheel marks from some sort of cart the assassin must have used to transport his cargo.

The tracks stopped at the closed doors of a freight elevator. Wayne couldn't believe that the power was on in this desolate place, but it seemed someone on the Vanguard's payroll had arranged for it to be working today. Undoubtedly whoever had been responsible would disappear or become the victim of a fatal mugging-gone-wrong or some other planned accident. The Vanguard didn't seem to be a fan of leaving loose ends. They had survived in one fashion or another for more than two centuries without being exposed. They couldn't let some patsy at the utility company unravel all of that.

Wayne was praying that Jon and Chloe were proving the loose ends the Vanguard couldn't cut off. If they were killed or otherwise unsuccessful in their mission to reveal the group's actions to the world, anything he could do here today would be of relatively little consequence. Yes, the president would survive, but Wayne's apprehension of the assassin without any independently sourced actionable intel would only serve to cast suspicion on himself. He might save the president—and hundreds of bystanders caught in the mortar's blast—from death, but his career and possibly his freedom would be in dire jeopardy.

*One thing at a time.*

Wayne didn't dare take the elevator up for fear that it would alert the assassin to his presence. Instead, he veered to the right, slipping into the stairwell and stealthily ascending.

The assassin wouldn't be on the lower floors. He would want to be relatively high up to ensure the mortar cleared the surrounding buildings en route to Fountain Plaza. Wayne didn't bother checking the first ten floors. Starting on the eleventh, however, he began poking his head out of the stairwell, checking the dust-coated floor in front of the elevator for telltale tire tracks. He also slowed his pace, tempering his footfalls to mask his approach. The last thing he wanted to do was alert the assassin to his presence.

On the landing between the fifteenth floor and the sixteenth floor, he stopped a moment to catch his breath. Still no sign of the assassin. Wayne was getting worried that perhaps he was barking up the wrong tree after all. The van and wheel marks could have been from some protesters planning to hang a massive political banner on the side of the building, from a bunch of ravers planning a killer overnight party, from a starry-eyed couple looking for a unique setting for an afternoon picnic, from a teenage runaway moving into his new digs, or from any number of other potential sources. Had he bitten too quickly at this potential site? Should he have had Aida keep looking for other buildings within range of the target? For that matter, was it possible that the target was not even Fountain Square, but perhaps the president's hotel, or the airstrip?

*Enough.* That was an endless hole of self-doubt and useless speculation. He had mere minutes before the president was slated to take the stage. If the assassin wasn't here, he didn't have time to go looking for him elsewhere. But if he was here, there was absolutely no time to waste.

He began to climb again, measuring his pace with the volume of his footsteps in the echo-prone concrete stairwell. No luck spotting the wheel tracks on the sixteenth floor, nor on the seventeenth or eighteenth. But when he reached the nineteenth floor, he did notice something different.

A scream. Then a wild-eyed man ran straight for him.

≈≈≈≈≈

Rafael Vargas sat bolt upright. He couldn't believe he had managed to doze off, but the overnight drive had taken its toll on him. He had set multiple alarms on his watch to ensure he awoke for the moment of truth.

He checked the time. Five minutes 'til four.

He shut off the alarms and dusted himself off. The shadows were a little longer and the sun a little lower than when he'd gone to sleep, but, other than that, his surroundings hadn't changed. Which was crucial.

The mortar tube was still bolted in place, its business end pointed out an empty bay window toward the sky. The quartet of bombs he would load and fire in quick succession waited patiently for their moment to shine. No one and nothing had disturbed him or his place of work. But his nap had nearly robbed him of his moment of glory. Of his nation's final redemption after a long history of being crushed underfoot by the neocolonial boot of American tyranny.

Thank God he had woken up. He was typically a fairly heavy sleeper, but he knew that the stress—and importance—of his mission would be enough to keep his slumber light enough for his watch alarm to rouse him.

But he had awoken before the first alarm sounded. Which raised the question: What had interrupted his sleep?

Voices. Somewhere downstairs.

*Not now. Of all the rotten timing . . .*

He was prepared for this possibility, but it wasn't how he had wanted things to play out. He would defend what he had been working for. What all of Venezuela groaned for. Within minutes, the president would be arriving at Fountain Square. And moments after he did, his death would rock the world.

Vargas grabbed his sidearm and prepared to make his move.

≈≈≈≈≈

"Down, now!" Wayne ordered in a low-volume yell. He didn't have to shout. The gun he had aimed at the homeless man's face was all the emphasis the attacker needed.

"I'm sorry. Take whatever you need," the man sobbed through blackened teeth.

Another time, Wayne might've taken pity on the man, given him a meal and listened to his story. But right now, he was not only in a hurry, but mad at potentially losing his stealthy advantage.

"Go over there and be quiet. If I see you or hear you again before I come back down here, I'll kill you. If you are quiet and still, I'll buy you dinner after this is over."

The man, quivering with a mixture of adrenaline, fear, and relief, held a shaking finger to his lips. He would either be quiet for the remainder of the operation, or he would bolt down the stairs and out of the building the moment Wayne was out of sight. Hopefully he'd choose the former.

Wayne nodded and retreated to the stairwell, climbing another floor, then another. No sign of the wheel tracks. But no more sounds below either.

A cough from somewhere above. The assassin was here after all. Wayne checked his watch. Four o'clock. The rally had begun, with some local dignitary no doubt introducing the president. Which meant the attack was imminent. He doubled his pace, being careful to keep his footfalls as quiet as possible.

At the landing between the twenty-third and twenty-fourth floors, he froze. In the dim light cast from the doorway on the next floor, he saw a thin reflection glinting across a stair. He crept closer and bent down.

It was a tripwire, tied to the detonator of a block of C4. More than enough to blow off both of his legs and otherwise ruin his day.

Wayne was definitely in the right place.

He stepped carefully over the tripwire and continued his ascent. No wheel tracks on the twenty-fourth or twenty-fifth floors. But on the twenty-sixth, he saw them.

A pair of tracks leading from the elevator doors to a source of light in the distance.

A window, no doubt. *The* window.

He slunk from the cloistered stairwell into the open-plan floor. A grid of load-bearing pillars would provide the best cover. Other than that, the space was broken up only by steel girders and buttresses forming the primordial skeletons of walls.

He followed the tracks as they wended their way through obstacles and aborted constructions. When he neared the far wall, he saw the tracks cut to the right. Illuminated by the afternoon sun, a mortar emplacement beckoned like a blast from his past. He had found it.

But where was the assassin?

Wayne's battlefield instincts kicked in not a second too soon. He tucked into a ball and rolled forward just as a fusillade of bullets plowed into the wall overhead. Sheet rock dust plumed from the holes and rained down on him. He came out of the roll with his gun pointed toward the site of the first shot, but the assassin was already on the move. Back toward the mortar.

It was now or never.

Wayne fired three shots at the assassin, all of them narrowly missing the moving target. The assassin returned fire, sending Wayne diving for cover behind the nearest pillar. Wayne blindly fired three more rounds, none of which seemed to hit home. His opponent shot back, both bullets embedding themselves in the concrete pillar.

This was a losing battle. The assassin didn't need to kill Wayne. He didn't even need to survive a shootout. All he needed to do was fire the mortar, and he won.

Game over.

So Wayne had to change the rules of the game.

"Hey!" he yelled as he stepped from behind the pillar. The assassin already had a mortar bomb in hand, but he turned, leading with his gun. Wayne dove to the side and sent two bullets into his opponent's chest. The assassin staggered back, but didn't go down.

Bulletproof vest. Wayne wished he had been as resourceful.

Still, Wayne had been in enough combat situations to know that bulletproof vests may stop most bullets, but it still hurt like the devil. He did some quick calculations. Ten-bullet clip, one in the chamber, meant he had three more shots before he was out of ammo. He had to make them count.

He ran toward his target, firing at the assassin center mass. Each bullet sent his opponent reeling just a little more.

*Just a little further.*

With his last bullet, Wayne went for a running headshot. It tore through the assassin's left ear. Hardly the kill shot he was going for, but the man dropped his gun and grabbed at his mangled ear.

But the assassin was unusually focused, as many true believers are. This man was a whole different caliber of patsy than Oswald had been. He may have been manipulated by the Vanguard, but he had the fierce determination of a battle-hardened soldier convinced he was fighting the good fight. He might die in the next few moments, but he would make sure he achieved his mission before he gave up the ghost.

Grunting through gritted teeth, the assassin twisted away from his enemy and moved the mortar bomb toward the mouth of the tube. Wayne knew well enough that the firing pin was gravity-triggered. When the charge at the base of the bomb hit the pin at the bottom of the tube, it instantly ignited. On the battlefield, that meant the instant after you dropped the bomb into the tube, you ducked and covered your ears. Today, it meant Wayne was seconds from failure.

With no time to reload, Wayne threw his pistol at the assassin and lunged toward him. The gun hit the man in the side of the face, but it wasn't enough.

The bomb slipped from the assassin's grasp and into the fateful darkness of the tube.

*No.*

Wayne slammed into the man's chest, knocking him backward with such force that he fell back into the mortar tube. He heard a crack as the tube was jarred from its foundations.

But it wasn't enough.

The bomb rocketed out of the tube and through the window, cutting a terrifying arc through the sky as it soared inexorably toward its destructive goal.

Wayne had failed. There was no stopping it now.

# CHAPTER 82
## Cincinnati, Ohio

Joanna Bixby struggled against her binds, but Molyneux restrained her. The gun at her temple also helped to stymie her efforts.

Jon's face was a portrait of shock, rage, and regret. He had surely been trying to contact her since their initial meeting, but she had been unreachable since Kellerman broke into her apartment two nights ago. At first, she was sure the intruder was going to kill her, but he had other ideas.

She hated being used as a bargaining chip for an exchange Kellerman had no intention of making. There was no way Jon or Chloe were walking out of here alive, no matter what they gave up. She had seen the way the Vanguard agent raged against the notion that the two youngsters had bested him multiple times. Molyneux too. This trap they'd laid wasn't just business. It was also personal.

Chloe seemed like a sweet girl, but Bixby's heart wrenched for Jon especially. He undoubtedly blamed himself for dragging his old professor into this mess. Of course, it had been her knowledge of the Society of the Cincinnati and its earliest conspiracy theories that had set him on the course in the first place. Without her pointing him in that direction, he might have bashed heads with the group for a few moments before conceding that the group's seal could have been in Bobby Kennedy's envelope for any number of reasons. Instead, he had drawn the ire of perhaps the most powerful secret society in American history, and the fullness of their wrath was about to pour out on their heads.

She felt awful, but there was nothing she could do about it now. He was a great kid with an incredibly bright future. One that, unfortunately, was about to be snuffed out forever.

≈≈≈≈≈

Anthony Kellerman sneered. Kidnapping Joanna Bixby and bringing her along for the ride as collateral was his tweak to Gaines's plan. Jon and Chloe may have been willing to sacrifice their own lives for this fool's errand, but with the professor's life also in play, their risk-taking would be mitigated. At least, that was his hope.

The two of them had come so far. To the very end, in fact. Right where he wanted them.

"Thanks so much for finding the Lafayette Confession for us," Kellerman said, his gun pointed at the two of them. "It will be an excellent addition to our archives here. Lay it on the table."

He gestured to the conference table with his weapon.

It would be a pleasure to kill them both. Chloe's family had been a thorn in the Vanguard's side for far too long, and the daughter had quickly proven to be far more of a problem than even her father. Jon, meanwhile, had shown himself to be a doggedly tenacious investigator. In a different life, perhaps he'd make a good Vanguard agent, hunting down loose ends and finding clever ways to manipulate the powers-that-be into action. Instead, he had chosen to fight against the national interest, endeavoring to derail the Vanguard's efforts at every turn.

Despite their best efforts, Jon and Chloe had both failed. But their failure was a victory for the Vanguard. Not only would they soon be rid of the neophyte troublemakers, but they would also be able to burn off the loose ends left by Kennedy, Washington, Anderson, and Taft.

So Jon and Chloe would both die. But first, Kellerman would ensure that the Vanguard's interests were fully secure.

"Now," he said in response to their lack of movement. "The letters you stole from Washington's grave."

Jon just grinned. "You really don't understand, do you?"

Kellerman had little patience for their games, but they stood between him and what the Vanguard needed. "Understand what, exactly?"

"The depths of your little boys' club's exposure. Washington's letters were discovered nearly a century ago. By one of your own honorary members."

Recent events had caused Kellerman to suspect as much. "Taft. We know."

That put Jon back in his place. His grin wilted at the realization that Kellerman knew more than he suspected.

"It's funny, actually," Kellerman gloated. "You got so close to the truth, but couldn't even see it. We're not the bad guys here, Jon. In fact, we're the true patriots, the only ones with the insight and the stones to keep this fractured nation intact."

"What are you talking about?" Chloe asked.

Kellerman shook his head. What did it matter? They would both be dead in a matter of moments. But something in him, perhaps the noble blood of his forefathers whose sacrifices had given birth to the United States, felt that, despite being on the wrong side of history, Jon and Chloe deserved to know why they were about to die. They had proven formidable foes, and despite being the enemies of the Vanguard, he needed them to understand that they were the true villains here.

But Jon beat him to the punch.

"You're trying to stop another civil war."

Kellerman was momentarily dumbstruck. Jon had figured it out after all. Or part of it at least. And yet he still fought against the Vanguard's mission?

"Do you have any idea how many times the Vanguard has pulled our nation back from the brink since Appomattox? Lincoln and Kennedy were mere pawns, sacrificed for the greater good, so the nation could live on. Wars and rumors of wars, false flag attacks, political scandals and assassinations, all of it to protect America from her greatest weakness: her own citizens. Our union almost didn't survive the first Civil War, and our nation was then far more homogenous in culture, religion, ethnicity, and values than we are today. One look at the news tells you how close to the tipping point we already are. Fragmented along every possible line, with click-hunting media pundits and unscrupulous politicians pushing every potential social division for personal gain. As a society, we are more divided than the 1960s and, in many ways, more divided than the 1860s."

"And without an enemy to unite against, you're afraid we'll devolve into anarchic chaos."

"Exactly. There's plenty of case studies from both history and modern world events to see the dangers of leaving a democracy to its own fickle devices. And as perhaps the least homogenous nation in the world today, the threat from within for us is far worse. We know firsthand. Even a century and a half ago, Lincoln had to go. Though he was a great man and a strong leader, he represented everything that the soon-to-be-defeated South hated. He was a Yankee who had proclaimed the freedom of all slaves in Confederate lands, had led a war against the seceded states, and had rendered all the sacrifices of the rebels for naught. His election to the presidency in 1860 had been the catalyst for the first Confederate states to secede from the Union. And now, after losing their sons, their land, their livelihoods, and their pride to Lincoln's forces, they were supposed to somehow fall in line behind him? Another rebellion was already brewing despite the war's impending end, and the only way to quell it was to remove him from the equation, putting a southerner, a Tennessean, in the White House instead."

"Did you ever think that instead of killing presidents, attacking American citizens, and instigating wars you might do something good? Give us something positive to unite behind rather than something negative to fear and loathe?"

Kellerman laughed. "And what would that be, exactly? Name me one major issue that Americans aren't split down the middle on, if not fragmented into a dozen deeply entrenched positions. All the potentially good things—medical breakthroughs, clean energy advances, public safety, effective immigration policies, improving our education system, growing the economy, more efficient government, cross-cultural understanding—have so many detractors on so many sides of the issues that they only serve to highlight our gaping differences. But kill a beloved leader or blow up a couple of skyscrapers and watch the national pride and unity sweep across the country."

"You've been drinking your own Kool-Aid so long you have no idea what Americans are really capable of," Chloe said.

"We are the original Americans, and we are the only ones willing and able to do what is necessary to ensure there is an America for the next generation to inherit. Were it not for us, we'd still be under the thumb of British tyranny. Were it not for the Vanguard's forward thinking, the South would indeed have risen again and destroyed the United States before Lincoln finished his second term.

"Last night, you decried us as war profiteers, but that couldn't be further from the truth. Time and again throughout the centuries we've protected the integrity of our national union and ensured the future of our country, fulfilling our original charge as Cincinnati. And yet you presume to lecture me on the capability of Americans. We know what they're capable of. And that's exactly why we must do what we do."

It was foolish to hope that they might understand the importance of the Vanguard's mission, but he had said his piece. Their failure to see the truth right before their eyes was further proof that men like Kellerman and Gaines were the rightful heirs to steer the nation's future. And it was further proof that he had to finish this, here and now.

"The documents," he said, reaching out his hand. "Everything. Give them to me."

"They're somewhere safe now," Jon said. "But if anything happens to us—"

"Oh, let me guess." Kellerman's voice filled with mock giddiness. "If anything happens to either of you, they'll be made public. Heard it before, pal. It was a lie when they did it in the movies, and it's a lie now."

He leaned forward and added in a more serious tone. "And just so you know, your CIA buddy topside failed. No one would listen to his crazy stories of a mythical assassin. Of course, after President Talquin is dead, President Finney may decide to prosecute him for being part of the Venezuelans' plan. He got cold feet at the end, but too little, too late."

Jon seethed, but said nothing. Instead, Chloe sent the next salvo.

"You really think you'll get away with this, Anthony?"

That froze Kellerman in place. They knew his name? How? Wilkins, no doubt. They had just proven to be even more of a liability. It was time to end this.

"You have until the count of three to place the Lafayette Confession, along with whatever you found in the *Victura* and here in Cincinnati, on the table. The count of three. There will not be a four."

"You stole that line from Hans Gruber in *Die Hard*," Jon ribbed.

He was clearly trying to unsettle him, to throw him off so he made a mistake. Kellerman was not in the mood. And he was done making mistakes with these two.

"One."

"There's more you don't know," Chloe said. "A smoking gun that will tie the assassination directly to the Vanguard."

Kellerman could see the desperation in her eyes, exposing her deceit.

"Two."

"Okay, okay!" Jon said. "You win."

Then he reached underneath his shirt for the documents the Vanguard had sought for two centuries.

≈≈≈≈≈

But it was all a ruse.

Chloe carried the documents now. Jon had the pistol Wayne had given them.

She charged Molyneux as Jon pulled his gun from his waistband. Kellerman was distracted by her sudden move, so he didn't see Jon's gun until it was almost too late.

Jon fired twice, both bullets flying high as Kellerman dove to the floor. Kellerman returned fire, sending Jon scrambling for cover behind the table.

Molyneux was slow to react, but react he did when he realized what was happening. He shoved Dr. Bixby to the ground and adjusted his aim toward Chloe. She was close enough now. She delivered a roundhouse kick to his gun hand, sending the weapon clattering to the floor behind him.

But he was quicker than she anticipated. He grabbed her leg on the way down and wrenched it to the side. She fell to the ground face first.

Molyneux scooped his gun from the ground and grabbed a fistful of her hair. Her scalp burned as he pulled her from the floor. Wrapping a surprisingly strong arm around her torso, he pressed the gun barrel to her temple.

*Well, crap.*

≈≈≈≈≈

Jon didn't have a shot. He could hear Chloe scuffling with Molyneux, but the Frenchman had a gun. Chloe was unarmed.

He peeked around the table, trying to get an angle on either Vanguard operative. Before his head even cleared the tabletop, Kellerman's next shot sent him ducking back behind the table. The table had a solid base, so he couldn't even shoot at their legs underneath it. The only person he could see was Dr. Bixby, crumpled on the open floor to his left, grunting and pleading with him for salvation.

The best way to catch your enemy off guard was to do the unexpected. So instead of moving to find a better angle to shoot at Kellerman or Molyneux, he changed the rules entirely. He tossed the gun to Bixby.

Bixby reached and grabbed the weapon with her bound hands, then spat out the gag. She raised the weapon and pointed it . . . at Jon.

*Please, no.*

Kellerman started laughing, a blood-curdling snicker that made Jon sick to his stomach.

"It looks like it's you who doesn't understand what's going on," Kellerman said.

Jon looked at his old professor pleadingly. "Dr. Bixby?"

"After I killed your buddy Vance, I was down one informant. She already knew so much about us, and she had your ear. She needed a little persuasion, but the life of her daughter turned out to be the right pressure point."

"I'm so sorry, Jon," Bixby said, a tear trickling down her dirty cheek.

Jon scowled. "Yeah, you look real sorry with that gun pointed at my head."

Chloe struggled against Molyneux, but his grip on her was like iron.

"So we come to the final play," Kellerman sneered. "The Vanguard wins. You lose. But if you don't give me everything you've stolen over the last few days, you'll lose even more."

Jon felt a deep-seated desperation take root in his soul. The Vanguard had all the guns, and every advantage. Barring some miracle from on high, he and Chloe were about to die.

# CHAPTER 83
## Cincinnati, Ohio

Special Agent in Charge Ian Hardwick couldn't shake the ghost of Wayne Wilkins from his mind. Fountain Square had been cleared in accordance with protocol. They had even double-checked the clearance of all the local officers assisting with security. No red flags whatsoever.

But Wayne's warning haunted him all the same. The CIA agent had even gone so far as to come here to Fountain Square to share his warnings of a vague threat to the president with Secret Service personnel and local police. Wayne had the president's implicit trust in the field, so he wasn't likely the sort of guy to go around making such claims without good reason. But he had been wrong. NSA, CIA, FBI, Secret Service, and state and local law enforcement had triple-checked their intel. No actionable threats had been made in relation to this rally.

So why did Hardwick feel so wrong?

President Talquin had taken the stage just minutes ago. He was slated to speak for twenty minutes before the mayor of Cincinnati, who was also running for reelection in November, would return to the stage for closing remarks. At that point, Hardwick and his team would escort Talquin back to the presidential motorcade. Then it was on to the airport for a remote cabinet meeting aboard Air Force One en route to another rally in Houston.

Election season was Hardwick's least favorite part of the job. Long stretches away from his family. Endless political blathering, campaign promises no one had any intention of keeping. And a heightened sense of danger for his team as the election frenzy brought all the crazies out of the woodwork.

Scratch that. It was his second-least favorite part of the job. His least favorite was when he felt like this.

Something was wrong.

But he had no idea what.

"We have accomplished so much in the past three and a half years," Talquin's voice boomed through the sound system. "Imagine what we can accomplish in four and a half more!"

Talquin was probably Hardwick's favorite president since he had joined the service. Some of his policies were controversial in some camps, but then these days it was all but impossible to get most people to agree on anything. Hardwick liked most of his politics, but, more than that, Talquin respected the Service's role in keeping him and his family safe. Previous presidents had made a hobby of trying to slip their security details, either for illicit liaisons or because they simply wanted a little privacy. It wasn't fun having a team of hired shadows following your every move for years on end, but Lincoln, Garfield, McKinley, Kennedy, Reagan, and countless near misses had clearly demonstrated the tantalizing target that the most powerful office in the world presented. More than that, though, Talquin learned everyone's name and asked about their family. He was polite even when he was in a hurry, and when he was unnecessarily gruff, he endeavored to apologize shortly thereafter.

For Talquin, the Secret Service wasn't just the help. They were the only thing standing between him and a bullet. And for that, he was regularly grateful.

Hardwick hoped he hadn't betrayed the trust the president had placed in him by not bringing Wayne Wilkins's concerns to him.

Talquin's voice cut through his thoughts. "There is still more work to be done, though. We cannot backslide in November. We must forge onward for a better, brighter tomorrow!"

The crowd cheered so loudly that Hardwick almost didn't hear the other sound. But he could never forget that. The sound that pierced the sky flashed him back to his Marine Corps service in Desert Storm. It had haunted his nightmares for two years after retiring from the military.

No matter how long it had been since he had last heard one, he could never forget the fear-inducing whistle of an incoming mortar shell.

That was what he had missed. Wayne had been right after all. And they were all about to pay the ultimate price.

Hardwick ran for the president, shouting into his radio. They knew what to do. It was the nightmare scenario every agent trained for. That they always prayed never came. But this one felt much, much worse.

*A mortar. My God.*

There was no time. His team's training was top-notch, but they couldn't outrace a rocket. If the mortar was aimed directly at the stage, they were all dead. Even a near-miss could be fatal, not only for the president and Hardwick's team, but also for hundreds of civilians attending the rally.

Still, they had to try. Long ago, he had sworn an oath to defend the president of the United States, whoever occupied that office. If his last act on this earth was to die trying to fulfill that oath, it was too good an end for him.

He should have listened to Wayne instead of so quickly dismissing him. And now they were all going to die.

He had failed his team. He had failed his president. And he had failed his country.

The faces of the crowd twisted into shock. Smartphones were whipped out and started recording. A rally was one thing. The stoic Secret Service leaping into action meant something historic was going down. And that had to be recorded on Instagram stories and broadcast via Facebook Live.

*You are all in mortal danger!* he wanted to scream at the social-media-obsessed masses before him. But it would have done no good. For his last few seconds of life, he had but one mission. Do whatever he could to protect the president.

His team was already hustling a hunched-over Talquin from the stage, shielding him with their bodies as they moved. Hardwick caught up to them and led them toward the waiting armored SUV. But even the so-called "Beast" would not escape a direct mortar blast unscathed.

*Just a few steps farther.*

The plaza erupted with a percussive boom, sending Hardwick's hands instinctively toward his ears. The ground beneath their feet roiled with the impact of the mortar. And then the screams began.

But something was off. Hardwick hadn't felt the heat he expected from the blast. Nor had he experienced even a minor pressure wave, something that he should have felt this close to the explosion.

He paused as his men shoved Talquin into the Beast.

Fountain Square was still there. Its occupants were shocked and terrified by the president's quick departure and the subsequent explosion. But no one here was dead.

A new source of screams caught his attention. Several blocks away, a fiery plume of smoke roiled from a crater that wasn't there a minute ago.

The assassin had missed.

Hardwick called in EMS support for the location and hopped in the follow car behind the Beast, which was already racing toward safety.

Somehow, Wayne Wilkins had been right about the attack. Perhaps he had even been responsible for the assassin's skewed trajectory that had destroyed one intersection but spared the Fountain Square crowd and President Talquin.

Which raised an even more terrifying question in Hardwick's mind.

If Wayne's intel on the attack was accurate, could the rest of his seemingly implausible tale also be true?

He keyed his radio for an agent he had seen get into the Beast with Talquin.

"I need to talk to POTUS," Hardwick said. "We may have a situation with the vice president."

# CHAPTER 84
## Cincinnati, Ohio

Jon was in an impossible situation. Two guns pointed at him. One more pressed against Chloe's head. And no chance of a passing policeman or helpful citizen to intervene in this hidden subterranean lair. He weighed his options. He could think of several scenarios where he might be able to kill at least one of his opponents. But in every one of those, he and Chloe died.

He had no moves.

Checkmate.

But he couldn't give up that easily.

"Any more bright ideas, Jon?" Kellerman mocked. "It's over. You've lost. Plain and simple. Now accept your defeat with dignity and hand over what you found before my colleague here starts redecorating the place with Chloe's gray matter."

"Let her go first," Jon called from behind the cover of the table.

"Not a chance," Molyneux seethed.

"You're not in much of a position to be negotiating here," Kellerman said. "You're in way over your head. But hey, you tried."

"Just promise you won't hurt her," Jon said, knowing any such promise the Vanguard might offer would be less than worthless. He was just stalling, racking his brain for any course of action that might allow him to gain the upper hand.

"She knows what will happen to her if she opens her mouth against us publicly. All we want are the documents."

Lies. But Jon would play along. "Then let her go first."

Kellerman seemed to realize the futility of Jon's tactics. "You're stalling and you know it. How about this? Give me what I want in the next three seconds, or I'll shoot you both and take it from your corpses."

"You actually think we are still carrying all of those historic documents around? Down here of all places?"

The Vanguard operative surely did think that, but he couldn't be sure. That was the only thing keeping them alive right now. But it wouldn't last long.

"I can think of one way to find out." Kellerman's voice was far closer now. Jon looked up to see his enemy standing mere feet from him. Without a gun, he was no longer a physical threat.

Kellerman leveled the gun at him. "Everything on the table. If something is missing, you and Miss Harper will be strip-searched. If that doesn't produce everything, we'll have to go with some alternative means of persuasion."

Jon didn't like the sound of that. Still looking for an opening that wouldn't come, he slowly rose to his feet and prepared to hand over the Lafayette Confession.

Suddenly, the earth shook as something exploded overhead. The lights flickered out, leaving the chamber in total darkness as shards of concrete rained from the ceiling.

It was the game changer Jon was praying for. He grabbed at Kellerman's gun and elbowed him in the nose. The gun fell from Kellerman's grasp and skittered away into the black.

"You son of a—"

Kellerman's invective was cut short by Jon's punch to his solar plexus, followed by an uppercut to his jaw. His brother had taught him that one-two attack. Michael would be proud.

To his right, he heard a grunt as Chloe fought with Molyneux. Then a gasp of pain every man recognized and feared.

Nut shot.

Rarely did Jon wish that pain on anyone. He was willing to make an exception for Molyneux.

His face erupted in an explosion of pain as a quickly recovered Kellerman blindsided him with a one-two punch of his own. The man hit like a prize fighter. Jon reeled, bracing himself against the conference table while he shook off the stars dancing in his head.

Footsteps running further away. Chloe? He prayed, if nothing else, she got away and survived to tell the world what she had found here. Even if he died here today, the Vanguard could still be destroyed.

He heard Kellerman coming this time. Jon dove out of the way just in time, leaving Kellerman to swing at air. Jon used the opportunity to duck around him, scrounging on the ground for where his assailant's gun might have landed.

A boot kicked him in the chest, cracking a rib. Jon crumpled to the floor, instinctively rolling into a ball. Kellerman straddled him and began pounding away with bloody fists.

"You have to learn to stop sticking your nose where it doesn't belong, Jon," Kellerman huffed along to the beat of his punches. "It got your brother killed. And now it's getting you killed."

The lights flicked back on with a fluorescent hum.

Chloe hadn't run after all. She was standing three feet away, a pistol pointed at Kellerman's head.

"This is for my dad, you sick—"

The last word was drowned out by the gunshot. Kellerman's eyes bulged and rolled as the bullet rocketed through his brain and out the other side of his head. Jon shoved him off and rolled away, bringing a fresh wave of pain to his injured ribs. The Vanguard operative slumped to the floor with a wet plop, his legs twitching as billions of neurons fired their last.

"Thanks," Jon said, taking Chloe's offered hand as she helped him up. She pulled him into a bear hug and he squeezed her back, ignoring his ribs' protestations. Her hug was the best feeling in the world, and he never wanted to let go. The way her hands clung to his back made him think he was not alone in that sentiment.

But their work wasn't done yet.

He let go and took a step back.

"You look like you've been through the ringer," Chloe said.

Jon chuckled grimly and motioned at Kellerman's body. "You should see the other guy."

Chloe laughed while Jon took in the room. Whatever had happened above their heads seemed like the miracle he was praying for. But they weren't out of the woods yet. Molyneux and Bixby were missing. The vault door was still closed, so they were likely still in the archives somewhere. Armed and dangerous.

"Let's finish this," he said.

"You sure you're okay?" she asked.

"I'll heal after this is over. How about you?"

She rubbed at a growing welt on her forehead where she had hit her head on the ground during her initial scuffle with Molyneux. "Me too. Let's do this."

They split up to cover more ground and not get caught in a pincer move between their two armed enemies. As he entered another section of the stacks, he found himself once again amazed at the size of these archives and the breadth of the national and global events its contents referenced. This would make the biggest news splash since 9/11, with even graver policy and international fallout implications.

And this time, he wouldn't be able to pass off all the credit for the revelation on his dead brother.

He'd already seen the trouble even the little bit of fame his role in the Rockefeller affair had gotten him into. First blacklisted from universities, then getting sucked into a life-threatening adventure up against an all-powerful secret society older than America itself. Then he thought of Chloe. Actually, maybe that last part wasn't so bad after all.

A shout from elsewhere in the archives. Molyneux. Near where Chloe had been searching. A bang, then click, click, click. Molyneux chuckling.

"I'm going to take my time killing you."

Jon couldn't let that happen.

But he was unarmed. And Molyneux was not.

He peeked through the stacks and saw Chloe running down an aisle away from the Frenchman. The rows were all parallel and laden with books, binders, and other materials from the centuries-long treasonous exploits of the Vanguard.

Which gave Jon an idea. The timing had to be perfect, but it could be just what the situation called for.

As with the powerful words penned by dead presidents that Kellerman had wanted Jon to hand over, knowledge could be a surprisingly potent weapon.

Bracing himself for pain from his injured ribs, he rammed into the bookcase, shoving with all his might. The bookcase rocked from its resting position, but would not go further. He let it rock back, then, using the momentum of its forward motion, hit the bookcase once more.

It toppled with a crash.

Then so did the next one.

And the next one. It was a lethal game of dominoes.

Jon raced alongside the cascading shelves, trying to reach Chloe before she was crushed. He reached her as she was mere feet from the end of the row.

The world slowed to a crawl.

Jon thrust his arm toward her.

She grabbed hold as he yanked her to safety.

Molyneux raised his gun, a look of defiant rage on his face.

"Down," Jon shouted as he shoved her out of Molyneux's sight.

A bullet ripped through the armpit of his jacket.

The next caught him in the bicep.

A third shot never came.

Molyneux screamed as several tons of steel shelving and paper crushed him to the floor. The dominoes continued to fall until the last one landed against the far wall.

Jon listened for a groan, grunt, or gasp. Nothing. Molyneux was dead.

"You okay?" Jon asked as he helped Chloe off the floor.

"I'll live," she said with a smile. "You should see the other guy."

Jon grinned. The exuberance of cheating death was like few other feelings in life. Adrenaline mixed with the euphoria at being alive. It made you appreciate living like nothing else.

"Help!" a weak voice gasped. "Please!"

Jon looked toward the sound. The toppling bookshelves had also forced Dr. Bixby from her hiding place. She had fallen while trying to escape the deadly cascade. Her legs were trapped beneath the end of the bookshelves. The gun Jon had foolishly trusted her with had fallen from her grasp and remained just out of reach.

He walked over to her and retrieved his gun.

"How could you?" he asked, his voice dripping with disgust.

She looked up at him, a pitiful wreck. "I'm sorry. He tortured me. They threatened my daughter. I'm so, so sorry."

Jon handed his gun to Chloe and helped Bixby extricate herself from beneath the shelves. The professor extended her bound hands.

*Burn me once . . .*

"Not a chance," he said. "Not until we're out of here and we don't have to worry about another double cross." He motioned with his gun toward the corner of the room. "You sit over there and play nice, and maybe we won't mention your aiding and abetting terrorists, traitors, and assassins to the authorities."

Bixby bowed her head and shuffled over to the corner.

"Now what?" Chloe asked.

Jon looked around the room. What was moments ago an orderly archive was now a shambles. Most of a whole row of well-organized shelves was now a multi-ton mess, each shelf weighed down by a dozen more, their contents fallen from their perch and scattered about.

"Now? We find the smoking gun. And then we bring down the Vanguard once and for all."

# CHAPTER 85
## Cincinnati, Ohio

Senator Stanton Gaines hated taking the stairs. Three flights down the narrow, dimly lit stairwell were not his idea of fun, especially when he was in a hurry. But he had no choice.

The attack had failed.

Somehow, the mortar had missed the president's rally, landing several blocks from Fountain Square. The tip about suspicious activity at Barnett Tower had gone out as scheduled, so Vargas would be captured soon enough, willing to share his tale about his secret mission on behalf of his home country with anyone who would listen. And then, before he could testify before open court, he would be killed by another purported Venezuelan operative who would die in a shootout with police moments later. A cover-up within a cover-up.

But it was all unraveling.

Perhaps the near-miss would still prove the tipping point that finally pushed Talquin toward a war footing with Venezuela. On the flip side, it could also raise his suspicions, considering how hard Gaines had been pushing Talquin for war in recent weeks. And that was the biggest problem. Talquin was still president. All of his grooming of Finney to be the Vanguard's latest man in the White House was for naught.

To make matters worse, he couldn't get ahold of Kellerman or Molyneux. The vault door sensor into the abandoned subway system had been triggered nearly half an hour ago. Plenty of time for those two to eradicate the threat Jon Rickner and Chloe Harper posed.

But he had heard nothing.

So much was riding on today. So much had already gone wrong. He had to salvage what he could. The fate of the nation was riding on it.

Unfortunately, the errant mortar had also briefly knocked out power to the building he used to access the Vanguard's subterranean archives. When the power came back on, the elevator was still out of service. The surge must have fried some circuit somewhere, and Gaines couldn't wait for the repairman to fix it.

So the stairs it was.

As he reached the bottom and prepared to swipe his keycard to enter the stairwell, he pulled his pistol from his concealed holster and checked the slide. Hopefully the signal was just bad down here and Kellerman had everything cleared up by now.

But if not . . .

He swiped his keycard and punched his private access code into the control panel. The panel beeped and flashed green as the lock disengaged.

As soon as he set foot into the archives, he knew something had gone horribly wrong. It looked as though a tornado had torn a path through the room. Shelves toppled, books, binders, and papers—centuries of documentation of the hard sacrifices the Vanguard had made in defense of the nation it served—were strewn everywhere.

At first, he thought the destructive blast that rocked the street above might have caused the chaos before him. But the lights were still screwed into their sockets, and several shelves had been spared. This reeked of intentionality. And he had little doubt who might've been responsible.

He ducked behind the fallen shelves and peered underneath each one. Four shelves down, he spied what looked to be the body of Patrick Molyneux, crushed beneath the weight of a thousand secret operations.

He feared a similar fate had befallen Kellerman. Which meant it was up to him now.

Kellerman and Molyneux were but soldiers in the Vanguard's centuries-long fight to keep America safe from herself. The group's future did not hinge upon their deaths. It did not even depend upon Gaines's own survival. The Vanguard was large enough and strong enough to carry on the good fight if it lost fifty good men today.

But it could not survive the exposure of this chamber.

This trove of information, the archives cataloging the Vanguard's secret contributions to keeping the United States from tearing itself apart, was the purest fulfillment of the original Society of the Cincinnati charter.

An unalterable determination to promote and cherish, between the respective States, that union and national honor so essentially necessary to their happiness, and the future dignity of the American Empire.

No one had done more to promote national union and the American Empire than the Vanguard. This archive was a testament to that fact, and served as a constant reminder of the importance of their work.

Without the Vanguard, there would be no United States today.

And if the contents of this room were revealed to the public, there might be no United States tomorrow.

He crept around the fallen bookcases toward the aisles at the far end that were still intact. He could hear voices at the other end of the room. Neither belonged to Kellerman. He was out of allies down here.

Once he reached the still-standing aisles, he made his first mistake. He stood, edging his way silently through the stacks toward the voices.

"Who's there?" a male voice called out.

Gaines looked toward the voice, realizing his error. He may have been quiet in his approach, but his cover was incomplete. The spaces between the books and the shelf above them betrayed his presence. He peered through the gap and saw Chloe and a pistol-wielding Jon standing over Kellerman's bloody corpse. They were both staring straight at him.

*So much for a surprise entrance.*

He smoothed his jacket and readied his gun. He was a combat veteran and an active member at a shooting range in Pittsburgh and another in northern Virginia. He had no doubt he could land kill shots on both Jon and Chloe before he succumbed to whatever wounds they inflicted on him. But he wasn't ready to die just yet. If it came to that, he would take both of them out and go down shooting, glad to offer the ultimate sacrifice to protect his nation's future.

But first, he wanted to try a different approach.

# CHAPTER 86
## *Cincinnati, Ohio*

Jon couldn't believe his eyes. He had thought Vice President Finney's companion at Anderson House sounded familiar. Now he remembered who it belonged to. The very man stepping out of the shadows behind the shelves at the far end of the archives. Senator Stanton Gaines.

The senior senator from Pennsylvania was a mainstay in the press these days. A moderate democrat who was perhaps the most hawkish member of his party in Congress, Gaines had pushed in recent months for an increased American response to the crisis in Venezuela. Jon wouldn't be at all surprised if the assassin Wayne had hopefully managed to stop was Venezuelan.

Another assassinated president, another pliant successor, another war to distract Americans from growing tensions at home. It was like JFK 2.0, just updating the playbook for a new century.

"So we meet at last," Gaines said as he emerged from the stacks. He held a pistol at his side, the barrel pointed loosely in their direction. The threat was implicit, but not the focus of his message right now. "I've heard so much about your exploits the past few days. It's quite something to finally see you face to face."

"It certainly is something," Jon said, keeping his own gun trained on the senator.

A few steps away, Chloe was tapping furiously on her phone. He hoped she wasn't trying to dial 911. Even if she could get a signal down here, by the time the cops found the archives, they'd all likely be dead. He glanced over at her, then took a few steps away to put some distance between her and where Gaines was focused.

"I'm just trying to figure out the part where a sitting senator decides assassinating his own president is a good idea," Jon said.

Gaines shook his head. "You make it sound so black and white. The world is far grayer than you realize."

"Enlighten me."

The senator gave Jon an avuncular smile. "My actions—indeed, all of the Vanguard's over our history—have been nothing if not noble. We make the hard choices that the public—and most elected officials for that matter—aren't ready to face in order to preserve the great Union that our forefathers fought and bled to create. Just look at the news these days. Our nation is rife with conflict. Liberals and conservatives at each others' throats on every issue possible. Millennials destroying the traditions of the Baby Boomers. White supremacists and anti-white iconoclasts clashing at rallies across the nation. Religious and anti-religious wars between Christians and Muslims and atheists and everything in between. Half the country wants to burn the second amendment, while the other half slips it into the Lord's Prayer every night. Millions have turned on law enforcement of any kind, which leads to less respect for the rule of law and further rioting and degradation of society. Even the press has gotten on board, with virtually every viewpoint on every issue finding some outlet that will support it enthusiastically. No one wants to listen to each other anymore. They just want to hear themselves screaming how they're right."

"And the Vanguard is the panacea for all the country's ills?" Jon asked with a heavy dose of sarcasm.

"No, not all of them. But our actions ensure there is a country at all. Without the Vanguard's protection, the United States would have devolved into an anarchic civil war years ago. And with all issues that divide America these days, it wouldn't just be a two-sided affair like the last time. When the smoke cleared from this one, the wasteland remaining would be wholly unrecognizable. The nation is already starting to break apart, with states like California, Vermont, and Texas flirting with secession. And our enemies—foreign and domestic—are far more numerous, well connected, and powerful than they were in 1861. If we've already got international agents trying to sow division in our elections, just imagine what they would do when we're on the ropes from a devastating civil war. We barely survived the first Civil War. We would not survive a second."

"And so, what, you kill President Talquin, frame some Venezuelan guy—"

"No, our assassin really was Venezuelan this time. Well, would-be assassin."

Jon felt his spirits lift. The assassination had failed. Wayne had come through. Now it was up to him and Chloe to finish their side of the mission.

"Why was that?" Jon asked, pretending to be interested.

"Easier for the powers-that-be to make the connection. When we used Lee Harvey Oswald, for example, his Soviet connections were too tenuous. And the Soviet connections to Vietnam were even less clear cut. Thankfully, Johnson already wanted to go to war, so it didn't take too much prodding."

Gaines seemed to be letting his guard down, talking more freely, though he kept his weapon aimed at Jon.

"But Vice President Finney wouldn't need much prodding either. We overheard you two talking at Anderson House last night. He assured you that once you put him in the White House, you'd have your war."

The senator seemed taken aback briefly by the revelation that his conversation was overheard in what was supposed to be an empty building. He recovered quickly, though, and continued on with his argument.

"No, Finney wouldn't have taken much prodding. But the American public might. After the sketchy WMD intel we used to go into Iraq, they're a little less war hungry than they used to be. The assassination of a sitting US President by a foreign national with a forged paper trail leading back to that country's government is just the sort of connect-the-dots simplicity the populace needs to support an armed incursion. And, after all, public support is the most important part of this whole exercise. This isn't about oil or neocolonialism, though those have made for convenient excuses to distract from the Vanguard's patterns and purpose over the years. It's about survival, plain and simple."

"I think you sell the American public short. Yes, we've got some serious issues, and, yes, the media seems to focus on those a lot these days for clicks or whatever. But, by and large, we stick together when the going gets tough. Just look at how we pull together after natural disasters. Strangers digging deep and helping other strangers in need. While FEMA is still sorting out their paperwork, it's volunteer firefighters and off-duty sheriff's deputies, corporate execs and soccer moms, bricklayers and college students who answer the call, from right next door or three states away. Across all races, creeds, and cultures, at our hearts, we're all American. And though we may disagree on a lot, at times even disagreeing on what makes us American, at our core, we're all bound together by a greater community."

"That's an awfully idealistic world you live in, Dr. Rickner. But you're surrounded by evidence to the contrary. You see, Kennedy was never the problem. Vietnam, the Soviet Union, Lincoln, Saddam Hussein, none of them held a candle to America's greatest threat."

Jon's theory was right. Horrifying, but right.

"Our own citizens."

"Exactly. You think Venezuela, Syria, or the Sudan have problems? They're far more unified than we are. And the only thing preventing the conflict-loving American populace from tearing this nation asunder forever is the Vanguard. Our forefathers gave up everything to forge this great nation. And I'll be damned if I'm going to let it fall to pieces on my watch."

"Who are you to force your vision on the nation? I thought liberty and self-determination were supposedly the core tenets of what our founding fathers—including the Cincinnati—envisioned for this country you claim to want to protect."

"Come now, Jon. You know better than that. The founders restricted voting rights to white male landowners. *The elite.* Even Cincinnati adversaries like Jefferson knew better than to entrust this country's survival to the whims of the proletariat."

"But all this death and destruction. Doesn't it eat at you? If you guys are so smart and *elite*, can't you figure out a way to heal the nation that doesn't involve treachery and mass distraction?"

Gaines laughed. "This is how it has been from the beginning. It's the only way. Even the original Cincinnatus knew this to be true. Any time a revolt was brewing at home, ancient Rome would launch a foreign invasion to give the unwashed masses a common enemy to rally against. That's what all this has been about. The preservation of congressional scandals, false flag attacks, presidential assassinations, international coups. Two centuries' worth, from Ford's Theater to Vietnam and beyond. All of it necessary to the continuance of our great union. Unfortunate, yes. But absolutely necessary."

Jon glanced at Chloe. She nodded.

"So you really believe that by killing President Lincoln in 1865, by killing President Kennedy in 1963, and by trying to kill President Talquin today, you and your Vanguard buddies have made America a safer, better place."

"Absolutely. Even with Talquin in power, we may still be able to salvage the war effort against Venezuela, as it's pretty clear that a foreign national *attempted* to kill the president. The American people will demand blood. And, once again, the Vanguard's guiding hand will have saved the nation from destroying itself."

Jon smiled, his eyes wide with wonder. "Wow. I've got to admit, it's absolutely incredible."

Gaines seemed to pick up on his impressed expression. "It truly is. And though we've clearly had some bad blood these past few days, I must say that we could use someone of your acumen to help with the restoration of this archive, and perhaps even to help identify future targets for manipulation. You wouldn't be a full member of the Vanguard, of course, as those are chosen from the ranks of the Society of the Cincinnati, and that membership is hereditary. But I'm sure we could come to some other sort of arrangement."

Jon feigned not having heard him. "I'm sorry, what were you talking about? Oh, no, I wasn't saying your *story* was incredible. I was referring to the fact that there's an LTE data signal down here. Who would have thought? The explosion up top must've broken something open. Chloe's been live-streaming your whole confession straight to Facebook and Instagram."

"Two hundred forty-six thousand current viewers and counting," she said with a grin at Gaines. "And hey, 'Vanguard' is starting to trend on Twitter. As are you, Senator."

Gaines's face melted as the realization of what had just happened took hold.

Jon smiled and took a step closer to the senator. "All this time you've been afraid we might discover the truth and expose your little treason club to the world. And after everything we've been through, it's you who breaks the story. Congratulations, Senator Gaines. You're going viral."

Gaines's face twisted in confusion, then rage, then a deep, mournful resignation. He angled the gun upward. Toward his own head.

Jon was prepared for this potential reaction. He shot Gaines in the arm. The shock of the impact caused Gaines to stall his suicidal impulse long enough for Chloe to rush in and disarm him.

"Come on, Senator," Chloe laughed. "You created this mess. Did you really think you would get out of it that easily?"

Jon patted him down and secured him as their prisoner until they could get above ground and turn him over to the authorities. But before they left the archives and prepared to retrace their steps through the abandoned subway system with two unwilling travel partners, Jon shared a poignant revelation.

"You know, Senator, you may be right on one point after all. Maybe having a common enemy does help to unite the people. And perhaps you've succeeded after all. Because today, all of America now has a common enemy to rally against." He cocked his head and stared at Gaines. "You."

# EPILOGUE
## *Arlington, Virginia*

Jon had just about had enough of cemeteries. He had been in more than his fair share over the past week. But this would be his last for a while.

Cemeteries were not just places for dead bodies and the bereaved. They were places to remember. To pay respects to those who came before. And to those who left before.

It was one reason he had accompanied Chloe to her father's grave in Tampa yesterday. He had helped her to lay a gladiolus bouquet on the grave. The flowers represented honor, faithfulness, and strength of character, something that Chloe hadn't realized her father embodied until it was too late. But his unheralded work and inspiration had paved the way for a staggering breakthrough that would have surprised even him. One spearheaded by his own daughter.

"He would have been proud of you," Jon had said, laying a hand on her shoulder after they set down the bouquet.

She had smiled as silent tears trailed down her cheeks. "I know."

Cemeteries were also places for endings. And, for believers in the afterlife, for new beginnings.

Both had come true in big ways over the past week. The fallout had started on social media where Chloe had set the fire, but it quickly spread to major media outlets, then to Capitol Hill. Senator Stanton Gaines was censured and arrested for treason among a host of other crimes. As for Dr. Bixby, Jon and Chloe had managed to keep her bout of forced complicity under wraps, painting her as a mere hostage when investigators questioned them, a deed for which the professor thanked them profusely, apologizing until she was blue in the face for her actions and promising them she'd never forget their act of forgiveness.

The Society of the Cincinnati simultaneously acknowledged the existence of the Vanguard and disavowed them, distancing themselves from the secret society within a secret society that held every national headline since the livestreamed subterranean revelation. With the Society's help, other members of the Vanguard were quickly identified and publicly outed. Three generals, a handful of senators and congressmen, and more than a dozen executives at major corporations were among those pulling the strings for the Vanguard, not to mention hundreds of power players and mid-level workers on the group's payroll or black-mailed into cooperation.

But the real *coup de grace* was the Vanguard's archives. The discovery of a stairwell and elevator leading straight to the subterranean chamber made extracting the material for analysis far easier than the circuitous route Jon and Chloe had taken through the subway tunnels. And fore-most on the team of researchers analyzing the material was Jon himself. Since their discovery, it seemed as though the university community's blacklisting of him had melted away, leaving him fielding dozens of of-fers from Stanford to Northwestern to Georgetown.

The Vanguard's faithful chronicling of their own treasonous ex-ploits since the closing days of the Civil War would revolutionize con-temporary scholarship in American History. Everything everyone knew about the past 150 years was instantly cast out the window, and new revelations would likely be coming for months on end.

Today, though, Jon was not poring over shocking discoveries penned by some Vanguard operative. He was walking with Chloe in another cemetery, one less of personal importance than of patriotic.

Arlington National Cemetery was the final resting place of more than 400,000 Americans, almost all of whom had served their country in the armed forces. Though the property was today one of the most som-ber and moving locales in the Washington metro area, the cemetery's Civil War origins were steeped in legend and wartime gallows humor.

The land had once belonged to Robert E. Lee, the great American general who later sided with the Confederacy in the Civil War. Arling-ton House, the neoclassical mansion that today served as the Robert E. Lee Memorial, was built in 1818 by Lee's father-in-law and George Washington's adopted grandson, George Washington Parke Custis. When Union troops captured the land during the war, they set up a field command post in his home. And to ensure Lee could never again return home, the Union started burying their dead on his property, claiming the land for the federal government and designating it as Arlington Na-tional Cemetery on June 15, 1864.

In the century and a half since, hundreds of thousands of American soldiers, sailors, Marines, and airmen had been buried on the property. Not far away, Old Guard sentinels guarded the Tomb of the Unknown Soldier around the clock and year-round as they had for nearly a century, paying homage to countless more men and women who had paid the ultimate price in wartime but whose bodies were never recovered. Numerous others who had served with distinction in the armed forces and died prior to 1864 had been reinterred here, including founding member of the Society of the Cincinnati Pierre L'Enfant.

Despite Arlington being the most famous cemetery in the country and perhaps its most revered, only two presidents were buried here. Both were well known to Jon and Chloe.

Though most of his family was buried back in Cincinnati, William Howard Taft was interred in a shady hillside glen a stone's throw from where Jon now walked. Taft, like many presidents before and after him, never officially served in the armed forces, but he earned the right to be buried in Arlington by virtue of his role as commander-in-chief during his tenure as president. Plus, a plot in this hallowed burying ground ensured he would be eternally near his beloved Supreme Court, even after death.

The second president who was buried at Arlington commanded a far more impressive gravesite. John F. Kennedy had served in the Navy during World War II, so he had doubly earned the right to spend eternity here. But his plot was unlike anything else in the cemetery.

Jon's palms sweated as they neared the top of the stairs stretching up the hill. As they climbed the last few steps, Jon saw the face of his old friend over the ridge.

Wayne Wilkins glanced at Jon and Chloe holding hands as they reached the top. He smiled but said nothing.

"We've got to stop meeting like this," he said.

Jon laughed, remembering an encounter two years ago in a cemetery across the city. He had buried his brother that day. If it hadn't been for Wayne, Jon's father would have buried two sons that day.

"Next time, we'll just have to hit up Applebee's instead. Livelier atmosphere, from what I hear."

Wayne shrugged, looking around. "That wouldn't be particularly hard."

Jon and Chloe had invited Wayne to meet them here as they tried to bring some sense of closure to this strange and turbulent episode in all of their lives. He had been more than happy to accept.

And the view didn't hurt. The hill sloped down into a green expanse of moss-covered trees and stone monuments to the honored dead. Beyond that, the iconic sights of the Washington Monument, Capitol Hill, the White House, and the Lincoln Memorial beckoned in the distance. As with all great Western societies through the centuries, the United States had carved their history in stone. Though a purposefully secular government compared to many of its predecessors, the US Government had filled its capital city with temples to their founding ideals and to Americans who had embodied them. Here, from another memorial to a fallen leader, Jon could see not only monuments to two of the nation's greatest heroes, but also the institutions integral to the continual functioning of this great American experiment.

He hoped the people working in those institutions could also see this memorial.

One of the hallmarks of the memorial was the eternal flame. It had been burning constantly since John F. Kennedy's interment here in 1963. Now, more than half a century later, it took on new meaning.

Bobby Kennedy had been laid to rest opposite his brother. Jon found that fitting, considering how the younger Kennedy had dedicated the last five years of his life to identifying and exposing those responsible for his brother's murder—and how he had ultimately been killed himself for the effort.

"I wonder if they're looking down right now, glad to know that their deaths are finally being put to rights," Chloe mused.

"Maybe so," Wayne said.

Jon looked at the flame. "It'll be interesting to see how the next few years and decades go. You know, it's crazy, but I can't help thinking that Gaines had a few good points about the problems the Vanguard tried to fix. Their solution was all sorts of screwed up, but he may not have been all that far off base about the problem. I'm just hoping we can carve our own even brighter future when we aren't being artificially dragged into conflicts every few years to 'unite' us again."

"I don't know," Chloe said. "I wonder if the United States, with the world's oldest essentially unchanged constitution, will still be recognizable in fifty years. Or if it'll even exist at all."

Wayne put a hand on each of their shoulders. "As your elder, I've gained a lot of experience and insight over the years. I've seen some of the worst America has to offer. And I've also seen some of its best. My parents both died in 9/11. They didn't have to. But they chose to try to save more people in the towers instead of saving themselves. This cemetery is full of self-sacrificing men and women who believed in that good and gave the best years of their lives—and many times even losing their lives—to fight to preserve it. Not because some twisted secret society was pulling the strings. Because they believed it was the right thing to do. Because they believed, as George Washington did, as Abe Lincoln did, and as JFK did, that America is worth fighting for. That hope and belief in forging a better tomorrow has been the lifeblood of the United States from its birth, and I have to believe it will keep going for a long while yet."

Jon reflected on the immortal words of the first victim of the Vanguard's machinations. "A government of the people, for the people, and by the people shall not perish from the earth."

"Indeed," Wayne said, pointing toward downtown DC. "And as long as those guys down there don't forget that, we hopefully won't have to water the tree of liberty with the blood of tyrants anytime soon."

Jon certainly hoped so. Without the Vanguard's interventions, perhaps the nation could reach deep into its institutions and culture to find an organic way to make those words even more a reality. If so, the future could be like the one Washington, Lincoln, and Kennedy had envisioned. One very like the symbolic flame that adorned Kennedy's grave.

A beacon, burning bright, forever.

# AUTHOR'S NOTE

I've been surprised in working on previous novels how interconnected much of history is (for example, this is the third Jon Rickner book where John D. Rockefeller has managed to find his way at least tangentially into the core history behind the narrative). But when working on this book, undoubtedly my most ambitious yet both in length and in scope, I was shocked when things would connect themselves in wholly unexpected ways.

For starters, this originally started as two separate book ideas: a Kennedy one (where, like Jack Harper's working theory, the culprits of the JFK assassination were some of the usual suspects in conspiracy lore working in conjunction in some new and unique way), and a Society of the Cincinnati one, which had been on my radar since high school. I even had working titles for the two projects (the relatively bland *The Second Shooter* and the tongue-twisting *The Cincinnatus Allegiance*, respectively). And then, as I started to research, I realized how intertwined both ideas could be, and the germ of *The Founding Treason* emerged.

Even once I had my main premise, the historical mystery, the modern-day conspiracy, and many of the key locations pinned down, I was surprised at how connected everything was. I had already explored all of the Ohio sites and knew that Taft was going to close out the book. I also had plans to integrate the French aspect of the Society, with particular emphasis on the Marquis de Lafayette, and Jon and Chloe were set to make a brief mid-book sojourn to Paris to find what he had hidden. And then I visited Anderson House. As the modern-day headquarters of the Society of the Cincinnati, Anderson House was always going to be in the book, and once I had seen the majesty of the palatial home firsthand, I knew it would receive a major role. But I had no idea before I took that tour that not only were William Howard Taft and Larz Anderson close friends, but the family-history-obsessed Anderson had a truly substantial connection with the Marquis de Lafayette through his great-grandfather, founding Cincinnatus Richard Clough Anderson. I didn't have to figure out how to get Jon and Chloe to Paris and back after all. History itself had already laid out the groundwork for a much more compelling and organic narrative.

Believe it or not, aside from the central conceit regarding the Vanguard, the vast majority of the history in *The Founding Treason* is absolutely true. Looking back on it now, having spent years researching and writing the book, it still astounds me how interconnected everything is and how much history supports the sweeping conspiracy I created for Jon and Chloe to discover and defeat. But now that the story is over, I will endeavor to separate the actual history, locations, and people from the fictional webbing helping to tie them all together.

The 1799 section of the prologue is rife with real history. The so-called "Quasi War" dominated French and American relations in the years following the French Revolution and saw a great deal of naval embargoes and privateer attacks on each country's cargo vessels, though it never escalated into a full-blown war. Napoleon Bonaparte was not a fan of the Marquis de Lafayette, and his prohibition against the marquis's attendance at the memorial services for Washington in Paris really happened.

The secret meeting in the 1865 section of the prologue is my invention, though it is grounded in theories espoused at the time and in the decades since. The theory that there was a greater conspiracy behind the Lincoln assassination beyond John Wilkes Booth, Mary Surratt, and the rest of the group convicted for their roles has been around for ages, with proponents pointing to the series of seemingly too-convenient coincidences that facilitated Booth's success in killing the president and in the assassin's ability to escape Washington DC after committing the most heinous crime the nation had yet seen. And though he is only mentioned in passing, Hamilton Fish was the president-general of the Society of the Cincinnati during the Civil War.

The prologue scene from 1963 is actually the first section I wrote for the project when I still envisioned it as *The Second Shooter*. Merging the official story (that Oswald shot at the presidential motorcade from the sixth floor of the Texas School Book Depository) with established conspiracy lore (that there were shooters on the grassy knoll) and adding my own twist (that Oswald had been contracted to shoot Gov. John Connally, whose wounds were part of the so-called "magic bullet theory," by powerful parties unknown) seemed like a compelling intro to the tale, especially when told through the eyes of the infamous assassin.

I tried to stick with the real settings, angles, routes of the vehicles, and timeline, though obviously the reason Oswald was up there and the additional shots coming from the grassy knoll are not part of the accepted historical record. There is a reason this conspiracy remains so enduring, though, and while the official story has remained virtually unchanged since 1963, there are still plenty of classified documents out there that may yet turn everything we think we know on its head.

The National Archives does house its main headquarters in College Park, Maryland at the so-called Archives II, but the original and most famous facility is in Washington DC. In addition to the publicly accessible areas, including the famed Rotunda displaying the US Constitution, the Declaration of Independence, and other founding documents, the historic building features a researcher-only section complete with archivist attendants, reading rooms, a modern-feeling lobby, and innumerable shelves stuffed to the brim with our nation's history. I've taken some liberties with the layout for story purposes, but many crucial elements, including the section's separate dedicated entrance, are real.

John Buchan's *The 39 Steps* was a seminal work in thriller writing, one of the earliest in the international intrigue genre. It was a tremendous success and inspired several sequels, as well as a film adaptation by Alfred Hitchcock. But among the book's biggest fans were four brothers from Massachusetts: Joe, Jack, Bobby, and Teddy Kennedy. The old Kodak film canister is based on real ones from the time, with the engraved Kennedy crest (and the spliced-together contents) my addition. The cipher encoded on the film strip is, as Jon describes, a very specific version of a book cipher, but instead of using the page, line, word/letter method commonly seen, the numbers at the top of the negatives identify the order of the specific letters underlined in the book itself. Since the underlining in the book is unique to that copy of the book, the code also includes elements of Cold War-era one-time pads, a unique cipher sheet used to encode and decode a single message by sender and receiver, then discarded forever.

The assassinations of John F. Kennedy and Robert F. Kennedy are staples in modern conspiracy lore. The only film the public has ever seen of the former is the famous Zapruder film, shot by Dallas dressmaker Abraham Zapruder, albeit released with a few crucial frames missing. The FBI confiscated all still photographs and film of the assassination, fueling rumors of a cover-up, and the hastily established Warren Commission's report only served to further fears of a greater conspiracy. The commission's membership—including CIA head Allen Dulles, Council on Foreign Relations chairman John J. McCloy, and future US President Gerald Ford—was similarly controversial, especially considering how the CIA and other groups represented on the panel were top suspects in the assassination itself for conspiracy buffs. The House Select Committee on Assassinations concluded in 1978 that JFK was killed as a result of a conspiracy, though most of the usual suspects—including the CIA, the FBI, the Secret Service, Cuba, and the Soviet Union—were explicitly mentioned as not being responsible for such a conspiracy. Which, of course, spurred me to think about unusual suspects, powerful groups no one had ever connected to the Kennedy assassination.

The President John F. Kennedy Assassination Records Collection Act of 1992, also known simply as the JFK Records Act, called for the declassification of all documents related to the assassination in twenty-five years, providing exceptions for documents that would imperil national security. In 2017, tens of thousands of documents were declassified en masse as ordered, though an untold number more remain declassified due to national security concerns. Of course, if there were some truly damning documents exposing some powerful conspiracy that actually killed JFK, that certainly seems like exactly the sort of thing that *could* present a national security crisis.

Bobby Kennedy was gunned down in 1968 by Sirhan Sirhan. At the time, Bobby was a sitting US senator and the Democratic frontrunner for president. His death, and that of Marilyn Monroe years before, have often been lumped in as part of the greater JFK assassination conspiracy. Sirhan's initial confession, followed by his recanting and claiming he couldn't remember anything about the assassination, is a matter of historical record. Alleged connections to MKUltra, which was an active but highly classified CIA program at the time, became part of the story after the program was revealed in the Church Committee hearings in 1975.

Bobby's dedication to his martyred brother cannot be understated. As attorney general until shortly before his election to the US Senate in 1964, he would have been well-positioned to launch secret investigations into his brother's killers alongside that of the Warren Commission, whose report was released just three weeks after Bobby's resignation from the Department of Justice in September. Perhaps his greatest accomplishment for his brother is the JFK Presidential Library and Museum. Together with Jackie Kennedy, Bobby worked tirelessly on his Oral History Project, gathering existing recordings and recording new ones to cement his brother's legacy for generations to come. And as it turns out, audio cassette tapes were in use in the 1960s, a big surprise to me in researching this book, since I was born more than two decades after JFK was killed. However, the cassette tape I have Bobby hide in the globe is, of course, my invention. But the globe itself, as well as the story behind it, is real and can be seen in the JFK Presidential Museum today. Indeed, the entirety of the library/museum is described as accurately as possible, though the exhibits are, of course, far more powerful in person.

The Kennedy boys's boat, the *Victura* is real and still sits outside the JFK Presidential Library and Museum today. JFK named the sloop as a boy, and sailing it along the Massachusetts coast was one of his great joys throughout his life. The compartment inside the hull is real, though the hidden panel and safe are my invention.

Faneuil Hall is one of the highlights of Boston's Freedom Trail, and the rich history behind it, as well as its importance not only to the early nation but also to the Kennedy family, is all real. The adjacent Quincy Market is also well worth a visit, though it is far more commercialized than its more historic neighbor. The *USS Constitution* is a magnificent warship and is the oldest working commissioned naval vessel in the world. It was named by President George Washington, who selected a fellow member of the Society of the Cincinnati to be its first commander. The history about its exploits during the Quasi War with France, conflicts with Barbary pirates, and the War of 1812 is true, as is the description of the boat's more recent history and its current role as a museum ship.

The rest of the Boston locations are also real. The Barker Engineering Library, with its famous dome and colonnade, is perhaps the most iconic place at the Massachusetts Institute of Technology. And there was a Radio Shack location just down Massachusetts Avenue from campus, though it shuttered its doors recently. The campus of Harvard University, and its nearby environs, is just as impressive and steeped in reverential history as you would think.

While I initially considered ways to fit it into the story, the Union Oyster House didn't ultimately survive the final cut. However, for chowder-lovers and history buffs alike, it is more than worth the trip.

Located a block from Faneuil Hall, the restaurant was established in 1826, though the building dates from colonial times. Prior to becoming a restaurant regularly patronized by the likes of Daniel Webster, it played a role in the Revolutionary War effort, serving as the headquarters of Ebenezer Hancock, the Continental Army's first paymaster—an issue that would later lead directly to the founding of the Society of the Cincinnati. The second floor later served as the home of Louis Philippe I, who was exiled from his homeland in 1796 as a youth and eventually took up residence in the Boston building, teaching French to young women to make ends meet, years before he returned home to serve as the last king of France from 1830 to 1848. In later years, as a restaurant, Union Oyster House started serving what, for my money, is the best New England clam chowder and cornbread around. But don't take my word for it; on the second floor, you can sit in a designated booth regularly used by one of the restaurant's most famous patrons whenever he was in town: John F. Kennedy himself.

The Jefferson Memorial is an incredible place and definitely gives off the reflective, contemplative vibe Jon mentions during his visit. The Tidal Loop Trail is also worth a visit, and the history about Mrs. Taft's planting of the cherry blossom trees with the Empress of Japan is true. The National Mall, too, is a great spot for reflection, both literal (via the Lincoln Memorial Reflecting Pool) and figurative. The Lincoln Memorial and Washington Monument are tremendous—if widely divergent—testaments to the lives and legacies of their inspirations. The memorials for veterans of World War II, the Korean War, and Vietnam are also moving, with the monolithic wall inscribed with the names of tens of thousands who died in Vietnam proving especially sobering.

The legend of Lucius Quintus Cincinnatus is real. So too is how George Washington was known as the American Cincinnatus for his role in leaving his estate to lead his people in times of crisis, then stepping down amid public calls for him to seize further, permanent power. While Washington has been rightly venerated in the centuries since his death, he was highly praised during his life as well. But he had seen the dangers that unbridled power could present, which led him to not only resist calls for greater power for himself but also to attempt to stymie the ambitions of some of his fellow Cincinnati.

The history about the Society of the Cincinnati's founding and early days is true, as is the controversy and conspiracy theories surrounding it and the opposition voiced by founding fathers like Thomas Jefferson, Benjamin Franklin, and John Adams. George Washington did seek to dissolve it initially, though his mind was changed by Pierre L'Enfant's gesture of the diamond eagle pendants he had designed for the group in France. The Cincinnati's relinquishment of hereditary membership under pressure from Congress, followed by a prompt restoration of that inheritance as soon as the pressure had died down is also real. However, the Vanguard and all of their machinations of American history from the shadows are entirely my invention, though many of the events, including the Gulf of Tonkin Incident, the September 11th attacks, the assassinations of Lincoln, JFK, Bobby Kennedy, and Martin Luther King Jr., and many other pivotal attacks and scandals that have rocked American society in the past two centuries are actually surrounded by conspiracy theories about an unseen man behind the curtain.

Similarly, the vast number of key historical figures mentioned as members, from presidents to titans of industry to the cadre of powerful men who surrounded JFK in his final days were all really members of the Society of the Cincinnati. However, the idea that honorary memberships were conferred upon presidents and other high-profile individuals who did the bidding of the Vanguard is, like the Vanguard itself, entirely fictional.

In fact, the real-life modern Society of the Cincinnati continues to do wonders to not only promote historical understanding of the Revolutionary War (in no small part thanks to their American Revolution Institute and their unparalleled collection of first-hand documents and artifacts from the period) but also to promote relations between the United States and her first ally: France. Though the original French chapter was indeed dissolved in the French Revolution as described in the narrative, the Society has since re-established a branch for descendants of French officers who joined the Patriots' cause.

Aaron Burr, however, was perhaps the most controversial of all the founding fathers. While his views on the Society of the Cincinnati's true mission and role as the inspiration for the founding of the Vanguard are my invention, his real-life treasonous exploits are a matter of historical record. The duel in which he killed Alexander Hamilton was, in fact, done while Hamilton was president-general of the Society of the Cincinnati. Burr's actions in the following years are equally controversial. He fled to the Ohio River Valley and tried to drum up support for a militia to take a chunk of the newly acquired lands of the Louisiana Purchase for himself. He also endeavored to foment revolution in, and war with, Mexico. President Thomas Jefferson had Burr arrested and tried for treason, but the trial ended in acquittal due to a lack of hard evidence. His treasonous efforts in the Ohio River Valley are now known as the Burr Conspiracy and helped establish Aaron Burr as the perfect founding father to inspire his own antagonistic subset of the Society of the Cincinnati, a radical fundamentalist offshoot that would pursue its twisted versions of the original charter just like Burr had—through any means necessary.

Anderson House, as amazing as the history behind it and the sights contained within are, is entirely real and described as accurately as possible. The road-map mural in the Winter Garden can be seen today, though the hiding place behind Mount Vernon's position on the map is my invention. The palatial estate is open to the public, with the American Revolution Institute offering free tours, which are highly enjoyable and informative. The house is replete with incredible details, including the Key Room (with the mythologized murals of Anderson's ancestors during wartime), the English Drawing Room (including the curtained dead-end doorway where Jon and Chloe thwarted Molyneux), and the upper gallery (where the very real secret entrance to Isabel Anderson's fire escape route is hidden in plain sight). The choir stall room, dining room, and Larz Anderson's study are also highlights of the tour, though the grand ballroom steals the show, as it has for more than a century's worth of visitors.

The Anderson family has a fascinating unsung legacy of American history, containing revolutionary leaders, war heroes, governors, diplomats, and celebrated explorers. Larz Anderson had some big shoes to fill, but his visions of grandeur were not fulfilled on the battlefield like many of his forbears but in the courts of high society. While Richard Clough Anderson helped leave behind a new country for his descendants, Larz left behind a magnificent monument to not only his own life and adventures but also to those of his beloved Cincinnati.

Exploring Mount Vernon is like stepping two hundred years back in time and comes highly recommended. George Washington's ancestral estate is described as accurately as possible. The Bastille key that the Marquis de Lafayette gave Washington still hangs in a shadow box in the main hall of the mansion today. The descriptions of the old and new tombs, as well as the history and timelines behind them, are all accurate as well. Graffiti from both Union and Confederate Civil War soldiers can still be seen near Washington's tomb as both North and South visited the neutral site to pay their respects to the most famous founding father. The Cincinnati brick in the rear of the old tomb and the hiding place it concealed are, however, my invention. But the Marquis de Lafayette did go to Mount Vernon and visit his old friend's original gravesite during his 1824 tour of the first nation he helped liberate, a tour he conducted while his Revolutionary War aide-de-camp, Richard Clough Anderson, was still alive.

The Taft political dynasty isn't as well-known today as that of the Kennedys or the Bushes, but it has certainly left its mark. With a litany of ambassadors, senators, and cabinet members, the Taft family has served the country for generations in the nearly two centuries since family patriarch Alphonso Taft co-founded Yale's Skull and Bones. Charlie Taft's influence on Cincinnati is well-documented, with the family as a whole being an institution in the city for more than a century. But William Howard Taft is undoubtedly the best-known member of the family.

Through his roles as solicitor general, secretary of war, governor-general of the Philippines, and provisional governor of Cuba during the tenures of Presidents Benjamin Harrison, William McKinley, and Teddy Roosevelt, he built a strong record of public service, ultimately culminating in the presidency. But though his residency in the White House was cut short by Teddy Roosevelt breaking his promise and tossing his hat in the ring for the 1912 election, Taft's ultimate goal was never the highest office in the land. Since long before even ran for president in 1908, he had set his eye on a Supreme Court seat, first being passed over for one in 1898, then again in 1916. During his brief one-term presidency, he filled six Supreme Court seats, more than any president other than George Washington (who had to fill the entirety of the original court) and Franklin Delano Roosevelt (who tried to pack the court with liberal justices to overpower Republicans in Congress).

Then, in 1921, he finally got his wish, becoming the tenth Chief Justice of the United States, and the first (and, thus far, only) to have also held the presidency. He sat on the Lincoln Memorial Commission and dedicated the monument at its 1922 opening in his capacity as chief justice. Meanwhile, at the other end of the National Mall, Taft was instrumental in the creation of a new home for the Supreme Court, which had to that point met in a relatively tiny room in the bowels of the US Capitol Building. Further, his establishment of the process by which the high court can choose which cases to hear not only cleared out the insurmountable backlog his court inherited but has allowed subsequent courts to be more efficient and effective, even today. While Taft is perhaps most infamous for getting stuck in the White House bathtub, that incident actually never happened and is based solely on a rumor circulated at the time, half-jokingly making fun of the president's not-insubstantial girth. But the legacy he left on Washington DC, the country, and his beloved Supreme Court, is one that has endured.

The Solomonic desk Alphonso Taft commissioned and used is real and is currently housed in William Howard Taft's childhood home as described in the narrative. The story of it being rediscovered by Charlie Taft is also true, as is the iconography echoing the Temple of Solomon. Most incredible of all is that the desk really does have secret compartments, including one that rangers during my visit said that they had discovered weeks before but had no idea how to access. That was the sort of detail I just had to use in the story.

Spring Grove Arboretum and Cemetery is one of the most expansive and interesting necropolises in the United States. The history and descriptions given on the narrative are real, as is Charlie Taft's gravesite, set far from the Taft family plot centered around Alphonso's grave. Charlie's tombstone, including the "Gone Fishin'" epitaph and the fisherman carving on the lake side of the stone, is also real. The missing gear and the hidden compartment, however, are my creation.

The Cincinnatus statue in Sawyer Point Park is real and can be seen today on the Ohio River waterfront as described. The four flags surrounding the statue are also there, including the Society of the Cincinnati flag, which is accurately described. While I wanted to ensure the impact of Jon discovering the flag at that point in their journey, the Society's flag can be seen displayed elsewhere in the city that bears its name, perhaps most famously in Fountain Square.

The abandoned Cincinnati Subway project is real, as is the history behind it. Many local Cincinnatians don't even realize that, beneath their feet, miles of never-used subway tunnels, platforms, and access points lay forgotten. The world wars, political infighting, and mounting financial concerns are typically pointed to as factors in why the project was abandoned, but there is no single smoking gun. A brief tour is given to a handful of lucky explorers one day per year, but the waiting list is often months long. That doesn't, of course, prevent some intrepid urban explorers from breaking into an access hatch and exploring on their own. The Vanguard archives and their location is, of course, my invention. With all those tunnels laying forgotten for nearly a century, and with the extreme restrictions on visiting, who knows what might be hidden beneath the streets of Cincinnati?

Arlington National Cemetery is one of the most somber and reflective places in the country, and for good reason. Nearly half a million men and women who dedicated their lives in defense of the United States and its ideals are interred there, and the endless rows of white headstones bearing testament to their sacrifice are incredibly moving. Influential founding Cincinnatus Pierre L'Enfant is, in fact, buried at Arlington, as are many important war heroes, high-ranking officers, and selfless young soldiers who have helped to keep America safe in the centuries since its revolutionary origins. William Howard Taft and John F. Kennedy are the only presidents to be buried in Arlington. In fact, all three Kennedy brothers central to the story are buried in Arlington. Bobby is buried at the edge of the hilltop memorial dedicated to JFK, while Ted, who died far later, in 2009, is buried in a plot near the foot of the hill. The eternal flame is also real and can be seen today. While a handful of brief, accidental extinguishments have occurred, staff were always quick to relight the flame, cognizant of what it signifies. Other than those brief interruptions, the flame has been burning constantly for more than half a century, illustrating not only the spirit of what JFK represented, but also of what he believed America herself represented.

Alongside the big conspiracy of the Vanguard, the story also makes reference to several real conspiracies. The CIA's mind control program of MKUltra, J. Edgar Hoover's massive blackmail campaign of high-profile officials and figures, the Hartford Convention plot for New England to secede from the Union following the War of 1812, and the Philadelphia Mutiny that Cincinnati founders like Washington and Hamilton had to put down were all real. And, of course, the Newburgh Conspiracy, which precipitated Washington, Knox, and the rest deciding to found the Society of the Cincinnati, was real and presented a potentially lethal threat to the nascent United States. Indeed, in those first years after the Revolutionary

War, the country's founding ideals and institutions could very well have been strangled in the crib by a military coup were it not for the creation of and intervention by the Society of the Cincinnati.

Finally, while the United States has never seen a division as clear and deep as the secession that led to the Civil War, there have been plenty of rumblings from pundits and activists on both the left and right that another one is brewing. The fears about the deep and widespread divisions along social, economic, racial, cultural, religious, and gender lines voiced by Stanton Gaines and his fellow Vanguard members in the book echo many concerns voiced by leaders today. But while Gaines makes some compelling points about the numerous divisions that are constantly highlighted by the media, politicians, and popular culture alike, I tend to hold out hope for Jon's counterargument. Living in the Florida Panhandle through the aftermath of Hurricane Michael this past year, I've witnessed firsthand the goodness of strangers across all races, creeds, and backgrounds. While our differences can and have divided us in the past, at our core, there is a shared unity that gets glossed over far too often. So while the news coverage tends to focus on what divides us from one another, often giving a disproportionately large voice to much of the chaos and hatred that unfortunately also lives among us, I think we're ultimately capable of being something greater.

A beacon, burning bright. Just like George Washington, the American Cincinnatus, would have wanted.

# ACKNOWLEDGMENTS

I began research on this book nearly a decade ago, with site research trips spanning several years. As such, I'm all but certain I've forgotten to mention some of the people who helped make this book what it is today. This list is not going to be comprehensive, so to all those who helped, encouraged, and otherwise contributed to *The Founding Treason*, whether or not your name is included below, I wholeheartedly thank you.

First, thanks to Mike Hickman, my AP American History teacher in high school, who first introduced me to George Washington as the American Cincinnatus nearly two decades ago.

Thanks to Meredith DeHart and everyone at the American Revolution Institute for the phenomenal tour of and incredible insights into the inner workings of Anderson House, past and present. Hopefully one day they'll let you all explore Isabel Anderson's secret escape tunnel!

Thanks to Donna Reynolds and Allen Weldman for the excellent tours of the mansion and grounds of Mount Vernon. My mind was awash with possibilities while I explored Washington's sprawling ancestral estate, and I have no doubt I'll be returning to Mount Vernon at some point for a future book.

Thanks to the park rangers and guides at the William Howard Taft National Historic Site, not only for the tour but also for answering all my crazy questions about Alfonso Taft's desk and its secret compartments.

Thanks once again to the incomparable members of International Thriller Writers. From my first nervous Thrillerfest a decade ago to the incredibly humbling outpouring of rave reviews for my own books from some of the best authors in the business to the host of friendships I cherish with A-listers and up-and-comers alike, ITW has offered a tremendous community that, one way or the other, helped me meet my agent, my publisher, and my wife. I look forward to the next decade of friendship, growth, and shared passion for thrillers of all shapes and sizes.

And while this book deals with those who make the decisions for America to go to war, I want to express my heartfelt appreciation for the men and women of our armed forces who have for centuries fought and died to protect the freedoms we take for granted far too often. Arlington National Cemetery is a haunting reminder of the cost of liberty, the sea of white tombstones bearing testament to the countless Americans whose lives were dedicated in selfless service to their fellow man. And that spirit of sacrifice is the same spirit that I think Washington – and, at their best, the Society of the Cincinnati – represented.

Now, on to the writing and editing of the book itself.

Thanks to my copyeditor on this project, Philip Newey, who polished the manuscript to a fine sheen and helped prevent more than a few potentially embarrassing gaffes.

Thanks to my incredible agent, Pam Ahearn, for fighting for me and my books in every arena she can and for sharing her robust insight into the publishing industry. Even before you were my agent, your eye for the strengths and weaknesses in my drafts was uncanny and continually helped me to hone my craft and make each book the best it can be. It's been a decade now since our paths first crossed, and as we stand together at the release of my biggest project yet, I am incredibly glad they did.

To my editor, Lou Aronica, who took a chance on an unpublished twenty-something aspiring author seven years ago and never stopped believing nor pulling the best out of my writing. You and Pam both have been incredibly helpful in building my brand and becoming the author I am today, and I remain forever grateful. I can't wait to see where we can go from here!

In the credits of many movies and larger video games, companies often list "production babies" who were born during the making of the project. My son, Graham, was born during the writing of *The Founding Treason*, and he continues to inspire me more with each passing day. Thanks for being so awesome, buddy!

Finally, thanks to my amazing wife, Meredith, who not only kept our family and home together during my long hours researching, writing, and editing, but who also helped with much of the travel research for this book – she was my adventuring partner in Boston, Washington DC, Mount Vernon, and Cincinnati. Her role in spurring me on and helping keep things together during crunch time cannot be overstated. For all the encouragement and inspiration you provide, for all the selfless evenings and weekends you went above and beyond to help me chase this dream, and for all the adventures we've already shared and will soon share together, this one's for you, Meredith.

# ABOUT THE AUTHOR

Jeremy Burns is the nationally bestselling author of *The Flagler Hunt,* *The Dubai Betrayal,* and *From the Ashes.* He is a lifelong storyteller and explorer whose travels have taken him to more than twenty countries across four continents. He has gained some unique professional experiences alongside his writing career, including working as an international educator in Dubai, a law enforcement consultant, a Walt Disney World cast member, and a journalist, writing for a number of award-winning publications on topics ranging from global terrorism to haunted asylums to end-time prophecies. He holds degrees in history, business, and computer science, and has far more interests than can possibly be healthy. He lives in Florida with his wife, son, and two dogs, where he is working on his next book.